Ruthe McDonald

I0632515

SOUTHERN COMFORT

A NOVEL

JOHNRUE PUBLISHING
SCRANTON, PENNSYLVANIA

JOHNRUE™PUBLISHING
www.johnruepublishing.com

Southern Comfort is a work of fiction. Names, characters, places and incidents are products of the author's imagination or are used fictitiously. Any resemblance to actual events or locales or persons, living or dead, is entirely coincidental.

SOUTHERN COMFORT
COPYRIGHT ©2009 by Ruthe McDonald

All rights reserved, including the right to reproduce this book or portions thereof in any form whatsoever.
For information address JOHNRUE™ Publishing, PO BOX 326, Scranton, PA 18501

ISBN-10: 0615599680
ISBN-13: 978-0615599687

Second Edition JOHNRUE™PUBLISHING February 2012

First JOHNRUE™PUBLISHING hardcover edition July 2010

Manufactured in the United States of America

ACKNOWLEDGEMENTS

Writing has always been a passion of mine. Even before I knew how to write! I thank the Father for blessing me, and allowing me to explore the creativity He has placed within me. It is a blessing.

All glory and honor goes to the Father for His continued grace and mercy. For His love and unmerited favor. Without it, I could not be.

I continue to thank my family and my friends for all of your support. It is a blessing to know that I have so many in my corner. I even take this time to thank my enemies. That's right! For you have become fuel to this rocket of success! Hey—even Jesus had Judas!

I can hardly believe the transitions that has taken place in my life since the first edition of Southern Comfort was released. It has been phenomenal. And here we are...the second edition. It is a profound joy in every way.

I could go on and list all the names of all my loved ones and all those that have contributed to my life. But...that's all in the first edition! You know who you are. However, I will say this: Hey Aunt Sharon! I love you to pieces! A promise is a promise.

Allow me to say this to you today: Whatever you have in your heart to do...do it! Don't procrastinate. Allow the gifts of God to flow in your life and bring you to that expected end that God has ordained just for you!

Ruthe McDonald

Southern~4~Comfort

JR

For John,
You never have to know...
That's a promise

Southern~5~Comfort

Ruthe McDonald

Southern~6~Comfort

S7R

PROLOGUE

July 4ᵗʰ, 1990

LORD, I JES DON'T KNOWS 'BOUT THIS. This is not what I expected. I never thought I'd be around this long. Don't get me wrong!—I'm grateful. Yes I am. I s'pose things could be worse. I jes miss my home, my things...my life. It jes ain't fair gettin' old!

Maybe I should jes stop complainin'.

Good Lord!—here comes another nurse. If she sticks me one more time...I ain't responsible for what I might do!

"Good afternoon, Ms. Emma. How are we today?"

How are 'we' today? Hell, she acts like she in this bed, being stuck like some damn pin cushion!

"We're going to just check your pressure..."

Again? This must be the hundredth time today. Hell, I'm still *breathin'.* Ain't any alarms goin' off. I wish they jes leaves me alone...and let me go home! It's the 4ᵗʰ...I should be preparin' for my family.

"Well, your pressure's just fine."

I could have told her that.

I realize that if I jes smile and nods my head they seem to get out quicker; except for that nurse in the mornin'. *Humph!* I swears she takes pleasure in stickin' me with them damn needles! Talkin' 'bout: *"Ms. Watson, we got to make sure your sugar's fine. We have to make sure all your levels are stable. You know, we ain't young no more".*

We?—I don't sees no one stickin' her! I'm sure as hell the only one gettin' poked and prodded! You'd think I was a turkey bein' prepared for Thanksgiving supper! And *'we ain't young no more'.* She has a hell of a lot of nerve! I know ain't *nothin'* young 'bout me anymore. Hasn't been for a *long* time. Hell, my breasts where my knees used to be, my knees where my ankles use to be. Don't even asks where my ankles went! And let's not talk about my behind, either. Lord, makes me cry jes to thinks about it. It used to be so round and tight. You could bounce a quarter off it! *Now?* Well, I don't know where it wents. Like it jes took off and ran away with the rest of my sexiness!

Damn!

If you can helps it, don't ever gets old. (Not that I'm that old, mind you! I'm only 68, and still gots a lot of livin' to do yet!) And whatever you do, stay away from hospitals! Especially doctors! —'cause all they gonna do is take your money and try to sticks you in some nursin' home, and gives you a bunch a pills. This pill for that; this one for that; this one to take cares of the side effects of the first one...and so on, and so on.

Hell if *I'm* goin' to one them places. As many Chilren as I have? *I better not!* I'd haunt every last one them Negroes for the rest of they lives! They thought I was hell when I was alive? Put me in some damn nursing home and see what happens!

I jes don't like havin's to depend on someone else. Don't gets me wrong; I'm glad I'm still around.

My doctor ain't, *too*, bad. Normally I'd tell you that I have no need for no doctors, but I s'pose that I need to listen to what they sayin'—at least *him* anyway.

It jes ain't no funs gettin' old, you know?

When did I gets so old anyways? Last time I look, me and Al B (that's my husband), were sitting under them stars and he was askin' me: '*what would I do without you?*' And I say to him: '*you never has to know*'. You know, I raised five Chilren. And some that wasn't mine. I s'pose I've lived a full life. I know it's been a good one. But hell!—I ain'ts nowhere ready to go...not yet.

Lord? Emma Jean here. We needs to have us a talk!

"Ms. Watson?"

It's that nurse again. I guess she ain't so bad...not like that mornin' nurse.

I turns my head and smile to let her know I'm still alive.

"You have a visitor." She smiles. "Come right in. She's awake. She's doing much better today." She opens the door wide and steps to the side, as someone enters.

My word! Look who it is.

I jes smile as wide as my cheeks would go.

"Hey Mama!"

It's *Macon*. My precious *Macon*.

"How are you today?"

She looks so good. Jes like me when I was her age.

"I know it's been a while, but I came as soon

as I got back. You know I can't miss our 4th of July celebration...just not the same..."

She places the flowers she's brought on the table next to my bed and bends over to kiss me on the cheek, then the forehead...jes like I do to her.

"You're looking good."

Liar! But it feels good to hear.

She sits down in the chair next to my bed.

She looks happy. I can tell. It's the glint in her eyes. Though I detect some sadness as well. I wonder how the kids are doing.

As if reading my thoughts, "The children are doing well. They miss you. They'll be coming in tomorrow. They can't wait to see you..." Macon's voice trailed off. She looked around the room taking in all the flowers and cards. "Well, one thing is for certain, you are definitely loved." She smiled, taking my hand. "Do you know what I was thinking about today while driving up?"

I bet I know. The same thing I started thinkin' when I saw her walk through that door.

I started smiling.

She laughed. "Yes. I was thinking about when you came to get me. That was the best day of my life."

I raised her hand to my cheek and kissed it. I saw tears begin to well up in her eyes. I tugged on her hand, and shook my head.

"I know you don't want me crying. You may not be able to speak, but I can hear you *loud and clear.* What I wouldn't do to hear you say my name, or call me 'suga'."

Damn stroke!—took my voice. But it ain't over yet! That's another thing me and God got to talk 'bout.

"God, it seems like yesterday that you came for me, and my life was never the same."

Your life wasn't the same, and neither was mine.

It's funny how things have a way of comin' out. Secrets never do stay buried. You can't run from your past forever. It always has a way of catching up with you—no matter how hard, how fast, or how far you try to run.

Memories rushed through Emma's mind, as though it were yesterday... remembering that time so long ago, and how it changed her life forever...

CHAPTER 1

April 25th, 1974

IF YOU WALK OUT THAT DOOR; don't think about walking back in! Do you hear me? Don't you even think about coming back!" Nadine Cooper screamed at her daughter. "Don't you come back! You hear? Never!"

Macon stood straight, her body trembling; more from anger than that of fear. *It was now or never*, she thought.

Picking up her bags, Macon turned to face her mother one last time. Her eyes filled with tears. Refusing to let them fall she swallowed hard, took a deep breath, and said, "I love you, Mama. But you won't hurt me anymore. I won't allow you to kill me like you did my daddy. Not as long as I can help it, and can think for myself. Daddy said I was strong, and I'm gonna prove him right." Macon walked out the door. Each step she made, feeling stronger. Every stride, a sign of freedom.

"Go! Get the hell out my house! And don't come back!" Nadine ran to the door and hollered, "You ain't better than me! You just like your damn father! Acts like him... dreams like him! You gonna ends up just like him!—nowhere, but six-feet under with no account dreams! You ain't strong! You're weak! Just like Nathan! Weak!"

Macon continued walking down the street,

ignoring her mother's rants.

"You'll be back!" Nadine laughed haughtily. "You watch! You can't make it without me. You no good without your mother! I gave you life. Me! You think that woman gonna help you? She got enough of her own! You a fool,

Macon! A fool. You'll see. You'll be back..." Nadine watched her daughter leave. She raised the pint of Jack Daniels into the air and said, "Good ridden. I don't need you. I don't need anybody!" She placed the bottle to her lips and gulped down quickly.

Nadine turned and looked around her dark, dank home. The air was stale, and smelled of carnations. She was all alone now.

She stumbled over to a chair just missing the seat.

"I don't need anyone," she whispered pulling herself up. "No one at all." Nadine sat quietly for a moment, and then began to sob. "Just me...and good old Jack...yeah...that's all I need...and..." Nadine reached for the phone falling out of the chair.

MACON never turned around. She continued walking, carrying her bags, gaining strength with every step. She loved her mother, but could no longer take the abuse. She was determined to get out before her mother not only destroyed herself, but her as well.

At fifteen, Macon was more mature than most girls her age. Sometimes life just makes a person grow up faster than they have to.

Macon Georgia Cooper: Her mother named

her after her hometown. Macon had never been there. She grew up in Philadelphia—the city of brotherly love: Although she never felt much love (except from her father).

Nathan Cooper showered his daughter with love. Macon often wondered what her father saw in her mother. He said that her mother was not always the woman she now was. Yet he never explained what happened to change her; turning her into an evil, hateful, and bitter woman—who seemed only to find comfort in a bottle.

Macon envied her friends whose mothers would dote on them and do the special things that mothers and daughters often did together. She recalled a time being invited to a mother and daughter brunch at a friends church. Nadine refused to go. Macon arrived alone, lying, saying her mother was not feeling well. Her friend's mother was kind and understanding, taking Macon under her wing. She knew the truth. People had often talked about Nadine Cooper, and the kind of woman she was.

Eventually Nadine put an end to it; informing Macon she was her mother, and no one else. She forbade her to continue the relationship, breaking Macon's heart. Macon continued to visit occasionally without her mother's knowledge. When her friend and their family moved away, Macon felt sore alone.

Macon had just turned fifteen when her father died. She remembered coming home from school, when their neighbor, Mrs. Johnson, informed her that her mother and father were at the hospital.

Nathan never recovered. Macon feared her mother did something awful to her father. She only knew her father to be healthy and strong. She never recalled a day—ever—her father being ill.

Neither Nadine nor Nathan told Macon that he'd had cancer.

Macon visited her father every day at the hospital (more than her mother). It was during these visits that Macon learned more of her great Aunt Emma, Nathan's Aunt. Her father often spoke kind of her, but not her mother. To suggest that Nadine did not care for Emma, would be putting it mildly. Macon did not understand the reason for her mother's contempt. She did know, however, her father loved his Aunt dearly; as a son would love a mother.

Nathan sent for his Aunt, asking her to come to Philadelphia. He wanted desperately to see her. It had been a long while, and it grieved his heart that he hadn't stayed as close as he should have. She'd no idea of his illness.

Emma came as soon as he contacted her.

When Macon met her great Aunt Emma—it was love at first sight. She was warm, kind, and feisty. To her, Aunt Emma was everything a mother should be.

Her father asked Macon to leave the room while he and Aunt Emma spoke privately.

Macon obeyed her father's request; curious though, as to what her father and Aunt were talking about. They talked for a long while. She tried to hear what they were saying, but their voices were too low.

When they were finished, Aunt Emma came out and got Macon.

Macon loved the way her Aunt spoke—with a deep, southern drawl. It made her chuckle.

"Macon, baby. You come on in here. Your Daddy wants to see you. I has to get goin'. Nevertheless, I aims to see you soon. All right? Now gives Mama some suga' so I can get this here train and be on my ways back to, Busby. Lord only knows what them folks done did to my house," she laughed.

Macon remembered the hug she gave her and the smell of her clothes— she smelled of Honeysuckle and a touch of peppermint.

When Macon went in to see her father, he was smiling. He told Macon that Aunt Emma would always be there if she ever needed her.

"She was a bit upset with me for not calling her sooner. But that's just her way. I love that woman with all my heart. And I want you to know something. Something very important..."

Nathan talked with his daughter for a long time that day. He had mustered enough strength to spend precious time with his beautiful daughter, and share with her what was in his heart.

Nathan Cooper passed a month later. Macon, heartbroken, never felt more alone.

Nadine made grieving even more miserable.

MACON handled most of the arrangements for her father's funeral. It was not difficult, since Nathan had the forethought to take care of the most pertinent details. He knew that he could not trust Nadine to do anything—but drink. What is more, that is exactly what she did—she drank herself senseless until she could not function; almost missing the funeral itself.

Macon did her best to sober her mother and prepare the house for the re-pass. It was a godsend when some of the women from her father's office came to help. Though, they did not stay long due to Nadine's antics.

They looked at Macon with pity in their eyes and a lump in their throats. No one understood how Nathan—the fine man that he was—could have been with someone like Nadine. They assumed he'd only endured because of their daughter, and perhaps some residual feelings of love that he once felt for his wife. He deserved better; so did Macon.

When Emma returned for the funeral, Nadine wouldn't let her into the house.

"You ain't welcome in my home! So you just take your nosy tail somewhere else," she said, slamming the door in Emma's face.

Macon ran and opened the door. "I—I'm so sorry Aunt Emma. I'm sorry. She—she doesn't know what she's saying." She held the door open for Emma to come in.

"The hells I don't!" Nadine yelled. "I know exactly what I'm saying." Nadine staggered over to the sofa and plopped down, spilling her drink. "Damn! See what that old hag made me do?" She got up, wiped her dress and stumbled into the kitchen.

Macon looked horrified. She was never so embarrassed.

"I'm very sorry, Aunt Emma."

Emma gave Macon a hug. "What you got to be sorry for? You ain't your Mama. Hell, better folks have called me worse—I might add. But ain't no name gonna stop me from doing what I needs to do." She smiled, and put her hand under Macon's chin. "Now you tells Mama, how you doing suga'? How's my precious grand-niece?"

Macon smiled, feeling better now that Aunt Emma was there. She felt safe.

"I'm all right."

Emma looked at Macon with skepticism. "Come on, Chile. I know you ain't all right. In facts, I know you hurtin' and missin' your Daddy. You ain't got to pretend with me. I understand. I understand a whole lot." Emma pulled Macon into her arms and held her tight. She watched Nadine sashay out of the kitchen with another drink in her hand.

"Good God, Emma! Ain't you got enough business of your own than to come here and gets in mine?" Nadine sat down, kicked off her shoes.

Emma let go of Macon, and walked towards Nadine.

Macon looked at her mother, shaking her head.

"What the hell you shaking your head for?

Don't make me get off this sofa and slap you."
Nadine took a gulp from her glass.

"You won't be slappin' anyone. Not in my
presence you ain't." Emma warned Nadine, "You put
one hand on this Chile, and it's gonna be me and you
sistah." Emma stood in front of Nadine.

"Oh hell, Emma. I done told you; this ain't
your home. That is my child and I does what I damn
well please." Nadine tried to stand up. Emma
pushed her down.

"What the hell?" Nadine tried again.

Emma pushed her back down.

"I ain't having this here sh—"

"Shut your mouth, Nadine! You sit right there
and don't move. My God! Looks at you! You needs
to be ashamed of yourself." Emma turned to Macon.

"Macon honey?"

"Yes, Aunt Emma?" Macon had never seen
anyone talk to her mother in that manner and not
receive a caustic earful of foul language. She was
impressed.

"You know how to make coffee?"

"Yes ma'am."

"Well go ahead and puts on a pot. Make it
strong." Emma turned and looked at Nadine. "I'm
aims to make sure your mama is sober, so she
understands what I'm about to tells her. Make it
black and strong—jes like me," she smiled, looking at
Macon over her shoulder. "I gots a feelin' it's gonna
takes a whole lot of coffee to make this here one
sober."

Macon went into the kitchen, and put on the coffee as Emma asked her to do. She wondered what Aunt Emma wanted to speak to her mother about. She wondered if it had anything to do with the long conversation that she and her father had the month before.

Nadine leaned back on the sofa looking at Emma with a scowl on her face. She swished her drink around in her glass.

"You ain't changed a bit!" She took a sip. "Still meddling in other people's affairs. What you want you insufferable hag?" Nadine put her head back, looking at Emma over her glass.

"I see you still the same intolerable, ungrateful, miserable soul. Why Nathan married you was beyond me. I suppose there used to be some redeeming qualities 'bout you. But you seemed to have drunk all of 'em away." Emma looked at her with disgust.

"What do you want, Emma? You ain't ever liked me. I was never good enough for you, or *your* Nathan! You just *knew* you could get rid of me! Well how you like me now? I'm still alive and your precious *Nathan* is gone!" Nadine laughed wickedly, gulping the rest of her drink.

Before the glass was from her lips, Emma lunged, slapping Nadine hard across the face, knocking the glass out her hand.

"You vile, disrespectful heifer!" Emma grabbed Nadine by the collar of her blouse. "No respect! None! None for yourself, your husband, or your Chile." Emma was seething. She pushed Nadine back against the couch and pinned her with one hand, while squeezing her face between the other.

Nadine struggled to get Emma off atop her. She could not budge the woman. Emma was too strong for her, and Nadine's body too lethargic from the alcohol.

Emma squeezed Nadine's face between her slender fingers and spoke through clenched teeth. "You disgust me. You were never good for Nathan. I saw your evil ways from the beginning. But God help that boy—he was blinded by his love for you and your pretty looks. I seens right through you. Oh yes I did. Nevertheless, he was a grown man, and had to makes his own decisions. But I warned you Nadine. I told you after the last time; if you ever did anything to Nate again, I'd be back, and you would have to deal with me." Emma looked at Nadine with fire in her eyes.

Nadine tried to free herself from Emma's hold, but could not. What she saw in the woman's eyes frightened her. Nadine knew Emma kept her word; she never made a threat she did not carry through.

"Let...go...of...me." Nadine wrapped her hands around Emma's wrist and tried to pull her hand away.

"I'll let's go when I'm good and ready. Now you listen up, and listen good," Emma drew closer to Nadine. Lifting her skirt, Emma straddled Nadine. Leaning into Nadine's face, whispering in her ear,

"We gonna have us a nice little chat later. When that Chile brings that coffee in here, you gonna drink it—every last drop—until you sober. You hears me?"

Nadine nodded her head.

"Good. Now I suggest—for your sake— that once I lets you go, you don't try anything stupid. I may have a few years on you, but I gots a whole lot of fight in me that came with this age. And I hasn't had me a good fight in a *long* while. So you jes sit there, keeps your mouth shut, and drinks that coffee. All right, I'm gonna lets you go now." Emma released her grip on Nadine and stood up. She backed away, straightening her skirt, fixing her hair.

Nadine did not move. She was sober enough to know that she was better off being still.

Macon had been watching the whole time from the kitchen. She heard when Emma slapped her mother. She came to the living room, astonished to see that Aunt Emma had her mother pinned to the sofa. Her first reaction was to run in. However, she decided to let Aunt Emma, "*handle her business*", as her father would say.

She stood back and watched. *Could that be fear that she was seeing in her mother's face?* She was not sure. She had never seen her mother quiet for so long. Macon wondered what else Aunt Emma had to say to her mother. She was sure she'd ask her to leave while they spoke.

To be a fly on that wall, she thought.

As soon as Macon saw Emma get up, she came in with the coffee.

"Um...the coffee's ready, Aunt Emma." Macon placed the tray on the coffee table.

"Thank you, baby. That smells right good... and strong," Emma said, lifting a cup. "Here..." she passed the cup to Nadine, "...drink this here coffee. It's black; jes what you need." She waited for Nadine to take the cup.

Nadine was going to say something, but decided against it and took the cup from Emma's hand. Taking a sip, it was bitter. She went to place the cup down.

Emma stopped her. "No sweetheart, I don't think so. You drink that coffee—all of it." Emma pushed the cup back towards Nadine. Watching, making sure Nadine drank the coffee.

Nadine slowly drank, scowling at Emma with every sip.

Emma ignored her, turning her attention to Macon. "Suga', thank you for the coffee." She took a sip. "Mm. You certainly can make a good cup of Joe," she smiled.

"Oh, thank you. I would make coffee for Daddy all the time. Every morning before he went to work and before I went to school..." Macon picked up a picture of her father, "...we would have breakfast together and have nice, long talks." Macon's eyes filled with tears. She put the picture down, wiping away the few tears that managed to fall down her cheeks.

"Oh, it's all right, baby." Emma wrapped her arms around Macon. "I understands," she said, rocking her. Emma understood exactly. She held

Macon in her arms for a while. She stroked the girl's long, black hair, and then whispered something into her ear.

Nadine sighed loudly, sitting back, crossing her legs.

"I'm sorry. I just miss him so much," Macon cried, burying her face deeper into Emma's shoulder.

"I know, I know. But you gonna be all right. Trust me. Mama knows these things. You come from good, strong stock. We have a way of bouncing right back. Yes we do." She stroked Macon's hair again. "So, you cry if you wants to. Let it all out. 'Cause you gonna be jes fine...okay?" She looked Macon in the eyes.

Macon nodded.

"Good. Now, you do Mama a favor?" Emma handed Macon a handkerchief.

"Yes," Macon answered wiping her eyes.

"I want you to go to the store for me while me and your mama has a little talk."

Macon looked over to her mother.

Nadine sat swinging her leg back and forth, rolling her eyes.

"What do you want me to get?" Macon asked, turning to her Aunt.

"Here," Emma took some money out of her purse. "I need you to gets me seltzer water, a pack of those peppermints—you know the kind I like, when I was here before?"

Macon nodded.

"And a pack of menthol one hundreds. I know it's a nasty habit. But Chile, sometimes I jes needs somethin' to calms my nerves." She glanced over at Nadine.

Macon took the money. "Okay. I'll be right back."

"Takes your time. And be sure and gets somethin' for yourself, okay?"

"That's all right. I'm fine. I don't want anything."

"You sure now?"

"Yes, Ma'am." Macon placed the money in her pocket and walked to the door. "Seltzer water, peppermints, and menthol one hundreds," she repeated.

"Yes," Emma answered.

"Okay...be right back." Macon walked out the door.

CHAPTER 2

EMMA TURNED TOWARDS NADINE. She sat quietly for a moment, staring at her. She took a cigarette from a pack in her purse, and lit it. Leaning back, Emma crossed her legs and smoked her cigarette. She sat blowing rings of smoke into the air, still watching Nadine.

Nadine glared at Emma. How she detested this woman; so high and mighty; always looking down on her ever since they met. She never was good enough for her *precious Nathan*. The woman hadn't changed a bit. A few gray hairs...but she was the same.

If I weren't so damn drunk...I'd whip her ass! Wipe that condescending look right off her black face! Nadine thought.

Emma continued smoking her cigarette. She could imagine what Nadine was scathing about.

She's probably over there wishing she could whip my ass! I wish she'd try!

Emma was not a large woman, but she definitely was in good shape. All the work she had done over the years—working with her husband, raising her children, working her garden—she had a naturally lean physique, with muscle tone that most women her age prayed for; especially after birthing four babies. She was a tall woman—five feet, nine inches—with a graceful stance. Her skin was flawless; like porcelain...not a wrinkle in sight. She had a mahogany complexion, deep-set, soulful, dark brown eyes—they almost appeared black—a slender nose, high cheekbones, and full lips, with a dip in the middle. Her hair was dark, with strands of gray that looked silver in the light. It was long, thick, and soft. She always kept it in a chignon.

Emma always dressed in clothing that flattered her beautiful, hourglass figure, and long curvy legs. Her hands were surprisingly soft considering all the work she'd done with them; her fingers long and slender. Yes. Emma Jean Watson was a beautiful woman...of that there was no doubt. Yet her inner beauty, wisdom, and strength were what made Emma such a formidable adversary and envy of many people...women especially.

Emma was not book smart—but she was people smart! It was this wisdom that helped Emma recognizes both the good and evil in people. It was also this wisdom which made some despise her. For they knew, that Emma could read them, knowing exactly what they were all about—and wasn't afraid to tell them about it! She was bold, brazen, and unapologetic. Emma spoke her mind—sometimes with regret.

Nadine became increasingly uneasy. Feeling Emma was taunting her, she lashed out. "Enough already! Say what it is you gonna say!"

Emma did not answer. She leaned forward, resting an arm on one leg, while taking in another puff.

"What the hell do you have to say, Emma?"

Nadine began fidgeting. She hated the way Emma was looking at her. "Macon gonna be back soon. So go ahead and say what you came to say!" She demanded.

Emma took one last drag from her cigarette. She picked up the ashtray and put the cigarette out...still silent. When she finished, she looked right at Nadine, clasped her hands, and began to speak in a slow and low tone.

"Don't pretend you care about when that Chile is coming back. You jes sits your tail back and be still. I've known you a long time, Nadine; Ever since you was that Chile's age. You was always wantin' something that either wasn't good for you, or belonged to someone else. The hells with anyone who got in your way of gettin' what you wanted. I warned Nathan that you would be the death of him! 'Cause you didn't cares about no one's but yourself. But God help him, he loved you. He loved you with all his soul and might. I tried to gives you the benefit of the doubt and helps you—"

"You did no such thing!" Nadine cut Emma off.

"You can tells yourself that lie. But you knows right well that I did. You jes wanted to see what *you* wanted to see. Except, none of what you seen was the truth. You have been selfish and cruel. Yes you have. What kinds of woman is so blind to the love of a man and her Chile? *Her own flesh and blood*? My God, Nadine! She comes from you! Did you not know that all your lies, plottin' and schemin' would catch up with you?"

Nadine did not answer. She sat back on the sofa and looked towards the window, avoiding Emma's stare.

"Of course you didn't. A lie always has a way of catching up with you. No, Nathan wasn't perfect. Hell, none of us is. He had his faults jes like the rests of us. But he was honest and he loved you. He loved you like no one's business, and would have done anything for you. Hell, he *did* do anything for you! He gave all he had for you. He gave up everythin', jes for you 'cause that was supposed to make you happy. And how did you repay him?" Emma leaned forward, uncrossing her legs.

Nadine turned and looked at Emma, unsure of where Emma was going with this conversation.

"Oh hell, woman! Just say what it is you gonna say!" Nadine picked up her pack of cigarettes, and then threw it down in frustration. "Listen, you come in my home and start babbling on like some fool. Why don't you just come out say what it is? I know you and Nathan had a long talk about me. I know he told you something. So what is it? Well, say it!" Nadine hollered.

Emma leaned back, crossed her legs, and laughed haughtily. "Hmm, you jes itchin' to knows what I know. You want to know what Nathan told me."

"You know damns well I do! What is it, Emma? So help me..." Nadine leaned forward with her hands balled into fists. "Tell me!" She demanded, pounding her fists on the coffee table.

Emma leaned forward, looking Nadine

straight in the eyes. "Did you really think Nathan did not know who you are? You really believed that you could hides the truth from him?" Emma shook her head. "You are some piece of work. Nathan knew about everything. He knew about the baby, too."

Nadine's eyes widen. She felt like someone reached in and grabbed her by the heart. She could not say a word.

"Oh yes. He knew. He knew about the man over in Walnut Hill. He knew about that stuff you been on, too."

"I-I don't know what you talking about. What baby? What man?" Nadine stood up and walked around the sofa. "You know, Nathan was crazy! Always accusing me of cheating and everything. When he knew full well he was the one!"

Emma sat back, shaking her head. "Uh-uh-uh! You know, Nathan said you would say that. You can deny it all to you blues in the face. But it won't change the fact that your lies have come back to bite you."

"You both crazy! I ain't had no other baby. I don't know any man in...Walnut Hill! And the only thing I does is drink now and again. I ain't never touch anything else...besides weed. And he did that, too! Hell! Even you have!"

"Whatever, Nadine! I knows you won't admit to nothin'. You'd lie to your dyin' breath. Howbeit, I intends to honor Nathan's wish."

Nadine glared at Emma. "And just what the hell is that?"

"Macon is comin' to, Busby, with me."

"Woman you crazy! What makes you think I'm gonna allow you to just come in here and takes my child?" Nadine went and stood in front of Emma.

Emma looked up at Nadine. "I knows you will. You don't has a choice in the matter."

"You a fool if you thinks you can just dictate to me how things are gonna go in my home!" Nadine said, getting in Emma's face. "You just as crazy as your nephew was!"

"I suggests you back it up," she warned Nadine. "You don't have a choice. If you don't allow Macon to come with me, I will and can takes her from you."

"And how do you suppose to do that?"

"Nadine, no one in their right mind is gonna jes sit back, lets you get high, drinks yourself to death, and abuse that Chile in the process. Not as long as there is breath in my body." Emma stood, facing Nadine eye to eye.

"That Chile's father is not here to protect her no more. Nathan told me what you've done to her. Especially when you get high on that stuff! I'm not gonna allows that baby to suffer at your hands no more. Even if it means taking you outta here myself."

Emma stood so close, that Nadine could feel Emma's breath on her face. She also saw the gravity in Emma's eyes. She knew she meant what she said. Nadine stepped back.

"You ain't taking my child, Emma. I don't care what Nathan said, and what you believe. You got no right to take my child from me." Nadine walked away. "No one does! That's my child. I'm her mother."

"Then why don't you acts like one; like you love her! Get yourself together, and I will gladly sends her back. I ain't heartless, Nadine. But I will fight for her."

Nadine was vehement. "Ain't no one gonna tells me how to raise my child, and how to lives my life! No one! You hear me?" She screamed.

"You don't has a choice, Nadine! If you don't gets yourself some help, you will never see Macon again. Lord knows you headed down a deadly path. I won't let you take Macon with you." Emma walked towards the sofa. "Do you think that Nathan didn't take steps to protect her? You have nothin', Nadine. Absolutely nothin'! Everything was left to Macon. Everything! The only thing you have is this house. And at the rate you goin', you will have drank and smoked it all up before years end. Is that what you want for your Chile?

"Do you wants Macon to come home one day to finds you dead? Or, will you be so high one day and beats her to death because you mad at yourself, and takes it out on her? Which is it? Huh? What, you think that man loves you? What he gonna do when you ain't got nothin's left to supports both you and his habits?" Emma grabbed Nadine by the shoulders. "Wakes up, Chile! Get it together before it's too late for yourself. Do it for Macon."

"Get off of me! You don't know anything!" Nadine began to cry. "You come in here all high and mighty like you know me. You don't know a damn thing about me. You don't know what I've been through. And you could care less! Yeah, self-righteous hypocrites! All of you! Always thinking I wasn't good enough for him! I wasn't stupid! I knew what I wanted. I knew what I deserved to have. And you right, I didn't care who got hurt, or in my way! Ain't nobody cared if *I* was hurt. Ain't nobody cared for *me.* So I did what I had to do! Nathan didn't complain. He knew what he was getting. Then he moved us here! Promising me that we gonna live the good life! I raised that child. Me! He was always at work, spending all his time making himself successful!"

"You ain't had no problem spendin' what he was makin'!" Emma retorted.

"You damns right I didn't! Hell, I had to look out for me. For me!" Nadine hit her chest with her fists. "I was here. Not anyone else. I made this house a home for that man. I washed his draws, cooked his food, and opened my legs to him whenever he wanted! It was me! His wife! No one else. I lived with him! I had his baby! Me! Not no one else but Nadine Alyse Cooper! By. My. Self! I wasn't nobody's slave. So you right; I made sure I was paid for what I did! I had to take care of myself. Ain't any one cared about me!"

"That's a lie, Nadine! I cared about you! Nathan loved you! He did whatever you wanted! But it still wasn't enough. You were so busy wantin' to be loved by the people who didn't matter, or care about you, that you stepped on, and spit in the face of those of us who did!"

"No. No," Nadine shook her head violently. "That's a lie! You are lying! Ain't no one ever gave a damn about me, but me! I don't care what you say!" Nadine stalked towards the kitchen, and turned around lifting her hands up. "Do you think I really give a damn about what you saying? Look around, Emma," she waved her hands, "this *is* my house! I worked for it." Nadine picked up a picture of Macon. "This here...is my child. I gave birth to her. And don't anybody has the right to take a child from their mother! No one!"

"I agrees with you. But when you ain't doing the job of a mother, then someone has to protect that Chile." Emma moved towards Nadine, speaking a little softer. "Nadine, whether you believes me or not, I do cares for you. I knows you love Macon—the only way you knows how. But that ain't enough...not for Macon. You can't give that Chile what she needs right now. She needs more, Nadine."

"Uh-uh," Nadine shook her head. "You just wants my child. You wants to take her and turns her against me. I won't let you do it, Emma. I won't!" Nadine held Macon's picture to her chest, pacing back and forth.

Emma knew that Macon would be walking through that door soon. She moved closer to Nadine. "Nadine, Chile. Look at me. Look at me for a minute," she said, touching Nadine's shoulder.

Nadine turned around, wiping the tears from her eyes, shrugging her shoulders from Emma's touch. "I don't cares what you say, Emma. My child is staying right here where she belongs—with her mother."

"Now you gonna listen to me. Whether you believes me or not, I do loves you. Oh yes I do. If I didn't, I wouldn't be here talkin' to you. I would've jes gone ahead, and let social services come here. But I does respect you as a mother."

Nadine shrank back.

"Social services? You called social services on me?"

"No, I didn't."

"You're lying! You just are trying to scare me."

"Nadine, looks at me. You knows I don't lie. I plays it straight and to the chase. I wants you to do what's best for that *Chile*."

"And that's giving her up?"

"No. It's letting her stay with me whilst you get yourself together and can be the mother that she needs. I ain't trying to take your place. I'm trying to saves your place."

"Mm-mm. You lying. You just want to punish me for Nathan. That's what you're doing." Nadine shook her finger at Emma. "That's what this is. So *you* called those people on me."

"No I didn't. I would never do that to you. You knows how I feel 'bout them people gettin' into our business. They don't know nothin's about no black folks home and how we are. No, honey, you did this one to yourself. The night you came up to the hospital, high as a kite, reeking of alcohol."

Nadine was confused. She could not recall

the incident. "No. I--I wouldn't do that."

"Well, you did. You passed out in the hallway. You hit your head so hard, you scared the hospital. Let's jes say, that one incident led to another, and here I am. Trying to makes sure you stay connected to *your* Chile, and that she don't be placed with no strangers."

Nadine walked over to the sofa, shaking her head. Disbelieving what Emma had just told her. "I still don't believe you."

"You don't have to. But them people will be here first thing tomorrow mornin'."

"What?" Nadine fell onto the sofa.

"Tomorrow. Here's the name and the number of the woman who will be comin'." Emma said, passing a piece of paper to Nadine.

Nadine looked at the paper. She was silent for a while. Emma sat down in the chair across from her. She gave Nadine a moment to digest what she had told her.

"Nathan knew about this?" she asked Emma.

"Yes he did. That's why he sent for me."

"How...how come he didn't tell me?" You could see the hurt in Nadine's eyes.

"He tried to. He said you was never in the right frames of mind on the occasions that you *did* make it to see him. I thought he would have told you. But I knows he didn't when that woman called my home this past week."

Nadine sat there, shaking her head.

"Nadine, I may be angry with you. And I am
tight as hell at you for what you been doin'. But I do
has love for you. I know that Chile loves you, too.
And I knows for a fact, as hurt and angry as he was
with you, Nathan loved you. Loved you to his dying
breath. I knows I can be harsh at times. That's jes
my way. But I does everything I can to help those I
love. You'd agree if you'd stop denyin' the truth."

Nadine did not respond. She sat still, staring
at the paper in her hand.

"I know this hurts like hell. However, it is
best this way."

"It's best this way? For who? You? Me? My
child? I love Macon. She is mines."

"Nadine, truth be told, we don't own chilren.
They's gifts from God. He jes lends them to us. But
sometimes we don't treat those gifts too well, and
we needs some help."

"You thinks you can do a better job than me?
You ain't perfect, Emma. I knows about your past."
Nadine shot a mean look at Emma.

"Yeah, that's right. I has me one hell of a past.
That's why I can reads your book so well—from
cover to cover. It may not have been exactly the
same. But it damn well comes close. The difference
is, I have learned from mine. Will you? I thanks God
I made it to see Fifty-two. Will you be able to say the
same thing? Will you even make it to your next
birthday? At least I can say at thirty-three I had
already mended my fences."

Full of anger and rage, Nadine still insisted
that Emma was lying to her. She was not going to

give up her child to anyone; especially not Emma.

"I don't care what you say. You will not have my child! I sooner see her with strangers than with you!"

"Now that's jes mean and spiteful, and downs right selfish!" Emma leaned forward and asked, "You mean to tell me, you'd rather see your Chile with some strangers than with her own kin—that loves her and will takes care of her like she should be?"

"You damn right!" Nadine said, mockingly. "At least I know she won't be brainwashed against me."

"Oh, of course not. She'll jes be put with some strangers that don't know nothin's about her. Don't loves her, and could cares less about who she is. Nadine, Macon is fifteen years old. She damn near grown already. It's already set whatever she feels and thinks about you—set by you. Technically, she can makes up her own mind as to what she wants to do. I jes wanted to give you the benefits of being her Mama, to makes the right choice for the both of you."

"I don't care what's you say, Emma. She ain't going with you to no, Busby."

Emma shook her head.

"Well, fine then. You want to act like some foolish Chile? You go right ahead. We'll jes let them people decide for you."

"Shut the hell up, Emma! I don't want to hear no more!" Nadine threw the paper at Emma.

"Well I tried. Don't say I didn't warns you. We could have taken cares of this ourselves. I'm tellin' you now; Nadine...gets yourself some help. Leaves that stuff alone. And for the love of, God and your Chile, leaves that man alone. Or marks my word, he will use you until you has nothin' left. And the only friend you will have is death itself." Emma looked at Nadine with such fierceness in her eyes.

Nadine didn't say anything. She sat still, looking towards the door. She was not going to give in to Emma, or her threats.

Macon walked in the door.

"I'm sorry it took me so long. I had to go to a different store for your mints, Aunt Emma." Macon looked at both her Mother and Aunt. She knew that their conversation had been a serious one, and it concerned her.

"They didn't have your brand of cigarettes."

"That's all right, baby. I sure appreciate it. I don't needs to be smoking no ways," she said, taking the bag from Macon. "Mm." She opened the mints, and placed one in her mouth. "These mints are the only things which settle my stomach."

"You're welcome. Here's your change," said Macon, holding her hand out.

"No, baby. That's your money. Keeps it."

"No, that's all right. I don't—"

Emma held up her hand. "No, no. I said you keeps it. I wants you to have it."

"All right." Macon looked at her mother. "Mama, are you hungry? Can I get you something to eat?" she asked. "You, too, Aunt Emma. Are you hungry?" She looked from one woman to the other.

Nadine did not answer. She sat quietly, looking coolly at Macon.

"That's right sweet of you suga'. But I has to be gettin' back to my hotel. I'm jes a little worns out. Tells you what, why don't you come with me. I needs to talk to you about somethin," Emma said, holding out her hand for Macon to take. Emma did not trust leaving Macon with her mother. She was uncomfortable with the state that Nadine was in.

Nadine sat up straight, angrily looking at Emma.

Macon noted the look on her mother's face. "Well, I –uh- I would like to. But...I think Mama might need me," she said, looking at her mother.

"I'm sure your mama won't minds. Matter of facts, I think it would be a good ideas for her to have some time to herself. She has an awful lot on her mind to think about," stated Emma, glancing over to Nadine.

Nadine rolled her eyes at Emma, and then turned to Macon. "Go ahead with your Aunt. She got something for you from your father that she needs to share with you."

Macon looked surprised. She gathered from the tone of her mother's voice, she was not the least pleased about it. The tension between her mother and Aunt was thick... it would take a bulldozer to knock it down. She was not sure how to respond.

"On second thought," Emma began, "Why

don't I stay here tonight?" she asked, looking wryly at Nadine. "This ways, I can cooks both of you a nice down-home supper. Would you like that honey?" she asked Macon.

Nadine shot Emma a look. If looks could kill, Emma would be six feet under alongside her nephew.

Macon was excited about the idea. Though, she knew that her mother would never go for it.

"Would you like that?" Emma asked again.

"I, uh...I would like that very much." Macon looked at her mother and asked, "Mama, is it okay?" Macon had knots in her stomach. She wanted Aunt Emma to stay, she was afraid of what her mother might do if she'd left.

Nadine looked at Macon, expressionless. "I don't care. Just as long as she stays out my way." Standing up, she said to Emma in a low voice, "this ain't over, Emma. Not...at...all."

Emma did not answer. She watched as Nadine went upstairs. She turned her attention to Macon.

Macon wondered what her mother meant by her statement.

"Macon, c'mon in here to the kitchen, so I can shows you how I used to cook for your daddy."

Macon smiled at her Aunt. "Okay. Aunt Emma?"

"Yes, honey?"

"Are you taking me with you when you leave?"

Emma was surprised. She looked at Macon and put her arms around her shoulders. Walking into the kitchen, Emma said, "Macon, *Chile*, you are a very smart young woman. Yes you are. We will talk later. But first, we gonna get in this here kitchen, and makes ourselves some good southern food. All right?" she said, smiling at Macon.

Macon agreed. "All right. So what are we going to fix?"

CHAPTER 3

MACON AND AUNT EMMA HAD A WONDERFUL
time cooking. Emma prepared for Macon some of
her father's favorites: Fried chicken, collard greens,
yams, macaroni and cheese, and cornbread. There
were plenty of desserts left over from the re-pass.

Macon enjoyed hearing stories about her
father's childhood. It made her feel closer to him.
Emma explained her and Nathan's special bond.
Although she was only thirteen years older than he,
she always felt like a mother to him. When her sister,
Clarisse—Nathan's mother—passed, she raised him
as her own. Nathan was ten. She loved him like a
son. Moreover, would do anything he asked of her.
She even respected his wishes when he asked her to
let him go live his life when he decided to move to,
Philadelphia. She had not agreed with his decision,
but respected him and honored his choices as a man.
It broke her heart when he left. Furthermore, it
pained her when they did not stay as close as they
once were.

Macon could see the hurt in her Aunt's eyes.
Aunt Emma did not have to say a word. Macon knew
her mother was the reason they fell out of touch.
Aunt Emma told her that you should never let
disagreements, or people keep you away from the
ones you love; because you never know where death
is waiting to claim a soul.

Macon thought about it, and about her
mother. How could one stay close to someone who

did not want to stay close to you? She did not know.

They enjoyed their dinner and conversation. Nadine did not join them. When Macon went upstairs to get her for dinner, she discovered that her mother was gone. She must have left while they were in the kitchen. Macon was somewhat relieved. This way, she could enjoy her time with Aunt Emma without feeling guilty, or having to be careful of what she said. It was the first time in a long while that she'd laughed. Aunt Emma had a delightful sense of humor. Just like her father. In fact, Macon realized just how much her father and Aunt Emma were alike. She marveled in their similarities.

****

Emma cleaned the house after sending Macon to bed at ten-thirty, telling her to get some rest. Emma explained to Macon about social services coming the next day. She had hoped that Nadine would have been there to talk with Macon herself.

Macon understood. Her father had briefly explained to her that she might be going to stay with Aunt Emma for a while; only until her mother was able to take better care of her. He wanted her to believe that her mother loved her; she just had to deal with some personal demons. He asked her to keep praying for her mother and to continue to believe that God would answer her prayers. He also said that the answers might not come the way she wanted them to. However God answered, though, it would be a blessing.

Macon did not understand all that her father said, but she would ponder it in her heart, as she did all of their conversations.

Macon was also smart enough to know that her mother would not let her go of her own free will. She was stubborn that way.

IT was six in the morning when Nadine returned home.

Emma was in the kitchen when she heard the door. She did not say a word. Nadine came in, got a cup of coffee, and went to her room. Four hours later, social services were knocking on the door.

When Emma answered the door, Macon went upstairs to get her mother. To her surprise, Nadine was sitting on the edge of her bed, as if she had been waiting for her. She did not say a word. Nadine got up, and went downstairs.

The environment filled with more tension. You could feel the nervous anticipation, and unraveled nerves circulating between Emma, Nadine and Macon.

Social services stayed for two hours. It felt like an eternity to the three. They talked with Nadine, then with Emma. They walked throughout the home, observing the living conditions, and then interviewed Macon alone.

When they were finished, they made their suggestions.

Nadine was advised to immediately get substance abuse counseling, as well as grief counseling. They suggested an inpatient program that would be willing to take her as soon as possible. They found no need to place Macon with a foster family, or group home, considering she had a willing relative to take her in, and finding that that was Macon's desire.

Nadine relinquished, and gave her consent to allow Emma to take Macon back with her to, South Carolina.

After social services left, no one was sure what to say.

Emma told Macon to meet her at the hotel. They would be leaving that evening. She wanted to give Nadine and Macon a chance to say their goodbyes.

Emma could see the fear in Macon's eyes. She told her not to worry. She did not believe that Nadine would be foolish enough to do anything to harm her.

Macon still was not sure, but agreed.

Nadine had not said one word to Emma. She acted as if she were not there.

After Emma left, she did not speak to Macon either. She poured herself a drink and sat in her chair.

Macon tried to speak to her mother to no avail.

Nadine refused to speak until Macon was leaving out the door. She resented the fact that

J7R

Macon had chosen Emma...over her—her own mother.

CHAPTER 4

MACON SLEPT THROUGH TO NORTH CAROLINA.
Waking only for a moment, she heard her mother's rants telling her to never come back home.

She did not know if her father was right. She did not believe that her mother loved her, or that she ever had.

Macon dosed off again.

This time, Emma was waking her, telling her that they were in, Columbus, South Carolina. Uncle Albert would be waiting for them at the train station.

"Now, where is that man? I told him we'd be here at ten o'clock." Emma looked around. "Here, let's go over here. There's a phone I could use."

She and Macon carried their bags over towards the phone, as a porter brought the rest of Macon's belongings.

"Hold this for me," Emma handed Macon a bag, while putting change into the phone. "Hopefully, he's on his way." Emma waited for someone to answer. "Hello. Did your father leave yet? How long ago? All right. Then he should be here anytime now. I missed you, too. Is my house clean? I ain't playin' with you all. My house had better be the ways I left it. All right. See you soon."

"Uncle Albert on his way?"

"Yes. He should be here shortly. C'mon, let's

go sit over here and waits."

Macon followed Emma to a bench near the phones.

Emma could sense the heaviness in Macon.

Macon had not said much when she met her at the hotel. Emma wondered if she should have stayed with her while she packed. She could only imagine the things that Nadine said to the Chile.

"C'mon over here," she said putting her arm around Macon. "You didn't say much at the hotel, and I let you sleep through the train ride. So before we gets home, do you wants to talk about it? I mean, 'bout what happened when I left?" She pulled Macon close to her.

Not saying anything at first, Macon leaned her head against Emma's chest and began to weep.

"It's okay baby. Let it all out. Mm, I'm so sorry you had to go through so much for such a young girl." Emma stroked Macon's hair.

"I really miss Daddy. He understood. My Mama...she told me to never come back," Macon stammered. "I don't believe she loves me. I don't believe she ever did." Macon sobbed heavily into Emma's chest.

"Oh no, Chile. She loves you."

Macon shook her head.

"No. No she doesn't."

"Yes she does," Emma insisted. "It's jes...well, your mama has a lot to contends with right now. But I knows Nadine loves you. She jes can't loves you the way you needs to be loved because she's havin' such a hard time loving herself right 'bout now."

Emma rocked Macon in her arms.

"Oh suga, there's jes so much you jes don't understands yet. But you will...someday."

Macon pulled away and sat up. Wiping her face, she looked at her Aunt and asked, "If she loved me so much, then why she hit me like she did? Why did she..." Macon shook her head and started crying again. She was too choked with emotions to continue.

Emma could not answer Macon. All she could do was allow Macon to express the hurt that she was feeling. She knew that Nadine had hit the Chile. She just did not know the severity of the abuse that Macon had endured.

Macon stood and walked a couple of steps away from the bench. She held herself, rubbing her arms. She turned and looked at Emma.

"Aunt Emma, I never did anything to her but love her. I tried to be like her. You know—my hair, my clothes. But nothing I ever did was good enough. I never told anyone the things she did to me. Daddy only knew some of the things. I didn't want him to leave. Maybe I should have told him the truth? I don't know." Macon stood in front of Emma.

Emma's heart was breaking. Tears began to fill her eyes. She wished to God that she had stayed closer to Nathan than she did. Maybe she could have done something. Maybe she could have been there for Macon, to save her from Nadine.

"Aunt Emma, am I a bad person?"

Emma reached out to Macon.

Macon pulled backed.

"Macon, honey. You ain't no bad person. You ain't even has time yet to live."

Macon shook her head.

"Then why she'd beat me? Why did she do what she did to me? I mean, if you loves someone, aren't you suppose to protect them?"

Emma stood up and took Macon's hands.

"Sweetheart, I don't knows why your mama did what she did. I don't have an answer for her. But I do know, that some people are lost in their own mind with their own thoughts... it ain't a safes place to be. Especially for someone likes your mama."

Emma pulled Macon into her arms and hugged her. She could feel her shaking. Emma knew in her soul that there was a whole lot more that went on between Nadine and Macon.

Things not even her nephew knew.

She did not want to push Macon into telling her everything right then. But she knew eventually, Macon would have to share everything in order to be free and move on with her life.

Macon cried softly into her Aunt's shoulder. She felt relieved to be there with her.

"Aunt Emma, I'm really glad that you came for me. I don't know what I would have done if I had to stay there with her." Macon exhaled deeply. As if she'd been holding her breath for a long time.

"Well, I'm really glad to have you with me." Emma pulled back, and looked Macon in the eyes.

"Baby, I wants you to know that I loves you very, very much. Jes like you mine. I don't ever wants you to be afraid to tells me anything. Anything at all. You hears me?"

Macon nodded.

"I got a whole lot of love for you. And I want you to be happy. I will moves heaven and earth for you. Hell...I'd whoop the devil himself if he tried to harm you. So, know that my heart and my ears are always open to you. There ain't a thing in this world that you can't tells me. And, there ain't a thing that could ever makes me stop lovin' you. Absolutely nothin' at all. You understands?"

"Yes." Macon smiled. "I love you so much, Aunt Emma." Macon hugged her.

"I loves you, too, baby. I loves you, too." Emma smiled and kissed Macon on the forehead.

"Now I wants you to know once we gets home everyone calls me, Mama. Even your Uncle Albert. However, it's all right if you calls me, Aunt Emma. I'll answer to that, too!" Emma smiled brightly.

Macon smiled up at her Aunt and said, "Yes...Mama."

"Well, I think that's jes fine. Yes it is." Emma smiled, hugging Macon tightly.

"Hey, is that my suga Mama over there?"

Emma and Macon turned around.

Uncle Albert was walking toward them smiling.

"Hey now! You two ladies need a taxi?" He

asked.

"Watch who you calling a lady!" Emma smiled.

"You better come on over here and gives me some suga, Mama. Papa been missin' you somethin' crazy!" Albert grabbed Emma by the waist and picked her up, swinging her around.

"Ooh! Albert! Lord, stop that for you gets me dizzy!" Emma kissed her husband. "I missed you, too. But look here, say hello to Macon."

Macon was giggling. She blushed when she'd seen her Uncle and Aunt kiss.

"Well, well, well. So this is the lovely Macon. Come here and gives your Uncle a hug." Albert held his arms out to Macon.

Macon was hesitant, but gave him a quick hug.

"Well, aren't you beautiful? Looking jes like your Aunt Emma." He winked at Emma.

"Thank you." Macon smiled.

Emma stood there with her hands on her hip, looking at Albert, tapping her foot.

Albert looked at Emma. "What is it woman? Go ahead; let me have it. I know, I know. I should have been here waiting for you two."

"And? You knows I told you ten o'clock. You knows I hate waitin' out here when it's late."

"Baby, I'm sorry. But I was a little caught up with somethin' at home."

Emma looked concerned. "What? What's going on at the house? Albert, don't tell me somethin's wrong and you—"

Albert cut her off, grabbing Emma by the waist and kissing her. "Mm. Jes like I remembers."

"Albert, tell me. Is somethin' wrong?"

"Mama, please. I jes had to get things ready for you, is all." Albert whispered something in Emma's ear.

Emma giggled like a schoolgirl.

"Albert, hush. You is too much!"

"Well I should hopes so!" He laughed, giving Emma a tight hug.

"C'mon, so we can gets home. It's been a long ride. And I cant's wait to get to my own bed."

"Me too. Good God! Me too!" Albert laughed.

Emma looked at Albert and smiled. "Man, what I'm gonna do with you?"

"Humph! Well if you don't know, I definitely aims to show you!"

"Albert! Not in front of the Chile!"

"Ooh, I'm sorry! Woman, I missed you so bad I done forgets we weren't alone," Albert said, looking at Macon.

Macon laughed. Uncle Albert and Aunt Emma were quite the pair. They definitely seemed to be in love.

"So, Macon," Albert said taking her bags, "how was the ride for you?"

"It was okay. I slept most of the way," she smiled.

"Well I'm mighty glads to have you with us. I'm sorry about your daddy. Nathan was a fine young man. Yes he was."

"Thank you." Macon's smile dimmed.

"I'm sorry. I don't means to make you sad. Sometimes my mouth moves before my brain has a chance to think. Forgive me?"

Macon nodded. "Yes, sir."

"Oh, please baby. Don't calls me, Sir. Makes me feel right old. Uncle Albert or jes plain, Uncle will do fine. Okay?" He said, smiling.

"Yes...Uncle." Macon did not care too much for the name Albert. She thought Uncle did not look much like an Albert. So she settled on calling him, Uncle.

"All right, my two fine ladies. Your chariot awaits you." He moved to the side as Emma and Macon walked passed.

"Chariot? Some chariot...*gold* colored Cadillac. Good Lord. Every times I thinks about when he drove up to the house in that thing." Emma shook her head.

Macon chuckled.

"Woman? You complaining about my car again? I'll leaves you right here. You can walks home. Me and Macon here will sees you when we sees you!" He winked at Macon.

Macon giggled.

"Man, please. You know right well you ain't fixin' to lets me walk nowhere. Especially if you plannin' on gettin's you know what tonight." Emma turned back and looked at Albert slyly.

"Woo! Woman you jes too much! I swears you are! *Come on*; hurry ups so we can gets home!" Albert started rushing them to the car.

Emma started laughing. It felt good to be back home.

She looked at Macon as she helped Albert put her things in the car. She looked so sad and lost. Nothing some good old fashion loving would not fix. Emma knew she could never take away the pain of losing her father, or replace her mother. Nevertheless, she was going to make sure Macon received plenty of love. Some good old fashion love. She needed to be loved on...a whole lot.

"All rights, Sweetie. You ready?" Emma asked Macon.

"Yes, Aunt Emma." Macon turned and looked out the window. All of a sudden, she felt an overwhelming loneliness.

She actually missed her mother. It confused her. She did not understand it; she just knew what she was feeling. She wondered if her mother was missing her, too.

"Okay, ladies. We'll be home soon." Albert turned around to Macon and said, "Don't worry, daughter. You'll be jes fine. Give it some time, though. With enough of Mama's love and good cookin', you'll be ready to take on the world. Trusts me. Uncle never lies." He smiled big at Macon.

Macon looked at him for a minute and smiled.

"Mama's love," she whispered to herself.

Sounds good. She turned her gaze back out the window, leaning her head against it. She took a deep breath. She was looking forward to something good happening in her life.

Emma stared at Albert for a moment, as he started the car. She reached over and touched his arm.

Albert turned and looked at her.

She whispered, "I love you."

He whispered back, "I love you, too."

Emma turned the radio on, leaned her head back and closed her eyes. They would be home soon. She could hardly wait. She hoped Macon would be comfortable and would feel at home.

THE drive home was so relaxing, that both Emma and Macon had fallen asleep. Before they realized it, Albert was waking them up.

"All right, sleepin' beauties. We're home!" Albert pulled into the driveway.

Macon woke up. Stretching her arms, she looked around. She could not see much; it was so dark out. What she did see, however, was a big, beautiful white house, with a large wrap around porch...with plenty of flowers and potted plants along the steps and railings.

Albert came around and opened her and Emma's door.

"Well..." Emma said to Macon, "...welcome home." She put her arms around Macon's shoulders. "You'll be able to see more in the morning. Chile, you jes can't see a thing in the country at night." She and Macon walked to the house.

Macon was nervous and excited at the same time. She stopped for a moment, and listened to the sounds of grasshoppers and cicadas singing in the night. She'd never heard anything like it before. It was soothing.

She looked at her Aunt and smiled.

She knew at that moment things were going to be different from now on.

She felt it—in her soul. It was a good feeling. She was not sure how to describe it. She just knew what she felt inside...peace.

When they stepped into the house, Emma turned the living room lights on. She looked around and smiled.

"It sure is good to be home. And I see you all cleaned up," she said looking at Albert.

Albert smiled. "Oh, c'mon, Mama. You knows we ain't gonna has you come back in here to no mess." He kissed her on the cheek.

"Here," he said taking her bags. "Let me put this in the room for you." He turned to Macon. "Here suga, give me your bag, too. I'll put it in your room. You'll be staying in Calvin's old room. Don't worry, Deeney and Shelby fixed it up real nice for you."

"Thank you, Uncle." Macon answered.

Macon gazed around the room. It was beautiful. It had a lot of charm.

It was a large living room. Larger than the

one back home. The walls were a soft yellow color—
almost like buttercups—with white crown moldings.
It had beautiful hardwood floors. There was a large
fireplace with a carved mantle; just like the
staircase. The carvings were similar in detail. On
each side of the fireplace were mounted two
hurricane lamps—with gold fixtures. On the ceiling
was a large dome. From it, hung an elaborate light
fixture, in the same gold color, which illuminated the
ceiling.

There were two large sofas facing one
another. Each covered with a duvet in a creamy, off-
white color. Between the two sofas stood an oval
coffee table, oak—just as the mantle and staircase—
with a glass top. It too, adorned with the same
beautiful decorative carvings. On top, a beautiful
vase sat, filled with the most breathtaking roses—
tangerine and yellow.

Two Wing-back chairs completed the
ensemble. Also Gold in color.

They sure like gold, Macon thought. Between
the Wing-back chairs sat a Tiffany lamp, on another
beautifully carved oak table...similar to that of the
coffee table.

To her right, a huge picture window with
flowing, butter-yellow curtains, and a window seat
adorned with big, cream colored pillows. Close to
the fireplace— farther to the right sat an old rocking
chair.

She noticed the many pictures on the wall
and on the mantle. She walked toward the rocking
chair—drawn to a photograph that sat on the small

table beside it.

Macon knew who it was right away—her father, when he was a little boy.

Emma watched as Macon picked up the frame.

"That was your father when he was ten. The woman in the picture was my sister, Clarisse. It was taken a month before she passed. Beautiful, wasn't she?"

Macon nodded. She stared at the picture a while before placing it back on the table. She turned and faced Emma.

"You have a beautiful home. Very beautiful."

"Why, thank you sweetheart. It's your home, too, baby. Always. For as long as you want."

Macon smiled.

"I'll gives you the grand tour tomorrow after breakfast. I'm guessing Deeney is asleep, and Junior and Shelby are probably out somewhere. Otherwise they'd been here to greets you. Are you hungry? You wants me to fix you a little somethin'?" Emma pointed towards the kitchen.

"No, I'm fine. I'm not hungry, just tired."

"All right. Well let me show you where you'll be sleeping. I hope you like it. The bathroom is right across the hall from you." Emma took Macon's hand, and walked with her down the hall. "I'm so glad you're here with us. I really am." She gave Macon a hug.

"Me too," Macon said yawning. "Excuse me."

"That's all right. You had such a long day. You go ahead and gets some rest."

Emma turned Macon around to face her.

"Macon, you are precious to us. I know right now things probably feel a little up in the air. But I promises you, it won't be that way for long. Okay? I got nothin but love for you. I knows you miss your Daddy...and Nadine, too."

Macon looked, surprised.

How did she know?

"It's all right. She's your mama, and you loves her. And I'm sure she's missing you, too. Now you go ahead and gets a good night sleep. Before you knows it, everything will be jes right. Trust me." Emma kissed Macon on the forehead.

Macon wrapped her arms around her Aunt's waist and closed her eyes.

"Thank you. I love you so much, Aunt Emma —Mama." Macon looked up at Emma and smiled.

"I loves you, too, baby. Good night." Emma watched as Macon sat on the bed and looked around the room. She closed the door and left.

Macon sat on the bed for a while studying her new surroundings. She was too sleepy to take in everything that night. She took off her clothes and took a large t-shirt out of her bag—too exhausted to fish through her belongings for her nightclothes. All she wanted to do was sleep. She reached over and turned the light off. As soon as her head hit the pillow, Macon was asleep.

AFTER taking a shower, Emma walked into her bedroom and sat on the edge of her bed.

Albert had been in bed waiting for his wife. He leaned towards Emma, placing his hand on her shoulder.

Emma grabbed his hand, gave it a peck and held it tight.

"It's been roughs for you, huh Mama?" Albert massaged Emma's shoulder.

Emma nodded her head. "Yes it has, baby. Yes it has," she whispered.

"I'm sorry I couldn't go with you. Maybe we should have sent Deeney with you?"

"No. No. You couldn't leaves the store, and Deeney still had school and all. Besides, it wasn't anything you could do," Emma sighed heavily.

"I loved him, too. We all did. I wished you would have let one of us come."

Emma shook her head. "I know. But it's what Nate wanted. And...it was the least I could to honor his wishes; especially after everything..." Emma's heart ached.

"Well, you c'mon over here and let me takes care of you." Albert scooted closer to Emma as she leaned back, resting her head on his chest.

"Albert, I don't know. I jes don't know."

"About what?"

"About Macon."

"Why?"

"That Chile has been through so much. More than any Chile should ever go through." Emma sighed heavily, turning to face Albert. "It's jes ain't right what Nadine put that baby through. Some of which we probably will never know. 'Cause I knows it's jes too much for Macon to talks about."

Albert listened to his wife as she spoke. He could see the hurt in her eyes, and hear the pain her voice. He knew his wife was hurting and remembering her own past.

He pulled Emma into his arms and kissed her on the forehead and held her tightly.

"I know this is hurtin' you, Mama. But with you on her side, that Chile will be jes fine. She couldn't ask for better comfort than you. No one could." He lifted Emma's chin.

Emma looked at her husband. He always knew what she needed to hear.

"Oh, I know of a better comforter than me...God."

"Naturally. But we both knows that the good Lord puts people here on this earth—jes like you— to bring comfort. He couldn't have chosen a better angel than you." Albert kissed Emma softly.

Emma smiled, then laughed.

"Me? An angel? Now that's funny. I ain't no angel—fars from it. But I do try my best. God knows I do. Especially after all I've done and been through." Emma stared into Albert's eyes. She stroked his face gently and smiled. "You have been my saving grace, Al B. I don't know where I would be without you.

Probably dead."

"Shush! Ain't no needs to say that," he placed a finger over Emma's lips. "I don't cares what no one says—you my angel, Emma Jean. You gave me a family, you showed me love, and you let me love you. You are home for me. And...I have definitely missed you. Now come on over here and let me get at you." He moved over as Emma climbed into the bed next to him.

"You are too much," Emma laughed. "But I certainly has missed you, too."

"Show me, Mama. Show me how much you missed me," Albert said slyly.

"Ooh, you dirty ol' man!" Emma laughed.

"Yeah, I'm your dirty ol' man! Now, c'mon over here and gives me some suga!"

Emma leaned over her husband and kissed him passionately.

Albert pulled his wife close to him and squeezed her tightly.

"Mm, Mr. Watson! You definitely have missed me!" Emma chuckled.

"You ain't lyin', Mama. You ain't lyin'! Now hit them lights!"

Emma reached over and turned the lights out.

She missed her husband. It was definitely good to be home.

God! It was *very* good to be home.

CHAPTER 5

EMMA TOOK A SIP FROM HER COFFEE MUG and stared out her back window. She watched as the sun came up over the tool shed and gazebo.

Albert came up behind her, wrapping his arms around her waist, kissing her on the neck.

Emma smiled, placing her hands over his arms.

"Good mornin', baby. Sleep well?"

Albert breathed in deep.

"How could I not?" he said, squeezing her.

"You want some breakfast?" Emma kept looking out the window.

"Now what kind of fool question is that? You knows I done worked up some kind of appetite." He kissed her on the neck again, and hit her on the behind before sitting down to the table.

Emma chuckled. Turning, she said, "Now don't you start nothin' this mornin'. You hear?" she said, raising an eyebrow.

"Ain't nothin' you can't handle!" Albert chortled. "Shucks, after last night I thinks *I* better works out some more!" Albert laughed, picking up the coffee mug Emma had placed in front of him.

"Albert!"

"What? You know you put a hurtin' on me last night!" He smiled slyly.

"You weren't too bad yourself," Emma retorted.

"Is that right?" Albert grabbed Emma by the waist, pulling her onto his lap.

"Albert, I thought you wanted breakfast?"

"I want that, too! But I wants my proper suga this mornin'. I don't like wakin' up and you ain't next to me. You knows that."

Emma put her arms around Albert's neck and kissed him.

"How's that? Sweet enough for you?" she smiled.

"Mm, I don't know. Try it again so I can see." He kissed his wife longer this time.

"Oh-my-goodness! Go to your room!"

Emma and Albert ignored their son's comment.

"You two act like teenagers! Early in the morning and you at it again?" Junior laughed as he went to the refrigerator.

Albert released his wife as she stood.

"Boy, this is *my* house. And I will kiss *my* wife, wherever, whenever and *however* many times I please." Albert took a sip of his coffee.

"C'mon over here and give me a hug," Emma said. "You weren't here when I got in last night." Emma hugged her son tightly. "You missed me?"

Junior hugged his mother. "Mama, you only been gone a week."

"And? What's that got to do with missin' your

Mama?"

"Yeah, I missed you," he smiled, giving his mother a kiss on the cheek.

"You bet he missed you," Albert said, looking to Junior. "Don't acts like you didn't. Trying to acts grown." Albert shook his head. "When he got home and found out you weren't here...you should have seen the look on his face." Albert laughed, picking up the newspaper.

"Pop!"

"What?" Albert kept reading his paper. "Ain't nothing wrong with a young man missin' his mama; especially when it's someone like *your* mama."

"I know," answered Junior.

"Now you two, don't start. He *is* a grown man, Albert." She turned to Junior, "You want somethin' to eat, *baby*?" She knew he didn't like to be called baby. But he was *her* baby—all of her children were. She didn't care how old they got.

"Yes Mama. You know I've been waiting for your cooking!" he said enthusiastically.

"I know you have."

Emma took the biscuits out of the oven she'd made earlier. She started cracking a few eggs into a large bowl and then beat them.

"So, tell me how you did this semester."

"I did real well. I made the Dean's list!"

"Oh, baby! I'm so proud of you!"

Emma went and gave her son a hug.

"Albert, how come you didn't tell me?"

"He wanted to tell you himself." Albert put the paper down and smiled. "Smart jes like his father. Good looks and brains too!" Albert grinned and stuck out his chest.

"Look at you!" Emma laughed. "Junior, I'm so proud of you. But jes 'cause you done well don't means you can acts a fool this summer," she warned him.

"I know, Mama. In fact...I was waiting for you to get home so I could tell both of you at the same time."

"Tells us what?" Emma asked curiously.

Albert looked over the top of his newspaper, slightly lowering it.

"Well, my Law School adviser got me an internship this summer at a law firm in, Columbus."

"What? Oh, that is wonderful!" Emma hugged her son.

"Junior, that's great." Albert put the paper down. "When you start?"

"Next week. I met with the supervisor two days ago."

"Oh, that is jes so wonderful! Our son the lawyer!" Emma hugged him.

"Yes...our son the lawyer." Albert looked at his son in awe. He was very proud of him. Although Junior got a late start, he was definitely making up for them three years.

"Didn't see too many colored folks in my day make it this far. I'm very proud of you, son. I mean, you works hard and you knows what it is you wants. I'm very proud of you...very proud." Albert got up and hugged his son, as well.

"Thanks, Pop. That means the world to me. I could never have done it without you or Mama. You two kept a tight rein—you still do," he laughed. "But I always knew it was because you wanted more for me—for all of us. I just want to make you proud."

Emma was crying. Her heart was filled with joy. She didn't think her heart could be this proud. She had a wonderful husband, a beautiful home and family. She was very much proud of her children, and Albert, too, for being such a wonderful husband, father and provider.

Albert Junior is about to become a lawyer (Thank God he survived Vietnam); Calvin is a teacher and Shelby is a nurse. She could not be more proud. And whatever Deeney wanted to be...she knew it would be something just as wonderful.

No one ever thought, especially her, that her life would be so wonderful...so full of love and joy. She took a deep breath, then exhaled.

"Thank You, Jesus," she whispered to herself.

Emma watched as her husband and son sat down.

"All right, time to fix my men some breakfast," she smiled. Emma continued preparing breakfast for her family.

"How was the funeral, Mama? I sure wish we could have been there."

Emma felt a lump in her throat, and the tears

stinging the back of her eyes. She looked out the window as she continued beating the eggs.

"It—it was beautiful. The service was nice. You know, Nate; always takin' care of everything. He took cares of it all." Emma put the bowl down and was still for a moment. She shook her head, and quickly poured the eggs into the skillet. "Yes, it was beautiful. My boy. I still can't believe he's gone." She reached for the salt and pepper. "I see so much of him in Macon."

"How is she doing?"

"As best can be expected. I can tell she's a little homesick and nervous about being here. She's been through a lot."

"How old is she again?"

"She jes turned fifteen last month. However, her soul is much older. She's a very wise young girl. Makes sure you all be careful with her, though. You know how you all likes to play around with one another. She's not used to that. She's somewhat shy; but very warmhearted, like Nathan was."

"She won't be shy too long after living here," Junior assured his mother.

"Ain't that the truth," agreed Albert.

"Jes the same, give her some time before you all start chiding with her."

"Yes Mama."

"Here you go." Emma placed dishes of food on the table.

"Here, Mama, let me help you." Junior put the

rest of the dishes on the table.

Emma had prepared scrambled eggs, grits, bacon, biscuits and gravy, and hotcakes.

"Mm...woman, you really out done you this mornin'," Albert smiled, helping himself to some scrambled eggs.

"Please, you know how you all eat. And I'm sure the rest of them be stirring up any minute now," said Emma.

She was right. Denise and Shelby walked into the kitchen.

"Well, look here; if it ain't sleepin' beauties."

"Good morning, Mama." Shelby kissed her mother. "Welcome home."

Emma hugged her oldest daughter. "Thank you, baby."

"Welcome back, Mama." Denise wrapped her arms around her mother's waist. "I'm so glad you're home! It was boring around here without you...and can't anybody cook like you," she smiled at her mother.

"Why, thank you Deeney." She kissed her on the forehead. "I missed you, too. It's definitely nice to know I've been missed."

Deeney was Emma's youngest child. Emma and she shared a very close bond.

"I tried to stay up last night. But I was just too tired."

"That's all right, baby."

"Did Macon come?"

"Yes she did. She's probably still sleeping."

"You want me to wake her for breakfast, Mama?" asked Shelby.

"No, let her sleep. It's been a while since she's had any good sleep. Let her rest."

Emma looked around the table before sitting down. She wished Calvin were there. "Go ahead, Albert. Say grace." Emma took his hand, and bowed her head.

"Father, God, we thank you for your bountiful blessings this here morning. We thank you for food on our table and the love in our hearts. We thank you for family and asks that you would remember those who don't have neither. In Jesus' name, amen."

"Amen."

"It's definitely good to have you back, Mama. You should've seen the mess Pop made in the kitchen!" Deeney laughed.

"I can jes imagine," laughed Emma.

"Likes you did any better," retorted Albert.

"You two's a mess. I'm surprised my kitchen is still in one piece." Emma shook her head.

"Well, I gots to admit, if Shelby didn't come when she did, you might not have a kitchen right now," Albert said, looking to Shelby.

"Thank you, baby. Mama sure appreciates it." Emma reached out and patted Shelby's hand.

"It's all right, Mama. It wasn't *too* bad."

"I bet," Emma answered looking at Albert.

CHAPTER 6

WHEN MACON FINALLY AWOKE, she sat up looking around, forgetting for a moment where she was. She rubbed her eyes and leaned back onto the pillow. She just lay there for a moment, still. She could hear voices coming from outside the bedroom door. She looked over at the clock.

Nine o'clock.

It was probably the family having breakfast.

Macon wondered why no one woke her. Then she figured Aunt Emma probably wanted her to rest.

Macon, still tired, yawned, stretching her small frame. Her body ached. Swinging her legs over the bed, she stood. Feeling a bit dizzy, she sat back down. She was not feeling very well. She'd been feeling quite sick for a couple of weeks now.

Opening her suitcase, she looked for something to put on. She noticed a towel and wash-cloth were placed on the dresser. Macon searched for her toothbrush. Just as she was about to open the door, there was a knock.

"Yes?" Macon asked timidly.

"Can I come in?"

Macon opened the door.

"Good morning Aunt Emma," she smiled.

"Good mornin' baby. I was getting a little worried about you. I made some breakfast. Would you likes somethin' to eat?"

Aunt Emma studied Macon for a minute. "Chile, you all right? You looks a little pale." She touched Macon's cheeks and forehead. "You ain't warm."

"I'm okay. I just feel a little sick in my stomach this morning." Macon rubbed her stomach.

"Well, I'm sure some of my biscuits and gravy will takes care of that," Emma smiled.

"That sounds good. I was just going to take a shower." Macon lifted the clothes in her arms.

"All right, you go ahead. We'll be in the kitchen. Your cousins can't wait to see you." She kissed Macon on the forehead.

"Okay," she smiled. "I'll be right there."

"Takes your time. Let me get back in here before they eats everything up," she laughed.

Emma went back to the kitchen, as Macon went into the bathroom.

Macon turned the shower on.

The warm water felt good on her skin.

Macon carefully washed. She soaped her legs, slowly moving the washcloth over the dark bruises. Her legs were somewhat sore. The bruises on her arms were starting to fade, however. But not much.

She stood in the shower and allowed the warm water to hit her face.

She began to cry silently.

Her body still ached. Macon began scrubbing herself fiercely, as she remembered what she'd endured.

As she dried herself, Macon studied the bruises on her back and her ribs in the mirror. Her body no longer got rid of the evidence as quickly as it used to. Bruises, as if like a banner, clung to her body so she would *not* forget.

How could she? How could she ever possibly forget? Macon did not need bruises to remind her. It was embedded in her mind, in her soul. Even if she assumed to forget during her awakened state, surely her subconscious would betray her during her sleep. Bringing every horrid detail back to her conscious, through life like dreams—awakening her to night sweats and violent shaking.

Although Macon felt that she could tell her Aunt anything, she was still afraid to share everything. Afraid, that she would be looked upon differently; afraid to be seen like her mother.

How could she ever explain what she went through, when *she* did not fully understand?

Love was a strange thing to, Macon. Love confused her.

She'd heard the word love used in many different aspects, and wondered which one was the correct one.

Which form of love was the real one?

She knew her father loved her.

She knew Aunt Emma loved her.

Her mother *said* she loved her.

However, in her heart, Macon knew that love should not cause you so much pain. Or, leave you with ugly scars and hues of black and blue all over your body.

Macon finished dressing and went to the kitchen.

"**Well**, hello there. We thought we were gonna have to send in the Calvary for you," Albert laughed.

"Come on over here, baby." Emma pointed to a seat next to her.

"Feeling better?" Emma asked taking Macon's hand in hers.

"A little," Macon whispered, as she sat.

"What's the matter?" Albert asked. "You ain't feelin well?"

"Her stomach was a little upset," said Emma.

"Oh. Well that's nothing some of Mama's cooking won't fix." Albert assured her.

Macon smiled and looked around the table.

"I'm certainly glad you're here," Deeney spoke first. "I'm your cousin, Denise. But I prefer to be called, Deeney," holding her hand out for Macon to shake. "I would hugs you, but I know how I would feel if some strange people came hugging up on me!"

Macon laughed, extending her hand. Deeney was funny. She liked her right away.

"I'm Shelby," Shelby smiled, extending her hand.

"And, I'm Junior," he said shaking her hand. "Don't worry," he said noticing Macon's nervousness.

"Give yourself sometime, and you'll be just as crazy as Deeney!"

"Hey!" Deeney hit him in the shoulder. "And I suppose you're not?"

"That depends on who you talk to," he shot back.

Macon giggled as the two shot words back and forth.

"All right! All right, you two. My goodness!" Emma said.

"Sorry, Mama." Deeney stuck her tongue out at Junior.

"Yeah. Sorry, Mama," Junior said.

Emma shook her head. "Well honey, welcome to my family...your family." She rubbed Macon's arm.

"Don't worry," Albert said. "I'll give her a good week or two, and she'll be jes like the rest of 'em!" he laughed.

Emma shook her head.

"Yeah, you probably right. Here you go, baby." She placed a plate in front of Macon. "You like biscuits and gravy?"

"I don't know...I've never had it before," Macon answered.

"*What*? You ain't never had no *biscuits and gravy*?" Albert exclaimed. "Mama, go on and give that Chile some." He shook his head. "No wonder you so slim. You ain't had no real southern cookin'. Well, you comes to the right place. Your Aunt Emma can really burn!"

Macon was very slender and petite.

"Oh, she's fine jes as she is. Besides, Macon knows I can cook. We had us a lovely dinner before we left, Philly," Emma said, putting a biscuit on Macon's plate. "Don't let her size fool you none either...this Chile can eats!" she laughed.

Macon blushed.

"So," Junior said, "what's it like in, Philly?"

"Okay, I guess."

"You must have had some fun—the museums and theater and all?" Deeney asked.

"Not really. I didn't get to do much." Macon put her head down.

Emma looked at her children and shook her head slightly.

A knot formed in the pit of Macon's belly, giving her a twinge of pain.

Changing the subject, Emma asked, "Shelby, when is Richard due home?"

"Not until next week. I didn't feel like being home alone this weekend."

"You know this is always your home. Where'd he go again?"

"Atlanta. He had an interview with a hospital out there. He's also seeing if there might be a position for me."

Emma looked at Shelby, sadness washing over her.

"I sure wish you all didn't have to leave. However, I'm glad to see you all making a life for yourselves. Yes I am. I hope he gets that position.

It'll be good for you both, and you all be closer to Calvin and Anna-Leigh. You jes don't forget to comes home every chance you gets." Emma looked at Shelby, raising an eyebrow.

"We won't, Mama. We won't," Shelby reassured her mother.

The phone rang just as everyone was finishing breakfast.

"I got it," Emma said picking up the phone. "Mama here, how may I help you?"

Deeney leaned over and whispered to Macon, "You want to go and check out Busby later? It ain't much, but I can introduce you to some real nice people."

Macon wasn't sure. She was still feeling a bit sick in her stomach. She thought eating would have settled it. It only made it worse.

"Maybe tomorrow," she answered. "My stomach still ain't feeling well," she said, patting her belly.

"All right. Tomorrow. You better ask Mama for some of her special tea. That always settles my stomach." Deeney thought for a minute, lowering her voice, "maybe it's that time of the month? My stomach always bothers me around that time."

"Perhaps," Macon said. "That's what it feels like."

"Yeah, get some tea from Mama. It will cure just about anything that ails you."

"Thanks." Macon smiled.

"Don't mention it. Like I said earlier, I'm

really glad you're here with us, Macon." Deeney smiled and gave Macon a slight hug. "I just had to give you a small hug! That's just how we do. See you later." Deeney left the kitchen.

"I'll be happy to sees y'all. Yes I would," Emma beamed. "I'll fix a beautiful Sunday supper. Oh, you want a peach cobbler? Well, I'll do that jes for you, baby. Yes. Uh-huh. All right. See y'all Sunday morning." Emma hung up the phone and turned, excited.

"Calvin?" Albert asked.

"Yes," Emma exclaimed. "He and Anna-Leigh are coming over Sunday. They want to share some good news!" Emma clasped her hands, "And I knows what it is... They pregnant!"

"Woman...now how you knows that?"

"'Cause, I done had a dream about eatin' me some fish. And you knows, when I'm the one eatin' it, it's one of mine!" Emma was thrilled.

Albert looked at Macon, "Ain't no use in arguing with her. When your Aunt dreams about fish, ninety-nine times out a hundred, she right," he said, shrugging his shoulders.

Macon laughed. Uncle and Aunt Emma were something else.

"So suga," Emma turned to Macon, "you feeling any better? I sees you didn't eat much."

"No...my stomach is still a little upset," Macon answered.

"Well, let me fix you some of this tea. It

should settles it right down."

"That tea can cure jes about anything," Albert said.

"Thank you Aunt Emma."

"No problem, baby." Emma put the teakettle on and prepared a cup of tea.

"So, you'll get to meet your other cousin, Calvin and his wife, Anna-Leigh, on Sunday. They live in Georgia. They'll be drivin' up."

Macon was curious. "Aunt Emma, why did you say someone's pregnant when you dream about fish?"

Emma thought for a moment. "You know, I rightly don't know the exact reasoning behinds it. But ever since I was a Chile, whenever someone dreamed about fish, a new soul was coming into the world. It meant somebody was either having a baby, or getting ready to make one. And if you is the one eatin' the fish, then it's someone very close to you—in your immediate family."

"They say that fish represent souls, or new life." Albert said.

Macon nodded her head. "Okay. Don't make much sense to me, but all right."

Emma laughed. "Not much does, suga, when it comes to old sayin's and all. Its jes somethin' that has been passed down through the generations: Folk lore."

"Yeah, Mama has a lot of those. Trust me; you'll be around long enough to get plenty folk lore. Your Aunt Emma's full of 'em," he said laughing.

"All right now old man!" Emma shot back, as she gave Macon the cup of tea. "Watch yourself."

"I'm jes jesting."

"Thank you," Macon said, taking a sip of tea.

"You welcome, baby. Jes takes your time. It's a strong tea. Takes some getting used to its taste." Rubbing Macon's back Emma said, "you'll be jes fine."

Macon smiled. She was glad to be around so much family. She wondered how she could miss something she never really had. But she did. She felt as though she missed out on a lot, and it was no one to blame but her mother. She knew it was her mother who kept her and her father away from their family. The more Macon thought about it, the angrier she became. And the more she resented her mother.

"You all right, Macon?" Emma looked curiously at Macon.

"Yes. I'm all right."

"Okay. You jes seem to be thinkin' rather heavy there. You know, you can tells me anything? Anything at all." Emma placed a hand under Macon's chin.

Macon smiled. "I know."

"All right, jes so you know." Emma smiled, and kissed Macon atop her head.

CHAPTER 7

MACON WAS FALLING IN LOVE WITH THE SMALL
town of Busby. Aunt Emma knew everyone, and
everyone knew her. Deeney had kept her word and
introduced her to a lot of nice people—people her
own age. She'd never had more fun.

Aunt Emma was right about the fish. Calvin
and his wife, Anna-Leigh, were expecting their first
child. Aunt Emma made a big fuss. She cooked all of
their favorites that Sunday. Macon could feel the
love. Everyone treated her as though she was there
all along. She felt very welcomed. Before she'd
known, two months had flown by.

Emma had truly been everything Macon's
father said she was.

Although Macon was feeling more
comfortable with each day that passed; physically,
she still was not feeling well. She barely had an
appetite, and she always felt tired. She accounted
her tiredness to a lack of sleep. She was
experiencing nightmares that would have her
waking up, shaking, and in a cold sweat.

One night proved to be most traumatic.

Macon's screams jolted Emma out of a sound
sleep.

Macon was screaming at the top of her lungs,
*"Let go! Let go of me! Please, leave me alone! I don't
want to! I don't want to!"*

Emma ran into the bedroom.

"Macon, baby! What's wrong?" She realized that Macon was still asleep. She ran to her bed. "Macon, Macon." Emma tried to calm her down.

Macon's arms were flailing, hitting at the air, as if someone was there. "No! No!" she kept yelling.

"Macon, wake up baby. Wake up," she gently shook her. "Come on, baby. You jes having a nightmare." Emma's concern deepened. This was not the first time Macon has had a nightmare since coming there.

Macon was soaking wet. Her hair was sticking to her face, and her clothes clung to her body. When she opened her eyes, she forgot for a moment where she was. She looked around quickly. When she recognized Emma, she leaped into her arms and held on for dear life.

"Macon, baby. It's all right. Mama got you. Shush. It's all right." Emma held Macon and rocked her. She could feel the child trembling in her arms.

Macon cried and cried. She would not let go of Emma; clinging to her, shaking.

"Oh, baby. What is it? What has you so frightened?" Emma tried to pull away for a minute. Macon would not let her go.

Albert knocked on the door before coming in.

"Is everything all right?"

Emma shook her head. "She had another nightmare," she whispered.

Albert nodded his head. "I'm gonna put on some tea, okay?"

97

Emma nodded.

Albert shut the door slowly.

Emma continued to rub Macon's back. The child was still trembling. She wondered what it was that had Macon so frightened. She was worried about her. Macon barely ate and was tired all the time. Even though she was loosening up a bit more each day, Emma still sensed that something just was not right.

"Macon, baby. Come on, suga. Look at Mama...looks at Mama for a moment."

Macon slowly released her hold on her Aunt.

Emma brushed the hair from Macon's face. She rubbed her arms, and bent to look her in the face. "Macon, baby. I can't help you if you don't tells me what is wrong."

Macon kept her head down. She kept folding and unfolding her hands in her lap. She wanted to yell out. She wanted to tell her Aunt everything; except she was too scared.

Emma took Macon's hands in hers. She raised them to her face and kissed them.

"Macon, baby. Please tell Mama what's wrong." She reached over and gently stroked her face. "I swears, baby. It'll be jes between you and me. But you has to tell me what's going on. I'm worried about you. You ain't been eatin' or sleepin'. You been so pale lately. Aren't you happy here?"

Macon nodded her head.

"Is anybody botherin' you?"

Macon shook her head.

"Does this have to do with Nadine and something that happen back home?"

Macon did not say anything. She was still.

"All right, it does. Doesn't it?" Emma determined.

"Yes," she whispered.

"Baby, please let it out. You gots to tell me so I can help you. I can't fix nothin if I don't know what's broke." Emma pulled Macon into her arms and hugged her tightly, reassuring her that everything was going to be all right.

Macon sat up straight, still trembling.

She was scared to tell what was wrong. She hated to think about what had happened to her. Moreover, the thought of even talking about it paralyzed her with fear.

However, she could no longer hold it in. She had to let it out before she lost her mind.

Every night since it happened, she has been reliving it in her dreams; some nights worse than others.

Macon stood slowly, wrapping her arms around herself. Shaking, she walked across the room, and sat in the armchair in the corner. Pulling her knees up to her chest, she began to rock.

Emma sat watching her. Not sure what to do, she walked over, knelt before Macon, gently touching her knee.

Macon looked into her Aunt's face, tears began to fill her eyes, and then falling down her cheeks.

Emma recognized the fear in Macon's eyes all too well. She'd been where Macon was now.

She reached forward, wiping the tears from Macon's face.

"Go ahead, baby. Tell me. I'm right here. I'm not goin' anywhere. I swears." She took Macon's trembling hands and held them tightly. "It's all right, I won't leaves you. Tell Mama and frees your soul, baby. That's the only way to make it stop."

Emma's voice was soft and soothing.

Macon felt reassured that Aunt Emma would not leave her. She would still love her—no matter what. She looked into Emma's eyes, as if she was looking right through her and began to tell Emma the most horrific thing.

It was so much more than Emma had anticipated.

She listened, and held Macon's hands as she spoke...slowly...painfully.

CHAPTER 8

TREMBLING, MACON SPOKE IN A LOW, monotone voice, recounting the events of a night two weeks before her father had passed.

"I just came back from the hospital from seeing Daddy. They wouldn't let me stay past visiting hours. When I got home, Mama wasn't there. I went into the kitchen and made myself a bowl of cereal. We hadn't gone shopping in a while. I was too busy with school and visiting with Daddy. I finished my cereal and washed out the bowl. I thought I heard my mother come in. When I called out, no one answered. I figured it was just the rain. It was a thunderstorm that night. I made sure I checked the doors and the windows—making sure they were all locked. Afterward, I went to my room. I had an exam the next day.

"I was lying across my bed studying when the lights went out. At first, I thought that it was a black out, because everything was so dark. I couldn't see my hands in front of my face. I felt my way to the hallway closet where I knew Daddy kept some flash-lights and candles. I was too scared to go to the basement and check the switch. Only Daddy knew how to do that, anyway. Then I heard a noise downstairs, but I wasn't sure. So I took a flashlight and went downstairs to see.

"I didn't see anyone, but the front door was

open. That surprised me, because I thought I locked it before going upstairs. I called for my mother, but there was no answer. I figured the wind from the thunderstorm blew the door open. Daddy was meaning to fix the lock on the door before he got sick. He never had the chance to.

"After locking the door, I went back to my room. But I felt weird. I can't exactly explain it; but I was scared. I lit the candle and placed it on my dresser. I went back over to my bed and lay down. I used the flashlight to study my notes. That's when I heard something. I said, '*hello*'. But no one answered. That's when I noticed the shadow in the mirror." Macon stopped talking for a moment, holding her breath.

Emma was not sure if she was ready to hear the rest of Macon's story. However, Macon needed her to hear. She needed to let out what she had been trying to hide for so long.

Heavy tears flowed down Macon's face. She finally exhaled. It was as though she was back in her bedroom. She let go of Emma's hands, stood, and began walking slowly towards the dresser.

Emma just watched, her stomach aching with pain for Macon.

"**WHO**—who's there?" Macon stammered. She eased her way off her bed, turning around quickly. Hands trembling, she tried to steady the flashlight between her small, slender fingers. She could not see anything or anyone.

"I said who's there!"

A deep voice came from the corner of her room near the closet, startling her.

"Relax, little mama. Relax."

A tall, lanky man came from out of the shadows.

"Relax, it's just me."

Macon knew who it was. She'd seen him many times before in their home; especially when her father was away. She'd seen him more frequently now that her father was in the hospital. It was Byron, her mother's friend.

He slunk out from the corner of her room, with his hands shielding his eyes from the glare of the flashlight.

"Can you put that light down? You damn near blinding me," he said.

"Ma-Mama isn't here. You're going to have to come back later." Macon was shaking. She never liked Byron. He always made her feel uncomfortable...nervous. Macon backed away slowly, trying to edge her way to the door.

Byron started walking towards her. "I know. Your Mama told me to meet her here. She...she had an errand to run. She told me it would be all right to wait here." He smiled slyly at Macon.

Fear gripped Macon. "What-what are you doing in my room?"

Byron came closer. "I was just checking on you...for your mama," he answered, smiling. He reached out to touch her.

Macon stepped back, stumbling over something. "You—you have to leave."

"I can't leave now. What? You want me to catch my death in this here thunderstorm?" Byron continued to walk towards her.

Macon regained her stability, making her way towards the door.

Byron stopped her.

"Now, where you going princess?" He placed his arm in front of the doorway, blocking her.

Macon stiffened. She did not like the way Byron was looking at her. "I...I'm going to go down stairs and wait for my mother." She tried to go under his arm.

Byron was now standing in the doorway, completely blocking her from leaving.

"I don't think that's a good idea. Why don't you just wait here with me? Your mama won't mind." He placed his hand on Macon's hair and began to caress it. "You got such beautiful, soft hair," he said grinning. He bent down and sniffed it. "Mm, smells way better than your mama's."

Macon was now trembling. She backed away, smacking his hand from her hair.

"I think you better leave...now." Macon knew she couldn't get passed him, so she tried to get him to move from the doorway. She walked toward her dresser.

"No, I'm gonna stay right here. I told you, your mama told me to come and waits for her." He advanced towards Macon.

Macon turned around quickly, not sure what to do. Stumbling, she dropped the flashlight onto the dresser, blowing the candle out.

Her thoughts moved rapidly.

Turning the flashlight off quickly, she made a dash for the door.

Byron tripped in the dark trying to catch her.

Macon too frightened to turn the flashlight back on, tried to make her way down the steps as quickly as she could, making it to the front door. She could hear Byron coming down the stairs. She fumbled to get the door open. She barely took two steps before she felt a pair of arms around her waist. She opened her mouth to scream, but a hand clasped tightly over her mouth, stifling her attempts.

Byron lifted Macon's small, five-foot- three frame off the ground, pulling her back into the house.

Macon kicked fiercely, trying her hardest to remove his grip.

"C'mon! C'mon! You ain't going anywhere!" Byron laughed.

Tears now blinded Macon's sight. She did not know what to do—so she bit into Byron's hand.

"Ugh!" Byron screamed, causing him to momentarily loosen his grip. "Damn little—"

Macon wiggled loose, running towards the

door screaming. "Help! Help! Someone, help me please!" She tripped over the crumpled rug.

Byron grabbed her again. "I said—you ain't going anywhere! Come here!"

"No! No! Let go of me!" Macon hollered.

On her knees, she grasped for the rug as Byron grabbed for her legs.

Macon reached for the flashlight that had fallen out of her hands earlier when trying to open the door. She continued to kick and scream as Byron tried to pin her legs in his arms. She managed to kick him as she reached the flashlight.

"Ump! You kicked me in the mouth! Come here!" Byron became enraged. He lunged at Macon on the floor, flipping her onto her back.

Macon swung the flashlight, just missing his head. She continued to swing, barely seeing in the darkness.

Byron ducked. The more she fought, the angrier he became. He knocked the flashlight from her hands, finally pinning her to the floor.

"No! No!" Macon screamed. "Get off of me! Get...off...of...me!"

"Shut up!" Byron yanked Macon up by the wrists, dragging her to the couch.

Macon screamed louder. "No! No! *Pleeeeeasssssse*, let me go!"

"Shut up, before I slit your throat!"

"Please let me go! Please," she begged.

Byron continued to drag Macon. "Stop fighting! Stop...fighting...me," he warned, throwing her onto the couch.

Macon screamed louder.

Byron slapped her across the face with the back of his hand.

Macon felt the searing pain across her face. Her ear ringing. She was helpless. He was too strong for her. She wondered where her mother was. She wished her Daddy were there to save her.

Macon whimpered, too afraid to scream out again.

Byron ripped Macon's blouse open. Leaning over her, putting all his weight on her, he kissed her hard in the mouth.

Macon cried.

His breath smelled of beer. Every now and then, she would get a glimpse of his face when the lightning shown through the window. His eyes were cold and evil. He placed one hand over her mouth, while he pulled on her pants with the other.

He whispered in her ear, "Now just relax, little mama. It'll be over soon. Relax."

Macon closed her eyes tightly. Tears burned her face. She could feel Byron's hands pulling down her panties, his rough hands between her thighs. She was horrified, and helpless to do anything to stop this monster, her mother's friend, from violating her—violating her body...her soul.

When Macon finished telling Emma the events of that night, she fell to the floor in a heap, sobbing.

37

Emma ran to Macon. She'd listened, holding her stomach and crying as Macon recounted the horrible events; sickened to her stomach by the whole thing.

CHAPTER 9

WRAPPING HER ARMS AROUND MACON, EMMA cried. "Oh sweet, Jesus. Oh, Jesus. Baby, I'm sorry. I'm so sorry! Oh God, what do I do? Oh baby girl, I'm so sorry." Emma rocked Macon back and forth in her arms. "I'm sorry. I'm so sorry," she continued whispering.

Macon held onto her Aunt; Weeping into Emma's bosom never wanting to let go.

Emma gently rubbed Macon's back. "Baby, Mama is so sorry. God, I'm so sorry." Emma held Macon tightly for a long while, telling her everything was going to be all right. She promised her.

Macon buried her face in Emma's bosom. At times, gasping for air from the pain that seemed to stifle her breath. Still, she had not told Emma everything. There was more that happened that night.

Macon began to tell Emma the rest.

"I—I didn't know what to do," she wept. "Then my mother came home. Oh, Aunt Emma..." Macon placed her head on Emma's shoulder.

"Oh, baby. It's all right. I'm here," Emma held her tightly. "Did you tell Nadine what happened?"

"Yes," Macon said.

Emma knew that Nadine was not there for her daughter as she should have been.

Damn that girl, she thought to herself.

"She—she said it was my fault," Macon cried. "She didn't care. She..." The words caught in her throat.

"What?" Emma could not believe her ears. "Oh, baby girl. None of this was your fault. None of it! Oh, Jesus, my baby," she insisted, squeezing Macon in her arms.

"He...he lied. He said that I came onto him, and...and one thing led to another. He lied on me, Aunt Emma. Mama believed him. *She believed him!*" Macon yelled.

"That no good bastard! Nadine didn't do nothing?"

Macon shook her head. "She told him to leave. I thought she was going to call the police. But she didn't. She wouldn't! I begged her to believe me. I begged her, Aunt Emma! Sh-she beat me!" Macon stuttered.

Emma was horrified. "Nadine whooped you?"

Macon bowed her head. In shame—nodded her head.

"She said I was no good—just like my daddy. She said I was always ruining her life. Then she beat me. She wouldn't stop. I begged her to *please* stop; but she wouldn't listen to me." Macon shook her head.

Emma cried; her heart breaking. She blamed herself for not seeing it when she went the first time. She blamed herself for not doing something sooner; for allowing Nadine to come between her and

Nathan.

"I ran to my bedroom and locked myself in. She kept banging on the door, screaming at me. She was high! I knew that she would kill me if I opened the door."

Emma held Macon in her arms tightly. "My precious. I'm so sorry I didn't see it. I'm so sorry I wasn't there. Please forgive me. Please, baby, forgive me." Emma's heart was in her throat. She was sickened by what Nadine allowed to happen to her child and the abuse she afflicted upon her by her own hand. She was also upset with Nathan. How could he stay—knowing what he knew? How could a mother be so cruel? She'd seen it many times before. However, the effect it had upon her was always the same.

"I was too scared to come out my room the next day. But I had to go to the bathroom. When I came out, she asked why I hadn't gone to school. I didn't know what to say. She didn't remember at first. Then she saw the bruises on my face. She didn't ask me anything else. She told me to get cleaned up because we had to go shopping."

Emma could not believe her ears. "She didn't take you to the doctor? You didn't get checked out?"

Macon shook her head. "No."

"She didn't mention nothing about the night before'?"

"No. She said it never happened. She said I had a nightmare. That Byron would never do a thing like that."

"What kind of..." Emma stopped herself from saying anything more. The look on Macon's face warned her to go no further.

She needed to get her mind together so she could help this child get through this. Emma was not sure where to begin. Macon was much like her in many ways. It was like looking in a mirror—watching her past relived through her grandniece. She was not going to allow Macon to go the same path she went. She was going to help her—anyway she could. Emma made up in her mind not to let the past continue to repeat itself. It had to stop.

"Did she let him back in the house?" Emma asked quietly.

"Yes," Macon whispered.

"Damn! Damn it!" Emma shook her head.

"I just tried to stay out their way. Mama said he was all she had left. He was the only one that really loved her and knew what she needed. She said she gave up enough for me. And she wasn't going to lose another man to me." Macon hung her head, tears flowing heavily from her eyes. Her heart ached, and her stomach began to do flips. She got up quickly, running to the bathroom.

Emma sat still, numb from the horrid revelation. She was not sure what to do. She wanted to *kill* Nadine. Though, what good does that Macon? —traumatized and barely holding on as it is. Her focus had to be Macon—helping her get through this.

"Lord, I jes don't understands why these things keep happening. I mean, why Lord? That baby ain't done anything to anyone, and she's suffering the most." Emma shook her head. "I jes don't understands." She stood and walked towards the bathroom, continuing to talk to herself. She heard Macon vomiting.

"Lord, jes let me get my hands on that bastard! I will make sure he never places his hands on another soul. Let alone be able to piss on his own! Damn it!" Emma hit her fists on the wall. "I got to get this baby some help. I got to get her checked out. No telling what he done left her with." She screamed. "Give me strength, Lord! Give me strength! That Chile needs me. I gots to be there for her...this is all my fault."

Emma knocked on the bathroom door, "You all right, baby?" She waited for Macon to answer. "Macon?" When she did not hear anything, Emma opened the door. Macon was passed out on the floor.

"Oh Jesus! Macon! Macon baby." Emma rushed to Macon. She patted her face, trying to wake her. "Come on, baby. Come on. Wake up for, Mama. Come on, baby." Emma began crying. "Oh, Lord! Albert! Albert!" she hollered.

Albert came running into the bathroom. "What's the matter? Oh Jesus! What happened?"

"I—I don't know. She's passed out. Hurry up! Get the car! We got to get her to the hospital."

Albert ran, slipped some pants over his pajamas and went to get the car.

Deeney and Junior came running when they heard their mother screaming.

101

"What's the matter, Mama?" Junior asked

"What's wrong with Macon?" Fear washed over Deeney's face.

"I don't know. She passed out, and won't wake up," Emma wiped Macon's forehead. "Your father went to get the car. We got to get to the hospital."

"Here, Mama, let me get her." Junior scooped Macon's small frame into his arms.

She looked like a rag doll against his six foot frame. Junior heard the car pull to the front as he carried Macon through the living room.

Deeney opened the door. "Be careful, Junior." She held the door open. "Watch her head." Deeney was shaking. She'd never seen her mother so visibly shaken before. Mama was strong. Always. It had to be something pretty awful to have her mother so emotional.

Emma rushed out behind Junior, tying a scarf around her head. She grabbed her purse. "Be careful."

"I'm going with you," Deeney said.

"No, no baby. You stay here. I know you don't like hospitals."

"It's all right, Mama. You need me. Macon needs me. I can sit with her in the back seat." Deeney was not taking no for an answer. She was already putting her sweater on.

Emma looked at her daughter. She knew there was no sense in arguing with her.

"All right, come on. We got to get there

Southern~101~Comfort

quick."

"I'm ready!"

Junior laid Macon in the backseat, leaning her head on Deeney's lap.

Albert looked at Emma, to ask what happened.

Emma shook her head, mouthing she would tell him everything later.

They rode in silence to the hospital. The nearest hospital was thirty minutes away. Albert drove as quickly as he could, praying that the good Lord would keep the police away.

Emma turned in her seat watching Macon, praying that she would at least open her eyes. Macon did not. Emma looked at Albert shaking her head. Tears welling up in her eyes, she prayed to herself.

"Lord, this is Emma Jean, here. Please, Father, let this Chile wake up. Let her be all right. Lord, you knows she has been through so much already. I done already lost Nathan. Please don't take the only thing I has left of him. Let her wake up. I promise, Lord. I promise You, I will takes good cares of her, raising her jes like she my own...because, we both knows she is."

Emma watched as Deeney rubbed Macon's forehead and held her hand.

CHAPTER 10

THEY ARRIVED AT THE HOSPITAL. Albert made it there in fifteen minutes. He drove right into the emergency entrance, carrying Macon in his arm; Emma and Deeney right behind him, yelling for help.

"Someone help us! Please, someone help us," screamed Emma.

A physician on duty rushed over to them. "Lie her down over here. What happened?" He asked, checking Macon.

"I—I don't know," Emma began. "She was in the bathroom throwing up and when I went to checks on her, she was passed out on the floor."

"How long has she been unconscious?" he asked.

"About twenty...twenty-five minutes." Emma was frantic.

"Has she regained consciousness at any time in between?"

"No." Emma shook her head. "Please, you got to help my Chile."

"Are you her mother?"

"No, I'm her Aunt. But she's in my care."

"All right; we're going to go in here and examine her."

"She...she gonna be all right?" Albert asked.

"I don't know yet. I have to examine her first." He turned to Emma, "Does she have any illnesses that you know of, or allergies?"

"No. None that I can recall. I can calls her mama, though?"

"All right. Do you know what caused her to vomit?"

Emma looked at the doctor for a moment. She had to tell him, but she didn't want to say it front of Deeney.

"Tell you what; come in here with me whilst I examine her. Just in case she wakes up, she'll see a familiar face."

"All right," Emma agreed, following the doctor. She turned to Albert. "Call Shelby, tell her to call Nadine and find out if Macon has any allergies or anything?"

"All right, Mama. Me and Deeney be in the waiting area." He hugged her and whispered in her ear, "Don't worry, the Chile will be all right." He then kissed her softly.

"I know. God got it. I'll tells you everythin' later. Okay?"

"All rights."

Emma went into the examining room with the doctor. Albert took Deeney's hand and walked to the waiting area to call Shelby.

"Is Macon going to be okay?" Deeney asked.

"I'm sure God got it. She'll be jes fine. We jes have to keep praying."

Albert called Shelby and told her what happened. He explained to her what Emma wanted her to do. He and Deeney sat waiting for Emma, to come tell them that Macon was going to be all right.

While in the examining room, Emma informed the doctor of Macon's abuse. She explained to him what Macon had shared with her that night, and her fears that something more may have happened.

The doctor assessed Macon's situation. He noticed several scars and bruises on various places of her body. Emma, horrified to see the scars, now understood why Macon wore the clothes that she did. She was trying to hide the scars.

After his initial examination, the doctor ordered blood work and more tests to be ran. He was concerned that Macon still had not awakened. She was not responding to any stimulation. And her breathing was somewhat labored. He did not want to speculate what was wrong. He waited for the tests to come back before he gave Emma a definite answer.

Emma waited in the room as the doctor assessed the results.

They'd started Macon on an intravenous drip.

Emma sat next to Macon's bed, holding her hand. She'd never been more frightened in her life.

"Macon, baby. Please wake up. Wakes up for Mama. Come on, baby girl. I promise you, I ain't gonna let no one hurts you ever again. I promise. Please baby, jes wake up." Emma shook her head. Her heart aching.

After a short while the doctor returned with the results from the examination and tests.

Although Emma was anxious to know what was wrong with Macon, she was also fearful. "Let's have it doctor; what's wrong with my baby?"

Closing the door behind him, he began to tell Emma.

Macon was expecting.

"Expectin' what?"

"You're niece is pregnant."

Emma's mouth opened, unable to utter a word, although, part of her was not surprised. She'd prayed her thoughts were wrong.

"She's about twelve to fourteen weeks along. She also has a virus, which has compromised her immune system. Complicated by the pregnancy, she is severely dehydrated and suffering from an iron deficiency. I am guessing she was never examined after the assault?"

Emma shook her head.

"So it's safe to say this is a result from that."

"Oh, sweet Jesus!" Emma shook her head crying. "Is...is she gonna be all right? I mean, is she gonna wake up soon? What about the baby? My God, she's jes a baby herself." Emma reached over, rubbing Macon's forehead.

"We started her on some antibiotics to fight the infection. We're also giving her some fluids to combat the dehydration. Her body is in shock. However, she's young and her resilience is remarkable." He placed a hand on Emma's shoulder. "She's holding up quite well. I expect her to make a full recovery."

"Why did she pass out? And why ain't she up yet?"

"Exhaustion: Plain and simple. Her body just couldn't handle it anymore—especially with the pregnancy. Our bodies have a way of making us do what we have to do. Her body needed rest. She will be all right, physically. However, from what you have shared with me; Mrs. Watson, your niece needs some counseling to deal with what has happened to her. As you said, she is just a child herself. And I am concerned how the knowledge of this pregnancy may affect her."

The doctor was very forthright and candid in his assessment of the situation. He advised Emma very carefully about the kind of care that Macon was going to need. He explained that if Macon was able to go full term, she would have a difficult childbirth. In addition, there is a slight possibility that the baby may have been affected by the stress and trauma of Macon's condition and the virus itself.

Emma listened carefully to the doctor's advice. All she cared about at that moment was that Macon was going to be all right. The good Lord saw every child as a blessing. No matter how they came into this world. Emma, however, was not ignorant to the fact that Macon was going to need a whole lot of love and care, and support through this pregnancy. It was going to be a very difficult pregnancy for her; physically, but especially emotionally.

After the doctor left, Emma sat quietly for a while studying Macon's petite frame, lying in the bed hooked up to the I.V.

"Looks at you. So frail; so innocent. Jes a baby, havin's a baby." Emma shook her head, tears rolling down her cheeks. "I knows baby girl, life jes don't seems fair to you. You only have been in this world fifteen years, and already you seen too much. But don't you worry none. 'Cause I'm gonna takes care of you; you and that baby. Yes I am. I won't let another soul hurts you. They'd have to kills me first. God knows I mean it!" Emma shook her head.

"Oh, suga', I knows what's you goin' through. I've been in your shoes. Yes I have. I've been jes where you at now. I've done walked this path. And Lord knows I know, it ain't s a pleasant one. Nevertheless, don't s you fret. 'Cause you see, you got me. Yes you do. Both you got me. I'm jes so sorry I didn't comes for you sooner. I'm so sorry I let Nadine gets between me and mine. *Yes I am.* But you know what baby girl? God got it anyway. Yes He does. We ain't gonna let that slick snake think he done got the best of us! No sir. We strong.

"You knows what? You jes like me: Strong, smart and a survivor. Yes you are. We takes a good lick, but we keeps on ticking," she laughed. "Oh yes. We fighters...me and you. I see so much of me in you. But you have much more sense than I had at your age. 'Cause my parents were gone already. And me and my sister had to raise ourselves. But God was good to us. I would've been dead a long time ago. Would've, if I didn't kills myself first someone else was goin to. That's why I thanks God for Albert. Yes I do. He saved me.

"We all needs a savior. Ain't no ones like Jesus. But we sure do needs to see him in the flesh once and again. And that was Albert. He changed my life. He gave me life." Emma took Macon's hand in hers, and stroked it softly. "See, that's why I know God sent you to me. So I can gives you what was given to me. My chilren don't knows all I been through. 'Cause I made sure that they never had to suffer what I did. They don't know about all the horrors that I know you knows, and that I done seen. Thank the Almighty.

"But you has. I 'm so sorry that you had to suffer so baby girl. Mama is so sorry. I jes don't understands why mama's hurt their babies the way they do. Why they abandoned them? Why they beat them unmercifully? Why they destroy them when they is supposed to protect them? I jes don't understands Nadine." Emma stood up, and walked towards the window. The sun had just risen. She turned and watched as the sunlight shined on Macon. She looked like an angel.

The sun was highlighting her long black hair. It sparkled like glitter. It brightened her face, which had been pale just an hour earlier. Emma smiled at the sight. She walked back towards Macon, and stared lovingly.

"How can your mama not love the hell out of you? You are so precious. Her own flesh and blood. I will never understands."

Watching Macon who looked so peaceful, it occurred to Emma for the first time. "Your mama is *jealous*," she whispered. "Well I'll be damned. Nadine is jealous of you." It finally made *some* sense to Emma. Nadine was jealous of her own child. She was no longer the center of Nathan's attention or affection.

"How sad. To try and destroy your own Chile, so you can feel important." Emma moved a strand of hair from Macon's face. "All she had to do was love you and enjoy you. But she couldn't. How could she? She doesn't even love herself." Emma sighed heavily. "Well, baby. I better gets in here and tells your Uncle what's goin' on. I knows he worried about you, jes as much as I am." Emma leaned forward and kissed Macon on the forehead. "I'll be backs a little later."

Emma closed the door behind her slowly.

"Lord, it's almost seven o'clock. I hasn't even had the chance to talk with Albert. He and Deeney are probably sleeping." Emma walked to the waiting room area. When she turned the corner, she saw Albert sleeping and Deeney curled up on the seat next to him with her head in his lap...asleep.

"Hey," she whispered in Albert's ear. "Hey Daddy." She gave him a kiss.

Albert opened his eyes. "Hey Mama. Mm, what time is it?" he asked, rubbing his eyes.

"It's nearly seven," Emma said. "Deeney, Deeney." Emma nudged her daughter lightly, as not to startle her.

"Umm...Mama. Is Macon okay?" she asked, stretching.

"She gonna be all right. Here," Emma placed some money in Deeney's hand. "Do Mama a favor?

Go gets me and your daddy some coffee?"

"Sure Mama."

"Be sure to gets you something too, okay?"

"Yes Mama." Deeney hugged her Mama tightly before she left.

Emma made sure Deeney was gone before she sat down. She plopped down hard in the seat next to Albert and placed her head on his chest and started crying. Her body was exhausted, and she needed the comfort of her husband's embrace.

Albert placed his arms around his wife, and kissed her atop her head. "Let it out, Mama. Let it out," he whispered in her ear.

"Good Lord, Albert. That Chile has been through so much hell. More than we knew. She's expecting, Albert."

"Expecting what?"

"A baby; it's such a long story. That baby has been through hell and back and it ain't over yet."

"What? How?" Albert said surprised.

Emma began to tell Albert all that Macon had shared with her the night before. She cried the entire time; breaking down in Albert's arms.

Albert was filled with rage. Not only concerning what happened to Macon, but for his wife—having to be reminded of her own wretched past. It disturbed him greatly.

CHAPTER 11

IT WAS A LONG, ARDUOUS FORTY EIGHT HOURS.
Macon still had not awakened. Emma sent Albert
and Deeney home. There was no sense in Albert
missing any more work; nor Deeney just sitting
around the hospital keeping her company. Although
she took comfort in their companionship, she
insisted that they go. She would call them as soon as
Macon woke up.

"Okay, Mama. I'll be back after work." Albert
kissed his wife.

"No, Baby. That's all right. You gets some
rest. Tell Shelby I'll see her later." Emma gave Albert
a tight hug.

"Listen, I don't cares what you say woman.
I'll be here after work." Albert put his hand under
Emma's chin. "You hear me?"

Emma smiled. "Yes dear. I hears you. What
I'm gonna do without you?"

"You ain't gonna ever find out." Albert smiled.
"She gonna be all right, Mama. God don't lie.
Besides, anybody who got you *and* Jesus on their
side can't go wrong."

"Oh Albert!" Emma wrapped her arms
around Albert's neck. "You always know what to say
to make me feel good. God, I love you!"

"I love you, too, Mama. Don't ever forget
that!"

"Never Baby. Never." Emma held onto her husband tightly. Thanking God for the day he sent Albert to save her life.

"Well, look who's here?" Albert said. "Right on time," he said giving Lynorra Washington a kiss on the cheek.

"Hey. I called the house looking for you," she said to Emma. "Junior told me what happened. I thought you could use a fresh change of clothes, and somethin' to eats. Lord knows how this hospital food is." Lynorra embraced Emma tightly.

"Oh, Sistah, you always knows what I need." Emma smiled at her best friend of twenty years. Emma pulled back, and cautiously asked, "Your husband ain't here is he? Lord knows, I ain't ready for that." She laughed.

"Now behaves, Emma. You know Reverend Washington cares about you." Albert chuckled.

Emma and Reverend Washington were anything but cordial. Emma detested him, but tolerated him because he was Lynorra's husband, and a man of the cloth. That had to count for something.

"Now, don't you two starts," Lynorra laughed. "No," she said turning to Emma. "He ain't here. But he did tell me to let you know he was praying for you," Lynorra said raising an eyebrow.

"What?" Emma feigned ignorance. "I wasn't gonna say a word...I swear!"

"Lord, lets me get out of here before the lightning strikes!" Albert chided.

"Oh hush! Go on, so you can gets to work."

Emma hugged her husband, and whispered in his ear, "Loves you, Al B. More than anything," she kissed him on the cheek.

"Same here, Mama. Don't you forget it. I'll see you at home tonight." Albert kissed his wife. "See you, Lynorra. You takes care of my girl, now." He smiled as he left, walking down the corridor.

"I got you," Lynorra called after him. Albert waved his hand, and disappeared around the corner. Lynorra turned to her best friend. "So, Sistah, you want to talk while we drink this coffee?" She raised the bag in her hand.

Emma smiled, comforted by her friends presence. "Girl, where do I begin?"

Lynorra put her arm around Emma's shoulder. "From the beginning. We can sits over here." Lynorra led her to the chairs in the small waiting area.

"Sounds good to me. But..." Emma said, "I really ain't in the moods for coffee."

"I know. But you don't think that I can just bring a jug of Mulberry wine in here, do you?" Lynorra winked at Emma.

"You didn't?" Emma said surprised.

"Of course I did! Shoot, these the best cups of coffee around...I just held the coffee, sugar, and cream." She smiled wide at her friend. "I warmed it a bit. I know you like it best that way." She sat down, and patted the seat next to her.

"Lynorra, you are jes too full of surprises today." Emma shook her head and sat down beside her friend, taking the cup from her hand.

"Girl, you ain't heard nothin' yet. Wait 'til I tells you about Artie. I swears; I almost rang his neck today."

Emma laughed, taking a sip of her 'coffee'. "Mm, this is jes right."

Lynorra took a sip from her cup. "Mm, you're right. So tell me," she said turning to her friend, "What's going on?"

Emma leaned her head back and sighed deeply. "Lynorra, Chile it's jes so much. So much more than I expected."

Lynorra took Emma's hand. "Well, you ain't alone. Remember that. I am here for you...always." She smiled squeezing Emma's hand.

"I know. And I loves you for that."

"So, start at the beginning..."

Emma began to tell her best friend all that had transpired in the last seventy hours. Lynorra listened to her friend, and then held her in her arms, as she cried on her shoulder.

EMMA kept vigil at Macon's bedside; praying for her to wake up soon. It was one o'clock in the afternoon; Lynorra had left a couple of hours ago. Emma fallen asleep holding Macon's hand, her head resting on the side of the bars to the bed. Emma woke up immediately when she felt something touch her hair.

"Huh?" Startled for a moment, Emma looked around quickly. She focused her eyes on Macon. She was awake! "Baby girl! You awake! Praise the good Lord," she leaned forward kissing Macon on the forehead. "I'll be right back. I'm gonna gets the doctor."

Macon didn't know where she was. Her eyes roamed around the hospital room. She felt somewhat confused, trying to remember what happened. She looked at the I.V. in her arm. She touched the tube that was in her nose, and began panicking. She did not like hospitals—not since the experience with her father. She began to pull the tubes out of her nose and the I.V. from her arm, just as the doctor and Emma walked in.

"Macon, no!" Emma rushed to stop Macon from pulling the I.V. from her arm.

"Now, you don't really want to do that, do you?" asked the doctor. "Just calm down, Macon. I'm Doctor Reese. Your Aunt and I have been waiting for you to wake up." Dr. Reese began to examine Macon. "So, young lady, how are you feeling? You gave your Aunt quite a scare," he smiled.

Macon looked at Emma, and began crying. "What...what's wrong with me? Am I dying too?" Macon was scared.

"Oh no, honey. You gonna be jes' fine," Emma assured her. "Your little body jes couldn't handles the stress you been under. So it made you get some rest..." Emma looked at the doctor. She was not certain how to explain to this *Chile*, that *she* was going to have a Chile.

Doctor Reese sensed Emma's concern and

uncertainty about what to tell Macon. He looked at Macon and smiled. "You're going to be just fine, young lady. As your Aunt said, your body just needed some rest. Our bodies are very smart. Sometimes they have a way of protecting us when we don't have the sense too." Dr. Reese checked Macon's pulse. "So tell me, Macon. What's the last thing that you remember?"

Macon thought for a moment. She looked at Emma and then put her head down. She whispered, "Speaking to my Aunt in my room." Macon did not look up. A sudden feeling of shame had come over her.

Emma took Macon's hand and leaned forward and kissed her on the forehead. "It's all right, baby. Everything gonna be jes fine."

"Do you know what today is?" he asked.

"Uh...Saturday?"

"Well, actually it's Monday."

"Monday?" Macon was confused. "You mean I've been asleep for two days?"

"That's right, baby."

"You sure I ain't dying or something?" she asked Dr. Reese.

"Yes, I'm sure. You are going to be just fine. You do have a little virus. But, we're taking care of that with some antibiotics. Your body was in a kind of shock. So it made itself go to sleep so that it could repair itself."

Macon wasn't sure if she believed the doctor. She sensed that there was something that he and

Aunt Emma were not telling her. She did not know if she wanted to know the truth or not.

"Excuse us for moment, Macon." Dr. Reese spoke with Emma quietly.

"I *must* be dying," she thought to herself. "They just don't know how to tell me." Macon strained her ears to no avail. The only word she heard was counselor.

"She's the best counselor we have on staff," Dr. Reese continued. "As I said, I think it would be better if she was here with you when you told her. I believe Macon would be more comfortable hearing it from you, than me. She trusts you, and I can see how much she loves you." He rubbed Emma's shoulder.

Emma nodded in agreement. "I completely agrees with you. Do you think that counselor's here today? I don't wants to linger in telling her. She needs to know."

"I agree. She is here today. I'll have her come right in. I'll inform her of the whole situation, then I'll join you afterward."

"Oh, yes, yes. Most definitely." Emma looked over to Macon. "Anything that's gonna help my baby gets through this."

"Give me about twenty minutes."

"Okay."

"All right young lady," Dr. Reese turned to Macon. "I'll see you in a short while. I'm going to see how soon I can spring you from here." He smiled and left the room.

Macon smiled halfheartedly at the doctor. She wondered what was really going on.

I'm probably going to die, just like my father. They're too scared to tell me. I wonder how long I got left.

Emma saw the concern on Macon's face and could tell that her niece was trying to figure out what was going on. Macon was a smart girl. You could not hide things from her for, too, long. She walked over to the bed and sat down taking Macon's hand.

"Now, what you over here thinkin' 'bout?"

"I'm dying, aren't I? Just like my daddy." Tears began to well up in her eyes.

"Oh, baby, no. You ain't dying. I swears," Emma said hugging Macon. "Whatever gave you such a notion?" She looked Macon in the eyes.

Tears began to fall down Macon's cheeks. "Be-because, it's just like when you came to see daddy. You two talked. And—and it was about him dying. Do I have the same thing wrong with me?" She asked, beginning to sob. "I have cancer, too?"

"Oh no, baby! Perish the thought! You gonna be jes fine. You hears me?" Emma pulled Macon close to her chest. "Sweetie, ain't nothin' wrongs with you that ain't been wrong with lots of people. You gonna be jes fine. I swears it. Else my name ain't Emma Jean Cooper Watson. Yes, Lord. You gonna be fine." She rocked Macon in her arms and continued to reassure her that all was going to be okay.

"Hello." A tall slender woman entered the

room. She extended her hand to Emma and Macon. "You are Mrs. Watson and Miss Cooper?" She asked cheerfully.

"Yes, we are," answered Emma, shaking the woman's hand.

"Please to meet you, both." She smiled at Macon warmly. "I'm Camille Alexander. Doctor Reese wanted me to come and speak with you, Macon." She rubbed Macon's arm.

"Why? Is there something wrong with me? Because Aunt Emma said I was fine!" Macon looked at Emma bewildered.

"Oh no! I'm sorry, dear. I didn't mean to alarm you. Your Aunt is right, you are fine." She reassured her. "But there are a few things I need to talk with you about. Things that Dr. Reese and your Aunt," she nodded towards Emma, "felt I was able to help you with."

Macon was not sure what was going on. But she knew she definitely was not as well as they claimed. "All right."

"First, let me ask you, how are you feeling?"

"I guess okay. I just want to go home. I don't like hospitals much." Macon looked at Emma.

Emma squeezed her hand. "It's all right, baby. We'll be goin' home soon."

"Yes, that's true. As soon as I'm finished and Dr. Reese signs a few papers, you'll be already to spring this joint." Camille smiled at Macon, trying to reassure her. "Well, I hear you have been through quite a bit?"

Macon nodded.

"Dr. Reese said he explained to you that your body was exhausted, and it was kind of giving itself a little rest?"

"Yes."

Emma turned to Macon. She had to be the one to tell her. "There is a reason why you have been so tired and your stomach has been all upset..."

Macon looked from Emma to Camille. She had a feeling she wasn't going to like what her Aunt had to say.

"Baby girl, you're expectin'..." Emma searched Macon's face.

Macon's face was blank for a moment.

Camille reached over and touched Macon's arm. "Macon, do you understand what your Aunt is telling you?"

Macon's eyes grew as big as saucers. She heard the words in her head, but she could not wrap her brain around what Camille had spoken.

"Macon, suga'? You all right?" Emma did not know what to do. Macon did not respond.

"Macon, can you tell me what you're feeling?" Camille asked. "It's okay, you know. However you feel."

"It's gonna be all right, Macon. I'm here with you." Emma looked at Camille, not sure what to do.

Macon could not believe it. It was not possible.

She finally spoke. "I-I'm only fifteen. I mean, I can't have a baby. I mean, how? I didn't do anything.

I know where babies come from. But I didn't do anything. I swear." Macon shook her head back and forth in disbelief. She looked at Emma, "You believe me Aunt Emma, right? I swear I never did anything. I would never disrespect your home or anyone else's. You believe me, right?" Macon began crying. She buried her face in Emma's chest.

Emma held Macon tightly, as the tears flowed down her face. She thought to herself: *What's I'm gonna say to this Chile? How I'm gonna explain to her, that this baby was 'cause of the rape? How, Lord?*

Emma looked at Camille and mouthed, "Do I tell her now?"

Camille nodded yes.

Emma took a deep breath. She stroked Macon's hair. "Macon, baby? Macon." She held her face in her hands, "You knows Mama believes you. I knows, as well as the good Lord, that you ain't got a disrespectful bone in your body."

"Then you know I can't be pregnant. I just can't," Macon cried.

"I know, I know. But I needs you to listen to me. I needs you to listen to Mama real good, okay?"

Macon nodded.

"It's true. You havin' a baby."

Macon shook her head. "No! I can't be. I didn't do anything, Aunt Emma. I swear!"

"Shush! Shush! I know. But I needs for you to listens to me." Emma shook her head, as if to clear her thoughts. "You are almost four months along."

She looked into Macon's eyes, and repeated, "You are almost four months along. So this ain't happen here. Do you understands what I'm saying to you, baby?"

Macon looked at Emma confused. "Four months?" She whispered. "But, I never did anything. Never. Not even back home."

Emma was not sure if she should continue. It was hard for her to explain to Macon. Moreover, she knew that it would be even harder for Macon to understand, and perhaps accept. She wondered if the Doctor, Camille and herself, was expecting too much from Macon at this time. But she knew that she could not hide the truth from her. The Chile was already three and a half months along, and ain't no hiding that.

Emma held Macon's face in her hands, brushing the hair away from her face. She kissed her on the forehead and took a deep breath. Looking straight into Macon's eyes, Emma began speaking softly, "Macon, baby, you know that I loves you like you mine. And I would never ever lie to you, or lets anyone else lie to you or hurts you anymore. I promised you that. Remember?"

"Yes." Macon whispered.

"Well, I needs you to think for a moment. Remember what you told me Saturday night?" Emma hated this. But she just couldn't risk being so bold and forward with Macon right then.

Macon looked at her Aunt, then to Camille.

Emma turned her face back towards her. "It's all right. Jes looks at me. Okay?"

Macon nodded. "I...I remember." Macon shut

her eyes.

"Now, I want you to understand, that because of what happened then, you are now expecting."

Macon opened her eyes. She stared at Emma for a moment, and then looked at Camille. She put her head down, and placed her hands over her ears. "No, no, no, no." She shook her head back and forth. "No, no, no....NOOOOO!" she screamed.

If it were possible, Emma's heart broke even more. She didn't know what to do for her niece. The tears ran down Emma's cheeks as she reached to comfort Macon.

"I'm so sorry, baby. I'm so sorry," Emma cried, while trying to hold Macon.

Macon continued to scream *no*, over and over again. She would not allow Emma to comfort her. Camille paged Doctor Reese. It was just too much for Macon to accept right then. She was becoming increasingly hysterical. Once Dr. Reese arrived, he gave Macon a sedative to help calm her down. He felt it best that Macon stayed for at least another forty-eight hours for observation. Although she profusely objected, he thought it best that Emma go home, and return in the morning. He explained that Macon would be out for the rest of the night.

To make her feel more at ease, Camille agreed to stay the night. She also insisted that Emma take this time to go home, get some rest, and inform her family of what's going on. She promised her that she would call if anything changed.

Reluctantly, Emma agreed.

Emma called Shelby to pick her up. She did not want to disturb Albert at work. Nor did she want to upset him by how distressed she was. Emma's nerves were really in a bundle.

She needed a cigarette.

Emma was waiting in front of the hospital when Shelby pulled up. "Mama, you all right?" Shelby walked over to her mother. "Mama?"

Emma was in a daze. She did not notice Shelby standing in front of her.

"Mama?" Shelby touched her mother on the shoulder.

"Huh?" Emma shook her head. "Oh, Shelby, baby. I didn't even sees you."

"You all right, Mama?" She sat down on the bench besides her mother. "I called you from the car, but you didn't hear me. Give me that." Shelby took the cigarette from her mother. "Mama, I told you these things are no good. They just make you feel worse than before." Shelby put the cigarette out.

"I know. I know, Chile. But my nerves were jes too bad."

"I thought Macon was going to be all right? What happened?"

"Chile, what *didn't* happen?" Emma shook her head. "Come on, I tells you on the way home."

"Okay." Shelby helped her mother up.

As they walked towards the car, Emma sighed heavily. Her heart was aching, and her mind was flooded with painful memories of her own past. Once they were on their way, Emma told Shelby everything that happened.

CHAPTER 12

SHELBY AND EMMA SAT IN THE CAR FOR A moment before going inside. Shelby looked at her mother and asked, "Do you think she'll be able to accept this...I mean, the pregnancy?"

"Shelby, honey, I don't know. I jes don't know. That Chile has been through so much in her short fifteen years. Especially these last ten months. The moment Nathan took sick, nothing has gone right for her. Without her father, she feels abandoned. I'm trying...I really am. But I don't know what to do that will make this all right for her."

"Just love her, Mama. Keep loving her the way you are and she will be fine." Shelby tried to reassure her mother.

"I don't know." Emma leaned her head back on the seat, and shut her eyes. "Did you get in contact with Nadine?"

"Well, I tried the facility, but they said they had not seen Nadine for two weeks."

"Oh, Lord!"

"I tried her at the house, and nothing. No answer. I've tried in the morning, the afternoon, at night...nothing. I tried the facility again this morning, and they still haven't heard from her. They even sent someone to her house, and nothing."

Emma shook her head. "Damn it!" Emma put her hand to her forehead. "Father, forgive me. I jes don't know 'bout that Chile! I really don't. I swears she tryin' to kill herself."

"I never understood Nadine. Not at all. And to treat your own child like that?"

Emma looked out the window. "Well, there are a lot of things people don't know about Nadine. Lord knows I tried my best to reach out to her and helps her. I only wish I never let her talk Nathan into movin'. Maybe if I would've..." Emma started crying. She could not finish her sentence. Her mind was racing with so many thoughts, and her heart was aching with much pain.

Shelby reached over and placed her hand on her mother's shoulder. "You did all you could do, Mama. You raised, Nate. And he loved you like you was his Mama. He was going to do what he wanted. You know how it is: We in love and we think we know it all."

Emma grabbed Shelby's hand and kissed it. "Thank you, baby. I knows you right. But there is jes so much you don't knows about. I jes wish I would have..." Emma shook her head.

"What is it, Mama? What do you wish?"

"A lot, Shelby. A whole lot. But this ain't the time or place. Let me gets myself into this here house. Albert be home soon, and I needs to cook him some good food. All he had these last two days is hospital food." Emma opened the car door.

"Don't worry, Mama. You get some rest; Miss Lynorra brought a whole meal over. She said she'd know you'd be too tired to even think about cooking," Shelby said, catching up to her mother.

"Oh, she's so thoughtful. 'Cause I sure am tired. I don't know if I'm comin' or goin'." Emma gave Shelby a kiss. "Sorry I'm keepin' you from work."

"It's all right. Just go ahead and gets some rest. Daddy will be home in a couple of hours, so you have a chance to take a shower and get some sleep before he comes in. I'll put the food in the oven on warm."

It felt like an eternity climbing up the stairs. Emma went straight to her bathroom and took a shower. The hot water felt good on her body. Her body was aching, her head was spinning. When Emma walked into her bedroom, she plopped down on her bed. She wanted to put on her nightgown, but she didn't have the strength to move. She kicked her slippers off, tightened her robe, and scooted back on the bed. She laid her head down on her pillow.

"Lord, I'm jes so tired," she whispered. "I don't know what else to do. How did this happen? Oh Father, help me. Please, help me..." Emma sighed deeply. She turned over on her side, her gaze falling upon a picture on her dresser. It was her sister, Clarisse. Emma stared at it for a moment.

"Clarisse, I'm sorry. I could have done better. I know I should have. Please, forgives me." Emma continued to stare at her sister's picture, growing wearier, until she drifted off to sleep...

"*EMMA Jean Cooper! You gets your narrow hide in this store! Right now!*"

"*Yes, Ma'am.*" *Emma slank her way passed her mother's glaring stare.*

"*Didn't I tells you about messin' 'round here?*"

"*Yes, Ma'am.*"

"*Gets in that back room and fix it up, before I tears your hide apart! I can never get a thing done with you 'round! I don't know why you're daddy ain't takes you with him!*" *Justine Cooper swatted Emma on the behind with the back of her hand. "Hurry it up!" She hollered.*

Trying not to cry, Emma moved quickly so not to get hit again. "Yes, Ma'am. I'm sorry." Emma, picked up the broom and started sweeping.

"*You always sorry! Jes like your damn, father! I swears, you two makes me sick. I don't know who's worse between you! Hurry up and gets that back room together!*" *Justine walked to the front of the store, mumbling to herself, "Damn fool! Chilren's! All's they do is get in the way. I swears, they ain't worth the pain of labor! Especially that little heifer back there!" As she was reaching for a cigarette, a customer walked in.*

"*Hey, Justine. How's it going today?*"

"*Hey, Miss Lorelei. Everything is goin jes fine. I got your order ready for you." Justine smiled, placing the cigarettes in her apron pocket.*

"*Thank you. We're having company tonight,*

and Lord knows I just can't seem to get it right in this southern heat." Lorelei wiped her forehead with her handkerchief. "I just don't know how you all do it in all this heat. I swears, I can't wait to get back to New York," Lorelei laughed.

"Oh, it ain't so bad once you get used to it. We manage. I suppose livin' here all one's life, you kind of don't notice it as much."

"Whew! I guess so." Lorelei fanned herself.

"Where's my manners? Here, haves a glass of tea." Justine turned and poured a glass of tea for Lorelei.

"Thank you, Justine. Exactly what this heat calls for." Lorelei wiped the rim of the glass with her handkerchief before taking a sip.

Justine watched her with a painted smile on her face. She thought to herself, "Hell, like she so much better than us all. High-yella heifer. Underneath all them fancy clothes, she jes as black as the rest of us." Justine watched, as Lorelei continued to drink her tea. "I should've spit in it."

"Mm, delicious. That really hit the spot," Lorelei smiled.

"Thank you. I'll be right back with your package."

Justine went to the kitchen to get the package she had prepared earlier.

Emma was watching from the back. She was fascinated by Miss Lorelei Hyde. Emma thought she was beautiful and very kind. Emma lost her grip on the broom when it fell.

Lorelei looked up and noticed Emma. She had a soft spot in her heart where Emma was concerned. "Well hello there, Emma. How are you today?" She waved her hand, calling Emma to her.

Emma looked to see where her mother was, and then walked toward Lorelei with her head down.

"Now Emma, what did I tell you? A young lady must always walk with her head up. It's not becoming of you when you walk with your head down. Besides, no one would ever see that pretty face of yours." She placed her hand under Emma's chin. "Now, that's better. Let me see that beautiful smile."

Emma smiled. Lorelei always made her feel special.

"So, how are you today? I'm surprised to see you here. I half expected to see you in my backyard, picking apples." Lorelei brushed the hair from Emma's face.

Emma put her head down, half-smiling. "No, Ma'am. If I dids that, then I surely would be in more trouble than I is now."

"Oh, I didn't means to get you in no trouble, Sugar. You know you can come and pick as many apples as you want." Lorelei looked at Emma with concern. "Did someone say you couldn't get apples from my yard?"

Emma shook her head. "No, Ma'am. I..." Emma looked up; she thought she heard her mother coming.

Lorelei saw the fear on Emma's face. "It's okay. I tell you what, whenever you have time, you come on over and we can pick apples together, and I'll even teach you one of my recipes for apple butter. Okay?"

Emma smiled brightly. The thought of spending time with Lorelei, thrilled her. But then she thought of her mother. "I...I don't know if that's such a good idea." Emma looked towards the kitchen. She saw her mother coming.

Lorelei saw the disappointment and angst in Emma's face. She leaned forward, and whispered in her ear, "It's all right. It'll be our secret." She looked Emma in the face and smiled. "Now, go ahead and finish what you were doing."

Emma looked at Lorelei with admiration. She could feel her mother's eyes on her. She turned around and ran to the back.

Justine looked at Emma, then to Lorelei. She fixed a smile on her face before speaking. "Well, Miss Lorelei, here is your package. I hope Emma Jean wasn't botherin' you none?"

"Oh no. I just noticed her back there, and wanted to say hello."

"She made a mess back there this mornin'. I has her cleanin' it up."

"Oh, I see. I was just surprised to see her in doors. I know how much she likes to be outside. She is such a free spirit."

"Yeah, I guess that's what you would call it." Justine looked towards the back.

Lorelei was beginning to feel uncomfortable. "Well, how much do I owe you?"

"That will be four dollars and thirty-five cents." Justine tapped her foot softly, as she waited for Lorelei to get the money from her change purse.

"Here you go. Keep the change." Lorelei gave Justine five dollar bills.

"Thank you." She handed Lorelei her package. *"I hope you enjoy."*

"I'm sure we will. We always do." Lorelei began to leave, when she stopped and asked, *"Justine, I was wondering if you might send the girls over to the house later? I have a bushel of apples that's just sitting there. You could be using it at home, or here in the store for your delicious apple pies."*

Justine did not answer at first. She wanted to say, *"Hell no! I don't needs your left-over!"* But instead asked: *"What time is good for you?"*

"Seven thirty?"

"All right." She couldn't afford to make no waves since Lorelei's Uncle owned the building her store was in. No building, no store. No store, no food to eat, or money to pay the bills.

"Okay." Lorelei smiled. *"Thank you once again. You are definitely a life saver."*

Justine half smiled and said, *"Oh, don't mention it. Jes doin' my job, is all."*

Lorelei walked out the store.

"Ooh! I swears I can't stand that high-yella heifer! She think she better'n everybody in, Busby." Justine took her cigarettes out her pocket. *"Emma Jean! Emma Jean gets your hide out here, rights*

now!"

Emma came running from the back. *"Yes Ma'am?"* Emma's voice was shaking.

"Did you finish back there?" She yelled.

"Yes. Yes Ma'am." Emma stood back. She knew her mother was angry.

"What was that woman whisperin' in your ear?"

Emma thought for a moment about what she should say.

"And, don'ts you even fix your lips to lie either!"

"M--Miss Lorelei told me that I should mind you, is all. Because young ladies mind their mothers." Emma swallowed hard, hoping her mother accepted her lie as the truth.

"Is that all? Don't lie to me, Emma Jean!"

"She said I should gets back to my work before I gets in trouble." Emma fixed her gaze on the floor boards.

Justine glared at her daughter before she lit a cigarette. Taking a puff, she looked at Emma and asked, *"You think her somethin', huh? Somebody important?"*

Emma didn't know how to answer her mother's question.

"I asked you a question?" She bellowed. *"Look at me when I'm talkin' to you!"* She grabbed Emma by the face, squeezing it between her fingers.

Emma looked into her mother's face, and just shook her head. *"No, Ma'am."* She said between squeezed cheeks. *"No, Ma'am,"* she repeated.

Ruthe McDonald

Justine leaned forward, and blew smoke in her daughter's face.

Emma coughed, but dared not move.

"Well, let me tell you somethin'; Lorelei ain't no better than no one in this here town. You hears me?"

Emma nodded. "Yes Ma'am."

"She pisses and messes, jes like the rest of us. She jes think her mess don't stink. But you hears me, Emma Jean?"

"Yes Ma'am."

"She ain't nobody special. And neither are you! Jes because she acts kind to you, don't means nothin'. 'Cause, at the end of the day, all you good enough for is to pick up her left overs, and wash her clothes. She may be a Negro, but she ain't no sistah to me. So don't you go gettin' no foolish notions in your head about being somethin' you ain't! Or, tryin' to be likes her! When all is said and done...you is mine. You hear?"

Emma swallowed hard. "Yes Ma'am."

Justine let go of Emma's face. "Now, gets to that kitchen and starts washin' them pots. And you better wash 'em good!"

Emma speedily walked to the kitchen. She started crying. She took the step stool so she could reach the faucet. As the water ran, so did the tears down Emma's face. "I hate her, Lord! I swears I do! I wish she wasn't my mama. She don't deserve no chilren's!" Emma wiped the tears from her face, but the more she wiped, the more she cried.

Southern~136~Comfort

Emma placed the two pots in the sink. As she reached for the mixing bowl, it slipped from her grip. Emma stood up straight, frozen with fear.

"What the hell?" Justine came rushing to the kitchen.

"I...I..." Emma stammered to get the words out.

"My good bowl!" Justine hollered.

"It—it was an accident, Ma'am. My—my hands were slippery from the soap." Emma stepped down from the stool and started backing up.

"I swears, you ain't nothin's but trouble! Do you think I got money to keep payin' for the things you bust up? Huh?" Justine grabbed Emma by the arm.

Emma began sobbing. "No, Ma'am. I'm sorry. I'll clean it up." Emma tried to get loose from her mother's grip, but Justine was not letting go. Her grip got tighter.

"How many times, Emma? How many times I tell you to be careful? You ain't no baby...you ten years old!" She began shaking Emma violently.

"I'm sorry! I'm sorry!" Emma cried.

"You always sorry! Always!" She slapped Emma, hard across the face.

Emma grabbed her face and yelled out. "Please, Ma'am, please. I'm sorry!" Emma tried to run, but her mother caught her by the hair.

"I told you, if you don't pay attention, I'm gonna makes you learn how!" Justine began beating on Emma.

Emma was balled up on the floor, shielding

herself from the blows.

"I'm so sick of you! I swears you are worthless! You hears me? Worthless!" Justine screamed as she continued to beat on Emma.

Emma cried out. "Please, Ma'am. Please! I'm sorry! I'm sorry!"

I'M sorry. I'm sorry…" Emma was turning back and forth in her sleep, mumbling. "I'm sorry, Ma'am. I'm sorry..."

"Mama?" Albert leaned on the bed next to his wife. "Mama, wake up. You dreamin', suga'."

"I'm sorry! I'm sorry! No!" Startled, Emma sat up. She looked around the room, then at Albert. "Oh Al-B!" She wrapped her arms around Albert's neck, and started crying.

"Shush, it's okay. Poppa's home." Albert sat down, and squeezed Emma. "It's all right. You were jes dreamin'." He stroked Emma's hair. "Tell me, what's goin on?"

Emma continued to cry into Albert's shoulder. Albert could feel his wife shaking.

"Mama, you shakin'. What happened today?" Albert grew more concerned with his wife's condition. She called him, Al-B. He knew she was in a bad place. He hadn't seen Emma this way in a long time. "Please, baby. Talk to me. Talk to me, Emma." He continued to hold Emma in his arms, gently rubbing her back.

Emma held onto to Albert, as if for dear life. She laid her head on his shoulder and sighed deeply. Crying, she began to speak, "Oh Al-B, I don't knows how much more of this I can take. I swear my past is in fronts my face yet again. I don't know if I am strong enough this time around. I jes don't know."

"Mama ain't anyone stronger than you. I done seen you go through hell and backs, and I knows for certain ain't no one stronger than you. Now tell me, what happened at the hospital. Where's Macon? I'd thought she'd be home today."

Emma sat up. Albert pulled out a handkerchief and wiped his wife's face.

"It was bad, Albert. Real bad..." Emma told Albert everything that occurred earlier at the hospital with Macon.

Albert listened to his wife, and knew that she was experiencing painful memories of her own. Exactly what he feared would happen.

After Emma finished, she walked over to her bureau, and picked up her cigarettes. Taking one out, she turned and looked at Albert. She could see the concern on his face, and the love in his eyes. He was the only one in her life that knew everything about her: The good, the bad, and the downright ugly. And he still loved her. He was amazing. He was her salvation; her peace of mind. She knew she would be dead if it were not for her Al-B—her nick-name for him.

She took a drag of the cigarette, and walked toward the window. Albert stood behind Emma, and placed his arms around her waist. Emma just leaned back into her husband's embrace.

"I love you, Emma Jean. And there's nothing in this world we can't get through together." Albert placed a small kiss on Emma's neck.

Emma put the cigarette out, and faced Albert. "We got to help that Chile. She needs us."

"We will, Mama. Macon gonna be fine. You hears what I'm sayin'? She gonna be jes fine." Albert hugged his wife tightly. Rubbing her back, assuring her that what he said was truth.

Emma closed her eyes and breathed in deeply, as Albert comforted her. "I knows she will...I knows she will. I jes wonder where Nadine is at in all this. She hasn't returned any calls. And no one knows where she at."

"Well", Albert began, "we can't worries ourselves about Nadine, right now. We'll cross that bridge once we gets to it. We gonna focus our attentions on that Chile." Albert looked into his wife's face, and gave her a small kiss. "And I needs to take cares my wife."

Emma opened her mouth to protest. However, Albert kissed her again more passionately before she could reject.

"I said," Albert's voice was low and sensual. "I needs to take cares my wife." He smiled at Emma. "Do I hears an objection?" He placed his hand under Emma's chin. "Hmm?"

Emma smiled. "No, Baby. Ain't no objections here." Emma placed her arms around Albert's neck, and pulled him into a long, tender kiss.

ⒿⓇ

Albert squeezed Emma close to him. He knew his wife well, and knew that she needed some TLC. He could tell from her kiss.

"Wait," Emma pulled away. "Shelby—"

Albert smiled, placing a finger to Emma's mouth. "Shelby done gone home. And before you can say anything, Deeney and Junior are eating out."

Emma's smile grew wide. "You mean..."

Albert nodded. "That's right, Mama. It's jes you and me." Albert pulled his wife towards him. He pulled on the belt to Emma's robe until it fell to the sides.

Emma blushed. Albert sure knew how to make her feel like that teenager he met so many years ago. She just stood there, as Albert began to caress her.

Albert gently massaged his wife's shoulders, pushing her robe until it fell to the floor. Without saying a word, Emma put her hands around her husband's neck and kissed him tenderly. Albert embraced his wife, running his hands down her bare back, resting his hands on her bare bottom and squeezing. Her skin was soft and beautiful. Every time with Emma was like the first time. Her body never aged to him. She felt exactly the same, and it made him feel like that twenty-two year old boy. It was Emma who truly made him feel like a man.

Emma helped Albert out of his shirt, as they walked towards their bed. Not a word was spoken between them. Nothing had to be said. They knew each other well enough to know what the other was thinking. Albert sat on the bed, as Emma helped take off his pants.

The passion between them could not be denied. Not even after thirty-three years of marriage. In fact, the passion was even stronger. What's more, the loving was that more intense. He knew every part of his wife's body. There was nothing about Emma that Albert did not know. And right now, he knew his wife needed some loving.

Albert lay back, and pulled Emma on top of him. He ran his fingers through his wife's hair, and held her gaze for a moment. She was more beautiful to him now, than ever before. The look in her eyes spoke volumes to his heart. She was speaking to his soul. She was all in his bones. And he loved *that* kind of ache.

Emma stared at Albert for a long while. His hands felt so good in her hair. His body beneath her was strong and hard. She studied his face, tracing it with her fingertips. Smiling to herself; remembering the first time they made love. Albert had the same, intense look in his eyes: a look of pure love, and fire.

He hadn't changed much over the years. He was a little bit leaner. A few gray hairs made his small Afro, a salt and pepper mix. He still had the same piercing, brown eyes. His beard and mustache shaped into a perfect go-tee, which accentuated his thin lips. Lips that knew had to set her on fire. He had a few age lines around his mouth...but that was solely from all the laughing he does. His skin was still smooth; a slight more golden—a deep amber— due to the Carolina sun over the years. His body was still strong. As was his hands. And God...when he touched her...it was always the same.

Emma felt the passion inside her growing fiercely with every touch Albert made.

She leaned forward and kissed him gently on the mouth. She began kissing him on his neck, then his shoulders, moving slowly down his chest. Emma knew every part of Albert. He taught her how to love, how to make love, and most importantly, how to be loved.

Albert moaned with pleasure, as his wife explored his body. He could not stand the desire that was welling up within him—ready to explode. He grabbed Emma by the waist and turned her over. He stopped for a moment, looking his wife in her eyes. What he saw in her eyes reflected his own desire. With his hands tangled in hers, he kissed her strongly; working his way down her soft, chocolate skin. He kissed her on the breasts, and then down to her stomach; working his way down to her thighs.

Emma shuttered with delight. Her body was exploding with so many emotions. A groan escaped her lips, as she and Albert became one flesh. His hands entwined with hers, she could feel every intense movement from the top of her head, to the sole of her feet.

Albert leaned forward and spoke into his wife's ear. "I loves you, Mama. I loves you... more... than anything... in this... here... world." His body shuddered with delight.

Emma rested her hands on his shoulders, and in between breaths said, "I know, Al-B. I know. And...I loves you... jes... the same." Emma squeezed her arms around Albert's neck, "Oh, AL-B!"

Emma lay on her stomach, as Albert played in her hair and rubbed her back. He circled his fingers over an old scar, on Emma's back. He leaned forward and kissed it. Emma, turning to her side, rested her head on Albert's chest.

"You all right, Mama?" Albert asked.

"Now, how can you asks me a question like that?" Emma chuckled. "After the lovin' you jes put on me?" She turned to face him.

Albert laughed. "Yeah, I did puts in some work there." He raised an eyebrow, looking at Emma.

"Ain't you full of yourself!"

"What?" He asked propping himself up on one arm. "You ain't had enough? Because, you know I got plenty more for you! Don't let these few gray hairs on this head fool you none." He chided.

Emma laughed. "Good God, no! Lord! Now you knows, baby, you done did this body here some good!" Emma closed her eyes, smiling.

"So what you sayin'? You don't wants no more?" Albert tried to stifle his laughter after seeing the look on Emma's face.

Emma opened her eyes, raised an eyebrow and said, "Man! Are you crazy, or what? You a dirty ole man! Yes you are!"

Albert laughed, and kissed his wife. "Yeah, but I'm *your* dirty ole man! And you's my *nasty* little woman! Jes the ways I like it!" He laughed, pulling

Emma into his arms.

Emma laughed, nestling her head against Albert's chest. "Yeah, well don'ts you go forgettin' that fact either!"

Albert squeezed her and chuckled. "That's my, Baby! She done marked her territory and ain't so afraid to let no one's know!"

"You damn right! You mine, and only mine. From the first day I met you. I knew, that man right there was gonna be mines." Emma smiled.

Albert kissed her on the forehead. "Yeah, you certainly staked out your claim, and took it. My heart and all! What would I do without you?"

"Like I've always said, you'll never has to know. Never." Emma leaned her head back and closed her eyes. She felt comfort and safety in her husband's arms. He was exactly what she needed. He had managed—for the moment—to make everything else seem so unimportant. Right now, only he and she existed. And that's the way she wanted it to be for a little while longer. Before having to tackle the rest of the world, and its pain that waited for her.

"Hey" Albert broke into Emma's thoughts. "Now stop all that thinkin, and rest." He placed a kiss on her cheek. "You hungry?" He asked.

"No...not for food, that is."

Albert looked at his wife; amused by the mischievous grin on her face. He asked, "You sure?"

"Well," Emma said, starting to get up, "if you's got to ask that question..."

Albert pulled her back down. "Don't plays with me, woman! You knows I got plenty more for you. I told you; don't let these few gray hairs fool you!"

Emma laughed. "Then...shows me what you workin' wit, Daddy."

"Nows you talkin' my kind of talk! Let me at you, Mama. Let me at you." Albert leaned forward, and kissed his wife, pulling the sheets over their heads.

J7R

CHAPTER 13

July 31, 1974

NADINE, THIS IS SHELBY AGAIN. *When you hear this message, please give Mama a call. It's an emergency. Macon's still in the hospital, and we need to talk. She really needs you, Nadine. It's really bad. All right. We'll be waiting to hear from you."*

Nadine listened to the last message again. Shelby had called her five times already. The outpatient center had called her four times. They even came to her house looking for her.

"Won't these damn people leave me alone!" Nadine yelled. She walked over to her couch, and plopped down. She picked up a cigarette to light it, but her shaking hands made it difficult.

"Where is Byron?" Nadine finally lit the cigarette.

She got up from the couch and began pacing; stepping over the mess that used to be her living room. The entire house smelled stale. It had not been cleaned since Macon left. She didn't care. It was dark and dingy, with no light coming in. The shades were drawn, the curtains drawn. Nadine didn't want anyone knowing she was there, or peering in being nosy—like those folks from the outpatient center.

Nadine's only concern was when Byron was

coming back.

It'd been four hours since he'd left!

He said he would be right back with the stuff!

Nadine looked out the window. Disgusted, she walked backed toward the sofa catching a glance of her reflection in the mirror.

Nadine looked dreadful. Her hair was undone; she had not combed it in weeks—Skin was gray and blotchy. She had dark circles under her eyes. Nadine was a sad version of the beautiful woman she used to be. The drug abuse was making Nadine look twenty years older than her thirty-three years. The bitterness and coldness of her heart also attributed to her ghastly appearance.

Nadine shook her head. She brushed her hand over her head, trying to pat down her hair that was sticking up all over the place.

"Hell, I need me a perm." Nadine stared at her reflection for a moment. Half believing what the mirror was showing her.

What happened to me?

She glanced to the left of the mirror; her eyes settling on a picture hanging on the wall. It was a picture of her, Nathan, and Macon at age one. She touched the picture.

Nadine recalled the first time she laid eyes on Nathan. Oh he was so fine, and so was she. She didn't know him personally, but she had heard a lot about him.

It was the beginning of the summer of 1958.

She'd just come to Busby, from Georgia a couple of months earlier to live with her Aunt, Celia. She refused to go to Beaufort with her grandmother. Celia was the only one who understood her, and did not fuss so much about her comings and goings.

Nadine was waiting tables at, Lula Mae's Rib Shack when she heard a couple of the local girls talking about a party over the weekend. The girls were exclaiming how they could not wait to see this young man named Nathan. They were fawning all over themselves. Lula Mae even had a sandwich called "The Nathan": a barbecue beef brisket sandwich, topped with a heaping mound of coleslaw and a sliced dill pickle on sour dough toast.

Nadine asked her Aunt Celia about who this Nathan Cooper was that everyone kept talking about...

June, 1958

Ooh, Chile," her Aunt exclaimed. "Nathan Cooper. That is Busby's own Ebony Prince. He's just as fine as he want to be. His Aunt and Uncle own the Watson Lumber-mill and Furniture store. His Aunt is a piece of work, but his *uncle*—whew! Now that is one fine man! Deep Amber skin—handsome—and a hard body..." Celia started fanning herself.

"Aunt Celia!" Nadine yelled, jolting her Aunt back to reality.

"Oh! Chile, I'm sorry. But that Uncle of his got

plenty of women folk around here buying furniture they knows they don't need." She fanned herself again.

"The nephew, Aunt Celia. What about Nathan?"

"Well, he fine just like his Uncle. And every girl and they Mama trying to catch that one. He just graduated from Howard University. I believe he got a degree in Business or something. Smart boy."

"What he look like?"

"He's about six feet, a strong physique, deep caramel complexion, dark wavy hair. None of that process mess—all natural. Deep dimples when he smiles, and nice teeth."

"Mm," Nadine smiled. "Where are his folks?"

"I don't know. His Aunt and Uncle raised him." Celia turned and looked at her niece. "Hey? Why you asking so many questions about Nathan Cooper?"

"Nothing really. Just curious. I heard a few girls talking about him at the rib-shack."

"Well," Celia began, "I'll give you a little advice —stays clear of his Aunt, Emma Jean. *She's* a piece of work. She don't like no one sniffing around her nephew."

"I was just asking about who he was," Nadine declared.

"Well...like I said, beware of his Aunt." Celia laughed and shook her head. Thinking to herself, *"That Chile is just like me. You'd think..."* Celia shook her head. There was no need in revisiting the past. "What's done is done."

Nadine did not have to wait for a party to meet Nathan Cooper. He walked into Lula Mae's one afternoon—one of the busiest in a long while—and sat down at the counter, at Nadine's station.

Nadine was busy bringing another customer their order when she finally got to Nathan. She did not even look up—she just asked, "What can I get you today?"

Nathan smiled. He had never seen her before. She must be new. He noticed how cute she was. He leaned back on the stool to get a better look at her. "Mm," he thought to himself. "Pretty little chocolate drop." He stared at her for a moment, and then decided to goad her into a little tit-for-tat. He wanted to see what she was made of. He loved a woman who could handle herself, and had a good sense of humor. "Uh, can you tell me what the specials are?" he smiled.

Nadine still had not looked up, or at him. Annoyed, she said to herself, *another illiterate Negro*.

"The list of specials is just as big as day when you come into the door." Exasperated, Nadine read off the list of specials from memory. "Today's specials are: Pinto beans with hammocks, with a side choice of dirty rice, white rice or no rice. As always, we have Lula Mae's ribs with special sauce. Since its Wednesday, you get two orders for the price of one, and a free dessert: Your choice of apple pie, sweet potato pie, or peach cobbler. The soup of the day of is Navy Bean, with hot Johnny cakes on the side. So, what can I get you?"

Nathan could sense that Nadine was having a particularly bad day, but he couldn't help but to chide her. There was something about this girl. He did not know what it was. Maybe it was the fact that she was not fawning over him like the other waitresses would. Or, it could be the fact of that beautiful round behind that she had on her. *Mm. Good Lord!* He noticed her as soon as he came in. *A petite thing; with the exception of that backside, and those big legs.* Nathan smiled to himself.

"So," Nadine said, breaking into his thoughts, "do you know what you wants?"

"How about your name? I mean, usually Lula Mae is very earnest about her waitresses being courteous."

Nadine looked up. She was about to give a snide remark when she became speechless. Sitting before her was the finest man she had ever laid eyes on. She didn't know what to say. He was sitting there smiling at her, with beautiful straight white teeth, deep dimples, deep brown eyes, and a golden caramel brown complexion. She felt her knees go weak for a moment. No one ever had that effect on her...never.

"I...I..." Nadine stuttered. She could feel the heat in her cheeks.

Nathan grinned. "What's that? Cat got your tongue? I mean...if I'm being too much of a problem, I'll be happy to move my seat. Although..." Nathan looks around the restaurant. "It does seem to be quite busy today." He turned back around and looked Nadine in the eyes. Beautiful eyes, he noticed. They were a chestnut brown, with flecks of gold in them. And her mouth...it was full. His eyes wandered down for a moment. Good- Googely- Moog! Mm! Ample breasts too! *This was one fine sister.*

Nadine shook her head, shaking herself awake. She noticed how this man seemed to be ogling her. As fine as he was, she didn't like any man checking out her goods; especially if she wasn't getting any benefits from it.

"Perhaps you *should* go sits somewhere else, then," she said sarcastically, placing a hand on her hip. "We very busy today, and you can't seem to makes up your mind as to what you wants."

Nathan laughed. *She caught me,* he thought to himself. He'd go along with her. "All right, if that's what you suggest. Maybe I should speak to Lula Mae?"

Oh hell! Lula Mae then already warned her once about her attitude. She can't afford to lose this job. If she does, she'll have no choice but to go live with her grandmother.

"Uh—no, that's all right." She picked up her pad, "What will you have?" She tried to sound more pleasant.

Nathan smirked. He had no intentions of really speaking with Lula Mae about her. He cleared his throat. "I'll have...your name please."

Nadine looked up; ready to say something

smart, when she noticed his smile. God! He is fine.
She smiled coyly, and said, "Nadine. Nadine Jackson."

"Well, Miss Nadine Jackson...it's nice to meet
you." He smiled wide, making his dimples deeper,
and held out his hand.

When he smiled at her, Nadine felt a warm
current run through her body as never before. She
felt it from the back of her neck, down her chest...
right down to her thighs.

*If he could have this effect on me with just a
smile, I wonder what other things he could do.*

Nadine felt herself blush.

"I won't bite..." Nathan said, referring to his
extended hand.

Nadine smiled, and shook his hand.

Oh, my sweet Jesus!

She'd sworn she felt electricity go through
her right then. She was dumbfounded again!
Nadine was too busy monitoring the waves of
currents running through her body that she had not
noticed Lula Mae standing next to her until she
spoke.

"Nadine? Are you fussin' with my customers
again?" She winked at Nathan.

Nadine fumbled with the pad in her hands,
and dropped it. "Oh no, Lula Mae! I... I was just
taking his order," she stammered.

Lula Mae looked at Nadine, then to Nathan,
and back to Nadine. *Good Lord*, she thought, *he done
got another one of my girls*. She noticed how flushed

Nadine was, and laughed. "Oh, sugar, it's all right. I'm jes playin' with ya. I knows ain't nobody fussin' over here but Nathan!"

Nathan! Nadine glanced at Nathan. Oh, my sweet Jesus! She should have known. He was finer than everyone had said. Hell, they hadn't done him *justice* in their descriptions.

"Nathan," Lula Mae said, "have you been givin' my girl here a hard time?" She put her arm around Nadine's shoulder.

Nathan smiled. With a sparkle in his eye, he answered, "No way, Miss Lula Mae! And have you ban me—again!—from this here fine establishment?" He winked at Nadine.

When Nathan was seventeen working there after school, Lula Mae suspended him for a couple of weeks. She said he was causing too much trouble between her waitresses. Unbeknownst to Nathan, it was his Aunt Emma's idea. Maybe he would be able to concentrate on his schoolwork more. She didn't know how he made it to college.

Nadine could feel herself blushing. Nathan was fine, and she wanted to get to know more about who this *fine* man was. Now she understood why all those girls were making such a fuss over him. He was definitely someone to fuss about.

It was not long before she got what she wanted. Nathan must have come to Lula Mae's every day that summer. He asked her out five times before she said yes. She didn't want to appear *too* eager.

She remembered the first time he kissed her. They were dancing to Sam Cooke's, *You Send Me.*

Nathan had held her so close, that she thought for sure he could feel the fast beat of her heart. As her head lay on his chest, she could hear the smooth beat of his heart, and the smell of his cologne. Nathan was a gentleman. She never experienced this before. Every guy she'd had known wanted one thing from her; but not Nathan. He had not even tried. She wondered if he was interested. When the song finished, Nathan had not said a word, he just bent his head, and kissed her, squeezing her tightly. She remembered how soft his lips were and how she felt his nature rise against her body. She knew then he wanted her, as much as she desired him.

Nadine knew her Aunt Celia was gone for the weekend when she asked Nathan to come in. She had no intentions of letting him leave. She wanted him. She wanted to know what it was like to be with him in every sense of the word.

They were lying on the couch kissing passionately when she took his hand and led him to her bedroom. He asked her if she was sure. She grabbed his face in her hands and kissed him, turned around, and pulled him onto the bed.

Just as Nathan began to remove her blouse, for some reason, Nadine felt she needed to be honest with Nathan before they went any further. So she whispered in his ear that this was not her first time. He just looked at her and smiled, and said, maybe not, but it would be the first time with him. Then he told her he was no choir boy either. She laughed.

Nadine remembered removing Nathan's shirt. He was beautiful. He made *her* feel beautiful. She could not remember when she had felt so much love. And they had not even been dating long.

It had not mattered with all the others, if she had never seen them again afterwards—which she seldom did. Yet, it was different with Nathan. She wanted more. She did not want this to end. It would hurt, too much, if she never saw him again.

Nadine was not one to pray, or believe that strongly in God; but while Nathan was making love to her that night, she silently prayed: "God, please don't let him leave me. Let him love me forever."

For the first time in her life, Nadine was in love.

God must have heard her prayers, because Nathan did not leave like the rest. He continued to see her. Nathan had in fact fallen in love with her, asking her several times to marry him. What is more, that was before she told him that she was pregnant.

She had conceived their first night together— the night she prayed. She had known for two months before telling him. She thought for sure he would run. At least, that is what her Aunt Celia said he would do. She said a baby would be a complication to Nathan's life. It would change everything. Furthermore, he would definitely think she did it on purpose—to trap him.

Nathan did not run. To Nadine's surprise, Nathan insisted they get married—not caring what any one said or thought.

There were all kinds of stories being told around town. How Nadine trapped him. How she did the same thing in, Georgia. How she was just like her Aunt Celia.

Nathan did not care. He loved her. They were married on Christmas day, in 1958, on her eighteenth birthday. Macon was born that following March.

In the beginning, everything was beautiful. She and Nathan were happy. Even she and Emma had been cordial. However, it did not last. Happiness never does. Something always comes to take it away. In the back of her mind, Nadine always knew that her life would always have sorrow and pain. She feared that someone or something would snatch away the peace and joy she found with Nathan, and their new little family.

Nadine did not start the downward spiral alone. Nonetheless, it was her fears that allowed it to grow and escalate...eventually destroying her own happiness.

CHAPTER 14

NADINE DECIDED TO TAKE MACON, and visit her grandmother in, Beaufort. She heard her parents would be there; she had not seen them since she'd left, Georgia two years earlier. She had not even invited them to her wedding. To say Nadine and her parents did not get along, would be putting it mildly.

Although it was grandma Jackson's birthday, her real reason for going was to prove how happy she was, and how good her life was going. Macon was already one year old, and they'd never seen her.

Nathan could not make it, so Nadine decided to go with her Aunt Celia, who was moving back home to Beaufort. Nadine had heard some rumors about Aunt Celia and one the ministers at First Baptist. However, she did not ask her about it. Because knowing her Aunt, the rumors were true.

"Hey, Gran! Happy birthday!" Nadine kissed her grandmother on the cheek, and gave her a hug.

"Well, hello there baby. Nadine, you looks so good. Is this my great-grand?" Grandma Jackson held out her arms to receive Macon. "Isn't she a beautiful little thing...looking jes like me!" She laughed, as Nadine placed Macon on her lap. She kissed Macon on top of her head and held her close to her bosom.

"Everybody looks like you, Gran." Nadine smiled.

"Well, better me than your grandfather!" She

laughed. "So, where's that husband of yours?" She said, looking for Nathan.

"He couldn't make it this time."

Nadine's grandmother looked at her with concern on her face. "Everything okay with you all?"

"Oh, we're fine. Nathan's in training for a new position, so he couldn't make it. That's all," Nadine reassured her grandmother.

"All right. As long as you all are doing fine. Come here, sugar." She patted the seat next to her.

Nadine sat down next to her grandmother. "Yes, Gran?"

Grandma Jackson held Macon close to her, and reached for Nadine's hand. "I wanted to speak to you before everyone gets here. I knows you had it rough. To be so young, you has been through much. But I wants you to know how proud I am of you. Marriage is doing you well. Now, I knows I've been awfully stern on you at times, but that's solely because I loves you, and always wants what's best for you, Nadine."

Nadine felt the tears welling up in her eyes. She could barely utter a word. Her grandmother had never expressed such accolades where she was concern. It was always a word of rebuke or chastisement. This was something unfamiliar to Nadine, and it warmed her heart. "Th—thank you, Gran." Nadine brushed the tears from her eyes.

"No, no, baby. Thank you. Because I knew you had it in you all along. And I am right proud of you. I prays for you all the time. Many a night, you have had my knees hurting," she chuckled. "But the good, Lord does answer prayers. Yes He does. I jes want you to remain happy, Nadine." She squeezed Nadine's hand.

"I am, Gran. I will."

"Listen to me, Baby. You've come a long way. And I may not be around to see this here child grow up, but I am sure happy to see your life turning around. I wants you to continue to grow. Don't lets no one or nothing keep you or your beautiful family from being happy. You's a mama now, and a wife. Keep your husband happy, and he will takes care of you. Raise your child with plenty of love, and she will love and respect you back. Confront your past. Deal with it, and it can't hurt you no more. Hold onto the happiness that you have right now and never let it go, Baby. Don't let no one takes it away from you. It's yours and you deserve it." She pulled Nadine close to her and hugged her tightly, kissing her on the cheek.

Nadine was shaking with emotion. It was as though her grandmother read the thoughts that have been plaguing her mind lately.

"Gran, I'm scared." Nadine whispered. "I...I feel like something or someone doesn't want me happy. That, I'm gonna wake up one day, and I will have nothing left. As if my past will come and ruin everything."

Grandma Jackson motioned for one of Nadine's younger cousins to come and take Macon. She waited until the young girl was out of ear shot. She turned and faced Nadine, taking both her hands in hers. She studied her granddaughter's face for a moment, before speaking. She took a deep breath, and wiped away the tears that were falling down Nadine's cheeks. "Nadine, I wants you to listen to me good. I don't know how many birthdays that the good Lord is gonna bless me with."

"Oh, Gran! Don't say that," cried Nadine.

"No, no. Now hush, child. You knows I ain't getting no younger, but I ain't complaining, because I had me a good life. With plenty of love and laughter. And yes; plenty of heartache and sorrow to last *two* lifetimes. But you hears me?"

"Yes, Gran?"

"I want to share something with you. I was stern with you all these years because I see myself in you, and I didn't want you to do what I did."

Nadine looked at her grandmother in surprise.

"I know. I know. You may find that hard to believes, but I was a hellion. I gave my parents more grief than a little. I suppose that's why the Lord gave me, Celia," she chuckled.

Nadine laughed also. Aunt Celia was the black sheep of the family. She could start more trouble than a fox in a hen house. Nadine always felt more like Celia, than her own mother. She even looked like her Aunt.

"Now, that don't mean that baby of yours is anything like, Celia. She has a sweet and gentle spirit. Celia was a handful from the moment she was born. But this ain't about Celia, this is about you. I know you scared. You scared that all this happiness you found with that young man ain't gonna last. You can't think like that. Because if you do, then it won't last, because you self-prophesied it. Do you understand me?"

Nadine nodded. She's heard that many times before. "But, Gran, I just can't help but feel like something *awful* is gonna happen."

"Well, you know what? Awful things do happen sometimes...tragic even. But we can't let them stop us from living, or being the best person we should be. You understand me?"

"Yes."

"Then let me ask you this, have you told Nathan everything? I mean *everything* about what happened in Georgia?"

Nadine turned away from her grandmother's stare. She had not told Nathan everything. She never even allowed herself to remember it. It was too painful, as well as shameful.

Grandma Jackson turned Nadine's face back towards hers. "I gather from your silence, that means no."

"No...I haven't. I just couldn't bring myself to tell him." Nadine began to cry. "I mean, I don't even wants to remember. It's my past, and I wanted to start new in, Busby. That's why I didn't come here... with you. Because I would just be reminded."

"No, you didn't come here because you didn't want to hears my mouth, or follow my rules." She raised an eyebrow. "Be honest, this is your grandmother you talking to."

Nadine shrugged her shoulders. "Yes Gran. But," she quickly defended herself, "I *did* want to start over, where no one knew me."

"Rightly so," her grandmother agreed. "I can understand that. However, you are a wife and mother now, and you got to understand that secrets can destroy one's life. I know for a fact that Nathan loves you to death—yes he does."

Nadine smiled.

"And I'd venture to say that he would do anything for you...including looking over your past. The only way from keeping your past from ruining your present, is by telling it to that young man of yours. This way, no one has anything over you."

"I know, Gran. But I'm just so scared."

"The truth can be scary sometimes. Especially when we've been practicing lying so much. Listen, child. This family of mine, I loves them to death, but there are just too many secrets being kept. Secrets that have destroyed lives."

"Secrets? Whose secrets?"

"Everyone's. And I ask the good Lord to forgive me for not stopping it sooner. Had I known better, I'd done better. But as much as I hate secrets, they ain't mines to tell. I wish I could, because I believe a whole lot of people wouldn't be like they are now. But I can't change the past. But I can prevent it from being repeated. That's why I want you to tell Nathan everything before someone else does. I see me in you, and I want to keep you from the kind of pain I suffered, because I didn't listen soon enough."

"Gran, I don't understand."

"Listen, tell Nathan everything. It will free you. And before I leave this earth I'm gonna make sure you knows everything you should know."

Nadine was confused by her grandmother's statement.

"I know you don't know what this old lady is babbling about, but it's about time the secrets in this family were dealt with. I love you, Nadine. And I couldn't be more happy for you, or proud of you. I wants you to stay happy, and never go back to that path of destruction. You have a chance now, and I wants you to hold onto it tight. But with truth. That's the only way that the past will not destroy you. You understand me?"

"Yes, Gran."

"Nadine," she stroked her granddaughter's face, "you have been through a whole lot to be so young. You grew up way, too fast. I don't know everything that went on in your parents' home, but I know it wasn't all good. Otherwise you wouldn't have been trying so hard to get out."

Nadine eyes widened. Her grandmother knew much more than she thought.

"Oh, don't be so surprised. I may be old, but I ain't senile. I knows my son may be a preacher, but he's *far* from a saint. And that wife of *his*? Well, let's just say that looks *can* be deceiving. I don't miss anything. I'm just sorry I didn't do more for you. I thought I was doing what was best for you all these years. But the good Lord has shown me the error of my ways. And I aims to fix it before I leave this earth. The truth can be devastating and very hurtful. But it can also be freeing. What's more, is that lies and secrets are more devastating and harmful. Some of which we never recover from.

"When you told me you were getting married, and having a baby...I have to admit that I was surprised and a bit concerned. I didn't think you were ready. I didn't think you were prepared to give so much of yourself. But when I saw you on your wedding day, I saw something in your eyes that I had never seen before...hope and happiness. I knew right then that that was your chance to make things in your life better. It got me to thinking about a whole lot of things, and these damn secrets that this family has kept. And, I am to blame for much of it. So, I made up in my mind to set things right before the Father calls me home. Now, I don't know if everyone is gonna follow what I asks them to do, but I'm gonna make sure I do what I can to set things right.

"What I want you to do is promise me that you will tell your husband the truth. Promise me that you will not let anything or anyone, turn you back. Promise me that no matter what you learn from here in out, you will not let it destroy your happiness. Promise me Nadine."

Nadine did not know exactly what to say but, "Yes, Gran. I promise." She had never heard her grandmother speak to her with so much love and concern. Perhaps she always had, but Nadine just never seen it that way before.

Her grandmother seemed almost desperate for her to honor her requests. Nadine could not explain it, nor did she want to tell her grandmother, about this overwhelming sense of dread that was flooding her. Despite what her grandmother said, she felt that the truth and the secrets she was referring to should be left the way they were...secret.

Nadine hugged her grandmother tightly. "I love you, Gran. I know I haven't been the best granddaughter, but I thank you for loving me. Even if I didn't know that's what you were doing...loving me." Nadine stayed in her grandmother's embrace for a long while. Overwhelmed by the warmth her heart was experiencing.

"I love you too, Baby. Never forgets that. Love is a powerful thing, Nadine. Remember that always. As well as forgiveness. Forgive yourself, and forgive others. Then you will always be free." She pulled back, and smiled at Nadine.

"Now, I don't know about you, but I am ready to celebrate my birthday. Not too many people get to see seventy. So I am very grateful to the good, Lord. Yes I am. Come on here, let's go get my great-grand, and celebrate. Whew! She gonna be a looker... looking just like me!" She chuckled, taking Nadine's arm, walking into the house.

THERE were two events from that day, burned into Nadine's mind. One was her conversation with her grandmother, and the other was what occurred that night.

The overwhelming sense of dread became the reality of an all-consuming tidal wave of pain: One that changed her life forever. Nadine knew that the secrets her grandmother referred to should have remained buried. Revealing them caused a lot more than just pain...it caused death.

Nadine recalled vividly how quickly things went from bad to horrific. The party had finally ended. Relatives and friends had departed. The only ones in the house were her grandmother, her parents, herself and Macon. She didn't know when her Aunt Celia returned. She had left earlier in the evening with some man.

Nadine washed the rest of the dishes, and brought her grandmother a cup of tea, then went to check on Macon.

That's when the beginning of the end to her happy life began.

As Nadine neared the bedroom door where she had laid Macon down, she could hear someone speaking. She wasn't sure, but it sounded like her mother. Nadine listened at the door before entering.

She could not believe her ears.

Nadine's mother, Claire was sitting on the edge of the bed looking down at Macon. She was stroking the child's hair as she was speaking to the sleeping child.

"Such a precious little angel. You know, you should be mine. Nadine doesn't deserve you. She don't deserve any children. How she managed to keep you...I don't know. It just ain't fair how some people can have children, while others can't. Especially people like Nadine."

Nadine's heart sank. She had heard enough when she pushed open the door.

"Is that right?" she asked her mother.

Claire turned around, startled. "Nadine. How —how long you been standing there?" she stammered.

"Long enough to be reminded of how much my own mother hates me!" Nadine grabbed her mother by the arm. "Get away from her! You stay the hell away from my daughter. You hear me?" Nadine pulled her mother to the door.

"Listen," Claire began, "I don't know what you *think* you heard, but don't go acting crazy again!"

Nadine couldn't believe the audacity of her mother. "What I *think* I heard? My God, mother! You were telling *my* child, I don't deserve to be her mother! You will not do this to me...never again. You will not..." Nadine felt a lump in her throat.

"What? Not do what again?" Claire snapped. "Keep you from ruining another child's life? You didn't deserve him, and you damn well don't deserve her either!"

Nadine pushed her mother out the door. "Get out! Stay the hell away from my daughter. Or, I swear..."

"Or, what? What you gonna do, Nadine?" Claire taunted her daughter.

Nadine stepped to her mother's face and inhaled, "You've been drinking again. Get out! Or so help me, I will forget the fact that you are my mother!" Nadine shoved Claire out the door. She turned to look at Macon. She was still sleeping. She closed the door behind her, and followed her mother towards the living room.

"Like I give a damn!" Claire spouted.

"I don't believe you! It's not enough for you to treat me like trash. It's not even enough for you to not love me...but to be so heartless? You took away my son, but you will never get my daughter! You ain't a mother! You are nothing! You hear me? You are nothing to me! You are not- my- mother!" Nadine screamed.

Claire began clapping her hands. "Well, well, well. You finally got something right for once in your pathetic life." Claire plunked down on the sofa. "You ruined my life! Yes you did. You were an ornery little witch! Selfish, manipulative, whiny...my God! You were horrible!"

Nadine knew her mother felt this way—that was no surprise; but to actually hear her admit it? "Wow! Bravo. You finally admitted how much you hate me. If I was such a burden to you, why did you have me to begin with?"

Claire glared at Nadine, and then a smirk came on her face. "*Have you?* Why did I have you? Good question. I think it is about time you knew the truth, Nadine."

"What truth?" Nadine looked puzzled.

Just as Claire was about to answer Nadine, Celia came through the front door.

"Hey, I could hears you both outside. What's going on? Where's Theo? He knows better than to leaves you two alone." Celia tripped over the footstool while walking towards them.

"Aunt Celia!" Nadine helped Celia up. "You were drinking, too?"

"Just a little celebration. You know; a welcome home drink or two. But I ain't drunk. Feeling good—but not drunk. I'm sober enough to know that something is going on with the two of you. Something bad." Celia looked from Nadine to Claire. She didn't like the expression on Claire's face. "*Oh hell,*" she thought to herself, "*it's about to hit the fan!*"

"My mother was about to tell me the truth. The truth about why she's hated me all of my life. Why she even bothered to have me in the first place." Nadine looked at Claire, waiting for her to continue.

"Yes, why don't you join us, Celia? I'm sure the truth will be freeing to *you*, as well." Claire sniped.

"Claire, you been drinking again, haven't you?" Celia was unnerved. "Don't do this Claire. Not now—not like this."

Nadine sensed that her Aunt knew a whole lot more than she. "I don't under-stand. Will someone please tell me what the hell this is all about?"

Celia shook her head. "Not like this Claire. Where's Theo?" Celia left the room to find her brother.

"What is it? What doesn't Aunt Celia want

you to tell me?" Nadine asked.

"The truth. You deserve the truth," Claire stated matter-of-fact. "I am not your mother."

"What? What are talking about?" Nadine was confused. "If you're not my mother, then who is?" Nadine waited for Claire to answer her when her father and Aunt rushed into the living room.

"Claire! What the hell is wrong with you?" Theo yelled.

"Ain't nothing wrong with me. Hell, like your mama said, the truth will set you free," she smirked.

"But not like this!" Celia screamed.

"Will somebody please tell me what she is talking about?" Nadine demanded.

"*I am not your mother!*" Claire screamed. "I did not give birth to you! She did!" Claire looked to Celia.

Nadine's mouth opened wide. But she couldn't speak. She stared at her Aunt. "Aunt Celia's... my mother?" She finally whispered.

"Damn it, Claire!" Theo grabbed Claire by the shoulders and lifted her off the sofa. "You're drunk again, aren't you? Why would you do this? Why?" His voice was filled with rage.

Claire yanked Theo's hands from her shoulders. "Because I'm sick of her! That's why! I raised her, and she was a brat. Then she took away any chance of us having our own children!"

"That's a lie, Claire. It wasn't Nadine's fault we couldn't have no babies. You know that!"

_97R_

"Oh please..."

"Hold it! Hold it!" Nadine screamed. "I don't give a damn right now about why she did what she did! Or, what she believes. I want to know how, Aunt Celia is my mother, and why no one ever bothered to tell *me*?" She turned to Celia, who was slumped on the couch sobbing, shaking her head back and forth.

"I'm so sorry, Nadine," Celia cried. "I wanted to tell you, but I thought it was best to leave things as they were. I couldn't take care of you. And they couldn't have any kids. So I just..."

"Gave me away? Do you have any idea the hell I went through with her as a mother?" Nadine was raging inside. She still didn't understand.

"You don't understand, Nadine. It's hard to explain. Everything isn't just black and white," Celia cried.

"All this time. All this time my Aunt is my mother. My father is my Uncle. And..." She turned to Claire. "My mother is nobody!"

"Least you had a home! You ungrateful little heifer," yelled Claire.

"*Ungrateful? A home?* You made my life hell from the moment I can remember. You tormented me. You ridiculed me. You stole from me. You took my son from me...I don't know where he is, or if he's alive. If you could have, you would have taken my daughter! And you," she turned to Theo, "you were no better. You left me alone with her, while you slept your way through half the church women. What kind of man of God are you? You let her take my baby. You could have stopped her." Nadine thought for a moment. "But how could you really? Between you beating me, her beating me, you beating her, her drinking, and you sleeping with everyone..." Nadine shook her head.

"Nadine," Theo started to say something, when he saw his mother standing in the door way.

The raised voices had awakened her.

"What is going on?" she asked. She looked from one to the next. "Celia? Theo? Nadine?"

"She knows, Mama. Nadine knows," Celia whispered.

"Knows what?" Her mother asked.

"The truth, "answered Celia.

Grandma Jackson looked at all the faces. She could see the most pain on Nadine's face. "How did this happen?"

"Claire told her." Celia looked at Claire. "The way she told her, *Mama.* It was wrong." Celia shook her head and began crying again.

"Claire, how could you?" Grandma Jackson asked.

"*How could I what*? Tell the truth? Ain't that what you been telling us to do?" snapped Claire.

"Not like this, Claire. Not like this." Grandma Jackson turned to Nadine. "Nadine, baby?"

Nadine looked at her grandmother. This is what she was talking about earlier. "Gran, how could you not tell me? The hell I went through. How come you didn't tell me? How come *you* just didn't keep me and raise me?" Nadine began crying.

"Oh Nadine, I wish I had. But I wasn't doing so well back then physically. And Celia was in no frames of mind to be a mother to you. We thought the best thing to do was to give you both a mother and father. I'm so sorry."

"Who is my father?" Nadine asked Celia.

"He died before you were born," Celia said between sobs.

"I don't understand. You all had to know what they were doing to me. And you did nothing! Absolutely nothing! I will never forgive you for this! None of you!" Nadine turned to leave the room. She had to get her daughter and leave.

"No, Baby. Not like this. We got to talk this out. You got to understands," her grandmother pleaded with her. "Remember what I told you this afternoon."

Nadine looked at her grandmother. A part of her wanted to run into her arms, and feel that love and comfort from earlier. But the other part of her wanted to get away as fast as she could. She was angry; especially at her grandmother. She could have stopped the hurt she endured. She could have prevented a lot of things. Nadine just didn't understand. And she didn't want to stick around for anymore lies.

Her grandmother reached out to her as she walked pass. Nadine pulled away. "No, Gran. I can't. I have to get Macon, and get out of here."

"Not like this, Baby. Not when you're so angry and hurting. And besides, it's late," her grandmother pleaded with her.

Nadine shook her head. "I can't. I have to go now, before..." Nadine couldn't say another word, for the lump in her throat was too painful.

"I know it's painful, sweetheart. And I am so sorry. Please forgive me?"

"I can't do that Gran ...not now. I don't know if I ever will forgive any of you." Nadine saw the pain wash over her grandmother's face.

"Please don't leave like this?" her grandmother begged.

"I'm...I'm sorry, Gran. I have to get out of here." Nadine went back to the room where Macon was sleeping, and started to put their things into a bag when she heard the yelling in the living room escalate.

"You had no right to do that, Claire. You had no rights to hurt that child like that." Grandma Jackson shook her in disgust.

"Oh please! You all have some damn nerve! She has brought me nothing but pain since I met her!" She shoved her mother-in-laws hands off of her.

"How can you be so cruel? Had I known...I swear!"

"What? Don't put this all on me, mother Jackson. You and your bad seeds!"

"Don't talk to my mother like that!" Theo hollered.

"You always were a mama's boy. That's what

wrong with you now!" Claire sneered.

Theo smacked Claire hard across the face!

"Theo!" Grandma Jackson yelled.

Claire laughed. "Oh, that's nothing. You should see him when he's *really* mad!"

"You're sick, Claire."

"No sicker than you, Celia. You see, my guess is, you feeling mighty guilty for tossing your brat on me. You should have kept your little bastard yourself!"

"Enough! Enough!" Grandma Jackson yelled. "There is plenty of blame to go around. But Claire, you ain't gonna disrespects my home no more. None of you will."

"Don't try to act so mightier than thou, mother Jackson."

"You will reap what you've sown, Claire."

"Maybe I will. Maybe I won't. But you sure in hell ain't gonna keep looking down on me. Maybe if you would have done a better job as a mother, you wouldn't have such a bastard of a son, or a harlot for a daughter!"

"You ought to be a shame!" Grandma Jackson began to cry.

"Don't talk to my mother like that," both Celia and Theo warned.

"Why? She can handle it. She's just getting back what she dishes out." She turned to her mother-in-law. "Truth hurts, doesn't it? Can't take it, can you?" Claire said smugly.

Grandma Jackson went to say something to

Claire. When she went to open her mouth, no words came out. She gasped in deep, clutched her chest, and fell to the floor.

"Mama!" Celia and Theo ran to their mother.

Claire stood frozen.

Nadine heard Celia scream—a loud piercing scream. It made the hairs on the back of her neck stand up. She knew it wasn't good. She ran to the living room.

She froze; her grandmother was lying on the floor, not moving.

"Gran?" she whispered. "Gran?"

The few hours that followed were a blank.

Her grandmother was gone.

She never got the chance to tell her she was sorry; that she loved her. Her last words to her grandmother haunted her. The look on her face stayed with her. Two weeks later, Theo beat Claire to death. He's been in jail ever since. And she hasn't seen Celia since her grandmother's funeral. She had briefly spoken to her, and learned that her real father was Celia's one true love. He never made it back from World War II. Celia was never the same after that. And there was no way she could have raised Nadine. No matter how much she wanted to.

Still, none of that mattered to Nadine. Because of their lies, her life was hell and she could never forgive that...ever.

Nadine never told Nathan all that happened that night. Or, what she'd learned. It surprised him

J7R

when she didn't go to her own "mother's" funeral. Or, go see her "father". He never pushed the issue. Nadine also kept the secret that she had given birth to a son a year before coming to, Busby.

Nothing in her life was ever the same. Everything changed: Her relationship with Nathan, and with Macon. Nadine could never understand what she did to deserve so much pain. Or, how her life turned out the way it did.

CHAPTER 15

NADINE TURNED AROUND ADRUBTLY, running up stairs to her bedroom. She ran over to her dresser, rummaging through the clutter on top. She found it...her hairbrush.

Nadine began brushing her hair vigorously. She stopped for a moment, and rummaged through the mess on her dresser again. "Found it!" Nadine picked up a barrette and fastened her hair back into a ponytail. Nadine looked at herself in her bureau mirror, still not satisfied, she whisked around, looking at her room. She stood for a moment thinking. "A shower...that's what I need. A shower. Maybe by the time I'm finished, Byron will have returned. Yes, I'll take a shower." She spoke, trying to convince herself it was a good idea.

Truth be told, Nadine did not like being in the house alone. She hated to be alone. Lately, however, all she felt was alone—though she refused to admit it—not to anyone. Not even to herself.

Nadine was growing tired of Byron; but he gave her what she needed. She didn't trust anyone else to get her stuff for her. (She couldn't bring herself to say the word Heroin.) She heard of plenty of people getting a hold of bad stuff and dying. She wasn't desperate like them. She had standards. She just needed to get through this little hump, and she'd be okay. She could stop using at any time. She did it for that first month just fine.

She was doing really well...going to the meetings and taking the methadone. She was making it. She had not even seen Byron for a while; although he was locked up for that month. But there he was, sitting on her couch when she came home one afternoon. She'd forgotten she'd given him a key a while back.

He was smiling at her, looking all good. And he had enough heroin for the both of them. She didn't have to pay for anything. It was a welcome home present, he said. He told her how he'd missed her, and all he could do was think about getting back to her so they could go forward with their plans. Nadine remembered telling him that she was clean now; that she felt better than she had in a while. Besides, she was getting ready to take a trip down South and sees how her baby was doing.

"How did this happen to me," Nadine thought to herself. Why did she get involved with Byron? Of all places, she met him at the grocery store a year ago. Now she couldn't get rid of him. A part of her was too scared to let go; for fear of being left alone for good.

Byron gave her a wide-smile grin, and patted the seat next to him. He said they'd had plenty to celebrate. He told her, "one more time ain't gonna kills you, baby." He pulled her down next to him. Nadine protested at first. Byron told her he thought she loved him and wanted to share his life with him. He claimed that this was a part of it.

Nadine wasn't sure. He got up to leave, and said she wasn't the woman he'd thought she was. He'd had plenty of females that he could get with.

Fear gripping her, Nadine stopped him and said, "Okay. Just this once. This is the last time."

That was a month ago. Nadine was now more strung out than before. She stopped going to the program two weeks ago; unable to hide her dependency any longer. There's no way she could say she had her menses for an entire month... avoiding the urine tests. Heroin had her mind, and her soul.

It wasn't Byron—it was the beast that had her, and Byron knew just how to use it to his advantage. He knew Nadine was strung out, and he knew she was the only one with enough cash to supply both his and her habit. In addition to using her home to do a little business—it was the perfect front for him; particularly since he was no longer getting his heroin from the same suppliers as everyone else.

He found a new supplier, and a purer product; the Asians. A few free samples here and there and people were lined up all over the place. He could make twice as much with the white heroin, than the brown. It was more potent, and gave a quicker and stronger high. This meant he could use less and charge the same price.

Now was the perfect time for him to step up his plan. Everything in Philly was changing. Word on the street that dealer, Big Willie was about to go down opened doors for Byron. Big Willie made a big mistake and started cheating his suppliers out of their full cut. He knew they ran everything in New York, Chicago, Atlanta, and Detroit, as well as Philly.

When he couldn't beat his rap, he cut a deal with the DA; information on his contacts, and everything he knew: suppliers, dates, drop-offs, pick-ups, distribution—all for a lighter sentence. You can't expect to make a deal like that and live.

Byron was ready to take over. He'd been waiting for this opportunity, and was not about to let some fool woman mess up his plans. He'd string her along for as long as she complied. But as soon as she became more trouble than her worth, he'd have no problem getting rid of her.

To ensure he got everything he wanted and needed—he had to make sure she married him and everything was placed in his name. In order for that to happen, how-ever, he had to make sure she stayed in-coherent. He definitely could not have her running down South either—at least not without him. Right now, Nadine believed him and that he had not touched Macon. He had to keep it that way. Although, he wouldn't mind getting another hit of that young tale.

It was a perfect plan. Soon he'd be in charge on the street. He did not have a problem paying a cut—so long as his cut was a sizable amount, too. He had big plans; make enough money here and eventually establish himself out on the West Coast. Maybe even get into the movie business. If Ron O'Neil could get a job, then a classy nigger as he would be a sure shot. He just needed capital—and Nadine was the perfect source—even though he did not intend to bring her along. Besides, she didn't look as good as she used to—she let herself go. He could not be seen with someone looking that bad.

He was only twenty-five, and ain't no way in hell he was gonna let her make him look bad.

NADINE stepped into her room. She heard music coming from downstairs. "Byron must be back." She wrapped her towel around her, and walked to the hallway.

"Byron? Is that you?" She waited for an answer.

"Who else would it be? You were expecting someone else?" He pushed the pillow to the side, and sat down on the couch. "Come on girl! I got something good for you. What you doing up there anyway?"

Nadine put on a pair of blue Bermuda shorts, and a pink tank top. It was the only thing that was clean. She hadn't washed clothes in a while. She grabbed a shabby gray sweater to put on, (to hide the site of the track marks on her arms,) the black and blue hues a reminder of her addiction.

"What took you so long?" she asked, coming down the stairs.

"Business. Now do you want this or not? I ain't in the mood for none of your questioning," Byron sniped.

"No, no baby. It's just that...well...you said you'd be right back. It's been four hours." Nadine sat down next to Byron on the couch.

"Yeah, well it took me a little longer to get what I needed."

"You got everything?" Nadine couldn't hide her deep need to feed her addiction.

"Look at this." Byron picked up a needle, and placed the cotton ball down. "Let's give this a try. It should make you feel really good. Take away those headaches you been having. Here you go." He passed Nadine the needle.

Nadine had already tied the rubber tube around her arm.

"Mm" Nadine was placing the needle to her arm just as the phone started to ring. "Damn it!" She stopped for a moment.

"Let it ring, baby. The machine will get it," Byron said, preparing to take a hit.

Nadine began again, plucked her arm a couple of times. As she stuck the needle in her arm, she heard Emma's voice on the phone.

"Nadine! I don't know where you are, but you listens to me good! Either you call me, or I'm comin there to get you myself! Just so you know, Nadine, Macon is pregnant!" The phone went dead.

Nadine did not hear a thing after her name. She was in a zone, and all she could concentrate on was the feeling that the heroin had over her. Nothing else mattered—just the numbing sensation that her body was feeling right then.

She may not have heard the message, but Byron did.

"Pregnant? She done went down there, and got knocked up. I knew she wasn't innocent." Byron sat back and placed the needle into his arm, letting the feeling of his hit take effect. He had a good thing here. "Yeah, everything is going my way." Amidst his high, Byron thought for a moment, "Pregnant... Huh."

JR

CHAPTER 16

THANK YOU SO MUCH, CAMILLE." Emma hugged
Camille tightly. "You definitely a god-send. Yes you
are." Emma squeezed Camille's hand.

"Oh no, Mrs. Watson. You are the god-send."
Camille smiled warmly at Emma. "I only wish that
all my patients had someone like you in their corner.
It truly makes a difference."

"You sure my baby's ready to come home?"
Emma turned and looked at Macon, who was
standing by the window.

"Yes. I talked with Dr. Reese, and we both
agree that she is ready," Camille reassured Emma.
"With continued counseling, physician's care, and
some old fashion love," Camille rubbed Emma's
shoulder, "Macon will be just fine."

"I pray so." Emma looked hopeful. "This has
been a long, hard two weeks. I reckon the rest of this
pregnancy ain't gonna be no cake walk either."
Emma shook her head.

"Well, it won't be a cake walk. But as I said,
with continued support, and the proper care, Macon
will be fine. She's a remarkable young girl, with a lot
more strength than *she* even knows." Camille
looked towards Macon. "Still no word from her
mother?"

Emma sighed, "Lord, no. I don't know where
that Chile is. She could be dead for all we knows,"
Emma said, disgusted.

"Well, maybe it's best this way. From what you've told me, and what Macon has shared, it may very well be the best thing. However, I admit, I actually am concerned about Nadine, as well. She obviously needs a great deal of help. She sounds like she's on a collision course with death."

"Yes," Emma agreed. "I jes don't understands it all myself. She has so much to live for, but she's jes so damn selfish!"

"Yes, it seems that way. But from what Macon has shared, her mother seems to have some very deep-seeded issues that probably stem from her own childhood. It's a shame; because in spite of everything, Macon really loves her...very much." Camille walked over to Macon.

"I know." Emma followed. "Macon baby, you ready to go now?" she asked smiling.

Macon turned around. "Yes, Aunt Emma. I've *been* ready." She looked at Camille. "Thank you, Miss Camille. I really appreciate your help."

Camille gently squeezed Macon's shoulders. "Oh, it's my pleasure. Now you remember what we talked about?"

Macon nodded. "Yes."

"Good. Then I will see you in two weeks. If you need to speak to me before then..."

"I can call you." Macon finished saying.

"Yes," she rubbed Macon's shoulder. "Now, you go ahead with your Aunt. I'm sure she has fixed you a meal fit for a princess."

"I sure have," Emma laughed, "all my baby's favorites. You more than welcomed to join us, suga?" Emma took Macon's hand.

"Thanks so very much. But my parents are in town for a visit this weekend."

"They's more than welcome. I got plenty of food, and room at the dinner table."

"That's awfully kind. Perhaps another time?" Camille smiled.

"All right...suits yourself. But I'll be sure to send my son by with some desserts for you," Emma smiled.

"No. That's not—"

"Nothin doin!" Emma cut her off. "I will be sendin' you some dessert. Now that's my final word. Ain't no use of arguing with me either." Emma was insistent.

Camille looked at Macon, who was giggling. "I guess no one wins against your Aunt?" she laughed.

"Nope." Macon agreed.

"And the sooner you learns that, the better," Emma declared.

"Yes Ma'am!" Camille saluted her.

ALBERT was waiting for Emma and Macon when they came out the hospital. He had a bouquet of flowers and a bag of Macon's favorite candy: lemon drops. He gave her a hug and a peck on the forehead.

"So, you ready to go home little girl?" he asked.

"Yes Uncle...more than ready," Macon smiled.

"Well...good; because we sure have missed you somethin terrible!" He leaned over and whispered in her ear, "Your Aunt has been drivin' me fool!" He laughed.

Macon chuckled.

"What was that, Al-B?" Emma looked at Albert with a smirk on her face.

"Oh nothin', Mama...nothin' at all. I was jes telling Macon here, how much we missed her." He winked at Macon, who was trying to stifle her laugh.

"Is that right?" Emma looked from one to the other. "Don't starts your mess, you hear?" Emma smiled slyly.

"Relax, woman! And get in this here car." Albert opened the door for Emma and Macon. Macon climbed in the back seat. Albert shut the door as soon as Emma was in. "Yes sir! God is mighty good," Albert said, getting in the car.

"He certainly is, baby," Emma smiled.

Albert turned and faced Macon. "You gonna be *allll* right! Trust your Uncle," he winked. "I tolds you before...with God and your Aunt Emma on your side—you can't *ever* go wrong!" He turned and kissed Emma.

Macon smiled. "I believe you, Uncle." For the first time in a while, she really did. Macon believed what her Uncle said. She looked at her Aunt and smiled.

"I loves you suga," Emma told Macon.

"I love you, too...Mama." The smile on Macon's face grew.

Emma looked at Macon, and smiled, a tear running down her cheek. "Take us home, Al-B...takes us home."

"You got it, Mama!"

CHAPTER 17

February 2, 1975

C'MON ALBERT! WE'S LATE AS IT IS!" Emma yelled up the stairs. "Deeney, Macon and the baby already in the car...we jes waiting on you!" Emma looked in the hallway mirror and fixed her hat. *Some Deacon...he's always late!*

"Mama, please!" Albert said, coming down the stairs. "You act as though we ain't ever been late before." He winked at Emma.

"Oh man, please! This here is different. Nathaniel and Ella is gettin christened today!" Emma was excited. "Calvin and Anna-Leigh are already at the church waiting on us. Now c'mon!"

"Yes Mama!" Albert chuckled. He was thrilled to see his wife so excited. The last couple of months had been very hectic on her...on both of them. Finally, they have something to celebrate.

"Did Junior say he would be there?" Emma asked.

"I reckon so. He said he had to pick up Camille. They's supposed to meet us at the church."

Emma smiled.

Albert looked at his wife with a smirk. "Proud of yourself, ain't you?"

J7Q

"What?" Emma feigned ignorance.

"Oh, like you ain't pleased as punch that yo' little match-makin done worked?"

"Why, Al-B, whatever is you talkin 'bout?" Emma giggled.

"Woman, you's a mess. A pure-d-mess!" Albert grabbed his car keys off the sofa table. "Alright, let's go." He held the door open for Emma.

Emma smiled to herself, and thanked God for His blessings. She wasn't much of a religious person; but she knew that it had to be the work of God that got them all through these last eight months. As she sat in the car, she had to think on His goodness.

She was very pleased that Junior and Camille were finally seeing one another. She knew right from the moment she met Camille that she was the right person for her son. Of course, it was not easy getting them two together. Camille was just as shy, and Junior was just as thick headed as his Daddy! Yet, just like his Daddy, he got the picture soon enough. They just needed a little push. God took care of the rest!

Emma was certainly grateful that Camille was there for Macon.

Macon had a difficult pregnancy. She didn't know if she was going to make it through that delivery. Emma had to give blood. Macon lost so much during the birth. Bless her heart, Macon was a trooper. Yes she was.

Nathaniel—named after his grandfather—was a few weeks early, born November 28th, 1974. Still, he weighed in at six pounds, thirteen ounces and eighteen inches long. Head full of hair, and red all over. He came in this world fighting and screaming. Yes Lord, he is going to be something else.

Then there's, Ella, Calvin and Anna-Leigh's little girl. It pained Emma that she could not be there in, Georgia for her son and daughter-in-law. Anna-Leigh had a rough pregnancy, as well. Each time Emma spoke with Calvin on the phone—she could hear the anxiousness and fear in his voice. She wanted to be there with them. This was their first child, and Anna-Leigh has no other kin. Her folks died in a tragic car accident when she was thirteen. She alone survived. Her grandmother that raised her, passed two years ago. Emma was torn.

Once Macon gave birth though, and Emma knew that she was all right, and that Camille and Shelby would be there, Emma drove to Georgia. She was happy that she did. As grown as Calvin and Anna-Leigh was—they needed their Mama.

It's amazing the kind of mess that a grown man can make! However grown he was, Emma knew her son well enough to know that he was worried about his wife and everything else came second—including his job.

Emma came just in time, so that Calvin could concentrate on classes and the final exams; while she tended to Anna-Leigh. Emma cleaned, washed—what seemed like two months' worth of clothes!—and went grocery shopping. Lord! They'd been eating take-out! That was definitely not good for the baby. Calvin never did learn to cook—not like Junior and Shelby. He and Deeney shared that trait.

Emma had been there two weeks when, Miss Ella Langston Watson came into the world—born on her Grandpa's birthday: December 19th, 1974. Oh, she was the tiniest thing Emma ever laid eyes on! Five pounds, six ounces and seventeen inches long— with a set of lungs on her! Yes, this one was going to be a singer and a heart-breaker. Emma knew when Calvin placed her in her arms.

Ella was sucking on her hand. She was beautiful—big, round, brown eyes, the cutest little nose. She had Calvin's forehead—bless the little Chile. And everything else was Anna-Leigh; her complexion—a deep olive tone—her small little fingers, her ten little toes, on the smallest feet. And the longest legs! The child was all legs. Maybe she'd run track like Wilma Rudolph.

Emma's heart was filled with joy. Just watching Calvin and Anna-Leigh fuss over Ella, gave her heart strength. She could not put into words the elation that her heart was experiencing. All she knew was that she didn't want it to end.

For two weeks—after Anna-Leigh came home with Ella—Emma continued to help her and Calvin. They were a nervous wreck. Emma understood: being new parents and both with no family around for miles. She reassured them, however, that they were doing fine, and that they would continue to be fine after she'd left. It was time for her to get back home, and tend to her own house.

Anna-Leigh cried and cried...and so did Calvin. It was just pitiful. Emma arranged for

Deeney to come stay with them while school was in recess for winter break. She knew Deeney would be a great help to her brother and Anna-Leigh. It was a good thing that Shelby and Richard would be moving to, Atlanta in February. That way, they would all have one another. It's not good for family to be so far apart...all the time. A little distance is okay; but you do need some kin-folk around—the kinds you can trusts! But, that's a whole other story!

****

"**Lord**, what a mighty fine day we are having today!" Reverend Washington's voice bellowed throughout the First Zion Baptist Church. "Isn't it a beautiful thing, that Deacon Watson and Sister Watson have brought their family here to celebrate the lives of these two new souls...?"

"Good Lord," Deeney whispered to her friend, Lynnie-Mae. "Does your daddy always got to go on and on and on?"

"Well, least you don't have to lives with him."

Both girls giggled.

"I can't believe your cousin had a baby," Lynnie-Mae said. "I mean...she only fifteen! Do you know who the daddy is?"

"Oh please! You act as though she the only one who ever had a baby young. And no, I told you before, I don't know who the daddy is...it ain't none of your business anyways!" Deeney sniped.

"*Sorry.* Sorry I asked. I didn't mean any harm. I like your cousin. I was just wondering...is all? She just don't seem the type..."

"The type...what?"

"You know...like Becca Moore?"

Deeney thought for a moment. Rebecca Moore had a bad reputation. She was seventeen and already had three babies—by three different guys. She didn't seem to care what people said either. Neither did her mother, for that matter. She had ten kids of her own...and no real daddy to claims none of them.

"Well, my cousin ain't like that. When she found out she was pregnant, she nearly loss her mind." She leaned in close to Lynnie-Mae, "and whoever says otherwise will have to answer to me... what's more, they'll have to deal with my *Mama.*"

Mrs. Watson was not anyone you wanted to cross. Lynnie-Mae knew of a few that had...and they're still talking about how they regret that decision.

"You ain't got to tell *me*...I *know* your Mama."

"—children are God's blessing. Never let us forget that." Reverend Washington prayed for each baby and their parents, and the godparents.

EMMA, I made a cake for you all," Lynorra said. "It's back at the house. I'll have Matt bring it by when we gets home."

"Oh, thank you," Emma exclaimed. "You didn't have to go to no trouble."

"Trouble? Now what kinda trouble is it for me to makes my best friend a cake?"

"Well...you right!" Emma laughed.

Lynorra chuckled. "Emma Jean, you's a mess! Let me get a look at these babies," Lynorra went to see the babies who were being passed around the congregation, for hugs, oohs, and ahhs.

"She ain't what you expects a first lady to be, now is she?" Albert asked.

"No she ain't. She's my kind of people—real and downs to earth. Wish I could say the same for her—"

"—Emma Jean...Deacon..." Reverend Washington was walking towards them.

"Mighty fine service, Rev," Albert said, while squeezing Emma's side.

"Yes, indeed. We really *enjoyed* the service today," Emma said.

"Why, that's certainly something coming from you, Emma. I must be getting better, huh?" He winked at Albert.

It was common knowledge that Emma was not very fond of Reverend Washington. He knew why. Although she loved his wife and their three children—she often wondered about him. He was the pastor; but he wasn't any of *her* pastor. That's just the way she felt. And he knew it, too.

Now, his *father*? That was *her* pastor; the late

Bishop Carl Washington, Sr. Now that man could preach! And you knew *he* knew God. He was real, too—just like Lynorra. Every time Emma thinks about it—it burns her up!—choosing that man to be the new pastor! So what if he was the son; that don't mean he know nothin about bein' no pastor. Hell, Satan was God's creation, head of the angels' choir... and look how he turned out! Damn Deacon Board! What they knows about selecting a pastor? Half they were corrupt anyway. With the exception of Albert, Deacon Wallace, and Deacon Wilson; Emma didn't hold much regard for the Board. They were out voted—five to three. Ain't that a damn shame?!

Yet Emma wasn't going to any other church. The only other church was, Mt. Bethel, and surely they'd run her out—again! (Another long story!) And she sure didn't feels like driving all the way to, Columbus every Sunday. So she'd just grin and bear it. But she knew one day, God was going to get that Reverend Washington. You can't keep shuckin' and jivin'; especially not the Lord. He sees it all!

"Everyone has their good days...I suppose," Emma answered flatly.

Albert nudged Emma, warning her to behave.

Reverend Washington was quiet for a moment, then cleared his throat. He looked at Albert. "Well, Deacon, I 'm certainly glad you all decided to have those children christened. They certainly do needs God's covering." He smiled weakly. Emma always unnerved him.

Albert took the reverend's hand, "Most certainly, Rev....Most certainly. We just happy you agreed..." Albert's voice went low. He wasn't ashamed of his family; but Macon's ordeal was difficult for him to handle sometimes.

"Oh, of course," Reverend Washington started to say, sensing the delicate nature of their conversation. "As I said, we all God's children...and babies are always blessings—no matter *how* they got here."

"My sentiments exactly," Emma spoke. "And... we do appreciates you doin what you've done," Emma said, sincerely. "Uh...you's welcomed to the house. We having a little gets together. You, Lynorra, and the kids, are more than welcome to join us." Emma tried her best to sound cordial.

With surprise in his voice, "Why thank you, Emma. I think we will do that. I...I knows Lynn made you a cake, so..."

"So, we'll sees you back at the house," Emma finished saying. She turned to Albert. "We best get goin, Albert. We has lots to do." She took Albert's hand.

Albert squeezed Emma's hand. He was proud of her. He knew that took a lot for her to do.

"Yeah, Rev," he said looking at the reverend, "we'll see you all back at the house." He reached for Rev. Washington's hand.

Rev. Washington shook his hand. "All right... we'll see you all later, then." He smiled at Emma before turning to leave.

Albert and Emma watched as he greeted another parishioner.

****

"**Thanks** for coming, Lynorra." Emma hugged her friend.

"Oh, you don't have to thank me. It's my pleasure," she smiled at Emma. She continued to dry the dishes, as Emma washed.

Emma was the first person Lynorra met when she moved to, Busby. She and Arthur were married a year, and she was pregnant with their eldest, Matthew. She would have lost her mind if she didn't have Emma to confide in.

"Suga, you knows I *loves* you!" Emma laughed.

She always enjoyed Lynorra's company. Never in a million years would she had ever thought she and another woman would be so close. Not since her sister, and Ms. Lorelei—Albert's Aunt. Emma shared things with Lynorra that only Albert knew. That's how close they were—like sisters.

"I loooooves you, too!"

Lynorra always knew when something heavy was on Emma's mind. She could tell from her laughter. It was the *way* Emma laughed, that let you know what was going on inside her. She knew this was one of those times that Emma needed her friend. She seemed happy; but Lynorra knew that there was deep concern tugging at Emma's heart.

"So...tells me, Sistah, what's going on? And before you says 'nothing', just remembers whom you speaking with," she looked at Emma with her head tilted to the side. "C'mon. Everybody's just about gone." She took the dish-rag from Emma's hand and placed it in the sink. "Let's go," she grabbed Emma's hand. "Let's go to our little spot, so we can haves us a nice long chat," she smiled at her friend.

Emma nodded, tears welling up in her eyes. It's been a while since she was able to speak in length with her friend.

Thank God for Lynorra. She knew what she needed at that moment: A friend to listen, and...a good drink.

"Lets me tell Albert—"

"No need..." Lynorra said, waving her hand, "...when he don't see either of us, he'll know where we at. Besides, before you say it: there's plenty of family in there to take care of each other. Shelby and them ain't leaving for a week. So you just c'mon here, and let's get our minds together. Lord knows we can both use it!" Lynorra grabbed two small glasses from the cupboard, and opened the back door.

Arthur must be working her nerves again, Emma thought. "Wait." Emma grabbed an apron off the back of the pantry door. It's where she kept her stash. "I really needs me a cigarette."

Lynorra smiled at Emma. Who was she to judge? We all had our vices. Emma's was cigarettes...hers was Mulberry wine...Just a glass every now and then.

Both women left the house quietly. All the dawdling guests had finally left...now that their bellies were full. Emma's family was in the family room, along with Lynorra's children: Matt, Lynnie-Mae, and James. Arthur had long since gone home—with a huge plate of food, and plenty of sweets.

Emma and Lynorra walked arm in arm, towards Albert's tool shed.

About ten feet beyond the shed, was a small gazebo underneath a hundred year old Oak. Albert had built it for him and Emma. It was an anniversary gift. After he surprised Emma, she never complained again about him spending so much time in his tool-shed. After all, a man needs his own space, too.

Sometimes, she and Albert would steal away and just sit there quietly, holding each other, staring up at the stars. Thanking God for his many blessings...and on occasion—make love! Ain't nothing like making love under the stars! But, that was a while ago. They still come out there...just not as much.

Lately, she's found comfort coming here with Lynorra. Emma didn't recall how they started coming out here; but it sure gave them a chance to get away from the kids and the men folks. Sometimes you just need to let your hair down and unwind. You know? Certain things that only women need to vent about. The kind of things you talk about with a sister. Emma realized how much she missed her sister when she began looking forward to her time with Lynorra. She's become so much more than a friend...she'd become a part of Emma's heart—she was family.

CHAPTER 18

BOTH WOMEN SAT IN SILENCE FOR A WHILE, trying to collect their thoughts. Emma smoked her cigarette briefly, and then put it out. Lynorra reached under the bench for the bottle of Mulberry wine; opened it, and poured a glass for her and Emma. They could hear laughter and music coming from the house in the distance.

The cicadas were singing.

It was much warmer for a February night. A cool breeze would blow every now and again. Emma could smell the salt water in the air. No doubt, Emma thought, Albert and the boys would take advantage of this time together and go fishing and crabbing. For certain they'd be having a fish fry tomorrow. She'd prepare the coleslaw when she went back in.

Lynorra spoke first.

"So," she began, "what should we toast to?" she asked, holding out Emma's glass.

Emma took the glass, and thought for a moment. "How about: To life?" She smiled, raising her glass.

Lynorra nodded. "Yes, to life, and...to sisters," she added.

"Yes...sisters." Emma smiled, and took a sip. She put the glass down and looked at her friend...her sister.

"So, Sistah, let's talk. I'm all ears."

"Chile, where do I begins?" Emma sighed. "I knows the good Lord don't puts no more on us than we can bear...but this here load? Feels like it's gonna break me," Emma shook her head.

Lynorra listened—nodding her head in agreement, and sipping from her glass of wine.

"And Albert's been so good through all of this," she smiled, thinking of her husband and the rock of support he has been. "Not once has he complained...not once. I know for a fact it's hurting him somethin awful. He sees me cryin'—and God knows, I tries not to cry in front of him all the time—and he jes holds me in his arms, tellin' me everything's gonna be all right," she shook her head. "I don't knows about that—everything being all right. 'Cause I knows for a fact, it's a long road ahead, and I jes hopes and prays we get through it all right." Emma stared off into the night sky, taking a sip of wine.

"Of course I'm worried about Macon, as well. I thank God for Camille. She really has worked with Macon a lot."

"How's she doing with Nathaniel?"

"She's doing much better. You know, that first two weeks she wouldn't even touch him. She wouldn't hold him, feed him, or look at him. I didn't know what to do. Then that day I tried to reach you...?"

Lynorra nodded, remembering the day Emma was referring to.

"I had to run to the store and bring some

work orders Albert left at home. Everyone was out the house. You had already left. It was just Macon, me and the baby. I jes lay Nathaniel down after givin him his bottle, so I figured he'd be sleep for a while. I told Macon I'd be right back...no more than fifteen minutes, twenty the most. Lord, the look in her eyes was pure fear. She started crying, not wantin' to be left alone. I promised her, everything was gonna be jes fine. That he shouldn't wake before I got back.

"Well, you know babies and husbands... always got to make a liar out you!"

Lynorra laughed. "Yeah, ain't that the truth."

"Albert kept me an extra ten minutes...he was the only one in the store. And by the times I got back home, I jes knew that baby would be awake. I called to Macon; let her know I was back. I went to check on the baby, and he wasn't in his crib. Lord, my heart nearly stopped."

"You didn't think she would harm him, did you?"

"I wasn't sure. You know I done seen plenty crazy things happen to some chilren? Anyway, I called out for Macon. She didn't answer at first. I started to panic a little, when I heard Nathaniel coo. Lord, I never saw a more beautiful sight. There was Macon, sittin' in my rocker in the family room, holdin' Nathaniel. She was smiling at him, and snuggling his small face with hers, whisperin' into his ear. I swears that baby was talkin back to her."

"Probably was."

"It was the first time in a while that I saw a

smile on her face. When she saw me, she told me that he had woken up, and wouldn't stop crying. She said she was scared at first, and tried to wait for me to come get him, but he wouldn't stop crying. So— she went and picked him up. She said he stopped immediately, looked up at her and smiled."

"God sure does work in mysterious ways."

"He sure does," Emma took another sip of wine. She leaned her head back and closed her eyes.

"You know," Emma began, "I know God is good; but I jes have this feelin' that somethin awful is about to go down. You know?" She opened her eyes and looked at her friend.

Lynorra didn't say anything for a moment; pondering if she should say what she was thinking. She knew Emma wouldn't mind her speaking what was in her heart. Yet, sometimes you don't want to hear no suggestions—you just want someone to listen.

As if reading her mind, Emma broke into Lynorra's thoughts.

"Now, c'mon and says what's on your mind. Ain't no needs in tryin to coddle me. I'm a grown woman...been so for a long time. And you already knows I love you and respects whatever you has to say to me. We don't have no secrets. You's my sister, and I wants you to tell me. 'Cause you know, I'd tell you."

Lynorra nodded in agreement. Smiling, she answered, "I know that's the truth. Can't anyone ever say of Emma Jean Watson that she don't speaks her mind and tells it like it is...with love, of course."

Emma smiled.

"Emma, I know you hurting. And I knows Albert is hurting, because he is hurting for you. I know all this here mess has been an awful lot on you. I know just as Albert, that this all has brought back some painful memories for you. Things I'm sure you have worked hard to bury...and even try to forget. But we both knows that ain't no forgetting the past—uh-uh—we know that it won't stay buried, or get forgotten until we confronts it, and reveals it, so that it never has a holds on us again...ever." She waited before continuing.

Lynorra knew that Emma knew where she was going with this. They had spoken about it many times before. She believed her friend needed to hear it again.

"I know how much Macon really means to you, as does Albert. And we both—Albert and I—know that in order to help Macon get through all of this, you gonna have to get through yours first. Who knew that your past would come back like this?" Lynorra didn't expect Emma to answer.

"I'll tell you, God knew. Because He knew that that little girl in there," Lynorra pointed towards the house, "was gonna need you...and that you was gonna need her."

Lynorra went and sat down next to Emma. She could see the tears streaming down Emma's cheek. She put her arms around her sister.

"It's gonna be all right. Albert's right...now, don't you tell him I said that!" Lynorra laughed.

Emma laughed, as well. Albert and Lynorra were always chiding one another.

Lynorra continued, "...and God don't lie either, Emma Jean. Yes, our past is our past. And no one has a right to hold it over us—not even ourselves. But if we don't deals with it: the past will always be there, trying to mess up our future.

"I've learned a lot from you, Sistah. Yes I have. I thanks God for you every single day," said Lynorra, turning and looking into Emma's eyes. "You are my best friend, and I don't know what I would have done without you. I know you are hurting; but it's time to take control and tell it all, so you can really help that child; because, both her and that baby needs you. Don't worry 'bout your children, and what they gonna say."

Emma *was* concerned about her children. She'd always taught them to be honest, and confront the past, so you can let it go. What would they think of her when they learned that she hadn't practiced what she preached? Would they even understand her reasons for keeping this secret? Would they forgive her? It was such a burden.

"Nathan was right..." Lynorra began, "...they will understand; If not at first, eventually. He understood. And he understood why. So will they," Lynorra assured her friend.

Emma sighed deeply, laying her head on Lynorra's shoulder. Emma was used to being the strong—no nonsense—give 'em hell—take charge— everybody's encourager— one. Now, she found herself on the receiving end. Melting from all the years of grief and pain; from regrets and secrets, she sighed deeply. Enough was enough; she knew what she had to do.

"Girl..." Emma began, "...you really have been listening to me all these years, huh?" Emma's shoulders shuddered from her stifled laughter.

"You damns right! Took good notes, too!" Lynorra laughed.

Emma sat up, and wiped her face. "Chile, I thinks you done had, too much, of that Mulberry wine!"

"Oh hell...I didn't even finish this one glass." Lynorra turned the glass to her head, and finished her wine.

"Lord, I can hears Arthur now: 'Emma, you done corrupts my wife. Don't no first lady need to be messin' 'round with you. In facts, *no* god-fearing woman needs to mess with a devil like you.'" Emma laughed.

"Ain't that the pot calling the kettle black?!" Lynorra hollered. "Whew, Chile! If half the folks in that church knew what we knew..."

"Oh hell, Lynorra, those damn Negroes know! Half them, if not most, been doin the same thing. Trusts me when I tell you...a lot of them folks ain't right. I may be far from perfects, but at least I admits to it! Humph!" Emma rolled her eyes.

"Yeah, that's the truth...but I don't think Artie could handle a church full of people like you."

"You's right. He'd been long gone from that church. Not even his daddy's name could keep him there."

"Emma, you is a mess!" Lynorra laughed.

"I know. I know." Emma agreed.

Emma and Lynorra were enjoying themselves.

After Emma poured out her soul, Lynorra told Emma what had been going on with her. Things she hadn't told Emma since the last time they'd spoken. Lynorra was exceptionally concerned about Arthur and James' relationship. She did not understand how a father—a minister at that—could seem to resent, or harbor ill will towards their own flesh and blood; especially their twelve year old son.

Emma and Lynorra had not realized that the music and laughter that they heard earlier was now replaced with yelling. Deeney was about five feet away, when they realized something was wrong.

"Mama! Mama!" Deeney was running towards her mother; Lynnie-Mae right behind her.

Emma stood up quickly.

"Deeney, what's wrong?!"

"You...got...to...come...to...the...house..." Deeney was out of breath. "All hell... is... breaking loose."

"What the hell is going on?" Emma's brow furrowed. She didn't like the feeling she was getting.

Deeney was still trying to catch her breath.

Lynnie-Mae answered, "Macon's mother is here."

Emma couldn't believe her ears. She shot a glance at Lynorra.

Lynorra's mouth flew open.

This was not good.

"Yeah…" Deeney said catching her breath. "Nadine's here…and Shelby's fixin' to whoop her behind."

"Mr. Albert told us to come find—"

Emma was already running back to the house before Lynnie-Mae could finish her sentence.

Lynorra and the girls were right behind her.

CHAPTER 19

EMMA RACED TOWARDS THE HOUSE. The closer she got, the louder the cussing and screaming became. World War three was breaking out in her home. Her feet couldn't move fast enough for her. She stumbled into the back door.

"—you can't tell me—"

"—you better leave—"

"—what to do. That's my—"

"—now, Nadine. So help me—"

"—daughter. And, I ain't—"

Shelby and Nadine were shouting and trading expletives back and forth. Richard, Shelby's husband, was holding her back.

Albert held Nadine by the arms.

Emma was out of breath.

Lynorra, Deeney, and Lynnie-Mae stood in the doorway.

"What in the hell?!" Emma yelled. "Nadine! Nadine!" Emma rushed towards her. "What in the hell are you doing here?"

"I ain't in the mood for you, Emma. I just came to see my child, and grand-baby!"

"*Now?* After all this time? Nadine, ain't nobody heard nothin' from you for eight months!" Emma couldn't believe the nerve Nadine had showing up.

"Well I'm here now, and that's all that matters!" Nadine wrenched herself free.

There was something different about Nadine. Emma couldn't put her finger on it, but there was definitely something very different about her.

"She doesn't want to see you," Shelby screamed.

Richard had a grip on his wife. He knew if he let her go, she would no doubt tear into Nadine's hide.

"Calm down, Shelby," he whispered in her ear. "Let your folks handle this."

"No...she just can't come in here, like that!" Shelby cried. "You don't know...that bit—"

"Shelby!" Albert stopped his daughter. "Listen to your husband. Jes go 'head. Me and your Mama will handles this."

Calming herself down, Shelby backed away, taking her father's advice.

Lynorra gathered her children and Deeney to take to her house.

"Emma, Albert...I'm taking Deeney with me."

Deeney started to protest, until she seen the look on her mother's face.

"Listen, I don't care about your family. I want to see my daughter...now," Nadine yelled.

Albert stepped to Nadine.

"Listen, little girl," Albert began, "you ain't gonna keep disrespecting my home, my wife, or my family. I will kicks you out my home before the door has a chance to hit you where the good, Lord split you." He looked at Nadine with fierceness and an intense anger.

It took a lot to get Albert angry. Nadine managed to push all the right buttons.

Emma looked at Nadine coolly.

She warned her, "I suggests you step lightly from here in out...you'd done crossed the line—yet again. One more thing out your mouth—and God help you!—I will let Shelby have at you, 'til there is nothin left of you."

Nadine stepped back, stumbling over a chair.

Emma looked around.

"Where's, Macon?" she asked.

"She's in the back with Camille, Anna-Leigh and the babies," Junior answered.

"Go get Camille."

Richard took Shelby to another room.

Calvin went and stood by his father.

He looked at Nadine, shaking his head. He couldn't believe that Nathan was married to this woman. He couldn't fathom being married to someone like her for all those years. He looked at her with disgust, and contempt. He knew she was bad news— from the beginning.

He could not contain the anger that had weld up in him—especially after learning what Macon had gone through, and suffered by the hands of her own mother.

"The audacity," he spoke. "The audacity you have to come into my parents' home, and disrespect them, after all you have done." Contempt was all over Calvin's face. If he believed in whooping a woman...Nadine would definitely be the first.

Nadine was surprised. She had always liked Calvin. But she'd never seen anyone look at her with such venom...so much hatred. Not even Emma.

"How could you even show your face in this home? The boldness of the devil!"

Calvin went and faced Nadine.

Nadine backed away, trying to avoid Calvin's glare.

"I always wanted to be like Nathan. I envied him, and his family, and how much he loved you. I wanted the same thing. I looked up to him. God, if I only knew what he was really going through. He never said one mean thing about you...ever. He'd call me, and see how I was doing—never once indicating how much hell he was going through."

Emma looked at Albert. It was a surprise to both of them that Nathan and Calvin had been in contact with one another on a regular basis.

"Don't...don't judge me," Nadine stammered. "Nathan was no saint!" she declared.

"I never said he was," Calvin retorted. "Neither did he claim to be."

Calvin folded his arms across his chest. He backed away.

Before turning away, he said: "I pity you."

"I don't needs your damn pity," Nadine spewed.

"I pity the fact that you don't even know how much you were loved. You're pathetic...a pathetic excuse for a woman. Any woman who would do to their child..."

Calvin couldn't get the rest of the words out. It was as though they were stuck in his throat. He walked away, waving his hands at Nadine.

"I'm going to check on the kids, and my wife," he said to his parents, and walked out the room.

Emma's heart ached. She knew that Calvin and Nathan were close; but she didn't know they stayed in contact over the years. She wondered how much of the truth Calvin already knew.

Did Nathan say anything to him?

No, Calvin would have addressed it immediately.

Junior returned with Camille following behind him.

Emma walked over to Nadine.

Nadine stood up straight, adjusting her jacket, and running her hand through her hair...a nervous tick she'd always had.

"Listen, Emma, I ain't come here to starts no trouble. I just came to see Macon, and my grandbaby...that's all. I'm still her mother. And *you said* that you weren't trying to get in between Macon and me."

"Don't try and use no reverse psychology with me, Nadine."

Emma shook her head. She really didn't know what to say to Nadine. All she wanted to do was wrap her hands around her neck, and squeeze the life out of her.

"You ain't got no right jes showing up like this, Nadine. Especially seein' how no one has heard a word from you since Macon left. You didn't return any phone calls, no letters. Hell, Junior drove all the way ups to Philly lookin' for you...and nothin'. So, don't you come here, to my home, trying to disrupts everything, and messin' with that Chile when she is finally getting' adjusted and all."

Emma stood face to face with Nadine.

"I won't let you hurt that girl, you hears me? You've done enough damage as it is. You will not get the chance to do any more."

Emma stood staring at Nadine—trying, with all her strength, not to put her hands around her neck.

Looking at Nadine, all Emma could hear was Macon crying, and telling her all she went through; seeing the fear, the hurt, and the pain resonating in Macon's eyes.

No, she didn't trust Nadine. Not for one moment. She was not going to give her another opportunity to hurt Macon, or that baby.

Albert knew his wife couldn't hold out much longer.

"Mama," Albert put his hand on Emma's shoulder. "C'mon, Mama."

Albert walked Emma away from Nadine.

Nadine was shaking.

Maybe it wasn't such a good idea to come.

But she had to.

They didn't understand.

No one understood.

Albert turned to Nadine, "I think you better have a seat."

With obeisance, Nadine sat down—unsure of what was going to happen next.

Camille sat down next to Emma, and took her hand.

"You all right, Emma?" she asked.

"Yes, yes," she nodded. "Don't worries 'bout me...how's Macon?"

Nadine looked up when she heard Macon's name.

She wondered who Camille was, and what she had to do with her daughter.

"She's okay," Camille answered. "And the baby's fine, too. Macon's just a little shaken right now. This is to be expected, considering..." Camille's voice trailed off, looking towards Nadine.

Camille leaned towards Emma, speaking softly, so Nadine could not hear.

"As soon as Macon saw her mother, she ran to the room. I still don't know if it was more fear, or trying to protect Nathaniel. She was afraid her mother brought *that man* with her."

Emma nodded her head, understanding what must have gone through Macon's mind at seeing her mother.

That poor Chile; hadn't she suffered enough?

Turning to Nadine, Emma asked, "You still haven't said; where in the hell have you been? And why did you come now...of all times? No letter, no phone call..."

Emma stared at Nadine, waiting for her to answer.

Everyone else in the room—Junior, Albert and Camille—waited for an answer, as well.

Nadine did not speak for a while. She looked at each face staring at her, and contemplated whether or not to tell them why she hadn't come sooner, or called, or written. She could see the contempt they had for her. It was in their eyes. The only one who seemed to not have a look pure hate was the young woman sitting beside Emma. And she still didn't know who she was. Should she tell them the truth?

It would be just one more thing for them to hold against her.

Nadine, not looking at anyone in particular, began to speak.

"I...I know I should have been here long ago," she stammered. "But, but I just couldn't. I mean, I knows I should have called. But I wasn't in any frames of mind to."

This of course was true.

Nadine looked at Emma.

"Emma, you know I was in a bad way, and I was angry with you for taking my child—"

J7R

"That's no excuse, Nadine," Emma interrupted her. "You could have at least returned the many messages we left for you."

"You're right," Nadine agreed. "But I was just so mad, and I didn't want to hear nothing you had to say...not even about Macon." Nadine tried to find the right words to say without revealing, too much, of the truth, and the real reason she was there.

"Listen, I took your advice, and those counselors advice...I've been clean for six months now. I got some help."

Yes, she'd been clean for six months. But she failed to mention that she was in jail for those last six months, too.

"I've been following a good program..."

Mandatory condition for her early release.

"I'm getting myself together..."

Part of her probation period.

Emma looked at Nadine, skeptical.

She knew Nadine looked different.

No, her gut was telling her there was more to this story than Nadine was sharing; and rightly so. There was a whole lot more to Nadine's story of 'sobriety'.

Nadine knew Emma was suspicious. However, she was not volunteering any more information than what she'd already shared.

This was the story she was sticking to.

CHAPTER 20

NADINE HEARD EVERY MESSAGE LEFT FOR HER.
She knew how important it was for her to call. But
she couldn't bring herself to do it. Doing that would
be admitting that something was wrong with
Macon...and that it was all her fault. She couldn't
face it. So she did what she did best...she ran. Ran to
the open arms of heroin, and to the arms of a man
she knew—but would never admit—was using her.

She'd married Byron.

Nadine knew in her sober mind, that Byron
did what Macon said he did. However, she couldn't
bring herself to face that fact. So—she anesthetized
the pain with heroin and Jack Daniels; numbing her
mind, and her soul to the reality that was around
her. She didn't want to face the truth. She couldn't.
If she faced the truth, and admitted it, she would
have to take responsibility and she would definitely
be all alone...forever. The one thing she was most
fearful of: being alone—especially with herself.

Nadine lied to herself, she lied to the
counselors, and she lied to child services. She even
lied to Byron. She told him she loved him, when the
truth of the matter was, she could barely stand him.

She needed the supply he could get for her,
and the company he gave her. Of late, though, it had
not been much.

He lied to her, too.

Byron needed a place for business and some cash. It's not like he had a job; or was even planning to get one.

Nadine asked about his parents. He said they were dead.

They lived in Ohio—very much alive. His mother was an elementary school teacher. His father was head supervising engineer (Lead Janitor), at Ohio State.

Byron would send money home every now and then to help his parents with his other five brothers and sisters. He wasn't completely *heartless*. At least this way, he could keep them at bay. They kept asking when they were going to see him. He had a selfish motive for everything he did.

His parents asked him what he was doing for a living. He told them the truth: pharmaceuticals. After all, he had become the number one Pharmacist in the neighborhood. He had to tell them something.

They believed him.

Just like Nadine *had* believed him...in the beginning.

People often believe what they want to believe. The truth is often harder to accept; a lie, much easier.

Nadine listened to all the messages. She read all the letters. She knew when Junior came. She didn't want to face the truth, so she acted as though it were all happening to someone else.

Byron was having another one of his "parties". An orgy is what it was! People were drinking, shooting up, snorting, smoking, having sex.

Sometimes, all at the same time.

Nadine was numb all over. Everything was one big blur. She walked from room to room. People groping her...men, women...it didn't matter. Her house had become the hottest spot in Philly.

Gone were the family photos from the walls, and mantle. Gaudy, loud, colorful furniture replaced the, soft comfortable sectional furniture that Nathan had purchased just a year ago.

All of Macon's awards and trophies were gone as well.

There was no trace of Nathan or Macon.

There was no trace of Nadine.

What remained was a shell of what used to be; now void of spirit and soul; given over to depravity and a disturbed mind.

The neighbors complained often.

Finally, someone listened.

Nadine doesn't recall everything that happened—just bits and pieces.

She remembered a loud crash at the front door, flashing lights, people screaming and running.

It was a raid.

Nadine recalled taking a swing at someone. The next thing she remembered was waking up in a cell, with five other women that she somewhat recognized from the night before.

Funny, Byron was free, and nowhere to be found. He'd managed to somehow get out the house when the raid went down.

Nadine called the house and left messages. No Byron. She was appointed a public defender. He couldn't get in contact with Byron either.

Nadine had to do six to nine months. She did six months before being paroled.

Byron eventually showed up: A month later.

He had a good excuse though; claiming that he'd had to stay clear from any trouble, or they might get him for violation of his parole.

"I'm your wife, Byron," Nadine cried. "You just left me here to rot!"

"No baby, it wasn't like that," Byron said, trying to talk soft and sweet to her. "I told you before; I got to keep my nose clean."

"You didn't even answer the phone, Byron. I... I could have beaten this with my own lawyer. I could have been out on bail," she looked at Byron, tears streaming down her cheeks.

"Look, I'm sorry Nadine. I told you, I didn't even know what was going on at first. I just ran as fast as I could when I heard them coming," he whispered, telling the truth for the first time.

"That was all well and good for you, but you left me behind!" Nadine raised her voice. "I ain't your girlfriend, Byron. I'm your wife!"

"Look, baby. What you want me to do?" Byron retorted, feigning annoyance. "I'm here now. Ain't that what's important?"

Nadine didn't answer him.

"Well," Byron got up like he was leaving. "I don't have to take this from you, you know? I got business to take care of. I came here for *you*. Because, I'm your husband and I love you. But if you want to start acting like that..." Byron turned away from Nadine, like he was leaving.

He took his time, waiting for her to stop him. *One, two, three...he counted.*

Nadine started crying and yelled out, "No, Byron, don't leave. I'm sorry baby. I just don't...I can't think straight in here." Nadine buried her face in her hands, sobbing.

Byron smiled to himself. *Yeah, he had her right where he wanted her: totally dependent on him.*

"Shush," he whispered. "You can't be crying in here like that. You want them to mess you over?"

Nadine lifted her head, and wiped her face.

"Listen, the most you got to do is six months. You be out before you know it. You got five months left. Just do what you told, mind your business, and I'll have someone looking out for you, all right?" He smiled.

Nadine looked puzzled. "Looking out for me? I'm in jail! Who in the hell cares about me?"

"Shush, baby. Don't worry." Byron leaned forward, beckoning Nadine to come closer. He looked around to see who was watching them.

"I spoke to Big Ty last week. He said he gonna make sure you okay."

Nadine didn't understand. Why would Big Ty care about her? She didn't know him personally. Hell, she didn't want to know him personally. She left all that black mafia business to Byron.

"I don't understand," she said. "Why would he do that?"

Byron was not sure either. But when Big Ty sent for him, he went. He just assumed he wanted to help Nadine, because she was his wife, and because he [Byron], has been bringing in a big profit with his new source of heroin.

Byron was clueless. And Nadine didn't know that she had more in common with Big Ty than she'd thought. She'd find out later, though.

"Listen, does it really matter? He looks out for his people. He knows I'm bringing in the cash. And you my wife. So he know that you a part of it, in a way. If the police looking at you, they gonna look at me...and then they might connect me to him. So that nigger probably just covering his own self anyway. But hey, so what? At least you get protected.

"Another thing, too, it's a good thing you ain't mention my name, or his. Because that really would've started something I know we *both* couldn't get out of."

Nadine looked at Byron. She was no fool. Too many people been getting blown up, shot up, or chopped up.

"I ain't stupid, Byron," she rolled her eyes. "I know how to keep my mouth shut."

"Well, that's good...for both of us," he said, looking at his watch. "Listen baby, I got to get out of here."

"You only been here thirty minutes, Byron.

You still got another half hour," she looked at him, her eyes pleading with him to reconsider.

"Sorry. You know I got to go. Time is money, and I got to take care of business," he stood up to leave, putting on his jacket.

Nadine knew it was no sense in begging him.

"When—when I'm gonna see you again? You are coming back, Friday?"

Byron didn't look at her. He pulled his zipper up on his jacket.

"Can't do Friday, babe. You know that's pick up day. I'll see you soon."

Nadine started to say something, but changed her mind. What was the use?

Byron turned to leave, then turned back to say something.

"Oh, by the way, I've looked everywhere... where's the bank book?"

BYRON came to see Nadine a total of six times in the following five months. He wasn't even there when she was released. To her surprise, there was a car waiting for her. At first, she thought it *was* Byron. At a closer glance, she recognized the driver...it was Spencer Thomas, Big Ty's driver.

Spencer held the door open for her.

Big Ty was waiting in the back seat.

She got in. You really don't say no to Big Ty.

Big Ty wasn't even *big*. Nadine guessed he was around five feet- eight, about 175 pounds. It was his attitude that made him big, and his ability to put fear into many people. (And a certain bodily endowment—so she heard.) When he said something, he followed through with it; whether it was an agreement, or a threat. His word was his bond.

He wasn't like your average hustler. He was about business all the time. He even dressed differently. He was not flashy or extravagant in his attire, nor did he ride around in a colorful Cadillac. No, he was more reserved; some might say classy. (If you could call a murderer, a pimp, a drug dealer and a mob boss classy.) Another thing about Big Ty that set him apart—he was honest. He never lied.

He sure was bold; picking her up in front of the jail.

He was like that, though. He didn't care about the police. As far as he was concerned, he was untouchable. He could shoot someone six times, point blank range, with a hundred witnesses, and still be found not guilty.

Nadine sat quietly, not knowing what to say, or what this was all about.

"So," he said smiling, "did they treat you all right?" He looked Nadine in the eyes.

"I...I guess so," she stammered.

He nodded his head. "That's good. That's good." He turned to Spencer, "Back to the crib, Spence."

Spencer nodded, and started the car, pulling off slowly.

"You're probably wondering what Big Ty is

doing picking you up...right?"

Nadine nodded.

"Well relax, Nadine. I ain't gonna bite," he said taking her hand. "Relax Mama."

His smile was wide, showing off his two gold teeth.

Nadine finally caught her breath. Slowly pulling her hand away, she said, "Well, I definitely wasn't expecting it. I mean, being picked up and all. No offense, but I don't know you." Her heart was beating a mile a minute.

He nodded. "No offense taken. I completely understand. But you might be surprised at how much I know about *you*."

Nadine's eyebrows rose. *How did he know about her? What did he know about her?*

"You know," he said looking straight ahead, "your husband was a good man. He had a lot of balls."

Nadine was confused. "Byron?"

Still facing ahead, "No, not that *fool*. I'm talking about Nate."

Nathan? How'd he know Nathan? "I...I didn't know he knew you."

"There's a lot you don't know. I'm surprised that you ended up with the likes of Byron. He ain't nothing but a two bit hustler, who's running out of time." He glanced at her, to see if she was following him. He turned his face forward again.

Nadine felt her stomach drop. She couldn't

respond. She didn't know what to say.

"It's none of my business who you keep company with; that's your prerogative. I just don't understand how someone as yourself, can lowers yourself."

"Hold on a minute," Nadine spoke up. She knew she was on dangerous ground, but she couldn't let him talk down to her like that. "You don't know me like that. You don't know anything about me." She thought about her words carefully. "And if you don't mind, I appreciate the ride and all; but if you just did it to get at Byron, then maybe you can just let me off at the corner here, and I'll walk the rest of the way home."

Big Ty smiled. "Yeah, you got guts...and plenty of attitudes. Not too many people stand up to me like that; especially no woman—with the exception of my mother. I like that. Nathan was right about you." He turned and looked at her, grinning. He asked her, "You ain't scared of me, are you?"

Nadine looked at him, not sure where he was leading with this conversation.

"No. To be honest, I ain't scared of you. I ain't scared of no one," she answered, lying. She knew every bone in her body was shaking with fear. Nadine didn't hear of too many people living that had spoken their mind to Big Ty.

He laughed. "All right, Nathan really knew you. You know, I ain't ever seen a man love a woman like he loved you."

Nadine grew more uncomfortable hearing

him speak of Nathan.

"If you don't mind me asking; how'd you know Nathan?"

"Not at all; Nathan did me a favor. I owe him."

A favor?

"Actually, the favor was for my mother. Nathan looked out for her."

"I don't understand."

"You know, ain't much you can count on in this world, or anyone for that matter. But there ain't no replacing your mother. You know what I'm saying?"

Nadine understood about not being able to count on anyone. But she couldn't relate to the mother part. She nodded just the same.

"Now, I ain't a liar, and I definitely ain't a saint either; but I love my mother more than anything. Mama held me down and took care of me and our family without any man. I owe her. Even though she doesn't agree with my life..." His voice trailed off, as if loss in a memory.

"Anyway, long story short. She was having some problems with her house and keeping the payments and all. That's when she went to Nathan's office for some help. I found out, and I had a talk with him."

Oh I see, Nadine thought.

"Like I said, Nathan had a lot of balls. You know I sent for that nigger, and he told me if I wanted to see him, I needed to make an appointment like everyone else?" Big Ty laughed to himself, remembering the guts Nathan showed. "Now him, he didn't fear me or no one. At first, I thought he was just some dumb house nigga—working for the man, and didn't know who he was dealing with." Laughing out loud, he said, "I never been more wrong. He was one classy brother. I liked his style. I didn't know he was a partner there. Anyway, he told me upfront he was going to help my mother the right way, on his term, and that I didn't have anything to worry about. He knew how to do his job, and he was damn good at it.

"Yo, I ain't ever seen a man so good with numbers like he was. You know, I offered him something on the side—you know, 'tax free'—and he turned me down? Yeah, I was real impressed. He didn't want anything. He helped my mother, and my mother couldn't stop singing his praises. She still does. It hurt her, you know, when he died. She said it was like one of hers dying. That's how I really got to know him...when he'd come visit with my mama."

Nadine was totally surprised. She could never picture Nathan and Big Ty just 'shooting the breeze'. It was incomprehensible to her. Nathan was no saint, but he was no criminal either. He wouldn't be caught dead with the likes of Big Ty. For that matter; she couldn't believe a ruthless person, such as Big Ty, could talk so lovingly about his mother. She almost forgot he was a cold-blooded killer. Almost.

"That's all well and good, but what does your relationship with Nathan have to do with me?"

Big Ty smiled. "You don't get it, do you? I

told you, I owe him. And, there are some things that you need to know."

Spencer pulled into a driveway in front of a brick, ranch-style house, in a quiet suburb of South Philly. Not exactly what Nadine had pictured. But then, nothing about this whole day was as she imagined it was going to be.

CHAPTER 21

NADINE WAS NOT SURE WHY, but she began to relax around Big Ty. He wasn't exactly what she'd expected. Yet, she was no fool to believe that if she crossed the line, that he wouldn't hesitate to slit her throat and have her chopped into little pieces, where no one would ever find her. He may owe Nathan, but that was Nathan. She also wondered what he meant, when he said that Byron's days were numbered. She didn't forget that little statement.

Nadine was sitting quietly in the living room when Big Ty walked in carrying a tray, with a coffee pot and two cups. He placed the tray down on the table beside him, and sat down.

"Would you like some coffee? If anything, I am hospitable. My mother did raise me to be a gentleman." He looked at Nadine, offering her a cup.

Nadine shook her head. "No thank you. I'm fine."

"Suit yourself," he said raising his cup. "I'm a little chilled myself." He took a sip, and sat the cup down. He leaned back, and studied Nadine for a moment.

"You know, although Nathan told me about you, I really wasn't expecting too much; considering that you took up with the likes of Byron," he said emphatically.

Nadine didn't know quite how to respond. He seems to be complimenting her, at the same time as belittling her. "Thank you...I think."

"Don't take offense," he said raising his hand. "Did you know that Nathan knew about you and Byron?"

Nadine bowed her head. She knew Nathan had known. But he never once said anything to her. She began to fiddle with her hands.

"I told him myself," he said taking a sip from the mug.

Nadine looked up. "And you proud of yourself?" she sniped.

"Umm, fire! I see you didn't like that one," he chided, putting his cup down. "To answer your question: no. I wasn't proud to be telling him that. Nathan was a good man. I just thought I owed it to him, to let him know that the woman he loved so much obviously wasn't digging him the same way no more."

Nadine's cheeks grew red. "You had no right. You know nothing about my relationship with Nathan or with Byron for that matter," she responded flatly.

"I know enough to know that you gave up prime rib for dog food! You went from a man to a boy playing like he's a man; who, by the way, is about to find out a hard lesson."

"You can't judge me!" Nadine hollered.

"Listen; don't raise your voice in my home. You are a guest, and I expect you to act as such," he warned her.

Spencer walked into the room.

Big Ty held up his hand, as if to say he had it under control.

The uneasiness in Nadine's stomach returned. She knew enough to know that that was indeed a threat. "Can you just tell me please, what you want from me?"

Big Ty sat back. He crossed his legs and took out a cigar, bit the end of it, then lit it. He took a couple of puffs, pulled it back, as if to admire it, then turned to Nadine.

"Normally, you won't catch me in any hospital. I don't like them. However, my mother asked me to visit Nathan. Nathan wanted to see me...it's the least I could have done," he took a couple of more puffs, before continuing. "I made it to see him just in time, too. He died the next day. How about that?" He looked at Nadine.

Nadine didn't say a word. She hadn't seen Nathan before he passed. The fact was she had not gone to visit Nathan for four days. When she finally had a clear head to go, he was gone. No one knew how she really felt. No one understood. Only Nathan understood...and he was gone, and she treated him with no respect. She pushed and pushed, yet he never left. He never even threatened to leave. She didn't know why he loved her so. Especially, since she did not—could not—loves her own self.

Nadine felt the lump in her throat. Tears were burning the back of her eyes, but she refused to let them fall. She simply said, "How about that, huh?" She turned her head towards the window. It was starting to snow.

Big Ty studied Nadine. She was a hard woman. Not like the women he employed; a different hardness...a hardness to her soul. Whoever messed her over did a really good job; because this sister was ice cold. In a way, he found himself drawn to her. And could understand and see what Nathan had seen in her. Funny, if this was another time or place, he would definitely have her for himself.

"Well, like I said," Big Ty broke the momentary silence. "I went to see Nathan. I met your daughter, Macon, the same day."

Nadine turned around and looked at him. Now it was coming together. This had to do with Macon.

"Fine young lady; looks a lot like her mother," he smiled.

Nadine didn't respond.

She wondered what all Nathan had said to Big Ty. And just what was it that Nathan wanted from him.

"She's a very intelligent young lady. By the way, how is she?" He already knew.

"I don't know. I guess she's fine," Nadine mumbled.

"You guess? You're her mama. You don't know how your own child is doing?"

Nadine looked towards the window.

"Listen," she began, "I know I'm her mama.

That fact hasn't escaped my mind. I will always be her mother. Just because I don't know how she is doing, don't mean I don't care." She turned towards Big Ty. "Besides, I've been a little locked up lately," she retorted.

Big Ty smiled. "True. But she ain't written you?"

Nadine didn't answer.

"Oh, I see. She ain't known you got locked up, huh?"

Nadine said nothing.

"Nathan asked me one thing that day. I'm sure you know what that is, don't you?" He stared into Nadine's face.

She turned from his gaze.

"No," she said, "why don't you just tell me."

"He asked me to look after Macon, and *you*."

Nadine wasn't surprised. She knew in her heart that Nathan still loved her.

"Ain't that something? I could understand looking out for your daughter, but you, *too*? He really loved you with his last breath," he said with awe in his voice. Then he said, "You must got some damn good stuff!" He laughed.

Nadine glared at him. "That ain't any of your business!"

"Maybe not; but it sure makes you wonder why a man like him would stay so long when he could have had anyone. Hell, I even offered him the cream of my crop. And still, he had class, and turned me down. I admired that about him. First, I thought he was just an arrogant s-o-b, but that was just him. I respected that. This is another reason that made me take to heart his request. It was the least I could do; especially after meeting Macon. I felt like she was my daughter."

Big Ty leaned forward in his seat, arms resting on his knees. He put the cigar out, and placed it in the ash tray. He turned his full attention to Nadine, getting a serious look on his face.

Nadine noticed the sudden change in his disposition.

Big Ty clasped his hands together, then rubbed his chin, as if thinking about what he was about to say. When he finally began to speak, Nadine saw this anger in his eyes she hadn't seen earlier. It was very intense, and unsettling. It scared her.

His voice was low and melodic when he spoke. "I don't know why people choose to do the things they do. I know I do what I do because I'm good at it, and it's what I know and a matter of survival. I'm not a saint; some may even call me evil. But I know that if I wasn't doing what I do, someone else would be, and I'd have to answer to them. There's a pecking order in this world you got to follow. And if you from the streets, you got to live by the rules of that street. You follow me?"

Nadine wasn't quite sure where he was going with this, but she nodded anyway.

"I'm a business man. I live by a strict code, and whoever works for me has to abide by the same rules. I'm not like these other cats out here; my word means everything. On these streets, your word is all you got. If you mess that up...then you have nothing. And you can best believe that someone is gonna come and try to take you out.

"You have to follow your word to the end—no matter what. And when you say you gonna do something, you have to follow through. I'll give you a chance to prove yourself. But you only have one. I'm not a liar, a thief, a rapist or a killer."

Nadine raised an eyebrow at that statement.

Big Ty held up his hands, "I ain't ever taken an *innocent* life. My hands are clean. And that's all I'm gonna say," he looked Nadine in the eyes.

She knew what he was saying, without actually saying it.

"If there's something I need to know about somebody—*anybody!*—I'm gonna find out. I'm gonna find out who I'm in business with and what they're all about. I trust one person in this world, and that's my mother. And when she says something is that's all I need to know. Mama never lies. And a mother should always protect her child at all costs."

Nadine wanted to say something, but the look in Big Ty's eyes held her mouth shut.

"My mother told me to do whatever Nathan asked me to do. He told me to look after his family—especially his little girl. I gave him my word. I gave my mother my word." Big Ty stood up and walked across the room. He looked out the window at the falling snow. He turned around to face Nadine.

"You're going to go see your daughter next month." He didn't smile. He didn't bat an eye. He said it matter-of-factly.

"Ex-excuse me?" Nadine stammered. "I can't just go *there*," she said.

"You can and you will." He walked towards her, until he was standing in front of her. "You will do exactly as I tell you, how I tell you and when I tell you."

Nadine was uncertain. She didn't understand what Big Ty exactly wanted from her.

"I—I don't understand," she cried. "What—what about Byron?"

Big Ty was incensed at the mention of Byron's name. He grabbed Nadine by the shoulders, lifting her out the chair, and shook her.

"What the hell is wrong with you? Do you not understand what that nigga did to your little girl? What he did to your own flesh and blood? Are you that blind? Are you that strung out and desperate?" He released his grip on her.

Nadine fell back down to the chair, crying.

"I swear to God, if I didn't give my word to Nathan, and to my mother, I'd..." he stepped back.

Nadine knew what he wanted to do right then.

"No, no," she whispered. "He didn't do anything," she cried. "He swore to me. He swore he never touched..." *She* didn't even believe the words she was saying.

After all that has gone down between her and Byron, here she was defending him, knowing that he was a liar. Deep in her heart, she knew he did to Macon what she said. She just couldn't bring herself to face it.

"*He didn't do anything?!*" Big Ty yelled. He picked up one of the cups and threw it across the room.

Spencer rushed into the room, and stood by the door.

"Woman, what in the hell is wrong with you? That nigga violated your daughter! He raped her! He beat her! He's robbed you blind! And has had the audacity to brag about what he's done! And proud of the fact that it was his seed that got your daughter pregnant! And you can sit there, like some silly woman and say he didn't do anything?" Big Ty screamed out in frustration.

It sickened him to his stomach what Byron had done to Macon. Ordinarily, other people's business was their own, as long as it didn't affect him. But he gave his word. More than that, he remembered what happened to his sister, Cicely, when she was thirteen. He was too young to do anything about it then. But that didn't stop him from making it right when he got in the position to do so.

Yes, he did some things in his life that he is not proud of; things for which his mother begs him to find a different way of life before it's too late. However it happened, this life chose him. He did not choose it, and it began with the violent rape and murder of his sister. He was only nine. But he knew that no man had a right to force himself on a woman, and especially not a young girl. Big Ty blamed his father for abandoning them and for the hood that took his sister's life.

Everyone knew who did it. But they were too scared to say anything for fear of retaliation. He knew at nine what he had to do; he had to protect his family and avenge his sister's death by any means necessary. When he was seventeen, he did just that, making a name on the street for himself. The man never saw it coming—not from his right hand protégé. From that day on, no one was ever going take away someone he loved again. And no one was going to dictate how his life was going to be, except for him. It's been thirty years, and he has never looked backed once. It was too late to go back and start over. He made his way in this world and he had to follow it through—even if it meant his death. You live by the sword, you die by the sword. That's the way it was on the streets of South Philly, and any ghetto in America.

This was not glitz and glamor like they posed it in the black-exploitation films that readily glamorized ghetto life. This was reality—every day, every night, with no easy escape route. Nothing was ever solved in two hours or in a three part series. There were new enemies' every day, jockeying to bump you off; ready to step in like they could do the job better. Young punks coming up thinking they ran the show; more determined and malicious than the ones before them, and with no respect for those who schooled them.

In Big Ty's eyes, this was Byron—whom he never trusted from the beginning; but gave him a shot to prove himself. When he found out whom Nathan was that changed everything. It gave him the opportunity to find out even more about Byron. And what he found out made his guts cringe. But what really enraged him about Byron, were the punks' attitude and the fact that he talked too much. Although this made his job much easier to find out all he needed to know; he was never happier to be taking out this trash. His concern, however, was Nadine. She was unstable and unpredictable. He had to make her wake up. He knew she was no stupid woman; but for some unseen reason, she purposely was turning a blind eye to Byron and what he did. It was to him, as though she were punishing herself. He'd made a promise to Nathan and his mother. And he would abide by it. Yet, if she chose not to follow what he said, he was not responsible for what may happen to her in the crossfire.

Nadine got up, pacing the room. She was holding herself, mumbling incomprehensible. She walked to and fro, shaking her head.

Big Ty walked to her, grabbed her by her arms.

"Are you ready to die, Nadine?" he asked her.

Nadine's head was spinning. She hadn't had a hit since being locked up; but she craved one right then. What she wouldn't give for one hit to numb what she was feeling.

As if reading her thoughts, "You can't afford to gets high now, Nadine. Do you understand me? If I catch you high…so help me, you won't have to worry about your PO—you'll have to deal with me," he threatened her.

She tried to free herself from his grip, and his gaze.

He wouldn't let her go. He tightened his grip on her arms.

"I asked are you ready to die, Nadine?" He said, more sternly.

Nadine shook her head. "No," she cried.

Big Ty released her.

Nadine stumbled over to the chair. Sobbing heavily, she tried to catch her breath. Her insides were shaking, and her head began to throb.

Big Ty walked over to Spencer, quietly speaking something to him.

Spencer nodded and left the room.

Big Ty walked towards Nadine, and stood in front of her.

Nadine looked up, and asked: "What do you want from me? What am I supposed to do now? I...I don't understands," she muttered.

"Do exactly what I tell you and everything will work out fine. But if you don't do as I say, you're on your own and I won't be responsible for whatever happens to you. I'm giving you the chance that Nathan wanted you to have. I'm trying to keep my word." Big Ty knelt down in front of Nadine. He placed a hand on her knee. He could feel her shaking.

Nadine wrung her hands, rocking back and forth. She wasn't sure she could do what he wanted.

"This is your last time Nadine. This is your last shot at a decent life, and to get yourself together. I don't give this to everyone. I could have easily walked away from all this, and you wouldn't have been any wiser of my promise to Nathan. But I couldn't do that; especially after what I learned about your daughter."

Spencer walked into the room holding a suitcase.

Big Ty stood up and nodded.

Spencer placed the suitcase next to the door and left.

Big Ty turned back to Nadine. "Here's what you're going to do. You're not going home. Not yet."

Nadine looked puzzled. "Where—where am I going?" She looked at the suitcase then back to Big Ty. "I can't go out of town; not yet."

"I know that. I made arrangements for you. You need to be clean...and you need to be somewhere safe." He stared at her intently.

"I can't just leave...I have to meet with my parole officer. I don't want to go back to jail. Not for three months or one more day," she cried.

"It's been arranged already with your PO. When you do this month, you will be free."

"I don't understand."

"My lawyer worked everything out for you; that's what he gets paid to do. You just do the month, follow the rules or the deal's off, and you go back to jail. And my promise to Nathan is over."

He looked intensely into Nadine's eyes. He

wanted her to know the severity of the situation that she was in; the fact that he didn't do this every day, or *any* day for that matter. He found himself in a peculiar position: doing something for someone else without any benefit for him. Sure, he would be getting rid of some trash that has been gnawing at him for some time now. However, he never did anything for anyone without there being something in it for him—with the exception of his mother. Even then, doing things for his mother, he was still looking to benefit. To benefit from her love and the satisfaction that she would never want for another thing in this life. Not if he could help it.

Nadine sat, her head spinning from the reality of what was really about to happen. It was no doubt in her mind that she would never see Byron again...at least not alive. *And why she should care?* She thought to herself. She knew Byron didn't love her. She knew that he had raped her daughter and had stolen from her; using her, her house and her checkbook for his own purposes. He'd been stringing her along, keeping her supplied and doped up. Half the time she didn't know what day it was, or who was in her house. She heard people whispering. She'd had heard some rumors. Yet, whenever she confronted him about it, he'd get angry and ask her: *Why she listening to them liars out in the street? Why she want to listen to people that were just plain jealous?* Yeah, he was real good at slinging his garbage, and she was real good at receiving it.

When—she thought to herself—*when did she let her life get so bad? How did it get so bad?* She did know that she had a problem with being alone. She hated it. Moreover, it was being alone with herself and her thoughts that she hated more. Truthfully, it scared her.

Big Ty walked over to a desk, opened the top draw and pulled out three manila envelopes, then sat down opposite Nadine.

Nadine watched him. He moved assuredly and with boldness. He was confident in everything he did, with no apologies. She understood then, that was the reason he was who he was, and could do what he did, and why so many people feared him, and aspired to be like him. She only knew one other man that exuded the same strength, confidence, and boldness: Nathan. Even when he fell ill, he still had this strength about him, and confidence. That was one of the things that drew her to him, and later repelled her. He expected too much from her, and she told him just as much. They had had several arguments about it. He wanted her to do more, be more. She accused him of trying to change her, and trying to mold her into one of those women from his office. He always denied it. He told her that he wanted it for her, so that she would feel fulfilled in whom she was as a person. He didn't just want her to be his wife or Macon's mother; he wanted her to have and fulfill her own dreams and desires.

Nathan always told her that she was bright, that she was smart and that he could always use her at the office. Nadine was not dumb. She was very good with numbers. She had learned a lot from Nathan over the years. She'd had her own bank account to prove it; one that Nathan didn't know about— nor did Byron. Yes, she'd readily admit that there were a lot of dumb things about her. She'd even admit to being foolish. But she would never call herself stupid. She was far smarter than anyone ever gave her credit for. She had security in case things did not work out her way. She had learned much more from Nathan, than anyone would have guessed. However, after hearing Big Ty, she knew that Nathan knew more than she'd thought. He always did.

In the beginning of their marriage, it was Nathan who first encouraged her to go to school. He said he would pay for it. He noted how she had a head for numbers and figures that seem to come naturally. She thought about it, and was going to. Then the bottom fell out from under her when the secrets, the awful secrets that her family had been keeping from her were revealed. How she wished over the years that she had never gone that day. The only reason she went was to rub her happiness in her parents face. The joke turned out to be on her. And the only one having anything rubbed in their face was Nadine.

As much as she did not want to leave; as much as she ached to get high; as much as she wanted to tell Big Ty, *to hell with him and his favor;* Nadine was smart enough to know, that Big Ty's way was the only way—the only chance she had to get her life back and begin to live again. Besides, she knew full well that if she *didn't* go along with his plan, there was no way she would live to see tomorrow. He'd probably have Spencer drive her somewhere; and the next thing you know, her death would be ruled an overdose. And no one would bother to question it. Not with her recent track record.

"So," Big Ty said, "have you had enough time to get your mind together?"

"Yes," Nadine nodded her voice shaky. "Yes," she repeated.

"I knew you were smart; Proving Nathan right once again. So," he lifted up the envelopes in his hands, "there are a couple of things we need to discuss before you leave. I believe it will benefit us both..."

CHAPTER 22

OKAY NADINE, I don't know what you're really doing here; but I don't believe a word that's coming out your mouth. Although..." Emma stood in front of the chair where Nadine was seated. She leaned forward, placing both hands on either arm rests, staring into Nadine's face. "...I must say, you *do* looks different." Emma stood up straight, backing away. "But I ain't buying it; especially when you're the one sellin' it."

"I ain't asks you to believe me, Emma. It's the truth. I got proof." Nadine rummaged through her bag, pulling out an envelope. She held out the envelope for Emma.

Emma wouldn't take it.

"Here," Nadine said. "It's a letter from the clinic I was at. It tells you I'm clean, and have been for a while now." She insisted Emma look at it.

Emma was skeptical. She took the envelope, taking out the letter. She read it briefly.

"How I knows this is legit? You could have faked this."

"Damn Emma! I swears! Call 'em! They'll tell you."

"May I see it, Ms. Emma?" Camille asked, walking towards Emma.

Emma gave Camille the letter.

"I'll find out for you— I'm familiar with some of the clinics in Pennsylvania."

Nadine looked at Camille. "And who the hell are you?" She snatched the letter from Camille's hands. "I don't know you. And this ain't none of your business!"

"Like hell it ain't!" Emma snatched the letter back, and gave it to Camille. "Go ahead and do that for me, baby."

Camille took the letter. "I'll be right back," she said, looking at the letterhead. "This place sounds familiar." She walked out the living room.

"Wait...waits one goddamn minute!" Nadine yelled. "Who is that heifer? And why'd you give her my letter?"

"Watch your mouth Nadine. Don't you disrespect Camille. Especially after all she's done for Macon!" Junior yelled.

"*Excuse me*. Must be your girl, huh? And what she got to do with my child?"

"A whole lot more than you!" Junior said. He shook his head. "Mama, pop...I'll be in the kitchen with Camille." Junior was exasperated by Nadine.

"Go ahead son. You don't needs to be in here no way. Let me and your Mama handles this," said Albert.

Junior left, shaking his head.

Albert waited for Junior to leave before saying something to Nadine.

"Nadine," Albert began, "you have caused nothin' but hell for that little girl in there," he said, pointing toward a room. "You have disturbed my home, my wife, my family. I will not allow you to come here and jes do and say whatever the hells you want! Do you understand me?"

Nadine did not answer at first. She didn't know what to say.

Albert asked her again. "Do you understand me, I said?"

Nadine nodded her head. "Yes. I understand. But," she started to explain, "I didn't come here to start trouble. I just came to see my daughter and my grand baby. I'm not the same person, Albert." She turned to Emma.

"Emma, I know we don't get along. Never had, and probably never will. But I'm telling you, I have been clean for over six months now. And all I wants to do is see Macon and the baby," Nadine pleaded.

Emma shook her head. She heard what Nadine was saying. But she didn't believe for a moment that that was all Nadine came for. There was more. She felt it in her guts. She looked Nadine straight in her eyes.

"Nadine, did you ever stop to think that maybe *Macon* did not want to see you?"

The thought never occurred to Nadine. Macon has always forgiven her. Surely she would want to see her?

"I know my child, Emma. Of course she wants to see me."

"Then how come she ran in the room as soon

as you came...and has not been back out since?"

Nadine had no response.

"Nadine, you have caused more trouble and damage than a fox in a hen-house. How do you expect that Chile jes to come and embrace you like this last year ain't happen? You's a fool if you believe that for one solitary minute."

"But she wrote me. She's been writing me and telling me about Nathaniel, and telling me about school..." Nadine said.

"That doesn't mean she ready to see you, or talk to you. Look, I don't want to hurt your feeling's Nadine."

"Oh yeah, like I'm gonna believe that for a minute," Nadine said, sarcastically.

"Not intentionally," Emma mused, "anyway. But if Camille hadn't told Macon to do jes that— write to you—she probably wouldn't have."

Nadine was incensed. "Who in the hell is this Camille? Can you tell me that?"

"Camille's been helping *your* daughter, to get through this mess that you caused," Albert interjected, "...cleanin' up after you."

"She's Macon's counselor," Emma stated.

Nadine sat back, feeling small and overwhelmed. She didn't mean to hurt Macon. And despite what anyone may have thought or believed; she did love her daughter. The best way she could.

"If it wasn't for Camille..." Emma felt a lump in her throat, "...I don't know what I would have done. So I better not hear another word from you in the form of disrespect concernin' her. Do you understand me?"

Nadine put her hands up, as if in surrender.

"I really don't know much about what's been goin' on with you, other than what you say. I ain't my wife—I'm no mama. But as a man; as a father, I can promise you this, I will protect that little girl as if she were mine; because she is." Albert turned to Emma. "Mama, I'm gonna go check on everyone. You got this?"

Albert wanted to be certain that Emma was calm enough before he left the room.

"Go 'head, baby. I'm fine. I won't do anything...I promise," Emma assured Albert.

Albert nodded his head as he left. He did not have to worry; Camille was walking in as he was leaving. He felt a little more comfortable.

"Well," Camille broke the silence in the room. "I called and verified that Nadine was indeed a patient at this clinic..."

"See. I told you. I've been totally clean for more than six months." She looked at Emma smugly.

"However," Camille interjected, rolling her eyes at Nadine, "she was an inpatient for *one month* only," she told Emma.

Emma looked at Nadine. She knew she wasn't telling the truth about everything.

"So—one month, huh? *Nadine!*" Emma glared at Nadine. "I want the truth, goddamn it! Right now or you get the hell out my house."

Nadine stood up. "Damn, Emma! What else you want...my blood? An agenda for every day of the last six months? When I slept, ate, pissed! Well I told you everything!"

"Actually," Camille began, "I did find out that —"

Nadine pushed passed Camille, cutting her off and almost knocking her over.

"I'm not leaving 'til I see those kids." Nadine tried to get through Emma.

"Move out my way, Emma!" Nadine yelled.

"Now I know you done lost your damn mind!" Emma pushed Nadine backwards.

Nadine fell on her behind.

Scrambling to get up, Nadine said, "I swear, I'm going to whip your ass, Emma!"

"C'mon! I have been waitin' a long time for this!" Emma charged at Nadine.

Camille tried to separate Emma and Nadine.

"Ms. Emma. Ms. Emma!" Camille couldn't get them apart.

"Junior! Mr. Albert!" Camille yelled.

Emma had her hands around Nadine's neck. "I told you...I wasn't gonna put up with your mess anymore!" She slapped Nadine hard across the face.

Nadine's arms were flailing. She was grabbing at Emma, trying to get a hold of Emma's hair.

"*I swear...I'm gonna kill you! I'm gonna make sure you right next to Nathan!*" Nadine was grunting. Emma was straddling her, and had Nadine's legs pinned.

"Yeah? Well you'll be there before I do. Why don't you say hello for me!" Emma punched Nadine square in the face.

Nadine's head bucked back and hit the floor with a loud thud.

Nadine put her hand to the back of her head and shook it.

Nadine made one last effort to grab at Emma's hair.

Junior, Albert, and Calvin came running in.

"Mama!" Junior and Calvin yelled.

"Emma Jean!" Albert yelled. He ran over and tried to pull his wife off of Nadine. "Mama. Mama. Come on. You told me you weren't gonna do anything!" Albert said.

Emma wouldn't get off of Nadine. "I lied!" Emma yelled, continuing to beat on Nadine. "I'm gonna give her as good as she gave Macon!"

Junior and Calvin tried to help their father. It was kind of amusing seeing their mother whip Nadine's behind. They hadn't seen their mother like that since they were teens, and their mother whooped Mrs. Anita Combs, at Mt. Bethel Baptist church.

Mrs. Combs had said something derogatory about their mother during one of them chicken dinner sales they always had. When Calvin heard it, he told Mrs. Combs off; just like his mother would have. Mrs. Combs smacked Calvin across the face, leaving her fat hand print across his light skin. When they came home, they tried to avoid their mother. Someone had already called Emma and told her what had happened. She demanded that they come down stairs and tell her what happened. Lord! When Emma saw Calvin's face…that was it! Needless to say, they're still not welcomed at Mt. Bethel Baptist Church! Not after what Emma did to Mrs. Combs; especially since she was the first lady!

"C'mon Mama." Albert pulled Emma by the waist.

Junior and Calvin grabbed Nadine.

Nadine was screaming. "No! No! I ain't finish with her! I'm gonna kill you, Emma!" Nadine struggled to get out of Junior and Calvin's grasp.

"Let her go! Let her go!" Emma shouted. "*Kill me? Kill me?* Let the heifer go so I can finish whipping her nasty tail!" Emma jerked herself from Albert's grip.

Nadine wrenched herself from both Junior and Calvin. She rushed toward Emma, spitting in her face just as she reached her.

Emma stood still, shocked and disgusted. "You foul, disgusting heifer!"

Before anyone could stop it, Emma drew back her arm, balled her hand into a fist, and threw a punch at Nadine's face. In what seemed like slow motion, Emma's right fist connected with the left side of Nadine's face. Nadine gasped and went down. Emma knocked Nadine out cold.

Nadine hit the floor with such a thump, causing the lamp to fall off the table.

Albert, Junior and Calvin winced. They knew there was no stopping Emma once Nadine spat in her face. That was the vilest, most disgusting thing that anyone could do; to anyone.

There was nothing to do, but let things play themselves out. Once Albert saw Emma draw her arm back, he knew that Nadine was a sure goner. All of Emma's strength was behind that punch. All the rage, anger, hostility, pain, guilt, animosity, and hurt gave that punch its impact.

Emma stood shaking.

Camille gave Emma a hand towel to wash her face.

Emma took the cloth without looking at Camille. She stared at Nadine sprawled out on the floor. Her body felt like jelly; her breathing became heavy. Emma began to feel as though she was suffocating. She couldn't catch her breath.

Albert grabbed Emma by the arm, and walked her to the sofa.

"Mama...Mama here, sits down. Calm down baby; it's all right. It's all right," Albert assured his wife. "Get your Mama some water," he said, to Calvin.

Calvin ran to the kitchen to get the water.

Junior ran and got Shelby.

Emma sat on the couch rocking, trying to catch her breath, and crying.

"Okay Mama, breathe. Take your time and breathe."

"I...I'm sorry, Al-B. I'm...sorry," she cried.

"Shush baby. Shush. You ain't got anything to be sorry about. Absolutely nothin'." Albert sat down next to his wife and held her.

"She...she jes...made me...so...damn...angry..." Emma said her breathing labored.

"I know. I know," Albert assured her. "Jes be still now. Catch your breath, Mama."

"Here Pop." Calvin gave his father the glass of water.

"Take a sip Mama." He held the glass for Emma.

"Al—" Emma tried to speak.

"Shush, don't talk. Take a sip."

Emma took a small sip, her hands shaking.

Shelby and Richard ran into the living room.

"Mama!" Shelby ran to her mother. She looked around the room and saw Nadine lying on the floor. "What in the hell happened?" She knelt down in front of her mother.

Although Emma was a dark woman, her face was red. She was sweating and breathing in short gulps.

"Richard, come check Mama out. It's her asthma." Shelby moved as her husband came over to Emma's side.

"Mama, do you feel hot?" He touched Emma's face and neck.

Emma nodded.

"Where's your pump?" He asked.

"In...my...bureau," Emma managed to say.

Shelby ran to get her mother's pump.

Richard turned to Albert. "Has she had a spell recently?" he asked.

"Not since September. She...she's been doin good," Albert answered.

"Okay, that's good." Richard turned back to Emma. "Mama, just relax. You've had too much excitement today. Were you smoking today?"

Emma nodded.

"Alright," he said.

"Here," Shelby gave Emma her pump.

Emma couldn't grip the pump; her hands were shaking too much.

"Here," Richard said, "I'll hold it. You breathe in on three. One, two, and three..." Richard held the pump in Emma's mouth and pumped it on three as she breathed in. He waited a few seconds and did it a second time. "One, two, three..."

Emma started to feel her chest open up. The tightness had begun to go away.

"Just relax," Richard told her. "Give it a couple of minutes. Alright?" He held Emma's hand and patted it.

Emma nodded.

"Just give her a couple of minutes," Richard said moving out the way so Albert could sit down. "She'll be okay, as long as she stays calm." He looked at Emma and said: "Mama, I wish you'd leave them cigarettes alone."

Emma gave him a look, as if to say, not again.

Richard held up his hands. "I know. I know. Not now. But I'm just concerned. I guess it's just the doctor in me; Patient first...family second."

Shelby took her husband's hand. "Thank you, baby," she said kissing him.

"It's alright, baby. It's my job." He smiled and gave his wife a hug.

Shelby looked at her mother. "I keep telling her she needs to leave them things alone."

Emma rolled her eyes, too weak to speak yet.

"What just happened here doesn't have anything to do with Mama's smoking," Junior exclaimed. "She was just fine. It has everything to do with that heifer over there on the floor," he pointed to Nadine.

"Somebody checks on her," Albert said.

"For what?" Calvin asked. "Let her stay knocked the hell out for a while."

"My sentiments exactly," Shelby agreed.

"No..." Emma spoke softly. "Do...as...your...father...said."

"I'll do it," Camille volunteered.

"Thank you, sweet," Albert said.

Camille bent down next to Nadine, tapped her on the face. "Nadine. Nadine." She turned around. "Nice right hook, Ms. Emma. She's out cold. She probably hit her head on the floor when she fell. She'll be okay. She'll have one hell of headache, though." Camille chuckled.

"I'll check her out—" Richard started to say.

"The hell you will!" Shelby interjected.

"But Shelby..."

"No! I mean it! Let that nasty witch stay there for a while. She was breathing, right?" she asked, Camille.

"Yes."

"Then she's fine. She lucky it wasn't me. She'd damn sure be on her way to the hospital," Shelby fumed.

Junior came back in the room carrying a pitcher of water. He walked over to Nadine.

"Junior, no!" Camille said, stunned.

Junior dumped the pitcher of water in Nadine's face.

"No—it's time for this disrespectful heifer to get the hell up! Get up Nadine!" he yelled.

Nadine jumped, disoriented, choking and gasping for air.

"What—what—what," gasped Nadine.

"It's time to get the hell up!" Junior snapped.

Nadine sat up shaking her head. "What the hell!" She looked around dazed. She rubbed the back of her head, and then touched her right eye. "Ouch," she winced. Then remembering that Emma punched her, she turned to Emma. "You punched me!" She yelled. Nadine struggled to get off the floor.

Camille tried to help her up.

"Get the hell off of me!"

"I was only trying to help you," Camille said,

backing away.

"I don't need your damn help," Nadine scowled, standing up. She stumbled to the chair. "I swear—"

"You swear, what!" Junior interrupted her. "What you think you going to do?"

"She ain't going to do a damn thing," Shelby interjected, "but get the hell out Mama and Pop's, house."

"You all a bunch of damn hypocrites! You all act so innocent, but you ain't nothing but a bunch of liars! You are trying to keep my child away from me. What you want me to do, walk on water?" Nadine stood up, brushing her hands through her wet hair.

"Enough of this!" Calvin yelled. "It's time for you to go," he said, taking Nadine by the arm, pulling her towards the door. "You had your chance, and when you spit in my mother's face..." he pulled her arm tighter.

Nadine struggled. "No! No! You can't do this to me! I'm gonna call the cops, Emma! You hear me! I have rights. I'm still her mother. You can't keep me away forever," she hollered. Nadine fought to no avail to get out of Calvin's grip.

"Good ridden!" Shelby yelled.

Emma had whispered something into Albert's ear.

Albert stood up. "Wait...waits a minute, Calvin. Let her loose."

"What? Let her *loose*; after what she did to Mama? No Pop, that's not happening. I'm taking out this trash." Calvin continued to pull Nadine towards the door.

"Son I know that, but jes listen; this is your Mama's call," he said nodding toward Emma. "Jes let her loose as I said." He moved toward Calvin.

"*Pop!* You got to be joking?" Junior asked.

"Mama, c'mon. Let Calvin toss her ass out!" Shelby cried.

"Watch your mouth Shelby," Albert warned. "I think we had enough."

"Sorry, Pop. I just don't understand," she said, turning to her mother.

Emma knew this seemed like an about face to her family. But she had her reasons. She regretted she allowed Nadine to push her that far. That was no way for her to react.

"I..." Emma began slowly, "...I think...we need...to take...a step back." Emma looked at Nadine.

Nadine yanked her arm from Calvin's loosened grip.

"It's about time you came to your damn senses, Emma," Nadine stated.

"Don't push it, Nadine." Albert warned. "I ain't but two steps away from knockin' you out my damn self. I ain't gonna tell you no more; watch yourself."

Nadine nodded. "Fine, Albert. I just want to see my child and my grand baby."

"That's all well and good; but you had no

right comin' into my home and causin' hell," Albert said.

Nadine started to say something.

Albert held up his hand. "Save it Nadine; because your excuses aren't worth the spit in your mouth." He turned to Emma. "Mama, go ahead and finish."

Nadine shrank back. She knew she was on even thinner ice than when she came.

Emma stood up slowly.

"Mama, you should stay seated," Richard said.

Emma waved her hand. "Thank you baby, but I am jes fine. A little winded, but jes fine," she assured her son-in-law. She walked toward Nadine.

Nadine took a step back.

"Nadine," Emma said, slowly. "I ain't fool enough to believe that you don't have more goin' on than jes wanting to see Macon. Now for some reason, you didn't want Camille to finish what she was gonna say." She raised her eyebrows up.

Nadine looked away.

"Thought I forgot, huh? Well I haven't. In fact, I know you started that fight on purpose, jes to stop Camille from saying what she was gonna say. And before we go any further here, I want to know what you've been so desperate to hide. Then, and only then, will I consider lettin' you see Macon and that baby...and that's only if *she* wants to see you." Emma turned to Camille, ignoring Nadine and whatever excuse she was about to give. "Camille baby, what exactly was it that you found out?"

In the entire ruckus, Camille nearly forgot
what she'd learned. If Emma had not mentioned it,
she'd probably not have remembered. Which was
Nadine's purpose: to distract her from telling the
truth.

"Yes, thanks for reminding me. Nadine has
been clean for more than seven months. She didn't
lie about that. However, she failed to mention that
she was in jail for six months," Camille stated.

Everyone turned to Nadine shaking their
head.

"Jail?" Emma said. "Well I'll be damned."

"What did she do?" Shelby asked.

"That ain't none of your damn business!"
Nadine yelled.

"The hell it ain't," Junior said. "That's why I
couldn't find you when I drove up there. I never
thought about jail!"

"Why not? That wouldn't have been such a
stretch of the imagination," Calvin retorted.

"Listen," Nadine said, "I didn't do nothing. It
was all a goddamn mistake."

"Six months for what, Nadine?"

"It couldn't be that bad." Albert gave her the
benefit of the doubt. "They only gave her six
months."

"And three months' probation," Camille
stated. "That was lifted when she did the thirty days
at the clinic."

"Do you know what she got arrested for?"

Junior asked, Camille.

Camille shook her head. "No, just that she did six months. But it won't take but a few phone calls to find out. Junior, you could find out easier than I could."

"You're right. I wasn't thinking."

"Wait a goddamn minute. You all act like I'm not even here. I did my time. It's over. And that's all you need to know. I don't have to answer to no one. No one at all!"

Camille lifted her hand. "Umm..."

"What is it baby?" Emma asked.

"There was one more thing I noticed about the letter." She picked up the envelope off the coffee table. "Ms. Emma, I don't think you paid attention to it. And Nadine probably didn't pay much attention to it either."

Nadine was puzzled. She had no idea what Camille was referring to.

"What'd you find, Camille?" Junior asked.

Camille handed the letter to Emma.

"Look at the name," she said.

Emma took the letter and looked at it closely. She hadn't noticed it the first time. But there was something different. She looked up at Nadine, disgust on her face. "You sneaky little heifer..." she said, in nearly a whisper.

"What is it Mama?" Albert asked.

"Mama?"

"When did you do it, Nadine?"

"What'd she do, Mama?" Junior asked.

"What you talking about now, Emma," Nadine said, angrily.

Emma moved closer to Nadine.

Nadine backed up.

"When did you do it?" Emma asked again.

"I don't know what the hell you're talking about!" Nadine wasn't sure what Emma was getting at.

Emma shook her head. *"Du-vall..."* Emma said, slowly.

Nadine's eyes got big as saucers. She forgot all about her marriage.

She couldn't speak. The words were stuck in her throat.

Oh Hell!

"Duvall? Who's Duvall?" Albert asked, looking from Emma to Camille to Nadine.

"I can't believe it." Emma shook her head, putting her hands on her hips, she turned around and looked at her family, standing there waiting to know who or what, Duvall was. "She married that *bastard!* She...actually...married him."

"What?! No. No..." Albert said, turning to Nadine.

"Oh my God!" Shelby cried. "I can't believe you!" She shook her head. "No, she got to get the hell out of here...now!"

"You married him?" Calvin asked. "Why am I not surprised!" He guffawed. "You are nothing but a whore!"

Junior couldn't say a word. He was shocked. He couldn't fathom the reason why Nadine would marry Byron. Was she really that desperate and strung out? He felt a pain in his chest when he thought about what Macon had endured by the hands of that man. He was no killer; but the murderous thoughts that now ran through his mind were not only for Byron, but for Nadine, as well. And given the opportunity, he doubted he would hesitate.

"You don't understand," Nadine began defending herself. "You don't know...none of you know a damn thing about me, or why I did what I did!"

"What in the hell is there to understand, Nadine?" Shelby asked. "You married the man that violated your daughter!" Shelby was sickened to her stomach. She did not think that Nadine could sink much lower.

"He raped your daughter!" Calvin shouted. *"And you married him*? How low can a negro get?" he said, through clenched teeth.

"It doesn't matter now!" Nadine turned looking at each one.

"Nadine, how can it not matter?" Albert asked, with tears in his eyes.

"Because...because I ain't with him no more. Yes, I made a mistake. But—"

"Cut the crap, Nadine!" Emma cut her off. "I asked you to tell me everything. I gave you the opportunity to come clean. I can't let you anywhere near Macon, or that baby!" Emma walked away shaking her head.

"No! No! You can't do this Emma. I told you things are different now. I'm clean; I ain't with Byron any more. And...and...and—" Nadine was flustered. How could she possibly explain what she didn't understand herself?

"It's time for you to leave," Albert said. "I can't let you around that Chile. I was willin' to give you a chance. But once she learns this...uh-uh. I ain't gonna let her get hurt by you again. No. You got to leave my home." Albert shook his head and walked towards the door. "Please leave now, Nadine." He opened the door.

Everyone stood around looking at Nadine with disgust and contempt.

"I can't...I can't leave without at least talking to her," Nadine cried.

"I don't think that would be wise," said Camille. "Macon is still in a very fragile state. And I know she won't be able to handle this."

"That's all I needs to know," Emma replied. "Leave now, Nadine." Emma stood by the door.

"I can't! You don't understand. Please!" Nadine pleaded.

"That's enough, Nadine," Junior said grabbing Nadine by the arm. "You have to go. Just do as Mama said. Please." He pulled Nadine towards the open door.

Nadine fought back.

"Let...go...of...me! Let go, goddamn it!"

Nadine kicked and screamed. "You all don't understand! You don't understand!"

Junior grabbed Nadine from behind and lifted her off the floor. Nadine's arms were flailing and her head was bucking forth. She was cussing and screaming and crying.

"Please!" she pleaded. "I have to see my baby! I have to set things right. I'm not...leaving...until...I do!" Nadine continued to struggle.

Calvin gave his brother a hand. He tried grabbing her feet and Nadine kicked him in the mouth.

"Damn it!" Calvin yelled, grabbing his mouth.

"Wait! Wait!" Albert hollered. "This is too much confusion goin' on. Too much fightin' and carryin' on! Enough already. That's it." Albert turned to Emma. "Mama, I'm gonna handle the rest of this. We gonna settles this once and for all."

Emma nodded. She recognized that look in her husband's eyes. Albert was not a loud and forceful man. And it took a lot to make his temper rise. But when he decided enough was enough, and he was going to handle things, the best thing to do was to let him.

"Whatever you want Al-B," Emma conceded.

"Let her go, Junior."

"But Pop—"

Albert held up his hand, cutting Junior off. "I said let her go. I don't want any arguments."

Junior released his hold on Nadine, causing her to drop to the floor. He backed away shaking his head, believing his father was making a mistake.

"Nadine," Albert began, "gets up and goes sit on the porch."

"But I—"

"No buts," said Albert. "You have caused enough mess up in my home this evening. You about a hair away from havin' me throw you out my damns self. So I suggest you do as I tell you, before I changes my mind."

Albert's look was intense. Nadine did not say another word. She limped to the porch.

"Pop, I don't understand," Calvin said. "What could you possibly think is going to help that has not been tried already?"

Albert looked at his son and nodded his head in understanding. He looked around at each of his family members, until his eyes rested upon Camille.

"Camille sweet," he said.

"Yes, Mr. Albert?"

"I want you to go back there with Macon, and check on how she doin'. I'll be back there shortly."

Camille nodded, and did as she was asked.

Albert turned back to his family. "I know what you all want to do, and I agree with you. However, there is one thing that we did not do that we should have, and I believe is the right thing." He turned and looked at Emma. "I done seen much in my day to know that this here mess is jes goin' to get worse. She gonna keeps comin' back, and comin' back until she gets what she wants. And ain't any of us goin' anywhere. So, we gonna handle this the way it should have gone from the start. We gonna finish this here mess once and for all!"

Emma understood what Albert intended to do. She herself had suggested it earlier. She knew in her heart he was right; because it was the right thing to do. Yet her gut was telling her something different. Emma's gut was telling her to get rid of Nadine, *now*!

"Now," Albert said, looking around the room, "I'm gonna go in here and see how Macon is doing. Then I'm gonna asks her what *she* wants to do. And if she decides she wants to see Nadine...fine. If she doesn't, then she can tell Nadine herself." Albert walked to the open door, and stuck his head out. "Nadine?"

Nadine looked up.

"You stay right there. Don't you moves a muscle. Because if you do, I swears, I'll take you all the way backs to Philly myself, and you won't be sittin' in my car either," he threatened. "You hears me?"

"Yes...yes," Nadine stammered.

"I'll be right back," Albert said.

"Mama," Shelby said, "you can't believe this is right? I mean..."

Emma held up her hand, shaking her head. "Shelby, I know. But your father is right; this is Macon's choice. I should have done it earlier when I said I was."

"C'mon, Mama. How is this gonna help Macon? Do you really think that Macon *wants* to see

Nadine?" Junior asked.

"Mama, you weren't in here when Macon saw Nadine walk through that door. All the color just left her face. She ran out of here, as if for dear life," said Calvin.

"I know. I know. I understands that. But your father is right. Even though I has a bad feelin' churning in my guts, I can only assume it will only get worse with time if we don't handles it now. I wants to protect Macon jes like you all, but I can't makes her choices for her. She needs to make up her own mind, and we will let her do that...okay?" she asked her family, looking at each one.

"I don't know, Mama. You know how she was when she got here last year," Shelby stated. "This might be a setback for her; especially if she learns about Nadine marrying that man."

Emma nodded in agreement. She understood Shelby's concerns very well; she felt the same.

"I don't know, Mama," Junior said, interrupting Emma's thoughts. "But I just can't shake this feeling that something worse is going to happen."

"So do I," Calvin agreed. "I really believe we should have called the police and just had them take care of her."

"I can still hear you out here, you know?" said Nadine, sarcastically.

"Who the hell cares?" Shelby yelled.

Emma shook her head at Shelby. "Ignore her...just ignore her."

JR

"You can ignore me all you want, Emma. But I still have rights. Even Albert has sense enough to see that," Nadine chimed in.

"Yeah? Well you keep runnin' your goddamn mouth, and we'll see who's got enough sense. Don't push it Nadine!" Emma warned.

Nadine didn't say anything else.

"You see, Mama? She's not going to make this easy. And despite what you and Pop believe, I really think Nadine shouldn't stay one minute more." Calvin walked towards the porch.

Emma agreed wholeheartedly with Calvin. But they had already made a mess of things where Nadine was concerned. She allowed her temper to get the best of her. She should have spoken to Macon from the beginning, instead of acting like a fool and tussling with Nadine.

Emma shook her head, and sighed. *Lord, you have to really help me this time. I really have a bad feeling that we ain't seen the worst yet. Lord Jesus, help me,* Emma prayed.

"She'll be out shortly," Albert walked into the living room. "She's putting the baby down, and getting a glass of water. Calvin," he looked at his son, "Anna-Leigh wants to see you."

Calvin left to see what his wife wanted.

"What did you say to her, Albert?"

Albert rubbed his hand over his chin. "Well, I told her the truths, Mama. And I let her know that the decision was hers, but she definitely had to be the one to make it."

Albert noticed the concern on Emma's face. He held up his hand. "Now, I know what you thinkin'. I understands. But Mama, she's goin' on sixteen, and she gonna has to make some decisions. Nadine ain't goin' away; as much as we'd like her to. As long as Macon is with us, Nadine gonna show up and raise hell, no doubt. But if we let Macon handles this once and for all. Let her mother hears it from her mouth what *she* wants, then we can deal with it after that; but not before."

Emma agreed with him. It was Macon's choice, and she knew that if it was not handled now, Nadine would surely cause them nothing but hell until she got her way.

Emma kissed Albert on the cheek. "Thanks, baby."

Albert put his arm around his wife. "Don't worry, she'll be fine. We all will," he reassured her.

Emma was about to say something when Macon walked into the room. She let go of Albert and went to her.

Emma held out her arms. Macon walked into her Aunt's embrace, her arms at her side.

"You all right, suga?" Emma kissed Macon on the forehead.

"Yes, I'm okay." Macon pulled back, and looked Emma in the face. "Really, I'm okay. I have to do this. I'm not scared. After all; I got Cooper blood in me," she smiled.

"Oh, baby." Emma caressed Macon's face. There was something in Macon's eyes; something she had never seen before, a vacant, distant look. It gave Emma an uneasy feeling in the pit of her stomach. She hugged Macon tightly.

Nadine watched through the window. It was the first time in ten months, that she had seen her daughter. She looked different. More mature. She had to give Emma credit for that; although she would never admit to it openly. Macon was beautiful. She looked just like her at that age. At that moment, it dawned on Nadine that Macon was the exact age she was, when she had given birth to *her* son; the son that she never told anyone about; the son that she still longed for.

Nadine walked toward the door. She had to speak to her daughter. She had to see her for herself. She knew that Macon loved her. No matter what she did; Macon always forgave her. *She* was her mother, and no one could ever take her place.

Macon turned to the doorway. She could see her mother from the corner of her eye. Her stomach clenched. It was a bundle of nervous knots. From the moment her mother arrived, Macon was torn in her emotions. She hated her mother for what she allowed to happen to her. She thought she could even forgive her, until moments ago.

Any residual feelings of love she harbored for her mother were now gone. It died the moment she overheard that Nadine had married Byron. Something in her broke. She was listening by the door when Camille stated what she'd found out. Macon went back to the room before anyone saw her. All she felt now was hate. She hated Nadine and everything she represented. She hated her for abusing her, for letting Byron rape her, and for how she treated her father.

Nadine walked through the door hesitantly.

Everyone stood still. The silence was deafening. Each one waited to see what Macon would do.

Emma held onto Macon's hand, not wanting to let it go.

Albert looped his arm through Emma's, and gently pulled her back towards his side. He whispered in her ear: "C'mon Mama, she gonna be jes fine. She's a lot stronger than you think. Trust me. *Trust her.*"

Emma nodded. She trusted Macon. It was *Nadine* she did not trust. The uneasiness she'd been feeling, grew more intense. She didn't like it. Her gut was telling her that all that happened earlier was calm compared to the storm that was about to hit. She felt helpless to stop it. It was too late. She knew that whatever it was—was going to happen whether she liked it or not. And there was nothing she could do to stop the impending course of events. The cards were already dealt, and had to be played until the end. Emma was frightened to her core to know what that end was. She wished then she had been more of a praying woman than a fighting one. She knew that only God had the power to calm this raging storm.

Nadine walked towards Macon, stopping a few feet from her daughter.

Macon turned, facing her mother completely.

She didn't move.

Nadine started to speak, but the look in Macon's eyes caused her to hesitate. There was a coldness that she had never seen before. It was as though her daughter was looking right through her. Nadine recognized the look. It was the same look she'd seen in her own eyes for years: hate. Nadine's mouth went dry. All of a sudden, she did not know what to say.

"Ma-Macon," Nadine stammered. She started to walk to her, but stopped. "You-you look good, baby. I just wanted to see you, and...and to see the baby." She smiled weakly.

Macon stared at her mother, not saying a word. She hadn't moved, hadn't blinked. She just stood there, staring coolly at Nadine.

"I—I have so much to say to you." Nadine walked tentatively towards her daughter. "I know...I know I have really screwed up, and haven't been there for you. But...but things are different now. I swear. I—I didn't come to start no mess. I swear I just wanted to see you and the baby, and let you know that I'm getting my life together. Baby?" Nadine reached out to touch Macon's hand.

Macon drew back her hand fiercely, as if she were just burned. *"Don't touch me,"* Macon said, through clenched teeth. *"Don't you ever touch me again."*

Nadine held her hand back. She didn't know how to respond.

"How dare you," Macon seethed. "How dare you come here? What do you want from my life?"

Macon's eyes grew to slits. "I want you to leave. You've seen me, and now I want you to go!"

Nadine shook her head, tears welling up in her eyes. "Baby, you don't mean that. I'm your Mama. I came—"

"You are not my mama!" Macon yelled.

Emma started to walk over to Macon, but Albert held her back.

"Macon, I will always be your mama. I love you," Nadine cried.

"You love me? You love me?" Macon took a few steps toward Nadine, until she was a few feet from her mother's face. "You don't love me. You don't love anyone but yourself. And you are not my mother. Not anymore. You...never...was." Macon stared at Nadine hard.

Nadine looked into her daughter's eyes. This was not the same girl from ten months ago. Nadine's mind began to swim. *What did she do? How could she possibly get Macon to forgive her? She had to get Macon on her side.*

"Macon," Nadine's voice trembled. "You don't mean that, baby. You know I love you. I—I just made some mistakes..."

"Mistakes? Is that what you call beating on me—mistakes? Is that what you call, letting your *husband* rape me? *A mistake?"*

Nadine's eyes grew wide. *She knows.*

Emma turned quickly to Albert. "Oh God!"

Macon shook her head. "No, *you are* the

mistake! I hate you! Do you hear me, Nadine! I hate you, and I never want to lay eyes on you again!" Macon screamed. She could no longer hold back the tears that were now running down her cheeks.

Nadine tried to reach out to Macon again. "No baby. You don't mean that. You—you're just hurting right now. Please Macon..." Nadine pleaded.

"Don't touch me!" Macon yelled, pulling her hands back, dropping the knife that she had hidden in her sweater sleeve.

Nadine froze. She looked at the knife, then at Macon, shaking her head. "No. *You can't hate me that much*?" Nadine covered her mouth with one hand, and grabbed her stomach with the other.

Emma gasped. "Oh Jesus! Albert! She got a knife!"

"Shelby! Get Macon out of here!" Albert yelled.

Shelby ran to Macon, putting her arms around her shoulders. Macon would not budge.

Macon stood there shaking, and crying. "No. No! She has to pay for what she's done! She has to pay..." she cried.

Macon tore herself from Shelby's grasp, and lunged at the floor to grab the knife before Albert could get to it. She was quick; faster than Albert. Macon stood up, waving the knife in the air.

"Macon, baby? Give Uncle the knife." Albert held out his hands. "C'mon baby. Jes gives Uncle the knife." Albert stepped lightly towards Macon.

Macon cried, as she held the knife in her

hands, shaking. She backed away as Albert came near. "No," she shook her head. "I can't. I can't do that, Uncle. Don't you see," she looked at her Uncle, tears blinding her. "If I let her get away, she'll just keep coming back. Uh-uh," Macon said. "I just can't let her do that. She's gonna keep coming and coming. She don't know how to take no for an answer." Macon turned quickly towards Nadine. "Isn't that right, Nadine? You never takes no for an answer. Everything got to be your way."

Nadine was still frozen in her steps. She couldn't speak. She just stood there, shaking her head, crying.

"Macon please..." Emma cried. "Please baby, give Uncle the knife. You don't want to do this. C'mon suga, let Mama have the knife. You don't have to give it to Uncle—jes gives it to me." Emma walked slowly towards Macon, holding out her hand.

Everyone was paralyzed, unable to move or think. They didn't know what to do. Richard held onto to Shelby, as she cried into his chest, her heart breaking for her cousin. Junior held Camille's hand tightly. Camille felt helpless. She did not expect this extreme response from Macon. There was no indication. She knew it would devastate Macon to learn of her mother's marriage to her rapist; but never assumed this far.

"Macon. Macon," Emma repeated softly.

Macon turned from her mother to her Aunt. "I—I can't. She—she's just gonna hurt me again," Macon sobbed, barely able to get the words out.

"She—she has to pay, Aunt Emma. She can't keep hurting people. My Daddy, you, Uncle...me." Macon shook her head. "Now she wants to get to my baby. I can't let her. I just can't."

"I—I would never hurt your baby," Nadine cried.

"Shut up! Just shut up! You're a liar!" Macon shook the knife at her mother. "You—you don't fool me. I...know...you. Better...better than anyone here. You...you didn't come here for me. You want my baby! He—he sent you here, didn't he?" She screamed.

"No. No, baby. I swear. He doesn't even know I'm here. I'm not with him—"

"Stop lying to me!" Macon cut Nadine off. "Stop...your...lying!" Macon hollered at the top of her lungs.

Emma cried. "Oh baby, please. *Macon*."

Macon would not, could not answer her Aunt. She glared at Nadine with such contempt.

"Macon, suga. It's all right. You can be mad at Nadine—"

"I hate her," she said, cutting Albert off.

"I know, I know." Albert walked closer to Macon.

Macon stepped back, out of Albert's reach. "I'm not gonna let her get away with this," she warned. "She—she just can't come in here and—and destroy everything!" Macon stammered.

"I know, baby. I know. But she won't. Me and your Aunt Emma ain't gonna let that happen. All right?" Albert tried to reassure her.

Macon shook her head. "No, I have to do it. *Me.* Otherwise, she gonna keep doing what she want...over and over again."

Albert saw as Calvin entered from the kitchen, just behind Macon. Calvin walked slowly, as not to alert Macon to his presence. Albert kept speaking to Macon, trying to get her to look at him.

"No she won't," Albert said. "You know Uncle won't let that happen. I promised you. Don't I keep my promises?"

Macon nodded, sobbing heavily.

"And you know if I didn't, your Aunt Emma would has my hide," he chided, trying to distract her.

Macon nodded again; looking from her Uncle to her Aunt, but tightly holding on to the knife.

Emma stood breathless. She couldn't move, praying that Albert and Calvin could get the knife away in time before Macon hurt Nadine, or worse—herself.

Albert reached into his pocket and pulled out his handkerchief. "Here baby, your nose is running. Wipe your face," he said, holding out his hand.

Macon took a couple of steps back. She didn't want to take the handkerchief. He might get the knife. She shook her head no.

"I'll just toss it to you," Albert said, tossing the handkerchief.

It fell on the floor in front of Macon's feet. She didn't move to pick it up. She stood there, full of rage, anger, and hurt. She couldn't let go of the knife. She had to protect her son from Nadine. Aunt Emma and Uncle didn't understand. She knew her mother better than any of them. She knew that her mother wasn't there for her. She could care less about her. It was her son. It was Nathaniel that she was after. No one understood her mother. Not like she did. Nadine was evil and selfish. She had to be stopped, once and for all. And she had to be the one to do it. If she let her go now, she'd just come back again and again, and worse—bring Byron with her. She would kill them both before she let them hurt her again, or go anywhere near Nathaniel. No. No. This was her fight. She had to make it stop. No one else.

Tears began to well up in Macon's eyes again, blinding her for a moment. She lifted her hands to wipe her eyes, and that is when Calvin rushed in and grabbed her from behind, causing her to drop the knife.

Albert picked up the knife.

"No! No!" Macon screamed, fighting to get loose. "You—you don't understand..." she sobbed. "She—she's evil. She gotta be stopped." Macon shook her head violently. "You. Just. Don't. Understand." Macon fell to the floor in a heap.

Calvin cradled her in his arms, as she wept.

"You don't know...." Macon said in a small voice. "You don't know her like I do. She's evil. She wants to hurt me. They want to take my baby..." Macon cried out from a place within her soul.

Calvin felt the pain in his heart, and cried for her.

Emma rushed over to Macon, falling on her knees. She pulled Macon into her arms and rocked her. "Shush. Shush. It's okay, baby. Mama got you. It's okay." She rocked Macon back and forth, rubbing her back and stroking her hair.

Macon sobbed into her Aunts shoulder, shaking from emotion. "No...," she cried. "She has to pay. They...want...my...baby. You...don't...know..." Macon tried to catch her breath. "She..."

"Shush. Shush. Don't you worry. No one's gonna hurt you again. I promise you. And ain't no one takin' your baby," Emma assured her.

CHAPTER 23

BYRON SAT BACK, confident that he had finally achieved a new status. He had made a name for himself. *Yeah,* he thought to himself, *a classy nigga like me deserves to be getting more out this game. I'm gonna get me a house just like this one—bigger.* He smiled to himself, as he smoked the cigar that was offered to him when he first arrived.

All his plans were finally coming together. Now all he had to do was take care of Nadine. She went and got into some drug program, which was bad for him. He thought for sure once she got out, all he had to do was start supplying her again, and he'd be rid of her for sure.

Why in the hell she gonna go and get smart now? He wondered. *Probably for that kid of hers.* A wicked smile crossed his face as Byron thought of Macon. He wondered if the baby looked like him. He wasn't sure at first if it was his; but when that cat from down South came looking for Nadine while she was in jail, he knew it was his. He ain't no punk; but he damn sure wasn't gonna get into some scuffle and bring unwanted attention to himself. No, he just laid low until he left. He remembered Spencer saying his name was Junior, kin to Nadine's dead husband.

Byron shrugged his shoulders. It didn't matter any way. By the time Nadine figured anything out, she'd be strung out again and he'd be rid of her. Nadine was too damn simple to think for herself, and too damn needy. Yeah, all he had to do was sweet talk her long enough so he could get some things in order. Knowing her, she'd OD. He was counting on it. He nursed his glass of Jack Daniels and continued to smoke his cigar, as he waited for his host to return.

A tall slender man walked back into the room. He sat across the table from Byron. He smiled and leaned back, crossing his legs.

"You know," he began, "you sure got a lot of balls." He picked up the bottle of Jack Daniels in front of him and poured himself a drink, sitting the glass down in front of him.

Byron smiled wide. "Well, you know..." Byron shook his head for a moment, feeling a bit lethargic suddenly. "You know, you get nowhere but six feet under being a coward." Byron sat back; thinking he should lay off the whiskey. He wasn't much of a drinker.

The man nodded in agreement. "True. True. So tell me, Byron, why should I believe anything that comes out of your mouth when here you are, ready to drop it on Ty like he was yesterday's trash." The man took a few sips from his glass, waiting for Byron to answer.

Byron nodded knowingly, his head feeling light. "Listen, we know how this works," he said rubbing his brow.

"How what works?" his host asked, feigning ignorance.

"I get you. I get what you saying," Byron

laughed. "Everybody knows that—that Big Ty ain't getting any younger. You know what I'm saying?"

The man nodded. "None of us are."

"Yeah, but...but you ain't afraid of...of giving someone...the chance...the chance to prove himself, and...and go after his, you know?" Byron was beginning to sweat, and he could hear his words beginning to slur.

The man nodded again, nursing his glass of Jack Daniels, watching as Byron began to sweat. "You all right, man? I generally keeps it warm in here."

Byron shook his head. "No. No. I'm good. I just ain't much of a whiskey drinker," he laughed hesitantly, wiping his forehead. "But, I'm cool. I'm cool," he insisted, lifting his cigar up and taking a puff.

The man nodded, sitting back. "All right, I hear you. Continue," he said raising his glass.

"Look...uh...Big Ty been running...been running this joint...a long time. So long, he done forgot...forgot what it's really like on the street. There's more opportunity out there. A bigger pie, so to speak..." Byron loosened his collar.

"And you ready for your slice of the pie?"

"Yeah, you could say that. You get where I'm going? It...it ain't like I haven't brought this to his attention; but he just brushed me aside, like...like I'm something he scraped off his shoe."

"Yes, Ty has always thought he was a high class Negro; too good for the same deals as everyone else."

"Yeah, well, I've been...been bringing in good money. That new stuff out here was my idea. Ain't... ain't no one was thinking about the Asians until I brought it to the table. Ev--everyone else was st-- still messing with the South Americans, and Me-- Mexicans. I was the one that increased the supply *and* demand on the streets."

"So, what you're saying is, you want a *whole* pie, not just a slice?"

"Yeah," Byron managed to say.

The man leaned forward a little, resting his hands on the table. "What do you suppose to do about it?" he looked, questionably.

"Well, that's why I came...came to you. I mean, you know what I can do. Things in Philly are changing, and we...we got to change with it. I can make it happen faster, by...by expanding. I'm not talking about your territory, but...but the West Coast. I just need some support." Byron took off his jacket.

"I see. You talked to Ty about this, you said?"

"Yeah, but he ain't interested in nothing else but Philly. He has no vision. All he wants to do is keep...keep the wealth for him." Byron sat back. "I figured like this; I want to leave Philly, anyway. I can easily set up somewhere else. Big Ty ain't trying to hear that. But...but if he wasn't in the picture no more, there wouldn't be a problem. All his territory would...would become yours, and I'm free to go and expand."

Byron looked at the man waiting for him to agree with him. He started to finish the cigar, and then changed his mind. His mouth was dry, and he didn't think the cigar would help.

The man leaned back in his seat. There are certain laws to live by in the street. Byron being at this meeting showed that he didn't respect those laws; which meant he wasn't worth the spit in his mouth, and could never be trusted.

There had been a long standing agreement between the man, and Big Ty. They made the agreement years ago, before either of them knew where their lives would take them. Ty was never interested in any area outside of Philly, and he wasn't interested in Philly at all. He and Ty shared a common tie; one that would prevent the other from crossing the line...ever. It was understood amongst their people where that line was. Obviously Byron was a man who did not understand respect, or loyalty.

It's a shame. Byron was right about one thing, Ty was an arrogant SOB and would never budge; although, he was part of that reason. Byron was also right about how much money he'd brought to the table. But as you come to learn in this particular way of life, there is always someone ready to take your place if you ain't looking; because they've been watching you and know exactly how to do what you do; especially if you talk too much, and believe your own hype.

He knew more about Byron than he cared to know. Perhaps if Byron had gone to another player in the game, they may have been foolish enough to take him up on his suicide offer, sealing both their fates. But who else *would* Byron go to? He was the best in this game, second only to Ty. Ty earned his place, and paid the price for it. He also earned his respect in this game they happened to call life.

The man leaned back and folded his arms. He rubbed his chin and smiled. "You present a good plan. How do you suppose *you* are going to get over on Ty, after so many have tried and failed, costing them their lives and their families in the process?"

Byron thought about it. "It won't be hard. Big Ty trusts me..." Byron's words trailed off. He could hear the words in his mind, but when he tried to speak, all he could do was mumble.

His host leaned forward. "You all right, man?"

His vision blurred, distorting the man's face. The words he was now speaking seemed foreign to him.

"I...I...don't..." Byron tried to stand up, but fell back into his seat, shaking his head.

The man stood up, swallowing the last of the contents of his glass. He walked towards Byron, grabbing a handful of his hair. He leaned forward until he was face to face with him.

"Hey! Hey!" he yelled, slapping Byron in the face. "You know, it's a shame you're not as smart as you think. But that's how it goes sometimes, huh? I give you credit, though. You definitely had guts to come up in here, and think you were just going to walk out." He released his hold on Byron and stepped back.

Byron tried to focus, as his heart began to

beat fast within his chest. *What happened? What did he miss?*

"One thing you should have learned: never do what your host doesn't do."

Byron was confused.

The man picked up the cigar and waved it in Byron's face.

The cigar! Byron began to panic. *It had been laced; but with what?*

The man placed his hand on Byron's shoulder. "Relax. Relax. You're going to give yourself a heart attack. And quite frankly, that's just too easy a way for you to go out. But don't worry; you won't miss anything that happens. Things will be a bit blurry for a moment. You still won't be able to move, but you'll definitely be coherent." The man laughed. "Oh, man. I haven't done this in a while. Sure brings back fond memories." He walked towards the door. "Don't worry," he said over his shoulder. "It won't kill you...directly anyway. It's one of my better blends."

Byron watched through glazed eyes, as someone else came into the room. The voice was familiar to him. He strained to see who it was. His heart nearly stopped. It was Spencer.

Oh God! Oh God, no!

He knew right then that Big Ty had set him up, and he was as sure as dead. The lingering question in his mind was how painful was Big Ty going to make it. Byron couldn't move. His body would not obey his brain that pleaded for it to move; to run; to do anything but just sit there waiting to be killed.

"Spencer, he's all yours."

Spencer placed both arms under Byron's armpits, and lifted him up.

Byron tried to speak, but only spittle came out.

Don't do this man. C'mon, Spence, not like this. Grow some balls man! Help me!

Spencer dragged Bryon out the door, as the man held it open. "Nice meeting you, Byron. Too bad it couldn't be on better terms," he smiled. "Oh, Spence?"

Spencer stopped for a moment, holding Byron like a rag doll.

"Tell my brother, we're even."

Spencer nodded, and took Byron to the car, placing him in the backseat on his stomach.

With that, Lester Smalls shut the door.

Brother? Brother? Byron screamed within himself. He lay there, unable able to move, and started crying.

CHAPTER 24

NADINE WAS NUMB. Her daughter hated her enough to kill her. She rocked back and forth, wringing her hands, waiting to see how Macon was.

Everyone was silent; not sure of what to do or say, wondering if Macon was going to be all right. Albert stood, looking out the window. He questioned himself, and whether he did everything the right way. Poor Emma; he knew that this was painful for her in more ways than one. No way had they seen this coming. He decided to check on them himself when Emma walked in.

Nadine stood quietly, as did Shelby, Junior and Calvin; no one saying a word, waiting with bated breath for Emma to tell them how Macon was doing.

"How's she doing?" Albert asked, first.

Emma sighed deeply. "She's resting now. Richard gave her a sedative, and Camille is with her. Anna-Leigh is with the babies."

"She's gonna be all right, Mama?"

"I don't know, Shelby. We jes have to wait and see. Camille wants to keep a close eye on her. We jes have to make sure she's stable...mentally. I don't know if she can handles anymore surprises," Emma stated, looking towards Nadine.

Nadine fidgeted with her sweater. "I...I never meant for any of this to happen."

"You never mean for *anything* to happen,

Nadine. But they always do where you're concerned," said Calvin.

"Listen, I didn't—"

"You didn't what? Want to destroy your daughter? Come here and make everyone miserable? Marry the man that raped your daughter?"

"You so damn high and mighty, Calvin. Just like your mother. Like she ain't ever made some mistakes in her life," hollered Nadine.

"I never said she didn't! But at least my mother is honest, and wouldn't think of hurting any of her children like you have Macon!"

"Oh really?" Nadine turned towards Emma.

"Enough! Enough," yelled Emma, looking at both Calvin and Nadine. "This here fightin' and carryin' on has got to end now!" Emma threw her hands up. "Nadine, I don't wants to fight with you no more."

Nadine rolled her eyes, and folded her arms.

"I've had enough. Enough of all this disturbance and foolishness. You have to leave. I don't want you in my home no more; not as long as Macon and that baby are here."

"What? I just can't leave. Especially not now. I...I told you, there are things you just don't understand," pleaded Nadine.

Emma shook her head. "I can't Nadine. It's no good for Macon. Surely you can see that?"

"She *doesn't* care, Mama. I told you, you

should've just called the cops and had her escorted off your property," Calvin said.

Nadine turned to Calvin. "You know, I am damn tired of you looking down your nose at me; acting as though you are so above me. I'd really like to see you knocked off your high horse," she seethed.

"Please, I don't have to *act* above you. You stay at the bottom. That's where you're comfortable."

"Calvin!" Emma interjected. "This has got to stop. It ain't doing anyone no benefit to continue to degrade one another." She turned to Nadine. "I'm sorry, Nadine, you have caused too much pain and trouble in my house as it is. It's time for you to leave; especially after seein' the state your daughter is in."

Tears rolled down Nadine's cheeks. This wasn't what she came for. She wanted to see Macon and the baby. She wanted to see for herself, with her own eyes, if the baby looked like Byron. She knew it was true; but she needed to see for herself.

"Mama, you're wasting your breath. She doesn't care about anyone but herself."

"Calvin," Junior began. "Leave it alone. Forget about Nadine."

"Yes," Shelby agreed.

Calvin couldn't believe his siblings. "Forget about her? Look at all the hell she's caused." Calvin shook his head. "You all just don't know. She is evil. She really is."

"Son, listen to your Mama," Albert spoke. "Ain't no need to continues with the name calling.

That is not how I raised you. You know better," he warned.

Calvin knew his father was right.

"Why don't you go ahead with your brother and sister; leave me and your Mama."

Calvin looked at his parents. Perhaps he needed to take a step back. "You're probably right. I'm gonna check on Anna and the kids."

"All right." Albert patted his son on the back.

Calvin turned to leave with Shelby and Junior.

Emma turned to Nadine. "I suggests you leave now, Nadine. If you needs a ride, I'm sure Albert won't minds takin' you to the train or somethin'." Emma tried her best to remain peaceful. She really didn't want another confrontation. It was beginning to wear on her nerves.

Nadine stood there, shaking her head. "Can't I just see my grandson?"

"That's not a good idea."

"Emma, please."

"Macon doesn't wants you anywhere nears him."

Calvin stopped and turned around. He couldn't believe the nerve Nadine had.

"You...you said she's sleeping, right? She doesn't have to know." She looked to Albert. "Please. I won't touch him. I just want to see him. It will probably be the only time I ever gets to see him."

"You don't know that," said Albert.

"Yes I do. I saw how Macon looked at me. She

hates me. She wanted to *kill me*." Nadine placed her hands across her chest.

"She wouldn't have done it," Albert assured her. "She was on edge."

"Rightfully so!" Calvin went and picked up the phone. "I'm sorry, but this has got to end. She's not going to leave on her own, and I really don't want to upset either of you. I'll call, Tucker. He's off duty." Calvin went to dial.

Tucker was an old friend of Calvin's and Nathan's.

"No," Albert said. "We don't need no more mess in this house. We gonna handle this." He turned to Nadine. "Nadine, come on, I'll drive you where you needs to go."

"I can't, Albert. I can't do it. You don't understand." Nadine shook her head.

"Nadine, please, enough already," Emma said. "Jes go ahead with Albert before somethin' else happens. You done caused enough upheaval, and I can't take no more this here night!"

Calvin hung up the phone and walked to his mother. He hugged her tightly. "I'm sorry, Mama. I'm just so angry."

"I know. I know." Emma rubbed her son's back. "Jes let your father handles this, okay?" She pulled back and looked at her son.

Calvin nodded.

Anger welled up in Nadine as she watched Calvin and Emma. She was incensed with rage.

How dare them! How dare they put her down?

How dare they steal her child from her, and make her look like the worst mother in the world? How dare they turn her child against her?

"You make me sick," spewed Nadine.

Emma and Calvin turned around.

"You all think you're better than me!" She looked straight into Emma's face. "All of this is your fault. You turned my daughter against me! You poisoned her mind with lies," yelled Nadine.

Emma shook her head in disbelief. "You have lost your damn mind, Nadine."

Albert grabbed Nadine by the arm. "Let's go, Nadine. Enough's enough."

"No, no. It's not enough until she hurts like I do," she said, looking at Emma.

"Let's go, Nadine." Albert pushed Nadine towards the door.

"I'm gonna wiped that smug look off your face, Calvin!" Nadine braced herself between the door posts.

"You are crazy!"

"Yeah? You think your mama's so special, huh? You think she walks on damn water, don't you? Well I know something she ain't tell you," Nadine gloated.

Albert and Emma looked at one another. Emma knew instinctively what Nadine was about to say.

"C'mon, Nadine," Albert grabbed Nadine about the waist.

"I don't care anymore! I'm tired of you all looking down on me, like I'm no good!" She wrestled with Albert, until she hit the floor.

"Your mama's a whore! That's right! She's a hypocrite! She gonna condemn me for the same damn sins she committed!"

Emma stood frozen, a lump caught in her throat.

"You know why she wants my daughter? Because she's trying to replace Nathan! She feels guilty! That's why."

"You're not making any sense!" Calvin yelled.

Albert struggled to pull Nadine out the door. "Nadine! Nadine!" He could not have her screaming for the world to hear Emma's secret. It was Emma's truth to tell, and no one else. He continued to struggle with Nadine, when he looked at his wife. Emma was shaking her head, eyes welling up with tears, and he knew in that moment, her worst fears were becoming a reality. Part of him wished that he allowed Calvin to call Tucker.

Albert resigned fighting with Nadine, and released his grip on her. There was nothing else he could do but be there for his wife. He walked to Emma's side.

"I'm making plenty of sense!" Nadine laughed wickedly, struggling to stand. "You...you all think you can hurt me and put me down, and treat me like trash? At least I didn't throw my baby away like trash! At least I didn't raise my own child as if he was my nephew!"

Emma bowed her head, as the tears spilled

from her eyes.

"What?" Calvin was confused.

Shelby, Richard and Junior walked into the room.

"Ask her! Ask your *saintly* mother! Nathan was your brother! That's right! He was her son! She was his mother, not his damn Aunt!" declared Nadine, pointing her finger at Emma.

Calvin looked at his mother, then to his father, confused and speechless.

"You ain't got anything to say now?" Nadine asked Calvin.

Shelby gasped. Richard put his arms around her waist.

Junior was too stunned to move. "Nathan was our brother?" he whispered to himself.

The pain in Emma's chest was like none she had ever felt before. Rage began to build up in her body. She could taste the bile on her tongue. She pulled herself away from Albert's embrace. All Emma saw was red. She watched as Nadine stood there smugly, and tauntingly. Nadine had no right. No right at all.

It happened quickly before anyone had a chance to react. Emma charged at Nadine like a raging bull, hell bent on tearing Nadine apart with her bare hands.

"You...no...good..." Emma screamed, launching onto Nadine.

Nadine fell backwards between the

thresholds of the door.

"How dare you!" Emma screamed, sitting on Nadine's chest punching and slapping her. "You had no right! You had no right!" She screamed between blows, while crying. "You don't know! You don't know anything!" Emma wrapped her hands around Nadine's neck and began to choke her. "I'm gonna kill you! You hear me? I'm gonna kill you!" Emma tightened her grip around Nadine's throat, trying to squeeze the life out of her.

Nadine kicked and bucked. She tried desperately to loosen Emma's hands from around her neck. She choked and gasped; her eyes bulging, face beginning to turn purple, close to unconsciousness.

Albert and Junior snapped out of their shocked, and raced to Emma before she killed Nadine.

"Mama! Mama!" Albert grabbed Emma by the shoulders trying to pull her off.

Emma wouldn't let go. Sobbing, and shaking her head, she continued to try and choke the life out of Nadine.

"Mama, she's not worth it," Junior said. "C'mon Mama, go with Pop." Junior tried prying his mother's fingers loose from Nadine's throat.

Nadine's lips were blue, and she had stopped struggling, finally losing consciousness.

Calvin stood frozen; unable to move from the shock of the revelation.

Shelby wept silently into Richard's shoulder.

"C'mon, Emma, I know it hurts. I know this is not how you wanted it. But please, Mama, don't give the enemy the satisfaction. We'll get through this." Albert assured his wife.

Junior managed to pry his mother's hands loose. He waved for Richard to come check on Nadine.

Emma fell back into Albert's arms, sobbing heavily, her body still shaking with anger.

Albert remained on his knees, cradling Emma. He wrapped his arms around her, and pulled her close to his chest. "Shush, it's okay, Mama. It's alright. Everything gonna be jes fine." He stroked Emma's hair, brushing the loose strands from her face.

Emma cried into Albert's arm. This wasn't how it was supposed to happen. This was not how the truth was supposed to come out.

Damn Nadine! Damn her!

Emma shook her head.

No, damn herself. Damn herself for not listening to Albert or Lynorra; for not telling her children the truth sooner.

Emma wept bitterly.

CHAPTER 25

EMMA TOOK A SIP OF COFFEE. Her hands were shaking, her heart broken. She placed the cup down, unable to drink anymore. She looked at Albert sitting next to her, and took his hand. She gently returned the squeeze that he'd just given her. She looked at the faces of her children—waiting for her to tell them, to tell them why she never acknowledged Nathan as her son; to tell them why she never told them, even after he passed. She knew they were waiting for answers. And they deserved answers. They deserved the truth.

Richard was gracious enough to take Nadine to the train station after he examined her. No one else would go near her. It was either Richard, or the police. They had enough trouble as it was. Nadine complied, and left with Richard.

As she looked at each of her children, Emma's heart ached even more. There was so more to the truth. So much that they didn't understand. She looked at their faces, and wondered if they would understand. Would they understand *why* she did what she did? Would they forgive her for what she did? She wondered.

Albert called and asked Lynorra to send Deeney home.

Calvin wouldn't look at her. Emma knew he was hurt the most. He was the closest to Nathan than any of them. He had a deeper bond with

Nathan; deeper than she had realized. She knew this was hardest for him.

Everyone sat quietly. Emma wasn't sure where to begin, but to acknowledge the hurt that she knew each of them was feeling, and perhaps the betrayal they felt, as well.

"I…I am so sorry," she began, her voice shaking. "I…I never wanted you to find out like this."

Calvin kept his face towards the floor, unable to look at his mother. "Did you ever plan to tell us?" he asked coldly.

Emma felt a lump in her chest. She nodded. "Yes…yes I was. I was planning on telling you all… soon."

Calvin shook his head.

"Mama, I don't understand," Deeney said. "How could Nathan be your son? You had to be, what, thirteen? Who's his father?"

"I don't think that matters right now," Albert said.

"Why?" Calvin said looking at his father. "Did *you* know all along?"

Albert nodded. "Yes I did. But there are things you don't understand."

"Did Nathan know?" Junior asked.

"Yes," Emma nodded. "Yes, he knew."

"He knew all along?" Shelby asked.

"No. Not all along. But he knew early on."

"So you told him, and you couldn't tell us?" asked Calvin, the pain evident in his eyes and in his voice.

"No, I didn't tell him. He already knew."

"I don't understand how come you never told us sooner. I mean, he was our brother, Mama. Macon. Macon is our *niece,* not our cousin," Shelby looked to her mother for answers.

Emma sighed deeply. This was hard for her.

Albert squeezed her hand. "Listen, I know this is hard for you to digest right now. But this is hard on your, Mama, as well."

"Oh c'mon, pop." Calvin stood up. "All our lives, you taught us to be honest with one another. Mama always said that it was better to tell the truth, because it'll just find you anyway. So how come you couldn't tell us the truth about, Nathan? To just tell us that this isn't your cousin, this is your brother." Calvin walked toward the door. "I mean, how easy would it have been just to tell us while we were growing up that he *really* was our brother? I mean, that's the way we grew up anyway."

Emma shook her head. "It wasn't that simple, Calvin. There is so much you don't know or understand."

"Then help us understand, Mama. Help us to understand what happened. It had to be something deep for you not to tell us, even after he passed," said Junior.

Emma nodded. "You're right, and I can't begin to tell you how my heart is aching and how I am so sorry for keeping this secret. For not allowing you all to know the truth. It's..." Emma looked at Albert. Even now, she didn't know if she could tell them everything. It was still too painful, even after all these years.

Albert looked at his children. "You know how much your Mama loves you all. And the last thing she'd ever want to do is hurt you. All she ever wanted to do was protects you— her chilren."

Calvin shook his head. "No, that's an excuse. Protect us from what? Our own brother? How can the truth about Nathan being our brother, instead of our cousin, have hurt us? Even now, you're still not telling us anything. Why?"

"Jes hold it, Calvin," Albert said standing. "You respect your Mama."

"I just don't get it," he said. "What's so devastating about Nathan being our brother? So what, we didn't have the same father. So what, you were thirteen. Surprising? Yes. But you obviously got through it, because you raised him anyway! What? Was Nadine right? You just threw him away? Was that it? Were you promiscuous and just threw him away because you didn't want him...a reminder?"

"Calvin!" Deeney yelled. "You ain't got any right to talk to Mama that way."

Emma sank back in her seat. She didn't think her heart could break any more than it already had. Calvin's words stung her deeply.

Albert approached his son with anger in his voice. "Don't you *ever* let me hear you speak to your Mama that way? How dare you show her disrespect?"

J7R

Shelby and Deeney went and sat on either side of Emma.

Junior walked towards his brother. "Hey, Calvin, I know you're hurting man. But you need to take it easy. You haven't heard everything. And for you to believe *anything* that Nadine said is crazy!"

Calvin looked from his father to his brother. "I didn't say I believed her; but Mama hasn't said anything to the contrary. Why did she let us believe all these years that he was her nephew? Why didn't Nathan say anything? Is that why he left all those years ago? Is that why he never came back? Is that why she barely talked about him all these years?" Calvin wanted answers.

"You need to calm down," Junior warned his brother. "I know you and Nate were close. But that's our Mama. And she would never do anything to deliberately hurt any of us...including Nate. You know I'm right."

"I don't know much of anything right now. All I know is, Mama's been lying all these years, and she's the reason Nathan left here and didn't come back!"

"What?" Albert looked at his son in surprise.

"No, you have it all wrong, baby," Emma cried. "That's not why Nathan left all those years ago."

"Why don't you *just listen*, Calvin?" Shelby pleaded with her brother.

"Son, I know you upsets right now, but I ain't gonna have you talkin' to your mama like that...like she done did somethin' wrong. Now, either you sit down and listen to her, or you can takes a walk until you calm down, and can listens with an open heart and mind. I ain't raised you to be judgmental, and you ain't gonna starts now with your Mama. Now," Albert looked at all his children. "What your Mama has to say is difficult. It ain't been easy for her these past years. Especially now with Macon here..."

"Albert," Emma's voice shook. "Let...let me. This ain't your place, it's mine. You ain't the one who's been lying all these years."

"You ain't been lying, Mama. You have been survivin'. And I won't have no one, including any Chile of mine, disrespects you." He shook his head. "I jes won't have it."

"It's not his fault. He's hurt and angry." Emma turned to Calvin. "I know you hurtin', baby. I know you don't understands. Consider how much you love your baby-girl, and would do anything to keep her safe and happy, and without any harm." She watched as Calvin faced the doorway. He couldn't face her. "That's all I did."

"No, I don't believe that," he said turning to her. "Mama, you always told us straight. You never kept us in the dark about anything this important. How could knowing Nathan was our brother harm us?"

Emma shook her head. "I never believed knowing Nathan was your brother would hurt you. But *me* being his Mama, and having to explain it all would have been harmful, and very painful. And yes, I'll admit to it now; I was selfish about it. Because, in order for me to tell you all the truth, it was gonna cause me more pain than I was willin's to face at the time. It would have opened some wounds that I still fight with to this very day." Emma stood up. "Calvin, I love you chilren—Nathan included. He was my first born. And God, yes! Forgive me, but at one time I tried to forget it. I acted like he wasn't mine. I pretended he was my sister's Chile. I couldn't look at him without cryin' and feelin' disgust. I even felt like I hated him!"

Tears fell from Shelby and Deeney's eyes as they listened to their mother. Junior stood quietly next to his father. Calvin kept his head lowered, unable to look up.

Albert listened to the pain in his wife's voice; knowing that her heart was ripping and her mind was aching with the memories that now flooded her. He knew the truth; the whole, ugly truth. Sometimes he wished he hadn't.

"I never in my life wanted to keep anything from you chilren more than I wanted to keep the entire truth about my past hidden. Yes, over the years I have thought many times about tellin' you all everything. But I wanted to be sure you were old enough to understand. As time went on, and you all grew older, I still found that I could not tell you. Not because I didn't want to; but for fear of havin' to revisit and face my past. And yes, Nathan was a big part of that.

"You may not believe this, but Nathan and I talked about this years ago. And it was *his* wish that I jes leave it alone. Why? Because he saw the pain that it caused me. I never loved him more than I did at that moment. Yet it didn't give me a right to keep that secret; to hide the truth. I regret it to this day. To this very day I wonder if maybe things would have been different if I had told the truth. Maybe I could have spared Macon all this pain if I would have revealed who I was. And maybe, just maybe, I would have had more time with my son, and we would all be better off. But I can't change none of that. No matter how much I wants to. And I wish to God I would have done things better. I wish to, God Almighty, that I was stronger in that area. That I wasn't so damn weak and selfish!"

Emma walked towards Calvin. She could see the hurt and pain on his face. There were just some things that couldn't be explained away; no matter hard you tried. The truth, all the truth, was a heavy load. All her life, since Nathan was born, Emma tried so many ways to bury the past. And yes, at first she didn't want to have anything to do with her own flesh and blood. Not because she didn't love him. She didn't know if she could.

Emma placed a hand on Calvin's shoulder. He didn't move. He continued to look at the floor, unable to look at his mother. "Baby, I am sorry that I hurt you." She looked at all her children. "I'm sorry that I hurt all of you, and robbed you of knowing Nathan as your brother. I swear to the Lord, if I could change things, I would."

She turned back to Calvin. "Calvin, I know you had the deepest bond with, Nathan. I knew you were close, but I hadn't realized until this day jes how close you two were. I don't know; maybe you are feeling betrayed. And yes, you were lied to but not to hurt you, son. Never that."

Calvin shook his head. He sighed deeply, with tears streaming down his face. "I...I just don't understand. We were family. We shared so much, and not once. Not one time did he tell me that we were brothers," Calvin turned and faced his mother for the first time.

"Don't you understand? I looked up to him. In my heart, in my mind, he was my brother. And when he left the way he did..." he shook his head, tears choking his voice. "He...he never said why. One day we were fine, and the next thing I knew, he was gone. Do you understand how I felt? I wasn't close to you like Shelby. I didn't follow Pop around like Junior. And Deeney was just a baby who got all the attention. Nathan was who *I* had. He was who I talked to. Then, just like that, he was gone and we didn't hear from him for a long time. And you, Mama, you never talked about him. It was like you was glad he was gone. I always believed that you had something to do with it because of your feelings toward Nadine." Calvin sat down on the arm of the chair, shaking his head.

"Mama, all our lives you taught us to be upfront. To be honest and face the truth. To face the truth no matter how difficult or painful it was; you said that the truth will always find you anyway, so it's always best to confront it, head on. *You* taught us that. Mama, what about Macon? You're her grandmother, not her Aunt. How is she supposed to deal with this revelation? You can't keep it from her. That wouldn't be fair. I don't know," he said standing. "Maybe I am being judgmental, as Pop said.

"Maybe I just can't handle anymore truth for today; but I wonder about how much more we don't really know. If there was one thing that I could always count on was you, Mama. You were telling the truth, no matter how hard it was. Don't you see? Maybe, maybe if you would have told the truth, Nathan wouldn't have moved away. And maybe, just maybe, none of this would have happened today." He turned, and started to leave the room.

Emma stood silent for a moment. She has said the exact same things to herself. She couldn't blame Calvin for his feelings. Nor could she blame any of her children if they felt the same way. She'd lied to them all their lives, and her lies had not only consequences for herself, but for the rest of the family as well.

"Now hold it jes a minute, son." Albert spoke up. "You has a right to feel what's you feeling. But you has no right to blame your Mama for things that was out of her control. Nate was a grown man; a grown man that made decisions for himself and his family. He was an adult when he moved away from here. A man, with a wife and Chile of his own. He did what he thought was best. He could have told the truth, because your Mama told him it was alright to do so. But he didn't. He made his choice. And apparently, he shared it with his wife, and she chose to put her own spin on things. But in any event, I'm not gonna have you walk out this home without hearin's *all* the truth. Even if I have to tell it to you myself." He placed his hand on Calvin's arm.

"Albert," Emma said. "I will tell what needs to be said. It's not your truth that needs to be told, it's mine."

"No," he corrected her, "it *is* ours. It became my truth the day I fell in love with you and the moment you told me."

Emma smiled at her husband of thirty-two years. She loved him more than her own life, and she knew he meant every word he spoke. No one understood her better than Albert. No one loved her more. "I know, but I have to finally put this ghost to rest before it drives me mad."

"I...I don't know if I want to hear this now," Calvin stated.

"It's not about you, Calvin. It never was."

"I know that, Junior. But I just can't handle anymore truth. Not today."

"Well you need to. You need to stop feeling sorry for yourself, like you were the only person hurt here by what we've learned."

"Please, please," Emma interjected. "I don't wants you two fightin'. Please," she asked.

"Sorry, Mama." Junior said.

Calvin was silent.

"Calvin, I can't make you stay. I can't make you hear what I have to say. But I am asking you not to leave before I tell you all everything, once and for all."

Calvin remained silent, and sat in a chair by the window.

Emma looked at Albert, who nodded his

head, assuring her that she was going to be fine. She took his hand as she looked around the room at each of her four children. Where did she begin?

"It's okay, Mama. I'm here with you," Albert whispered in her ear, before placing a kiss on her forehead.

Emma could feel her insides churning. Although Albert was holding her hand, it didn't stop it from shaking. Emma was quiet for a moment, her head bowed. Shelby and Deeney sat solemnly, holding onto one another. Junior sat across from them, as Calvin remained facing the window.

Emma's voice was shaking as she began to tell her children the truth for the first time.

"I...I was twelve years old when I got pregnant, thirteen by the times I gave birth. I didn't even knows I was pregnant at first. I tried to deny it when I found out. I was so scared. I didn't know what I was gonna do. God forgive me, but I tried everything I knew how to do to get rid of it. Nothing worked. I was more scared of my mama than anything. 'Cause I knew that she was gonna kill me," Emma closed her eyes shaking her head, a lump forming in her throat. "I...I tried so many times to forget what happened. I tried so hard to jes act like it wasn't me. Clarisse was there for me. She never left my side; especially when mama found out." Emma stopped for a moment, wanting to stop but knowing she couldn't.

"I'll never forgets that day. The day mama found out. I was getting dress to go work at the store. That was my job on Saturday mornings. I was certain she was still asleep. So I had times to hurry and wash and gets dressed before she seen me. I could camouflage with the kind of clothing I was wearin', and I could hide under the apron from the store. I wasn't showin' much, but I had gained some weight.

"I remember gettin ready to pull my dress over my head when mama walked in. I froze. I didn't know what to do. She walked towards me, and she yanked the dress out my hands, and looked at me. I knew then, that she knew and was gonna kill me. I wouldn't have to worry about no baby, because we would both be dead once mama was finished with me..."

"You heifer, you! I knew it! I knew you done went and gots yourself pregnant! Whose is it?! Who's the damn father, you little whore?"

"I stood there, too scared to move, and too scared to say anything. She grabbed me by the shoulders and likes to shake Nathan right out of me. The rage in her eye's! I still couldn't speak. It—it was like she scared the voice right out of me. She slapped me across the face so hard, that my ear was ringing. I stood there crying. Crying from the pain, but more so from fear. She shook me again."

"Didn't I tells you to keep your legs closed? I done told you, walkin' 'rounds here like you so goddamn special and cute! I knew it! I knew my gut was tellin' me right! Look at you! Your breasts damn near as big as mine! Damn it, Emma! If you don't tells me who you been messin' round with? I ain't fittin' to raise no babies around here. I done hads

enough with you and your sister. Now tells me! Who is it? Who is it? I swear, I'll beats the truth out of you, alongs wit that baby!"

"I knew mama well enough to know that was no idle threat. I remember opening my mouth wantin' to say who the father was, but knowing she wouldn't believe me, and knowing that if I told her I was as good as dead."

Emma stood and began pacing back and forth, wringing her hands. Her family watched her with pained expressions.

"I jes wanted to run, to run as fast as I could. But I knew she'd catch me before I reached the door. She jes kept yellin' and screamin'; wantin' to know who the boy was. But it wasn't no boy. Oh God, I wished I'd died. I prayed that the good Lord would jes kill me!"

"Emma Jean Cooper, I swears to God, if you don't opens your damn mouth, I'll make you dead as your father! I swears, I will buries you right next to him! Who'd you lay down with?"

"She grabbed me by my arms, and began to drag me towards the door. I cried, and begged her to let me go."

"You don't want to talk? Fine, I will drags you to every door, and ask every damn boy if they the father, until I finds out!"

"I remember screamin', and pleading with her, until I jes blurted it out: *It was Joe! It was Joe!"* Emma put her hands over her mouth, stifling her cries. Albert rushed to her side, and held her. But she pushed him away, overcome by the pain of the memory.

Shelby and Deeney cried. Junior could barely stay in his seat. He never saw his mother like this. Calvin was still, unable to move, watching his mother as she relived her most painful memories.

"Oh, God," Emma cried. "I—I jes wanted the pain to go away! I told her, that her husband, my stepfather, raped me. He raped me more than once and it was his baby!" Emma sat down, holding her stomach, rocking back and forth.

"I—I don't know if deep down I wanted her to believe me. But I knew...I knew she wouldn't. She let go of my arms, like she was holding fire! She began slapping me, over and over and over. Calling me a liar..."

"You liar! You liar! How dare you blame, Joe! How dares you? He ain't been nothin' but kinds to you. He treats you like you his! You stop lyin'! You hear me, Emma Jean? Tell me the truth! Tell me the goddamn truth!"

"She jes kept shakin' me, demanding that I tell her the truth; to tell her that I was lyin' jes to break up her marriage. She said he was the best thing to happen to her since my no good father went and got himself killed! She told me I was a worthless, no good, spoiled brat, who hated her for being happy! She called me a whore and everything in between. Everything but a Chile of God." Emma cried out, her vision blurred by the tears, her face soaked with them. She wiped her nose with her sleeve.

"I—I can't say I didn't believe what she was saying, because it was nothin' new. I tried to tell what he did. How he crept into my bedroom, night after night. How, the only way I could get away from him, was to sneak out my window and goes to Clarisse." Emma nodded her head. "Clarisse was smart. Uh-huh. She knew he was no good. The moment mama brought him home, Clarisse left, getting' herself a room. I wanted to go with her. But mama wouldn't let me go. Oh, he didn't do nothin's at first. He waited, and he waited, bidin' his time. He made it look like he was kind and fatherly. Taking care of my mama, and payin' all the bills at the store and then bought the store outright for her, so she didn't haves to rent anymore. He was the devil himself, come to make my life a living hell.

"Mama whooped on me that day like there was no tomorrow. I hated her. God forgive me, but I hated her. With every hit, I hated her more, and wished she were dead. She cursed the day I was ever born. She was gonna kill me that day. As sure as I am breathing right now, if she could, she would have killed me. I managed to run out the room. She followed me. I made it to the living room before she caught me by my hair and pulled me back..."

"Where do you think you runnin' to? I swear I'm gonna kill you! You no good tramp! You little heifer! As good as I am to you. As good as Joe is to you! You gonna lie? I feeds you, put clothes on your back, and this is how you repays me? By lyin' on my

husband? I will kill you dead before I lets you out this house spreadin' them lies!"

"I remember fallin' to the floor on my stomach, trying to shield my face with my arms pinned beneath me. She was sittin' on my back, beatin' on me. Then all of a sudden, I felt this searing pain on the back of my shoulder," Emma touched the back of her right shoulder. "I screamed out. She must have had the flat iron on. She burned me with it."

"Oh Mama," Deeney cried. "That's where— where you got that scar from."

"I—I couldn't believe it, I really was gonna die. I started kickin' and screamin', until I knocked her off of me, and the flat iron out her hand. I know it must have been God that gaves me the strength to get loose from under her..."

"Mama, no, you don't have to tell us anymore," Shelby cried.

"Shelby's right, Mama. You don't have to say no more," Junior agreed.

"No," Emma shook her head. "I know I don't have to, but I got to, because now *I* need to. There's so much more. That wasn't the worst of it. When I pushed her off of me, she must've hit her head. She wasn't out cold, but she was down long enough for me to runs. I didn't care. I ran as fast as I could without lookin' back. I ran all the way to Clarisse's in my panties and bra. It was early yet, and there were a few people out, but I didn't care. I wouldn't stop 'til I got to my sister's.

"I banged on Clarisse's door for what seemed

like forever. I woke up her landlady and some of the other tenants. When she opened that door, I jes fell in her arms crying. I told her everything. I told her about the repeated rape, the baby, and our mama. She jes hugged me and said everything was gonna be alright. That she was gonna takes care of it. She had me take a shower. When I finished, she gave me one of her gowns and told me to get in bed. She said she'd be right back. I was to stay there 'til she came back; to not open the doors for anyone. She said she was gonna see mama, and fix everything. I begged her not to leave. I begged her to stay with me.

"Clarisse wasn't scared of mama like I was. Even at sixteen she stood up to her, and said what she wanted. She was jes like our daddy. Clarisse said she was gonna make sure everything was fine, and that I didn't needs to be scared no more. But I was. I was terrified—terrified of Joe, terrified of my mama, and terrified for Clarisse if she confronted them. She jes shook her head, and said there was no reason for me to worry no more. Jes lock the door behind her, get in the bed and she'll be back soon.

"It seemed liked hours had passed. But it was only one. I couldn't sleep, too scared of what happened to Clarisse. I didn't listen. She told me to stay, but I couldn't. I started worryin' 'bout her and what happened. I put on some of her clothes and I went lookin' for her. I snuck back home to see if she was there. I jes had a bad feelin.

"I saw Joe's car in the back as it always was. I snuck around to one of the windows. The living room was empty. The light in the kitchen was on. I didn't see my mama, or Clarisse. But I knew Joe was there. I could feel him. I figured Clarisse probably was at the store confrontin' mama. I started to leave when somethin' made me go to the back of the house, to my room. I jes couldn't shake this awful feelin' that somethin' wasn't right.

"The window was open. I looked in, but I didn't see nothin' at first. I started to leave when I heard a faint sound. I knelt down, and I crept closer. My heart stopped beatin' for a moment. Joe—Joe was on my bed attacking Clarisse. She wasn't movin'. She looked dead. I—I didn't know what to do. I had to think fast. I didn't have time to run for help. I ran to the front of the house. I came in as quietly as I could. I went to my mama's room and got her gun from out of her wardrobe. I ran to my room as quick as I could. I could hear him, breathin' and moanin'. I pushed the door open, and yelled for him to get off of her! I held the gun in both hands, shaking. I told him to get off of her, or I was gonna kill him. He stood up, smilin', tellin me to put the gun down before I hurt myself. I tolds him to shut up, and move away from my sister.

"I didn't know if Clarisse was alive or dead. She wasn't movin'. From where I was standin', I could see blood on the side of her face and her head. I started screamin', and askin' him what he did to my sister. He jes kept smilin', saying that she's fine. I told him he was lying. I asked him how come she wasn't movin'. He shrugged his shoulders, and jes said she must be tired from all the fun they had, jes like me and him. I told him to shut up before I shoot him. He said I wouldn't; that I didn't know how to

use that gun. He started to walk towards me, tellin'
me to give him the gun before he has to punish me. I
told him...I told him not...to come...any...further, or I
was gonna shoot. He laughed at me and came closer.
Before I realized it, I squeezed the trigger and shot
him in the groin. He fell to his knees, yelling out,
cussin'. But he was still comin' towards me, so I shot
him again, and again, and again! I shot him four
times, until he fell over near my feet.

"I stood there for a second, not sure if he was
dead. I kicked him, but he didn't move. I dropped
the gun and ran to Clarisse. She looked so bad; I ran
and got some towels and water from the bathroom.
I jes couldn't lose my sister. After a while, she
started to come through.

"Clarisse had confronted our mama at the
store. She said she came over to the house to get
some of my things when Joe had snuck in on her.
They started fightin when he pushed her into the
dresser, knockin her out. She turned and saw him on
the floor. I told her I killed him. I was so scared; I
didn't know what to do. I knew I was gonna go to
jail. She said I wouldn't; she promised.

"I don't know how we found the strength; but
desperation will make you strong. We got his body
and dragged him to the back of the house where his
car was. We managed to put him in the back seat.
We wasn't sure what we was gonna do yet, but we
had to put mama's gun back and clean up the blood
as best we could. We had to hurry before our mama
got back. We were in the middle of wiping' up the
blood, when my mama burst in the door. She started

hollering' when she saw us. She stopped when she noticed the blood. She looked at our faces, then around the room. She asked what we two heifers did. I started crying. Clarisse didn't say anything. She asked us again, and then started running through the house callin' for, Joe. She asked us what we did to him. We still hadn't answered. She went to the kitchen, and was about to turn around when she saw the blood near the back door.

"She ran out back to the car. She started screamin'; calling Joe's name over and over again. She tried to wake him up, but couldn't. She ran back into the house, threatening us. She told us we was gonna rot in jail for what we did. She grabbed the keys to the car; she was taking him to the hospital. Clarisse told her it was no use, he was dead. She slapped her across the face. Clarisse told her not to drive the car, it wasn't safe. Mama didn't listen.

"I looked at Clarisse, scared, wonderin' what we were gonna do. Clarisse told me not to worry. It was all over. And none of it was our fault. She had us finish cleaning up, like nothin ever happened. I didn't understand how she could be so sure and calm.

"Later, someone came knockin on the door, saying that our mama and Joe was jes in an automobile accident. They said that they must've lost control, and slammed into the refinery jes over the bridge. It exploded on impact.

"I couldn't believe it at first. As much as I hated my mama at that time, and I did want her dead; when it actually happened...I—I couldn't believe it. Clarisse didn't bat an eye. I don't know exactly what happened to cause that car to lose control, but I know my sister knew, and she took that secret to the grave with' her. We never spoke on it. Not once.

"I jes knew God was gonna get me for killin' Joe and my mama. I was so scared. But Clarisse told me to forget about it. That nothin that happened was my fault; especially not my mama's death, or defending myself from the likes of Joe. But I couldn't. I couldn't let go of what happened to me, or the fact that I killed someone, and caused my mama her life, too. I was haunted every night. I swear, my mama reached out from the grave and made my life a livin hell. I closed my eyes, she was there. I walk around the corner; I could feel her watchin' me. Clarisse tried everything to make me believe that I didn't have nothin' to worry about.

"When I finally had Nathan, I couldn't even looks at him without seein', Joe. He didn't favor him, but that's all I could see. I didn't wants nothin to do with him. God forgive me, but I left him with Clarisse, and I ran off. I ran and didn't look back. I was in a bad place mentally. I was jes like Nadine— maybe worse. I never thought I would ever leave, Busby; but I found myself on my way to New York, to Miss Lorelei, your daddy's Aunt. She took me in, and showed me love. And if it weren't for her and your daddy; I would have never come back...never."

CHAPTER 26

BYRON'S HEAD ROLLED BACK. He stumbled in and out of consciousness. His body felt like a Mack truck had run over it a few dozen times. He hoped, for a brief second, that Big Ty had a change of mind, and was going to let him live. He quickly gave up that notion when he felt a blow to his ribs, and ice cold water hit his face causing a stinging sensation. His body somewhat numb, aware of his surroundings, and feeling a dull pain, Byron still couldn't get his body to follow what his brain commanded.

"You coming around, nigga?" Big Ty slapped Byron across the face. "I want you to see everything coming! And know who sent you to hell!" He smacked Byron again, with the back of his gloved hand, the leather snapping hard against Byron's flesh.

Blood trickled from the right side of Byron's mouth. Gaining some control in his arms, he tried to move them, but they were tied behind him to the chair. "No..." he cried. "No man. I—I'm sorry. Please —"

"Please? Ain't this some--" Big Ty looked at Spencer.

Spencer was silent.

Big Ty turned back to Byron, and leaned in his face. "I don't have sympathy for trash," Big Ty said, coolly.

"I—I'm sorry. I—I wasn't...I wasn't trying...to
—"

"Save it, nigga!" Big Ty leaned in closer. "You
have the *audacity* to think you can take *me out*? And
use my own brother to do it?" The look in Big Ty's
eyes was chilling.

"I—I didn't—"

"What, you didn't know? So what! You really
thought you could get away with it." Big Ty shook
his head. "I always knew you were a snake from the
beginning; a high-yella snake. Well, I'm about to
help you shed your final skin!"

Byron began bawling like a baby; mumbling
incoherently.

Big Ty stepped back. He looked towards
Spencer, nodding his head.

Spencer opened up a black case on the table.

"Do it," he said to Spencer.

Spencer walked over to Byron carrying a
machete.

"What—what you doin'?" Byron looked at
Spencer in bewilderment. Spencer didn't answer.
He grabbed Byron in one hand, holding the machete
in the other.

"No! No! Oh, God. No!" Byron began
screaming, demanding the rest of his body to move
to no avail; realizing what Spencer was about to do.
"No! No!"

"This is for Nate and his daughter," Big Ty said
coldly.

Spencer lifted the machete, coming down in one fluid motion, making one clean cut.

Byron screamed, but no sound came out; his body convulsing. His head rolled back, then forth, his gaze resting upon Big Ty.

Big Ty stood in front of Byron, silent. He placed a gun to the middle of Byron's forehead. A single tear ran down Byron's face.

"I do know how to show mercy," said Big Ty, his voice void of all emotion. "This one's for me," he said, pulling the trigger; the silencer stifling the sound of the shot.

Big Ty turned to Spencer. "Let's go. We're late for dinner. You know how Mama is." Big Ty handed the gun to Spencer, and then fixed his scarf. He looked at Spencer. "Make sure you clean yourself. You know how your grandmother is."

CHAPTER 27

EMMA SAT AT HER KTCHEN TABLE, nursing a warm glass of Mulberry wine. Calvin and Anna-Leigh were over to Shelby and Richard's. Everyone else was still sleeping; she saw no need in preparing a big breakfast. She doubted if anyone had an appetite, anyway. She wondered if her family would ever be the same.

She bowed her head, all cried out from last evening. She had no more tears, just heartache and regrets. Emma felt as though her heart had been wrenched from her chest. That she had singlehandedly caused her family to suffer great pain, because of her wretched past.

Why, God? Why couldn't I spare my chilren? They don't deserve it, Lord. Emma shook her head.

Emma stood, not sure what to do, then deciding to go out to the gazebo. She needed to be alone, away from this house, away from her family. She grabbed a sweater from the back of the door in the mud room. She reached in her apron pocket and got her cigarettes. She turned, and looked around her kitchen, sighing deeply, a loneliness filling her heart. Weighing even heavier on her mind was what, and how she was going to tell Macon, and when. Emma's chest grew tight. She turned and slipped through the back door, being sure to not to make too much noise.

J7R

It felt like the longest walk. Emma could see the beginning of a sunrise. She sat quietly, wrapping the sweater tightly around her. She lit a cigarette, and leaned her head back. She drew in long, and held it for a moment before finally exhaling. She watched as rings of smoke circled to the top. She laughed to herself. *Jes like my life...up in smoke!*

The look on her children s' faces burned in her mind; especially that of Calvin's. She knew he was the most devastated. She always knew he would be. Despite his rough exterior, Calvin was the one with the tender heart, and the easiest hurt. He'd been that way all his life. Maybe she babied him too much when he was first born, then didn't give him enough attention when the other children came along.

Calvin was right: he did have Nathan. They were inseparable. Calvin was Nathan's shadow. How could Emma not see that they would still maintain a close bond? And it was for that same reason that she knew that Calvin felt betrayed by Nathan, as well. Oh, he was sure enough angry with his mama; but he was also angry with Nathan for not telling him about this, and so many other things. Calvin was feeling left out, and abandoned. She understood her son, she understood all of children. She knew each one's strengths and weaknesses.

Emma didn't believe that Calvin would get over this quickly. Even after hearing the whole truth. Calvin was not only hurt, but angry. He sometimes allowed that to pull him away from his family—one of his weaknesses. Emma wondered if he and Nathan became close again when he and his father had that argument about six years ago.

     Calvin hadn't spoken to his father for an entire month. Emma called Nathan and asked him to speak to his brother. She remembered Calvin wanted to quit school and teaching, to enlist in the service. Albert wasn't hearing of it. Junior was already over there, and he wasn't going to have both of his sons gone.

     "Listen, son. You have a wife to thinks about. There is no need for you to go into that godforsaken war! You need to stay where you are needed...at home!"

     "But Pop, I can still teach when I come home. Anna-Leigh understands. How come—"

     "No! You may not make it back home alive. Did you think of that? I've been in war, son. And if you don't haves to go, then ain't no needs for you to be volunteering'. Stay in school, and continue teaching. That's where you belong. You ain't cut for war," Albert told his son.

     "But Junior *is*? Are you trying to say I'm, too weak; I cannot cut it? That, I'll get myself killed?"

     "No! That's not what I'm sayin', son. Calvin, you and Junior are two different people. Junior is tougher in some ways than you are. Do you understand?"

     "Yes, I understand. You believe I'm, too weak, a coward! And Junior is the strong one—just like you. I'm the weak one, unable to fight for myself!"

"No! Son, that's not what I'm sayin' at all. You don't have a mean bone in your body. You have always been the peace maker, not the one to fight. Listen Calvin, I know what war can do to you, do to your mind. If you are one that leans closer toward a peaceful disposition, rather than confrontation, war will eat you up and spit you out. It will mess with' your mind, and never lets it go. Even if you make it back home, you will never be the same. Calvin, I know you don't want to hear this. But you are not a fighter. You are a teacher. By nature, you are a peacemaker. And son, I'm tellin' you now; Vietnam will eat you, and spits you out faster than you can blink."

Calvin was angry and hurt. It only proved Albert's point the more. Calvin knew his father was right. He had no business enlisting. Emma knew, however, why Calvin wanted to enlist: to make his father proud of him. So he could finally say that he and his father had something in common, just as Junior had. Although Calvin was older, he envied Junior and Albert's relationship. Calvin still didn't realize how proud his father was of him. Albert's heart filled with joy to see his son accomplish so much in life, and have a family of his own and to already own his own home. Yet, Calvin always felt like he was in competition with Junior. Nathan had brought a balance to the equation. And when he left, Calvin felt it most—perhaps more than Emma.

Emma sat back, folding her arms across her chest. She was exhausted. The sun was barely up when she felt her eyelids grow heavy. Her body ached just as much as her soul. She rested her head on the lattice, closing her eyes.

"Lord, Emma Jean here." Emma began to pray, "I know I have made a mess of things here. I should have told my chilren long times ago the truth. I ask that you would forgives me for that. I really can'ts complain, seeing how good You have been to me and mine. But, Lord, if You can see Your way to stop by here, jes one more time, I'd surely appreciates it. I knows I doesn't deserve it. Father, you have shown me much grace. But it ain't for me this time. It's for my chilren and my grand baby. I know. I'm finally sayin' it out loud. My grand baby, Macon. Lord, I don't even knows how to begin to tells her the truth. I can only imagines how she gonna takes it. But God, I trusts you to help me with that.

"Father, I especially prays for my son, Calvin. Father, I had no idea jes how much losing Nathan had affected him. My son is hurtin', Lord. And I am sorry for my hurtin' him with my lies and all. He don't deserves to be hurtin' so bad, but he is, and I can't change that. As much as I wish I could; I knows I can't. All I can do is continue to loves him. He's my son, but I know he was Yours before he was mine. So, I'm trustin' in You to takes care of him. Heal his heart, and please, Father, please heal our relationship. It jes broke my heart to see him looks at me like that. Bless him and Anna-Leigh. Let them gets stronger and stronger as husband and wife. Let him cling to his wife, Lord. Because I knows she loves him greatly. Let him, let her in. Don't let him shut her out. Not now. Watch over Ella. Help my son to find comfort in his little girl, and strength in his wife. And if it's not too much to ask, bless them with some more babies.

"Father, I asks You to please watch over Junior. Let him be there for his brother. Don't let them pull further apart. They's family, and they need to sticks together; especially brothers. Thank You for bringing Camille into his life. She is jes what he needs. She's such a sweet girl, and so smart. She brings my son balance, and she has brought him much comfort and healing from his past. Thank You for that.

"I know Shelby gonna be jes fine. Shelby has Richard, and he is good for her. He jes like my Albert: strong, compassionate and thoughtful. I knows they fixin' to move at the ends of this week, and it's gonna breaks my heart some more. But it'll be goods for Calvin and Anna-Leigh to not be alone. Please grant them Your favor, and sees to it that they don't fuss too much. Lord knows how brothers and sisters can be some times. But I trusts You with that one, too. And bless them soon with a baby, too. I know Shelby's been tryin'. Even though she doesn't say it, I know she wants a baby real bad. Bless her womb, Father, so she may know what I feel, being her mother. There never was a more deserving daughter than my, Shelby. She'd make a great mama.

"Let me be a good listener to Deeney. Father, don't lets my past stop her. But let it make her strong. She's a feisty one. But she's also my baby. And I wants her to have what is best for her. She's a spitfire sometimes. And that scares me; because I see so much of me in her when I was that age. So, I ask that You would keep her safe and her head on straight. 'Cause, I definitely don't wants her given her daddy no heart attacks or nothin'."

Emma stopped for a moment, yawning. She stretched out her arms, and tightened her sweater around her arms before continuing, her eyes becoming heavier.

"While I gots Your attention, remember Al-B. Father, You indeed blessed me with a good man. A strong, capable, beautiful black man. I couldn't have asked for a more perfect soul-mate. Surely You knew what You were doing when You sent him to me. And I knows it were You that sent him. Because as soon as Al-B came into my life, it started to get better. Keep him healthy and strong. Don't let him worries about me so much, 'cause I know he does. Bless him real good, Lord. He always asks me, what would he do without me? But in my heart, I wonders what would I do without him? And where would I be, if You never sent him along? I already knows the answer to that, so You don't has to say it. I prays I'm a good wife to him. I pray that I have made him as happy as he has made me. I knows for sure I didn't deserve him; but I'm so happy You gave him to me anyways.

"Lord, thanks You for my sistah, Lynorra. I couldn't have asks for a better friend. She has been here for me and never once judged me, or complained. All she has done is shown me love. And for that I am very grateful. She is a blessin' and deserves to be treated as such, along with her chilren. Keep Matthew, Lynnie-Mae, and James Perry, healthy and safe. Let them stay strong. And gives my sistah the strength she needs to get through her trials. I can only hopes that I am there for her, as she has been for me. Now Lord, You knows right well hows I feel concernin' Reverend Washington. There have never been any love lost between us. But that's Your man of the cloth. So— I'm gonna tries and keeps my mouth off him. But I'd be lyin' if I said I didn't want to see some fire put under his feet. Then I thinks, who am I to judge? I knows you said in the good book, 'let him who has no sin, cast the first stone', and we both knows, I've gots too many to be throwin' anything at anybody. But I do ask, that You look out for Lynorra. She don't deserve no more pain in her life. She too sweet a person to be someone's scratchin' post. Well, you know what I mean. Jes bless her.

"I guess it wouldn't be right of me to asks for forgiveness if I couldn't at least prays for Nadine. You did say, we supposed to pray for our enemies. And Lord, I do—even after all she has done to me and my family—has love in my heart for her. I won't lie—it ain't much. 'Cause she nearly destroys that last night. But she was my son's wife, and she is the mother of my grandchild. And I know too much 'bout her not to have at least a little sympathy for her. I'm afraid for her, Lord. Nadine is hell bent on destroying what's left of her life, and she looks as though she gonna win. Nathan asked me to reach out to her; to extend her an olive branch. Well, it ain't easy when she keeps tryin' to bites my hand off, and destroy my family. All I asks of You, Lord, is that You grab her before the Devil gets her for good. Because, no matter how much Macon thinks she hates her mama now; I knows for certain, if anything was to happen to Nadine now, Macon would never be the same, and she would be haunted, jes like I was. And I don't wants that for my grand baby. So please, get a hold of Nadine, and yoke her up by the collar before she destroys herself and Macon, in the process.

"All this, I pray, in the name of Jesus. Amen."

Emma stirred on the bench. The sun had fully risen. Its heat felt good on her skin. She looked towards the sky, yawning, and closed her eyes once more. Leaning back, resting her head, she drifted off into a deep sleep.

CHAPTER 28

NADINE'S BODY ACHED. Her head pounded in her skull like it was trying to escape. Emma really whipped her good. Not that she could blame her. Nadine shook her head. *What in the hell was wrong with her? Why did she mess up everything good in her life?* Nadine's heart ached knowing that her own child—her own flesh and blood—hated her enough to try and kill her. She wished she could believe what Albert said, that Macon wouldn't have done it. Yet, the hate in Macon's eyes was real. Nadine could blame Emma for the rest of her life, until the day she died. But she knew that there was no one to blame but herself. She was pathetic! She hated herself more than Macon could ever hate her.

What kind of mother was she? Who in the hell marries the man that raped their daughter? What kind of mother never looks for her child that was stolen from her? What kind of *woman* would allow herself to become someone like she had? Nadine didn't know the answers.

Once again, Emma was right—she was on a collision course with death, and she had not cared. She wanted to die. At least, she thought, death would stop her pain. Macon would be better off. No one will ever know just how much it hurt her to see the hate in her daughter's eyes. To know, that she hurt her child as much as her family had hurt her. She recognized the look in Macon's eyes all too well. For it was the same look she saw in the mirror many times growing up. All Macon did was love her, and all *she* did was destroy her daughter. Nadine believed that there was a special place in hell just for her, right alongside Byron. It was a shame that Nathan—from his grave—was doing more for their daughter than she.

Nadine rubbed her backside as she walked from the train station. For the first time in two years, she had no desire to get high. She had no craving for heroin. "I guess, having your own child try to kill you will do it for you," she whispered to herself. For the first time in years, Nadine felt she knew what she needed to do. She thought about it during her train ride into, Philly. She needed a change; a change of everything. The very first thing she needed to do was to get rid of Byron, and get her life back; for her, for Macon, and for her grandchild.

Nadine made her way to the taxi stand. She tightened her coat, and pulled her hat over her ears. The cold had bitterness to it. It was a far cry from the warm weather down South. Nadine shivered, pulling her purse towards her, looking for an available taxi. She needed to get home. She was sure that Byron had been looking for her—if he was even there. She didn't know exactly what Big Ty was up to; but she really didn't want to know. As she neared a taxi, someone grabbed her by the elbow. Nadine whipped around. Something told her that Byron was no longer a factor.

Spencer led her to a waiting car.

"How come I get the feeling I'm not going to like this very much?" Nadine said looking at

17

Spencer.

Spencer shrugged his shoulders. "I'm just the driver," was all he said, as he pointed her towards the waiting car.

Nadine followed. Spencer was a young man of few words. It was no use in trying to get anything from him. Big Ty wanted to see her. Hell! He already knew she was back in Philly. This was *definitely* not good.

Nadine recognized the neighborhood she was in, as she looked out the window. It was South Dorchester, another Philly suburb. They had many older homes and working class people in this part. It was one of the first neighborhoods that she and Nathan had considered.

She had never been to this house before. It was a nice older home, with lots of family photos and nick-knacks. Nadine walked towards a piano that was adorned with hundreds of photos. She looked at the pictures. *Must be of the family that lives here*, she thought. She looked around studying her surroundings. *Why on earth would Big Ty bring her here?* Spencer had walked her in, and said he'd be right back, as he went upstairs. That was five minutes ago.

Just as Nadine was turning to look out the window again, an elderly woman walked in, carrying a tray with food. She must have been in her late sixties, early seventies, Nadine guessed. The woman smiled at her, as she placed the tray on the dining room table.

"Have a seat, baby. And takes off that coat

before you catch pneumonia. I'll be with you in a minute."

Nadine started to say something, but the woman had already gone back into the kitchen. Nadine just stood there, not sure what to do. "What in the *hell* is going on?" she said, in low voice.

The elderly woman came back out, this time carrying a teapot. She looked at Nadine and smiled. She placed the teapot on the table. Placing her hands on her hips, she walked towards Nadine and asked: "What's the matter? You still chilled, baby? I know its cold out there today. Would you like a cup of tea, or maybe some hot coffee?" she said helping Nadine take her coat off.

Nadine still didn't understand why she was at this house, and who this woman was. "Uh, no thank you. Excuse me. I don't want to seem rude or anything..."

"Yes," the woman said, looking at her smiling. "What is it, sugar?"

"Who are you? And why am I here?"

The old woman laughed. "I see Tyrell didn't bother to tell you, you were invited for dinner. *That boy!*" She shook her head. "He probably had Spencer just pick you up, and brings you over here, huh?" She looked at Nadine, studying her face. "Ooh, honey, what happened to your face?" she asked, touching the left side of Nadine's face.

Nadine winced, putting her hand to her face. She'd forgotten all about that. "Oh, it's nothing. Just had a run in with a wall," she said.

"Hmm, that's some wall. Sure packed a mighty punch. Let me get you some ice." The woman turned to leave. "There's a bathroom to your right. You can freshen up in there. Dinner will be ready in a few minutes," she said over her shoulder before disappearing through the doors again.

"Damn, she did it again." Nadine shook her head. As she was walking to the bathroom, she stopped. "Did she say, *Tyrell*?" Nadine laughed. "She must be Big Ty's—wait!—*Tyrell's* mother. Why in the hell did he bring me here?" Nadine continued to the bathroom.

When Nadine came out of the bathroom, Big Ty and Spencer were sitting at the dining room table.

"Uh, thanks for the ride and all," she said, walking towards them. "But can you tell me what I'm doing here...at this house?" Nadine asked Big Ty.

"I see you had an eventful trip," he said pointing to her face.

Nadine touched her face. "Well, let's just say I made quite an impact on someone."

"Seems like *they* the ones that had the impact," Big Ty laughed. "Guess your reunion didn't go quite so well?" He said raising a glass to her. "Here, have something to drink, and take a seat." He pointed to a chair near him.

"No thank you. I just want to go home."

"I'm sure you do. And you will, as soon as we finish dinner."

"Listen, this is...nice of you and all. But—"

"Oh, don't get it twisted. This has nothing to do with being nice. My mother has wanted to see you. I felt today was as good a day as any. Now," he stood up, and pulled a chair out. "I suggest you sit down, and show some respect for my mother. You are *her* guest and I will not discuss it any further," Big Ty said, waiting for Nadine to sit.

Nadine didn't attempt to argue. She knew there was more to Big Ty bringing her here than he let on. She wondered what reason his mother, of all people, could have in wanting to see her. She didn't know the woman; although she seemed nice.

As Nadine took a seat, Big Ty's mother walked in, carrying a basket of dinner rolls, and an ice pack. She looked at Nadine and smiled, handing her the ice pack.

Big Ty pulled a chair out for his mother. Spencer took the basket of rolls and placed it on the table.

"Thank you baby," she said, patting Spencer on the cheek. "So," she said turning back to Nadine, "I sees you gonna stay for supper. That's good. You look like you could stand some home-cooking. You need a little meat on them bones."

Spencer laughed.

Nadine didn't know how to answer. "I guess I could stand to gain a few pounds," she smiled weakly, unsure of what else to say.

"Mama, according to you, everyone needs to gain some weight," Big Ty said, sitting down.

"Well, it's true. And," she began, slapping Big

Ty's hand, "how comes you didn't tells this young woman where she was coming? I taught you better than that."

"I didn't have a chance. I had some business to take care of," Big Ty answered.

His mother stared at him sternly. "Tyrell, one of these days..." she raised her hands to the sky. "Lord, gets a hold of my son." She shook her head. "And Spencer, too," she added.

"Not today, Mama. I'm sure the good, Lord has heard enough about me," Big Ty stated.

"Not if you keep doing what the devil wants," she said. "But, I believe God hears me."

"Yeah? How you know that?" Big Ty asked smiling at his mother.

She touched his hand, and reached for Spencer's. "Because you here at my table, ain't you?" she asked, looking at one then to the other.

"Okay, Mama," Big Ty submitted. "We're here, and we're gonna have a good meal."

Nadine watched the dynamics between Big Ty and his mother. *What the hell was this; the black version of the God Father?* This was, too much, for her. *A gangster and his mother; good God!*

Big Ty's mother looked up at Nadine. Smiling, she said, "Since my son has lost the good sense that God gave him, let me say that I thank you for coming, Nadine."

"Thank you, Miss..."

"Oh sugar, I'm sorry. I guess the apple don't fall far from the tree after all. All this time, I just started talking and never once introduced myself. You can call me Ms. Smalls," she smiled, extended her hand.

"Thank you, Ms. Smalls." Nadine shook her hand.

"Now, let us pray and eat this food before it gets cold." Ms. Smalls had everyone hold hands as she prayed.

Although dinner had gone well, Nadine was anxious to leave. She wanted to deal with Byron once and for all, and get things in order. Throughout dinner, her mind wandered, and she kept seeing the look in Macon's eyes. She really needed to go. She still hadn't learned why Ms. Smalls wanted her to come for dinner.

Big Ty and Spencer excused themselves after dinner, saying that they would be back in a minute. Ms. Smalls had finished clearing the table. Nadine offered to help; but Ms. Smalls insisted she was a guest, and wouldn't hear of it. There was something familiar about Ms. Smalls; something that struck Nadine as if she had met her before. But she knew she hadn't.

"Come, sugar," Ms. Smalls said holding out her hand to Nadine. "Come with me for a minute."

Nadine took her hand, as Ms. Smalls led her to the kitchen. Pointing to a chair, she asked Nadine to sit. Nadine obliged. The older woman sat down across from her.

"I know you're probably wondering since you

came here, *what does this old woman want from me?*"

Nadine shook her head. "No. No. I was just wondering—"

"It's okay. I understand," she smiled knowingly, taking Nadine's hand and patting it. "Baby, it's okay. I'd been saying the same thing myself," she smiled.

Ms. Smalls reached into her apron pocket, and pulled out an envelope. She held it in her hands, closed her eyes, as though she were praying, and then looked directly at Nadine; the expressions of her face now somber.

"Nadine, I want you to know that I loved your Nathan. Yes I did."

Nadine was silent. She remembered Big Ty telling her something to that affect.

"He was such a darling young man; strong, clever and wise. I'm sure his mama was proud of him."

Nadine flinched at that statement. "Tha— thank you. I'm sure she was extremely proud."

"Yes, I gathered so from the way that Nathan carried himself and his treatment of others. He was a real go getter. You don't find, too many, like him around these days." She smiled and was silent for a moment. "Anyway," she said, looking into Nadine's eyes, "Nathan helped me more than I can say. I spent some time with him near the end. I also met your lovely daughter..."

"Macon," Nadine whispered.

"Yes. Macon. Oh what a lovely young lady, and so beautiful. She favors you, you know?"

"I don't know about that. She's much more beautiful than me," Nadine said quietly.

"Oh stop. You're beautiful. You've just been through some really tough times," she said, patting Nadine's hand. "But, I got a feeling you gonna be okay."

"I don't know about that," Nadine stated, unintentionally out loud.

"You need faith, honey. Without it, we all lost. But I don't want to preach to you; but I would like to encourage you; become a friend maybe? And perhaps," she held up the envelope in her hand, "this will help you as well." She handed it to Nadine.

Nadine took the envelope, turning it over in her hand. "I don't understand."

"It's from Nathan. He wanted me to give it to you."

Nadine's eyes grew wide.

"I know I've had it for some time. But he told me that I would know when to give it to you. Nathan felt that you may not receive it from someone else. But for someone reason—only God and him knew—he felt that you would receive it from me. I asked him was he sure? He was adamant about it."

"That was Nathan."

"All I know is sugar, he loved you *very, very much*. And he was awfully worried about you and his baby girl. Now, I had plans to gives this to you shortly after Nathan passed, but I wasn't doing so well myself, and my son told me you kind of had your hands full. So I waited. I kept asking Tyrell about you, and he finally told me today that you were coming. I'm so glad you did. I'm just sorry I couldn't get it to you sooner. But," she took Nadine's hand, "God is always on time. And I have a feeling that you need this letter today. It just may be an answer to a prayer."

Nadine stared at Ms. Smalls for a moment, tears welling in her eyes. Then it hit her; she knew who Ms. Smalls reminded her of: her grandmother. Grandma Jackson. Nadine put her hand over her mouth to stifle her cry. The tears fell from her eyes. *That's why Nathan gave her the letter, and no one else.* He wanted her to meet Ms. Smalls. Yes, Ms. Smalls was just like her grandmother. Nadine's chest felt heavy with ache.

"You alright, sugar? Can I get you something?" She looked at Nadine with deep concern in her eyes.

Nadine held up her hand and shook her head. "No. No. I'm—I'm fine. Just a little bit overwhelmed," she managed to say, taking the tissue that Ms. Smalls was offering her.

"I understand, sugar." Ms. Smalls stood up. "Well, I'm gonna go in the living room and gives you some privacy. Unless...unless you want to reads it in the privacy of your own home?" she asked.

"No. No. I want to read it now. I don't think I can wait until I get home."

"Okay. I'll just be in the living room if you

need anything."

"Thank you, Ms. Smalls."

"You're welcomed, sugar." Ms. Smalls went into the living room, closing the kitchen door behind her.

Nadine sat at the table, holding the letter in her hand, too scared to read it, too scared not too. She put her hand over her mouth, stifling her cries. Her heart was racing, and all kinds of thoughts running through her mind. What could Nathan possibly have written? She was awful those last couple of months. She wasn't even there when he took his last breath. She betrayed him, and their family. She used him, and blamed him for things that were not his fault. She purposely tried to drive him away. Yet, Nathan never left. He never blamed her. Instead, he loved her. Yes, he yelled, screamed, and a few times threatened to leave. But, he never did. And Nadine knew he wouldn't. Her last words to him now rang loudly in her ear. *"Stop trying to save me, Nathan! You can't. I don't need a savior. So just leave it alone! Just die already!"*

Nadine shook her head; tears ran down her face, remembering the awful things she said. *How could she be so heartless?*

Still, Nathan loved her. She saw the hurt in his eyes. And his voice shook as he tried to speak. *"Don't worry; I think...I...have...that one...covered. Just do me a favor? Remember...that our...daughter... loves you...and...so...do I, Dee Dee. Forever...no matter...what."*

Nathan was the only one who ever called her, DeeDee. It was his nickname for her. He only called her Nadine when he was truly angry and disgusted with her. But not once, not once while he was in the hospital those last four months, did he ever call her Nadine. It was DeeDee, all the way to the end.

Nadine hung her head, closing her eyes for a moment. She held the envelope tight in her hands. She lifted her head, and wiped her face. "C'mon, girl. You can do this. Just read the damn letter," she told herself.

Nadine carefully tore the letter at one end, running her finger along its length. She took her time to unfold the letter; her heart breaking from the first line. She put the letter down for a moment, covering her mouth. "Damn you, Nathan. Damn you."

She lifted the letter again, this time reading it in its entire.

Dear DeeDee,

I know that I do not have much time left; so I wanted to write this letter to the woman I love; to my beautiful black queen. The woman that I married; the woman that I fell in love with so long ago; who I first laid eyes on at, Lula Mae's Rib shack. That was the day my life changed. I never told you; but I knew then that I was going to be with you for the rest of my life.

DeeDee, you have no idea how I wish

and pray to God that I could go back in time and make everything better. I wish that I could have taken away all your pain. I wish that I had been a better husband to you. Maybe I put, too much, pressure on you; I don't know. Maybe I just didn't understand how deep your hurt was inside. For this, I am sorry. Please know that I never stopped loving you. Never. You were the only woman that held my heart.

Remember the first time we kissed? We were dancing to 'You Send Me', by Sam Cooke. And you surely did. I knew then that I had to marry you; because I didn't want any other man to have you. You belonged to me, and I belonged to you. We were perfect for one another. I wanted to fill your life with joy and happiness. I think we had that for a while. Don't you?

At one time, I thought maybe we should have stayed down South. But the truth is I don't believe location had anything to do with what went wrong. We both were running— running from our past and the hurt that we experienced. The only problem was; I got through mine, but you didn't get through yours. And I should have helped with that. I'm sorry, and ask that you would forgive me.

Never think for one moment that I ever stopped loving you, or that you are all alone in this world. I know you, DeeDee. Better than anyone. Better than you know yourself sometimes. And I'm worried about you and Macon. More so you. Why? Because I know you are still struggling with some very strong demons. I know you don't want to hear this, but you need help, DeeDee. You cannot do this alone any longer.

I'm sure by now, that you have spoken to Emma. I asked her to look after Macon— only until you can. I know you love our baby girl. But you need some time to yourself. I wanted to tell you about the social service people; but I couldn't. Anyway, I asked my Emma to take care of her. Please, DeeDee, please try and get along for Macon's sake. And I trust you to keep my confidence about her being my Mama. That's my mama's place to share that, and no one else.

Please know that she really does love you. You have no idea what my mother has done for you. Remember when we first saw our house, and how you fell in love with it? It was way more than we could afford, but you had your heart set on it. Well, it was Mama that gave me the money. I tried to talk you into something else; but you had already fallen in love with it. I called her the next day. She told me that maybe this was what you needed. So she wired me the money the next day from her own personal account. She never told anyone. She made me promise not to tell you. She said it was best if you thought it came from me. She said you deserved a new start after all you had been through. She understood what it was like to be a new mother and wife, and have gone through so much at a young age. She said you didn't need to know anything about her involvement. She told me that if I was happy, then that's all that mattered. And I was happy. So please, give Mama a break, and know that deep down, underneath all her brashness, she really does love you.

Words can't express how much I already miss you and Macon. Thank you for a beautiful daughter. No father could be prouder. Each day I see her, she reminds me so much of you; her smile, her sense of humor. She is you, DeeDee. And she loves you so much. She really worries about you. I try and assure her that everything will be okay. Keep her safe. I know you would give your life, before letting harm come to her. However, in order for you to do that, you must be well. So— please get the help you need, so that you can be the mother that Macon needs and deserve. I love you, DeeDee.

There is so much I want to say to you. I want you to know something. I know about the baby boy you had before you came to, Busby. I also learned about Celia being your real mother. I guess we had more in common than we thought, as well as you and Mama? That's probably why you two butt heads so much; you are too much alike. In any case, I knew. And it made me understand so much

more. How did I know? I received a letter
from your father; well, I guess your uncle,
sometime last year. It was a real surprise.
Celia forwarded it to me at the job, so it
wouldn't come to the house. He told me
everything. Forgive me for not telling you
sooner. But I figured since you had not told me
in all these years, you didn't want to. So I left
it alone.

    Now, as I lay here in this hospital bed,
dying, I realized many of my mistakes. I fear I
should have told you, and maybe it would have
been what you needed. But then this cancer
came, and I forgot about the letter. I want you
to know that it's never, too late, to make
amends. As long as you have breath in your
body, it's never, too late, for redemption and to
start all over. That's what I want for you,
DeeDee. God, I love you so much, and I want
you to have a fresh start. And I think the best
way to do that is to get out of Philadelphia,
and go find your son. DeeDee, you can't keep
hiding from your past. There is nowhere else
to run. And I believe with all my heart, that
you deserve some happiness. Find that missing
part of you. Sell the house and move back
down South. It don't have to be South Carolina;
maybe Georgia. That way, you'll be able to
search for your son. Make a fresh start for you
and Macon. She'll be grown soon, and going
off to college. You need this time together. I
want this for you. I want this for our daughter.

    By now, you have met Ms. Smalls. Isn't

she something? She reminded me of your grandmother. That's what made me think to give her the letter. I know if Mama gave it to you; you'd probably torn it up before reading it. More importantly, I wanted you to meet Ms. Smalls, and be reminded of someone you loved dearly. To make you think of down South. Please, DeeDee, sell the house and get out of Philly.

I have set up trust funds for you and Macon. By the way, I knew about your secret account. Come on, how could I not? But I was proud to see that you were thinking for yourself. And that's what I need for you to do now. The trust funds will be available a year after my death. You will receive all papers and instructions. I had them mailed to Mama for safe keeping, just in case you are still having some trouble. Which I pray you are not.

Listen, my love. You made me happy. Know that I forgave you long ago. And no matter how much you said you wanted me gone, I knew in your heart that was just you, trying to protect yourself. Please know, I loved you with all of me, and I forgive you for EVERYTHING. Do you understand me? Everything, DeeDee. I miss you. I miss who we were. I miss my wife, my friend, my lover. I miss your laugh and your sense of humor. I know you miss it, too. I miss holding you in my arms. I miss making love to you, and holding you afterward. I miss the scent of your hair,

*and the sway in your hips, and the soft
tenderness of your lips. I am so grateful for my
memories; because they keep me alive. I love
you forever.*

*Here's to the woman I love. To the
woman I fell in love with. To the woman I will
love even when my essence leaves this earth. To
my beautiful, black queen. You are loved.
Always.*

With All My Heart and Soul,

Nathan

Nadine cried in silence. She wrapped her
arms around herself, rocking back and forth, crying
for the love of her life. She cried, finally feeling the
loss of Nathan. She cried for the love she would
never feel again. She cried for the touch she would
never experience again. She cried for the man that
knew her better than she knew herself. She cried for
the loss of her heart and her soul. Most of all, she
cried, knowing that Nathan loved her more than she
loved him, or even herself.

Nadine cried for another half an hour, before
wiping her face and saying good bye to Ms. Smalls.
She thanked her for her kindness and for all she did.
Ms. Smalls asked her to stay the night. She didn't
think she should be alone. Nadine declined, stating
that she needed to get home, and start getting her
life together. Ms. Smalls understood. She asked
Nadine to wait for Tyrell or Spencer to come back, so

that they could give her a ride home. Nadine called a taxi instead. She really wanted to be alone. She kissed Ms. Smalls on the cheek, and promised to stay in touch. She thanked her again for all she'd done, and agreed that the letter was exactly what she needed. Ms. Smalls hugged her tightly, and reassured her that God will work it out for her; just have faith. Nadine smiled.

During the ride home, Nadine, flooded with so many emotions, hadn't realized the yellow police tape on her front door, nor the police officers and detectives until she was a few feet away.

"What?" She looked around the front of her house.

"Ma'am," a detective startled her.

Nadine turned around. "What's going on here?"

"Is this your home, ma'am?"

"Yes. What's this tape doing on my door?"

"I'm Detective Johnson. I'm gonna have to ask you to come with me."

"For what?"

"Please come with me," the detective insisted.

"I ain't going anywhere until someone tells me what the hell is going on."

"Are you, Mrs. Duvall?"

"Cooper."

"You said this was your house?"

"Yes," Nadine said.

"You lived here...with your husband?"

"Yes. And my daughter."

"Where's your daughter at?"

"With family. I don't understand, what's going on?"

"Please, are you Mrs. Nadine Duvall?" he asked, looking at his police pad.

"No...Yes. I mean..."

"Can you please come with me?"

"Why?"

"There's been an incident in your home, ma'am. I need you to come with me," the detective answered, leading Nadine to a waiting car.

"What kind of incident?" Nadine asked.

"It concerns your husband. We need you to identify the body."

"*Body?*" Nadine whispered. "*In my house?*" she said to herself. Nadine didn't say another word as the detective helped her into the car. She looked back at her house, wondering what Big Ty had done to Byron. Then it dawned on her; that's why he had her go down South. He'd planned this all along. Just then another thought occurred to her: *The police probably thought she did it.*

Oh hell!

CHAPTER 29

ALBERT STOOD AT THE BACK DOOR. He looked to see if Emma was on the back porch. He was so tired; he hadn't realized that Emma was not lying next to him. He did not like waking up without her next to him. He didn't even know when she'd gotten up. It was already nine o'clock.

"Hey Pop," Junior walked into the kitchen. "Where's Mama?"

Albert turned to his son. "I don't know. I think she might be in the gazebo."

"How was she last night? I mean—I know she wasn't doing so well; but did she say anything else?"

"No. She didn't speak at all. Which is unlike your Mama. I went to hold her, and she pulled away from me. She wouldn't let me touch her." Albert's voice choked with emotion. "Your Mama is a strong woman. *But this here*? This nearly killed her." Albert shook his head. "I knew it would."

Junior placed his hand on his father's shoulder. "I know, Pop. I have never seen Mama seem so..." Junior searched for the right word.

"Defeated?" Albert suggested.

"Yes. You know how Mama is: strong, quick tongued. I'm not used to seeing her this way."

Albert grabbed his son's hand. "I am, son. You all truly don't know *all* that your mama has had to endure; especially to keep this family strong and together. Yeah, Mama can be loud, and speaks her mind with ease."

Albert looked intently at Junior.

"There's also a part of your mama that only I know. That part of her that hurts and aches, and has nightmares. The part of her that's vulnerable. You know..." he said walking towards the back door, "... you chilren really don't know, or understands jes how far your mama will go to protects any of you."

Junior started to protest.

Albert held up his hand. "No, let me finish son. You know she loves you with fierceness; but you don't know what it cost her, and how much she fought to keep this family together. There are things that are between a man and a woman—a husband and wife. You'll find out. There are also things that stay between parents, and you'll understand when you have some chilren. Son, the depths of your mama's love is endless and it's fierce. It even goes beyond her family; her own flesh and blood. That's one of the reasons I loves her the way I do. And I'll be damned if I let anyone—even a Chile of mine, hurt her."

Junior nodded his head, conferring his understanding. "I guess we didn't do such a great job as children last night, huh?"

Albert looked into his sons eyes. "Ain't no one blaming you. It's jes that, sometimes in life we are so certain about how things should be. And when we gets our picture broken, we tend to be a bit accusatory, rather than understandin'." Albert opened the door. "But, wisdom comes with age...and with trials." With that said, he walked out the door towards the gazebo.

EMMA could hear a faint voice in the background. She didn't know if she was dreaming, or if it was real. She opened her eyes, twisting her body, and stretching her arms. "Good Lord, I done fell asleep. I wonders what time it is." She yawned, her body aching with every stretch.

"Mama?" Albert called. "You back here?"

It wasn't a dream. It was Albert she'd heard calling her.

"Yes, baby," she said, standing. "I'm back here." She smiled slightly as she saw Albert come into view. She could see the concern on his face.

"Hey, Mama," Albert pulled his wife into a hug. "You know I don't like wakin up without you next to me." He kissed her on the forehead, then the lips.

Emma wrapped her arms around her husband's waist, resting her head on his shoulder. "I know, Al-B. I'm sorry. I just couldn't sleep."

Albert squeezed Emma gently. "I know. It's okay...this time."

Emma looked at Albert, her mouth forming a slight smile.

"How're you feeling this mornin?"

"I'm doing better. I had a little chat with

Jesus."

"Is that so?" Albert smiled.

"Yes. Jes give me some time, though. I jes have so much to sift through, yet." Emma leaned into her husband's embrace.

"I understand, Mama. I understand."

"I'm scared, Albert. I don't know what's to expect no more. My chilren upsets with me. My grand baby tried to kill her mama. And how's I'm supposed to tell her the truth?" she asked, looking at Albert. "I mean, if I do, will it hurt her more?" Emma shook her head.

"Shush. Don't you worries none about that right now."

"How can I not? I mean, I've jes made a mess of everything."

Albert grabbed Emma by the shoulders. "Listen. Listen to me, Emma. You don't haves to worry, because God gonna takes care of everything. Didn't you jes say you had a little talk with Jesus?"

Emma nodded. "Yes. But—"

"There ain't no buts about it. Now you gonna haves to trust, God, Emma Jean. He ain't never failed us. And there ain't no needs to believe that He gonna starts now," Albert looked into his wife's eyes intensely. "You are a strong woman. Stronger than *anyone I* knows. Now, it's 'bout time you let someone else starts takin' care of you. Do you understands?" he asked, placing a hand under Emma's chin.

Emma started to say something when Albert

placed a finger over her lips. "All's I want is a yes," Albert said.

Emma smiled and said, "Yes."

Albert hugged her tightly, then pulled back and looked at her. "That means, you gonna let me takes care of *you*, right?"

Emma nodded.

"That means, whatever I say goes, right?"

Emma hesitated.

"Right?" Albert said, smiling. "Well, at least most of what I say...deal?"

Emma smiled. "Deal, Mr. Watson."

"Good. And don't you worry about them chilren. None of 'em. They gonna be jes fine. You'll see. We can ask Camille about Macon. And, we'll jes haves to give Calvin a little more time than the others. He's a little bruised right now. But he'll be all right. I think havin his sister, and Richard close by is gonna do a lot of good for him."

"I surely pray so," Emma said, wrapping her arm around Albert's waist side.

"Jes gotta keep the faith. God never let us down before. And He never will." Albert placed his arm around Emma's shoulder and began walking.

"I know. It's jes a little hard right now."

"I know. But that's why you got me."

"Thank, Jesus," Emma said. "I love you, Al-B," she said softly, as they walked toward the house.

"I loves you too, Mama. What would I do without you?"

J7R

"You never has to know."

"Promise?"

"Promise," Emma said, taking Albert's hand in hers.

Albert kissed her on the forehead. "Me too, Mama. I promise, too."

"**NO**. SHE WENT backs to sleep. I brought her somethin' to eats a couple of hours ago. Oh, he's fine. I jes gave him a bath not too long ago. He's in the room with Deeney right now." Emma poured hot water into a cup.

"Yes, I know. He wasn't going to, but I told him to go for at least a couple of hours. We still have bills to pay. Listen, Lynorra. I want to thanks you for Sunday night. Yes I do. Well, I'm still sayin' it anyways," laughed Emma. "Yeah, it's alright. I could use some company right 'bout now. Okay. See you in a bit." Emma hung up the phone. She poured some honey into the cup with hot water, and sat down to the table.

"Hey, Mama." Deeney walked into the kitchen, holding Nathaniel in her arms.

"Hey, baby. Everything okay?" Emma asked, getting up.

"Yes. Everything is fine," she said, her voice hushed. "I was just letting you know that I was going to lay him down in the family room. He's sleeping right now," she said, swaddling the baby. "I didn't want to put him in the room with Macon; she's

Southern~367~Comfort

still sleeping, and I didn't want to disturb her."

"Oh, okay. That's good. I'll be in there in a few minutes myself. I'm jes waitin for Lynorra."

"You okay, Mama?"

"I'm fine, suga'," Emma smiled. "Don't you worries 'bout me."

"Alright," Deeney smiled. "I love you, Mama."

"I loves you, too, baby." Emma stood and kissed her daughter on the forehead, and then placed a soft kiss on Nathaniel's, causing him to stir a bit.

"I better lay him down, before he wakes up." Deeney turned to leave.

"Deeney?"

Deeney turned around. "Yes, Mama?"

"Did I ever tell you how proud of you I am?"

Deeney smiled. "All the time."

Emma smiled. "And thanks for helpin' out with the baby."

"It's no problem. Now, we'd have a problem if he was a *screaming baby*," she laughed.

Emma laughed. "I hear you. But still, thank you. By the way, I hasn't forgotten about your birthday."

"I know."

"Any plans? You'll be seventeen. I guess I has to stop callin' you baby?"

Deeney laughed. "Well, since you asked... David has tickets to the Marvin Gaye concert in,

Atlanta. He, George Lee, and Nancy were going to drive down there. He asked if I wanted to go for my birthday," Deeney said, with hope filling her face.

Emma nodded. "Well, we have to asks your father first. I think he trusts David. Maybe you all can spends the night with Richard and Shelby, instead of driving back that night?"

"Really, Mama?" Deeney asked excitedly.

"We'll see," Emma smiled. "You deserve it anyways."

"Thank you, Mama."

As Emma watched Deeney leave to lay Nathaniel down, a knock came on the back door before opening. Emma turned, just as Lynorra was walking in.

"Hey sistah," Lynorra said. "How're you holding up? I made you a seven-up cake," she said, lifting the cake plate in her hand. "How about some coffee?" She smiled, giving Emma a hug with her free arm.

"Mm," Emma hugged her friend. "What you tryin' to do, fatten' me up?" She laughed.

"Oh girl, please. You know Albert likes some meat on them bones. And besides, ain't nothin' fat about you. You look good, Emma Jean. Makes me sick sometime," laughed Lynorra, placing the cake on the counter.

Emma put some water in the kettle. "Oh stop. These hips of mine have their own address. And you know you jes as fine as you want to be, Lynorra Washington. I see the way those men be lookin' at you. Rev better watch it!" Emma laughed.

"Now I know you have lost your mind!" Lynorra chuckled. "Artie ain't a bit concerned about me than the man on the moon!"

"What you tryin to say? You ain't gettin any?" Emma turned, putting her hands on her hips.

"The Sahara dessert is wetter than I have been in the last three months!"

"Ooh!" Emma laughed out loud, covering her mouth. "Lynorra!"

"What?" Lynorra grinned taking a seat at the table.

"You needs to cut it out. What kind of first lady are you?" Emma chided.

"*One with needs*! Shoot! You don't see Nun stomped on my forehead. But one would swears it was written across my draws! N-o-n-e! Because, that's exactly what I'm getting—none!"

Emma and Lynorra laughed until their sides ached.

Emma made two cups of coffee and cut a slice of cake for both her and Lynorra. They went into the living room, so that Emma could keep an ear out for Nathaniel and Macon.

SO, did Camille say how long it would be before you could tell Macon the truth?"

"She said to give it some time. I'd know when she was ready. It's better to let her know sooner rather than later; especially before someone else says something."

"You mean Nadine?" Lynorra sighed.

Emma nodded.

"I can't believe she did that. No, I can believe it. She's just like her Aunt Celia, in that respect. Don't care who gets hurt; just as long as they gets what they want. Now, what I'm having a hard time believing is her marrying that man."

"I did at first; but the more I thinks about it, the more it makes sense to me."

"That will never make any sense to me." Lynorra shook her head.

"Well, I look at like this; that girl is, or *was* so hooked on that heroin stuff, that she wasn't thinkin 'bout what she was doin. She jes went ahead and did it. No feelin, no thinkin, no nothin. And I knows that the one thing that Nadine hates more than me, is being alone. She can't handles it."

Lynorra reached over and felt Emma's forehead, with the back of her hand.

"What are you doin?" Emma laughed.

"Checking to see if you feel all right," Lynorra laughed. "Sounds like you gone soft."

Emma laughed, waving her hand.

"As much as I want to hate Nadine for what she did, I can't; because I actually understands her. Even though she thinks I don't, and that I hates her. But I don't. And I also know that she misses Nathan and she misses Macon. And I wouldn't be a bit surprised if havin your own Chile try and kills you, wouldn't change a person."

"I pray it's for the better."

"So do I. Truth is Lynorra, a part of me is glad the truth is out. I'm not happy with how it came out; but jes the same, it was a burden lifted. Now all I has to do is tell Macon the truths, and continue praying that Calvin will come around."

"Oh, he will. You know how stubborn he is—just like you. Give him some time. He'll come around soon. You'll see."

"I pray so. 'Cause he wasn't, too thrilled with me; even after I told them everything." Emma stood, taking Lynorra's cup. "You wants some more coffee?"

"No," Lynorra shook her head. "I'm good."

"I'll be right back. I'm gonna check on the baby."

"Alright," Lynorra called after her. "Hurry's back so I can fill you in on *my* drama." Lynorra stood and walked over to the window, looking out towards the garden. She always loved Emma's garden.

"Now," Emma said. "What's goin on?" she asked, sitting down.

Lynorra sat down across from her friend. "Remember what I was sharing with you, Sunday night?"

"Yes...about Celia. She ain't been around has she?"

Lynorra shook her head. "Not as far as I know. But I have been getting a lot of phone calls... well hang ups, anyway."

"You think it's her?"

Lynorra nodded. "I just have this feeling that

I can't shakes."

Emma shook her head in disgust. "That nasty heifer. Did you talk to Artie?"

"Um-hm. He said he hasn't heard from her in years."

"Do you believe him?"

"I want to."

"But you don't?"

"I can't." Lynorra looked sullen. "Am I wrong? I mean, I have no proof it's her. But..."

"But somethin in you is tellin you different."

"Yes. It's the same feeling I had years ago. So am I wrong, Emma? Am I wrong not to believe him?"

Emma thought for a moment before answering. She knew firsthand how devastated Lynorra was before when Artie and Celia Jackson had gotten together. Bishop Washington was not around to clean up his son's mess, or keep him on the straight and narrow this time.

"Lynorra honey, you are not that same woman as back then. You are much stronger and wiser. You know what to do. Jes make sure you positive about what's goin on. Now, I ain't one to stick up for Artie; but I will say, give him the benefit of the doubt before you makes up your mind. Make sure first. It could be somethin, or it may well be nothin. Jes be certain. Ain't no needs to yell fire, when you don't even sees no smoke."

"I understand. But I swear Emma, I have gone through too much hell being married to that man. I'll be damned if I lets him destroy me or my children. Not this time. I am not that same young, naïve girl I was back then. No, I am a different person than I was when I first came to, Busby."

"Tell me about!" Emma laughed. "You sure ain't that same girl."

"No, I'm not. I went through hell in New York with him. And if it weren't for Bishop Washington, I would never have come to, Busby. I was ready to leave Artie. But you know how Bishop was."

"Yes, he was special. Now *he* was a man of God! Not tryin to say anything against Artie; but I often wonder if he took after his mama's side or something. He is *nothin* like his father, or his brothers."

"No, I understand. I sometimes wonder myself. Artie was so different when I met him. Then —I think—I was just blinded by his good looks and his charisma." Lynorra looked at Emma.

"You *think*!"

They both laughed.

"Girl, I was young and stupid. I believed everything he told me. I *wanted* to believe it. The truth was, I was running from my own mess—out of the frying pan, and right into the fire. I'd believe just about anything he said with his slick-tongued self. And he sure knew how to sling it; even back then," Lynorra said.

"Don't they all?"

"You're right. Then we act so surprised when *we* ain't blind anymore."

"The light will do that for you. Love can make us *stupid* and *blind*. You *know* the things I did."

Lynorra laughed. "Yeah, you *were* something else. How did Albert put up with you?" she chided.

"Girl, I don't know." Emma laughed. "But I am so glad he did. Lynorra," she took her friend's hand in hers and squeezed it gently. "Make sure you certain. Because you have worked hard over the years, and I don't want to see no one's come in and mess up your family."

"I know. The thing is, Emma; it wouldn't bother me so much if Artie and I were handling our business."

"Mm."

"I mean, it's been a *couple of months*. And that ain't like Artie. Sometimes I can barely catch a breath he's so on top of me. *But lately?* It just makes me wonder." Lynorra stared down at her wedding ring. "It ain't been easy for me. I mean, *you've* been there. And, God, I am so grateful for that."

Emma nodded knowingly.

"It's just...I'm tired, Emma. I don't know if I have it in me anymore to go another round with, Artie." Lynorra shook her head. "Matt will be eighteen in two months. Lynnie will be seventeen next month. And James...he's only twelve right now; but it's been hardest on him." Lynorra looked at her friend, pain in her eyes, hurt in her voice. "Emma, I ain't ever seen anything like it—Artie acts as though he can't stand to be in the same room with James. Have you ever seen such a thing...for a father to treat their own child like that?"

"Not often; but it happens. But you know I always believed that James Perry scares his father. James Perry is jes like his grandfather. And you know the gift he has is special. He jes has a way of lookin at a person, as though he is reading their very thoughts—seeing into their soul. That's a bit scary for some people; especially someone like, Artie. You know how he and Bishop never got along; always bumping heads? It's because Bishop Washington knew his son, and could no one tell me he didn't hear straight from God. Yeah, I believe that scares Artie to see the same thing in his son."

Lynorra sat quietly, pondering what Emma had said. She, too, believed the same thing. But, it still didn't give Artie cause to treat his son in that manner. He was sometimes just down right cruel to James.

"You know, over the years, and growing up, I was taught how important the role of a Pastor's wife was. How, being a first lady is some kind of honor." Lynorra shook her head. "I sure don't feel that way. I mean, I used to—I used to think it was gonna make me important, and give me what I was missing in my life...,"

"Chile, ain't no title can give you that. Being a wife and mother is a job in itself. But add on top of that being a first lady and messin' with church folk, and you adding in a whole other set of problems."

"You ain't lying." Lynorra agreed. "But what I have learned, Emma, is that can't nobody gives you what you need in your soul but, God."

J7R

"Amen."

"Can't no one make what's wrong in you right. Can't anyone fix what's broken in your spirit, but God himself. I can honestly say, that being married to Artie, I have called on God more than I ever have. There are some times, though; that I feel God is far away. Like He has forgotten about me."

"Oh, God don't forget about us."

"Oh, I know. It just feels that way sometimes; especially when it seems like your prayers go unanswered for so long." Lynorra set her gaze upon the window. "I often ask myself: what would I be doing now if I *hadn't* married Artie? Or, what if I would have left him back then? Then I looks at my children, and couldn't even imagine my world—my life without them. You know what I mean?"

"Yes. I sure do. I asks the same questions myself."

"I don't feel superior, or better off because I am a Pastor's wife. I don't feel privileged. To be honest, I feel trapped, and like I'm being punished. I love, Artie. I really do. But I don't like him. I can't stand his ways. And I just find something wrong with him being a man of God, and treating his son the way he does. Or for that matter, having treated me the way he has over the years."

Both women sat quietly for a moment; neither saying a word, but knowing what was in the others heart. They've been friends a long time to know that their bond went beyond words. It was a knowing that each other knew the heart of the other. And just their knowing that the other was there to listen—anytime—always brought comfort.

"Aunt Emma."

Emma looked up to see Macon.

"Macon, baby. What's wrong?" Emma said, going to her.

Macon stood shaking, holding herself, crying. "I—I...," Macon began to sob.

Lynorra stood, and picked up the coffee cups and plates. "I'll put this in the kitchen on my way out," she whispered to Emma.

"You sure?" Emma asked looking at her friend.

Lynorra nodded. "Yes. You take care of Macon. Call me if you need anything."

Emma reached out to Lynorra, placing a hand on her arm. "I will. You do the same," she kissed her on the cheek. "I love you, sistah," Emma whispered.

"I love you, too...sistah. Talk to you later," said Lynorra, leaving.

Emma turned her attention to Macon, who was now sitting on the sofa, rocking and crying.

"Macon, baby. What's wrong? Tell Mama what's wrong," she said, sitting next to Macon, wrapping her arms around her.

Macon continued to sob; unable to get the words out. "I...I...," she shook her head.

"Did you have a bad dream, or somethin'?"

Macon shook her head.

"You gotta tell me, or else I can't help you."

Emma brushed Macon's hair from her face. "Shush. Shush. It's okay. Mama's here. I ain't goin' nowhere," she pulled Macon closer to her, rubbing her back.

Macon turned, and looked at Emma. "I...I tried to kill...my...mother...," Macon cried out, her eyes growing wide.

Emma hugged Macon tightly. "Oh, baby. No, no. You didn't know what you were doin. You were jes overwhelmed. That's all. You didn't know what you were doin. It's not your fault." Emma continued to rock Macon in her arms, trying to reassure her that everything was going to be okay.

"But...but I tried to...kill...her!"

"Oh, baby. I know. But, it's okay."

"How? How can it be okay? I tried...to kill my own mama," Macon looked into Emma's eyes, pleading to understand. "I didn't mean it," she cried. "I didn't mean it, Aunt Emma. I swear! I swear!"

"Baby. Baby. I know. I know. It's okay. We know you didn't mean it. We know you were jes upsets," Emma pulled Macon closer. "Everything gonna be jes fine. I promise."

"I didn't mean it. I...I was just so mad. I didn't know what else to do. I wanted her to hurt...I wanted her to hurt, like she hurt me," Macon cried into Emma's chest.

"Shush, baby. Shush. I know. I know you didn't mean it. I know you were jes overwhelmed. It was too much for you. And don't no one blames you."

"I was so angry," Macon cried. "I...I just don't

understand how...how she could have married him."
Macon looked at Emma, wanting to understand.
"Why would she choose him over me? How come she don't love me?" she wept.

"Oh no, baby. Your mama loves you..."

"No," Macon shook her head. "I will never believe that."

"I know. And I don't expects you to, right now. But your mama was not in her right mind. I truly believes she didn't know what she was doin."

"Uhn-uhn. She knows what she was doing," Macon insisted. "I know her. I know her better than anyone. She doesn't love me. She never did."

"No. I won't believe that...ever."

"How can you defend her?"

"I'm not defending, Nadine. But I'm tellin you what I know. She loves you; she jes don't know how. There are some things you don't understand about your mama. And I pray to God, she gets herself together so she can tell you. But I don't believe for one moment that Nadine doesn't love you...the best way she can."

Macon shook her head in disbelief.

"Baby, you didn't see your mama after what happened. She was scared for you. It wasn't fear for her; but *for you*. And you don't get that kind of look in your eyes when you don't love someone. That was a look of pain and regret."

"Why are you saying this, Aunt Emma? Especially after how she's treated you? "

"I know Nadine better than *she thinks*, and better than *you think*. We ain't that much different."

Macon disagreed. "No, you are nothing like her. You have been more my mama than she has my entire life. I don't care if I ever see her again."

"No, Macon. Don't say that."

"I mean it. I'm sorry for what I did. I truly didn't mean it. But she is poison. She married that man, and now they want to take my son. That's why she came here!"

Emma shook her head. "No, Macon. I don't believes that for one second. I do believe she came here to see you; but I don't believe for a second that she wants to take Nathaniel back to that man."

Macon continued to shake her head. "I don't want her near me or Nathaniel...ever."

"I understand. And baby, that's your prerogative. It's totally ups to you. But," Emma said taking her hands, "there are some things we gonna have to talk about. Things that you need to know. Also, you gonna has to forgive your mama..."

Macon was shaking her head no, before Emma could finish. "That's never going to happen, Aunt Emma. *God*, I am so sorry for what I did. But I will never forgive her—never."

"I know you feel that way now—"

"No. I can't, Aunt Emma. I could have forgiven her for everything; because I always have. But this time is different. She married him. She married that monster. And by doing that, she proved to me that she doesn't love me, and never did. She chose him over me. I can never forgive her for that.

I can never trust or believe anything she ever says again. Please, Aunt Emma," Macon cried. "Please don't make me see her again."

Emma wrapped her arms around Macon, and held her in her arms. Her heart was breaking. There was no way she could tell her the truth right now. Macon was still, too, fragile. She didn't want her to think that someone else that says they loved her, has lied to her yet again. She could not tell her. Not now.

"Don't you worry, baby. Mama ain't gonna make you do anything you don't wants to, or aren't ready to do. Okay?" Emma reached in her pocket and gave Macon a handkerchief. "Okay, baby?" she asked, lifting Macon's head.

Macon nodded, wiping her face.

"Okay, everything gonna be jes fine. You'll see. Everythin' gonna work out jes fine. God don't lie. No He don't."

Emma prayed within herself. *Lord, help me. Help this Chile. And please help Nadine. This ain't easy, Lord. I know You don't put more on us than we can bear; but this load here is a mighty heavy load.*

CHAPTER 30

NADINE WAS EXHAUSTED. All she wanted to do was get out of her clothes, and lay down for a couple of hours. But she knew that was going to be impossible. The police didn't allow her to go home until they determined that she hadn't killed Byron, and that there was no threat to her. She could only imagine what Emma must have thought when the police called her to verify that she was indeed there. She could hear her mouth now. They wouldn't even accept her ticket receipt as proof.

Nadine dreaded walking into her home. She could care less about what her neighbors thought. But the idea that Byron was killed here; that *anyone* was killed in her home that she, Nathan, and Macon shared, disturbed her.

After she was done at the police station, she had to identify the body. At first, Nadine had declined. The last thing she wanted was to have anything else to do with Byron; including his dead body. But she decided to, so his body could be released for burial. The sad part was, that Nadine had felt no remorse or grief. She was married to this man, and yet, she felt nothing. Byron had stolen from her, cheated her, raped her daughter and got her pregnant, used her, and lied to her the entire time she'd known him. He didn't deserve to live. And he damns sure didn't deserve a funeral. As far as she was concerned, they could burn him.

Finally at home, Nadine removed the yellow tape from the door. As soon as she entered the house, the smell of blood and death lingered in the air. She walked into the living, unable to ignore the blood stained carpet.

This is where he died, she thought. She walked around the empty room. There was hardly anything left in her home.

"That son of a—" Nadine walked into the kitchen and came back out. "He cleaned my house out!" She stood still for a moment, staring at the blood. "You lucky it wasn't me. Because, I'd of cut you into a million little pieces!" she screamed.

Nadine filled with rage.

"YOU BASTARD! YOU...DAMN...BASTARD! YOU RUINED MY LIFE! YOU DESTROYED MY DAUGHTER! I HATE YOU! I HAAAAATE YOU!"

Nadine screamed at the top of her lungs, raising her fists in the air. "You stole my life from me! I'm glad you're dead! I'm just mad I didn't get to kill you my damn self!" Nadine turned in circles, tears beginning to fall down her face. "I hope you're rotting in hell! Do you hear me? I hope your yellow ass is burning in Hell!"

Nadine began to weep. "Oh, God, Nathan, forgive me! Please...forgive...me." She fell to the floor in a heap, wrapping her arms around herself, rocking.

"I'm sorry. I'm so sorry. I didn't mean it. I swear I didn't mean it. Oh, Nathan! Naaaathan!" she cried out. "Why? Why'd you leave me? Why'd you leave me alone?" she sobbed. "You...you promised me. You promised to be with me always! You said... you...would never...leave me...alone!" Nadine buried her face in her hands, weeping and wailing. "Oh, God! Oh God! I'm alone...I'm all aloooone..."

CHAPTER 31

March, 1975

HEY BROWN SUGA. How 'bout you dip that finger in my coffee and makes it sweet the ways I like?" Albert wrapped his arms around Emma's waist, and kissed her on the neck. "Mm...jes the way I likes it; dark and sweet!"

Emma laughed. "Now you know you needs to stop it before one of them chilren come in here," she swatted his hand.

"Oh, don't acts like you don't like it. C'mon," he turned Emma around to face him. "I've missed you, Mama. It's been quite a while since you did what's you did to me last night!" He leaned in, kissing Emma passionately.

"Mm," Emma returned his kiss, wrapping her arms around Albert's neck. "I know, baby. And Mama's sorry. I promise...that will *never* happens again."

"Good. 'Cause I don't like it when I can't get my arms around you, and some good lovin'," he said, kissing her, running his hands down Emma's backside, resting his hands on her behind.

"Mm, I missed you, too, Al-B. But I'm backs now," she said, smiling coyly. "So, what's my fine husband wants for breakfast?" she asked, staring into Albert's eyes.

"Whatever you makes is fine...you know that," he said, patting her behind before pulling away to sit down. "But I know one thing—I need me some of this here coffee," he said, taking a sip. "I need me some strength," he winked at Emma, holding up the cup. "You put a hurtin' on *me* last night," he chuckled, taking another sip.

Emma smiled. Though you couldn't see it, she was blushing. "You weren't so bad yourself, Daddy," she looked at him with raised eyebrows.

"Mm, have mercy!" Albert laughed.

Emma and Albert laughed. It had been a while since Albert heard his wife's carefree laugh. He missed that. He missed her.

Emma felt good inside. For some reason, she felt lighter in her spirit today. She knew part of that was due to Albert. She hadn't felt in the mood for a long while. Not since everything that happened with Macon, and Calvin. However, when Albert came home last night, and they were getting ready for bed; she needed him. She needed him with such urgency that she couldn't explain it. She wanted him more than she had ever wanted him. She needed to be made love to. It was as though he filled her soul. And gave her a part of his spirit; because she felt more alive today than she had in a long while.

"So, what's the plan for today?" Albert asked.

"I'm gonna be cookin' most of the day." Emma answered.

"You gonna talks with her today?"

Emma turned, wiping her hands on a dish towel. "Yes. I thinks she's ready."

"Good. I thinks so, too. Macon will be sixteen tomorrow. She has been through a lot to be so young; but she strong—jes like you," Albert said, reassuring Emma.

Emma smiled slightly. Albert was right; Macon was strong. It was time she knew the truth, as well. "Thank you, baby."

"For what? Telling the truth?" Albert walked to his wife. Taking her hands in his, he looked Emma in the eyes.

"Emma, I have never met, or have known a stronger woman than you. I know better than anyone how difficult this has all been for you. But you ain't alone. And I am most certain that Macon will not be hindered, or hurt, by what you tell her. In fact, I believe she gonna feel better knowing' that you her grand-mama," Albert smiled, kissing each of Emma's hands.

Emma shook her head. "You know what man? You are somethin else, and I am so grateful to, God, that you are on my side." She placed her arms around Albert's neck.

"Is that right?" he said, smiling at his wife, wrapping his arms around her.

"Yes it is." Emma kissed Albert gently on the lips.

"Mm," Albert looked at his watch. "I still have some time..."

"You gonna be late for work," Emma whispered.

"Then it's a good thing I'm the boss, huh?" he

smiled, taking his wife's hand.

"Ooh, you dirty ol' man," Emma giggled.

"Yeah, I'm *your dirty ol' man!*" he said over his shoulder. "Now c'mon and shows me what you workin' wit!"

"Ooh, Daddy, let's go!" Emma laughed, running behind Albert towards their bedroom.

CHAPTER 32

MACON SAT QUIETLY at the kitchen table, nursing a glass of milk, and picking at the sandwich which Emma made for her.

"What's the matter, suga?" Emma said, sitting across from her.

Macon shook her head. "Nothing."

"Oh come now. You expect me to believe that? Especially since you ain't touch that sandwich." Emma stared at Macon. Reaching across the table, she opened her hands for Macon to take.

Macon placed her hands in Emma's.

"So," Emma began, squeezing Macon's hands, "I have a feelin you has a whole lot goin on. Do you wants to talk?"

Macon remained quiet.

Emma leaned forward. "You've been very quiet these last few days. I haven't said anything, because I wanted to give you your space."

Macon bowed her head, biting her lip, still not saying a word.

Emma breathed deeply. She wasn't sure how to approach Macon; how to tell her that she was her grandmother, and not her Aunt. She patted Macon on the hand, and released her hold. "I understands if you don't feel like talkin'. You've had lots to deal with lately, and I know a lot has been on your mind.

So—I ain't gonna push's you none. When you ready to talk 'bout it; you know I am here." Emma stood, and walked over to Macon. Placing one hand on her shoulder, Emma kissed her granddaughter on top of her head. "It's alright, suga'. I know it's been hard. But I promise you: it's gonna get better. I may not know when, but I know it is gonna get better. God don't lie. We jes has to believe Him and trusts that He gonna do what He says."

Emma stroked Macon's hair.

"Oh, baby. I wish I could take your entire pain and jes make it all disappears." Emma wrapped her arms around Macon, resting her chin on her shoulder.

Macon placed her hands on Emma's arms, and began to cry; her shoulders shaking from the well of emotions within her soul.

Emma hugged Macon tightly, kissing her on the cheek. "Go 'head, baby girl. Let it out. I ain't goin nowhere," she whispered in her ear.

Macon wept into Emma's arms. Her heart was aching. There were so many thoughts and feelings that she had inside her. She didn't know where to begin. Everything had changed so much in her life. She was scared. She couldn't let go of the fear that gripped her every day. Each day she wondered if this was the day her mama showed up again...this time with Byron.

She never thought that anything good could come from what happened to her. But when she looks at Nathaniel, her heart gets filled with love and she couldn't imagine her life without him. She asked

God to forgive her every day for the way she behaved when he was first born. She asked God to forgive her for asking him to take Nathaniel before he was ever born. She never told Aunt Emma. She only shared it with, Camille. She didn't want her own baby. She wondered what her father would have said about that.

Macon also asked God to forgive her for trying to kill her mama. She didn't really want to kill her; she just wanted her to hurt, and be scared like she was. She wanted her mother to feel helpless and afraid. In that moment, Macon knew what it was like to hate your own mother. And she prayed that Nathaniel never felt that way about her; that he wouldn't fear her, but respect her.

"It's all right, baby," Emma said softly, gently stroking Macon's hair and hugging her. "You go 'head and cry. Ain't nothin's wrong with cryin'."

Macon sobbed heavily.

"I...I..." Macon stammered. "I...miss...my father," she finally said.

Emma felt a sharp pain in her chest.

"Oh, baby. I knows you do. God, I know you do," she said, kissing the side of Macon's head.

"I...I wish he was here," Macon cried.

"So do I, suga. So do I." Tears began to fill Emma's eyes.

"I miss him so much." Macon choked on her tears, a heavy lump making its self at home in her throat. "I...I just wish he didn't die," she shook her head. "He...he would have never –" Macon couldn't bring herself to finish the sentence.

"It's okay, baby. I understand." Emma continued to keep her arms around Macon, trying to comfort her.

"Daddy...daddy knew what to do—about everything. I miss him so much. It hurts, Aunt Emma. It hurts so badly." She leaned her head into Emma's embrace, and wept some more.

Emma was silent, listening to Macon cry in her arms. What could she say? How could she bring comfort to this Chile? How could she possibly tell her the truth now? However, in her heart, Emma knew that was exactly what she had to do. She knew that the longer she waited, the greater the chance that someone else might say something, and the greater the odds that Macon would never forgive her.

Emma straightened as she released her embrace. She sat in the chair next to Macon's. She held onto Macon's hand, while brushing the hair from her face with her other hand.

Macon squeezed Emma's hand tightly, and looked up.

"I—I'm sorry, Aunt Emma," Macon took a deep breath in. "All I been doing is crying lately. I just miss him so much."

Emma patted her hand. "Oh, baby, you don't ever has to apologize for that. I knows how much you miss your daddy; jes as much as I missed mine when he died. That ain't somethin you jes move on from. That was your daddy, and I know that he was also your best friend. Because, my daddy was mine."

Macon looked at Emma. She wiped her eyes

and blew her nose, and asked, "Really?"

Emma nodded. "Oh, yes. Besides my sister Clarisse, my daddy was the person I talked to about everything. He took me fishin' and boatin'. We went camping. He taught me how to shoot. To this day, I can shoot a tick off a dog from fifty feet away," she laughed.

"You know how you and your daddy used to have breakfast together?"

Macon nodded.

"Well, my daddy and I used to do the same thing." Emma nodded her head and smiled. "He would make this big ol' breakfast: grits, eggs, ham, catfish, home fries, biscuits. Oh, what a spread!" Emma chuckled to herself. "How I jes loved that man. He knew how to make me laugh. He knew how to make my heart feel right. And...he protected me," Emma closed her eyes, shaking her head.

"He protected you from what?"

Emma opened her eyes, looking straight into Macon's.

"From *my* mama." Emma squeezed Macon's hand before releasing it. "Baby, there is so much I needs to tell you. I know how you feels, because I been where you at. But you a whole lot stronger than I ever was. Yes you are," said Emma, smiling sadly.

Macon didn't say anything. She wiped her face with a tissue. She could see pain in Emma's eyes that she had never seen before. She saw something she couldn't quite identify.

J?R

"You know how much I loves you?" Emma asked.

"Yes. I know you love me very much."

Emma smiled. She looked down at Macon's hands in hers. She looked at their similarity. She laughed to herself, a small laugh, and then looked into Macon's eyes.

"Suga, there is so much in my life that I regrets. There are many things that I wish I would have done differently. Perhaps if I had, some people wouldn't be hurtin' right now; especially you..." A lump formed in Emma's throat. She swallowed hard to keep the tears from flowing. She could feel the tears burning behind her eyes, threatening to fall. But she dared not cry; she dared not shed another tear. Not now. Not until she'd told Macon everything. This was not about her; but about Macon—her grand baby.

"You could never hurt me, Aunt Emma," she said, taking Emma's hand.

"Oh, I didn't mean directly; but my actions have caused you hurt, nonetheless."

"I don't understand."

"I know. I know. But I'm fittin' to explains all that, right now."

Emma shook her head, and breathed in deep. She shook her body a little, summoning up the courage and strength to continue.

"There's something you need to knows the truth about; the truth 'bout me and your daddy..." Emma searched for the right words.

"You see—"

"—you were his mother," Macon said softly.

Emma's mouth opened, but nothing came out. She couldn't believe what Macon just said. Then she wondered who told her, or if she'd overheard everything that Sunday night.

"How—how—"

"My father told me...before he died," Macon said gently.

Emma sank back in her seat.

Nathan told her?

"You mean, all this time..."

Macon nodded. "...I've known."

"I don't understand," Emma shook her head in disbelief. "Why didn't Nathan tells me he told you?" Emma placed her hand over her mouth, tears running down her face, she cried. "I—I don't understands..."

It was now Macon's turn to comfort her grandmother.

Macon took Emma's hand in hers. "Please don't cry, Aunt Emma. It's alright...really. Daddy told me how hard it was for you to give him up. He told me that you would tell me everything when you were ready, and felt the time was right."

Emma looked into her granddaughter's eyes. All this time she knew, and never said a word.

"How comes you didn't say anything?"

Macon shrugged her shoulders. "I'm not sure, really. I guess, since my daddy said you would tell me, I was okay with just knowing."

"You—you ain't upsets with me for...for not... tellin' you I'm your grandma, and...and not your Aunt?" Emma searched Macon's face.

"No. Why should I be?" Macon asked. "Aunt Emma, you have been my mama ever since I got here," Macon smiled. "Daddy said something really bad happened back then; but he knew you would tell me the truth."

Emma was quiet for a moment. She was still trying to digest the fact that Macon had known the truth all along. Emma marveled at her granddaughter's strength. She looked at Macon, shaking her head.

"I still don't understands *why* he told you to begin with?"

"My mama," Macon said flatly.

Emma understood.

CHAPTER 33

HEY LITTLE MAN. How are you doing this morning?" Macon picked Nathaniel up from his cradle. "Guess what? You missed your mommy's birthday. You slept right through the party." Macon sat down in the rocking chair that Albert had specially made for her birthday. She held Nathaniel close in her arms, and began rocking slowly. "That's okay, we'll have plenty more to celebrate together," she smiled.

Nathaniel cooed at his mother. Smiling, he nestled his face into his mother's bosom.

Macon smiled. She couldn't believe how much she loved this little boy; despite the fact of how he was conceived, she couldn't love him any less or any more. Nathaniel was her heart, and she understood for the first time how difficult it must have been for Aunt Emma.

She laughed to herself.

"Aunt Emma," she said softly. "I guess we should start calling her grandma. What do you think, Nathaniel?" she said, taking his small hand in hers.

Nathaniel looked at his mother and cooed, blowing a spit bubble.

Macon laughed.

"Yeah, I think she'll like it, too," she smiled.

97

Macon leaned her head back; thinking. She marveled at the past year. Her heart still ached for her father. It even ached for her mother, somewhat. She meant what she told her grandmother yesterday; that she had been more of a mother to her than Nadine ever was.

"Yes," she said looking into Nathaniel's smiling face, "We will call her, Mama from now on." She placed a kiss on her baby's forehead. "You are going to love it here, Nathaniel. Yes you are. Mama is the best. She loves us so much; just like she loved my daddy—your grandfather. I wish he could have seen you. I believe Mama though, when she says that he is looking over us." Macon studied her son's features, and the little faces he was making. Probably gas, she laughed to herself.

"I promise you, Nathaniel, I will love you always. I will never let anyone hurt you. I don't care who they are. I will die before I let anyone hurt you. I promise you that." Macon fell silent for a moment. Her throat began to ache, as tears burned behind her eyes. "I'm sorry I didn't hold you when you were first born. I'm...I'm sorry I did not feed you and tell you that I loved you. I hope you don't remember that."

Nathaniel began to fall asleep. Macon lifted him to her shoulder, and gently rubbed his back.

"I promise to love you forever, and be the very best mama to you," she whispered in his ear.

Macon lightly kissed the side of Nathaniel's face. She got up slowly from the rocker, as to not jostle her son, and gently laid him in his cradle.

A small knock came on her bedroom door.

"Come in," she said softly.

"Hey, Macon," Deeney said coming in. "How are you doing today?" she asked, walking over to the cradle.

"I'm good."

Deeney smiled as she looked at Nathaniel. "He's getting big."

"I know. I think he's teething, too." Macon smiled.

"Really?" Deeney asked sitting on the bed.

"Yeah. At least that's what, Aunt—I mean, Mama says," she smiled.

Deeney smiled. "So, I guess you're alright with Mama being your grandma, and not your Aunt?"

"I guess you could say that. I mean, I knew already that she was. And to tells you the truth, she been more like a mother than anything to me. I mean, I think I would have died if it wasn't for her." Macon sat down next to Deeney.

Deeney nodded. "Yeah, I can see that. You know...this means we ain't cousins? You're actually my niece," she laughed.

"I *know*," Macon giggled. "How weird is that?"

"Girl, this is down South—this ain't weird. Now, if they said you were my *sister*? Girl, I don't know" Deeney laughed.

"You're crazy!"

"What? That mess *would be* weird!"

"Uh...yeah...you right. That would be some funky stuff!"

"You ain't lying!" Deeney shook her head laughing.

"So, should I call you, *Aunt Deeney*?" Macon chided.

"Only if you want to gets slapped!"

Macon laughed.

"It doesn't change anything between us," Deeney said, her tone becoming serious. "I love you just the same. You family, girl. Always was, and always will be. Just like that big boy over there," she pointed towards the cradle. "I can't say I understand all you have gone through; but I definitely know my Mama does. I'm just glad she was able to tells you, and that you took it all well. No matter what; that's my Mama, and I loves her to death. All she ever wants to do is protect the people she loves."

Macon nodded knowingly.

"I never knew everything my Mama went through. I knew that sometimes she would get sad and depressed; but she never once let it keep her down. I've always seen Mama as strong, unbreakable, bold—always speaking her mind. I never realized how much she went through to protect our family. She never lets us see that side of her. But it just made me see how strong she *really* is, and how much I admire her." A lump formed in Deeney's throat.

A small tear escaped from Macon's eye, rolling down her cheek.

"I don't know; saying I love her just don't

seem enough." Deeney bowed her head, and fiddled with an envelope she had in her hands.

"I know...I feel the same," Macon agreed. "Is Calvin still upset?"

Deeney nodded. "Yeah. But, he'll come around. Calvin's like that—stubborn and takes everything personal."

"I know it's hurting, Mama. I saw her crying the other day. She'd just got off the phone with, Anna-Leigh. She didn't see me; but I heard when she hung up, and went on the porch." Macon shook her head.

"I know. She's been doing a lot of crying lately."

"But she's strong. I know she'll be fine."

"I only hope that I am half as strong as, Mama. Then, at least I know I can handle anything that comes my way. And of course, marry someone like my father," Deeney smiled. "He loves my Mama so much. It's..." Deeney searched for the right word.

"...it's one-of-a-kind, special," Macon said.

"Yes—one-of-a-kind, special. That's what I pray I have."

"Do you feel that way about David?"

Deeney turned her head quickly to Macon, her mouth gaping.

"What?" Macon asked, incredulously.

"*David?* Oh God, no!"

"Why? What's wrong with David? Everybody knows how much he likes you. And you don't seem to mind."

"Girl...David is gay!"

"Noooo!" Macon slapped Deeney in the arm. "Shut your mouth! You're lying!" she said, covering her mouth, trying not to wake Nathaniel.

"No I ain't either. He sweeter than Lula Mae's sweet tea...and we both know how sweet that is!" Deeney laughed.

"I had no idea. I...I just thought he...wow," Macon shook her head. She couldn't believe it.

"I've known David forever, and he's always been gay. He told me so from the beginning. You know how he is. I remember him telling me not to fall in love with him. Although he knew it would be hard not to; it would never work, seeing how he liked the same thing I did," Deeney laughed.

Macon shook her head laughing. "He said that to you?"

Deeney nodded.

"How old was he?"

'Twelve."

"Yeah," Macon thought about it. "That sounds like David. Cocky, isn't he?"

"Uh-hm. He has a big heart though. He'd give you the shirt off his back."

"Must be hard for him being a Pastor's kid?"

Deeney shrugged her shoulders. "I guess. His parents don't know. Well, at least his father doesn't. I suspect his mom does."

"Wow."

Both girls were quiet for a while; thoughts running through their minds. Deeney looked at the envelope in her hands. She had stalled long enough in giving it to Macon. She turned to Macon, taking her hand.

"Hey," she said softly.

"What is it, Deeney?" Her eyes searched her face. "I suspect it has something to do with that letter in your hand?"

Deeney smiled, looking down at the envelope. "Yeah," she nodded. "Can't gets nothing over on you," she chuckled.

"What is it?"

"It came yesterday...it's for you. A letter from Nadine," Deeney finally said, placing the envelope in Macon's lap. "I didn't open it, or anything."

Macon stared at the envelope. "Of course you wouldn't," she whispered, not looking up.

"I don't know what's in it, but I didn't want to ruin your birthday. So I waited until today. I didn't tell anyone. You know, like Mama."

Macon nodded understandingly. "It's—it's okay. I wonder what she could possibly have to say." Macon stared at the letter, almost afraid to open it.

"Who knows? You don't have to read it, you know. In fact, you could just rip it up if you..."

Macon shook her head. "No, I think it's better if I read it. I don't particularly care for any more surprises, you know?" She laughed nervously.

"Do you want me to stay, or get Mama?"

"No, I think I better do this alone. After all, I'm sixteen now. I definitely ain't no little girl no more. I'm a mama. I have to grow up some time. And that includes facing Nadine….even if it's just a letter."

Deeney stood. Opening the door, she turned around before leaving. "If you want me to stay, I can?"

"No. That's alright. I'll be fine. It's just a letter. She can't hurt me no more…not if I don't let her, anyways." Macon stood, and walked towards Deeney. "Thanks for asking, though," she said, hugging her. "But, I'll be okay. After all, I come from good stock," she smiled. "They don't come any stronger than, Emma Jean Cooper-Watson."

Deeney laughed. "Yeah, you right. We are a strong family. You are definitely one of us. I can see Mama rubbing off on you," she chided.

"That makes me feel *real* good," she said softly.

"Well, you just remember: you ain't alone, Macon. You got family that loves you, and will do anything for you." Deeney took Macon's hand and squeezed it. "If you need me…just let me know," she smiled.

"I will. I will." Macon shut the door behind Deeney. She stared at the letter in her hands. She looked over towards the cradle. Nathaniel was still sleeping. Macon walked to her rocker and sat down. She held the letter in her hands, running her fingers over it. She sat for a while, contemplating what she should do. A part of her wanted to rip it up; but another part of her was curious to read what her mother had to say. She held the letter up. It wasn't a very thick letter; but she could tell it was a few pages.

"Oh God, what do I do?" Macon asked looking upwards. "Should I read it? Or, just get rid of it and leaves the past alone?"

Macon's stomach started to do flips. Nervous anticipation was running through her body. She wanted to know—no, she *needed* to know what her mother had to say. It was the only way to put closure between her and Nadine.

Macon carefully tore one end of the envelope, and slid the letter out. She unfolded the letter, and began to read, then stopped.

"Oh God, help me," she prayed.

With her hands trembling, she began to read the letter again. Tears started to fall down Macon's cheeks, as she read her mother's words...

March 24th, 1975

 Dear Macon,

 Happy Birthday, baby! I know I am probably the last person that you want to hear from. But I just had to write you, and tell you how sorry I am. Macon, I am so sorry for all the hell that I have put you through. I know you may find this hard to believe, but I swear to God, I am so sorry, baby. I never meant to hurt you. I never meant to cause you any pain. I know I has no rights to asks for your forgiveness; but I would hope in time that you would find it in your heart to forgive me. You don't ever has to see me again if you don't wants. But, I beg of you to at least finish this letter. There is so much I has to tell you. So much that you need to know. I love you, Macon. I swear I do. And no matter what happens in this life, I will always be your mama. And you will always be my baby.

Like I said, there are some things that I need to tell you......

Macon rocked quietly, reading her mother's letter—tears flowing heavily, as she read each of Nadine's words. She could hardly believe the things she was reading. Her heart became increasingly heavy with each word; with each paragraph.

Once finished, Macon leaned her head back, closed her eyes, and held the letter to her chest. She covered her mouth, stifling the cries that resonated deep from her soul. A lump of pain lodged itself within her throat. Her heart was racing with emotions; her thoughts were tumbling, trying to make sense of all she read. She wanted to believe most of what her mother said, and forget the rest. Her body began to shake from the heavy sobbing that she was holding in. She dared not cry out, for fear of waking Nathaniel, and having him sense her pain and discomfort. Mama said that babies were very sensitive, and could tell instantly when their mother was upset.

Macon stood, her legs feeling weak. She had to find Mama, and share the letter with her. She walked quietly to Nathaniel's cradle.

He was still quietly sleeping.

She wiped her face, and eased her way towards the door. She opened it slowly, as not to disturb her son. She left it ajar, so she could hear him when he awoke. She quietly made her way to the kitchen. She could hear Mama's voice from the hallway.

Macon stood in the doorway for a moment.

Emma was talking on the phone, and did not see Macon come in.

"Ooh, Chile!" Emma jumped. "You scared me..." Emma noticed the tears and sullen look on Macon's face. She held up her hand. "Hey, Sistah, let me call you back. Yeah. I'll talks with you later. Love you, too. Bye." Emma hung up the phone and rushed to Macon.

"What is it, baby? What's wrong?" she asked, placing her arms around Macon.

Macon leaned into her grandmother's arms, and wept.

"Ooh, suga, what happened? You were fine a couple of hours ago?" She pulled Macon back, to look at her.

Macon rubbed her eyes. "I...I..." Macon was too overcome with emotion to speak. Instead, she gave Emma the crumpled letter that was in her hands.

"What's this; a letter?"

Macon managed a nod.

"Well, what kind of letter would have you so upset?" Emma unfolded the crumpled letter. "Nadine," she whispered. Emma guided Macon to the kitchen table. "Here, baby, sits." She handed Macon a tissue, as she sat down across from her. "Do you want me to read it?"

Macon nodded.

"Okay," was all Emma said before reading the letter from Nadine.

The kitchen was quiet, with the exception of Macon's occasional sobs.

Emma read the letter silently, covering her mouth after a while.

"Oh my sweet, Jesus...." she whispered after a while. "Oh, Lord, no..." she said soon after.

Emma continued reading, shaking her head. Not so much in disgust; but rather in horror, disbelief and pain...Pain for Macon, for Nathan, and even pain for Nadine. Once she finished, she folded the letter and placed it on the table. She took Macon's hands in hers.

"Come here, baby."

Emma stood, pulling her granddaughter into her waiting arms. "I'm so sorry, baby," she said, squeezing Macon tightly. "But I promise you, that the worst is now over. And we *will* get through this... together. I promise you. Do you hear me?"

Macon nodded.

Emma was silent for a moment, as she

continued to comfort Macon. She finally said, "I'm not gonna lets anyone hurt you. I loves you, too, much. I'd die before I lets anything else, or anyone else hurts you. You hears me?" Emma said, lifting Macon's chin.

Macon nodded, brushing away her tears.

Placing both her hands on Macon's face, Emma leaned in and looked her granddaughter in the eyes. "You are all I has left of my Nathan. I made many mistakes where he was concerned; but I'll be damned if I do the same with you. I promised him I'd takes care of you and protects you, and that's what I'm gonna do. So—if you needs to cry, you cry. If you needs to scream, you scream. If you wants to hit something, hit it! Jes as long as it ain't me!" Emma laughed.

Macon managed a smile.

Emma straightened, and pulled Macon closer to her, kissing her on top of her head. "Oh suga', you are a blessin to my soul. You jes don't know. And you may not believe it, but things are gonna be better...you'll see. The worst is over. And you ain't gots to worries about nobody comin to takes that baby of yours. Yes, you have a beautiful road ahead of you—you and that beautiful baby boy."

"I'm glad he's dead. He can't ever hurt Nathaniel," Macon said, burying her face in Emma's chest.

Emma stroked Macon's hair. "Yes baby, he's dead. He can't hurts no one no more." Emma continued holding Macon. She believed in her soul that things were going to get better.

Emma wondered about Nadine, however, and how she was faring in all of this. She hoped she was doing well in, Beaufort. She didn't know how well she would do around her Aunt Celia. Celia had her own demons to contend with. However much Emma detested Nadine's ways, she understood her, and was genuinely concerned. No matter what, she was still Macon's mother, and Nathaniel's grandmother. She only hoped that Nadine would use this opportunity for a new start wisely, and get the help that she truly needed.

CHAPTER 34

CELIA, DO YOU THINK I DON'T KNOW THAT?"
Only three weeks in Beaufort, and Nadine was ready
to leave.

"I was just saying, Nadine. Maybe you should
leave well enough alone, and move on with your life,"
said Celia, lighting a cigarette.

Nadine glared at Celia. *Why did she come back
here?* She had no choice. She couldn't stay in Philly.
She knew that in order for her to get herself
together, she needed to be far away from all of that;
especially if she had any hopes of a new relationship
with Macon, and getting to know her grandson. *But
God! Celia was driving her crazy!*

"Celia, *unlike you,* I care about my child. I
want to know what happened to him, and if he's
doing okay; are the people he's with loving him
right?"

Celia put her cigarette out.

Nadine could tell she'd hurt her feelings but
didn't care.

"Looks, Nadine. You can do whatever the
hells you want. But you ain't gonna comes into my
home, and start no mess. You can take that mess
somewhere else!"

"Don't you mean *my home?*" Nadine retorted.
Nadine's grandmother had left the house to her
when she died. Nadine could never bring herself to

accepting it, knowing what had happened the night she passed, and how much guilt she still harbored.

"*Whatever Nadine!* What; you wants *your* house now? I mean, me and Russell don't has to stay here! He makes good money, you know?" Celia shot back.

"Oh relax! Ain't nobody said you had to leave." Nadine shook her head. She wondered how Russell put up with Celia and her antics.

Nadine was surprised when she showed up three weeks earlier. She hadn't even known that Celia was married—for two years, nonetheless. Celia never bothered to tell her the few times they had spoken. She wasn't sure what kind of work Russell did, but he sure seemed crazy about Celia. Russell was the exact opposite of her mother—a small, quiet, laid back, unassuming kind of a man. Whereas Celia's, loud, flashy, and annoying! To see them together was strange. Nadine kind of felt sorry for the man. Celia seemed to walk all over him, and Russell seemed to take it all in stride. He'd just say: "Oh, that's just Celia. You can't harness the wind, you know? You just got to flow with it." Yet, it was something underneath; something you couldn't quite see with the naked eye that struck a chord with Nadine concerning Russell. She hadn't figured out what it was, though.

"I mean, me and Russell can move you know? You can have *your damn house!*" Celia continued to rant. "You got some nerve, Nadine. You ain't changed a bit. Still selfish as the day is long! I don't know how Nathan ever—" Celia stopped herself from going any further. "I'm sorry, Nadine," she said, changing her tone. "I didn't means nothin by that."

"Save it, Celia! You ain't change either. I guess the apple *don't* fall far from the tree, huh?" Nadine shook her head. "I didn't come here to takes the house from you. I just needs some time to gets myself together, and find my son so I can start getting my life back." Nadine took out a cigarette. "I won't be here much longer...*that* you can bank on!" Nadine stormed to the front porch.

Celia quickly followed her.

"I didn't mean no harm, Nadine. I'm sorry. Really I am. I know how important it is to you to find your son and all, and get Macon back. But maybe you should just wait. I mean, takes your time. Give yourself time to get used to being on your own."

Nadine took a puff of her cigarette. "I don't have time," Nadine whispered to herself. She turned to Celia. "I've wasted too much time as it is, Celia. I'm not gonna keep running from my past, and watching it come back to bite me. I'm gonna do what I gots to do." Nadine studied Celia for a moment. She stopped, and really took a good look at her mother. Celia hadn't changed much in the past fifteen years. She was a few years older; but no wiser. She didn't want to end up like her. Nadine shook her head. The only reason Celia married Russell was for his money. No one could convince her otherwise.

"What?" Celia asked. "Why you lookin' at me like that?"

Nadine shook her head again. "Nothing...just

thinking to myself." Nadine had been running all of her life—running from who she was, and her past. She ran away from her family so she wouldn't be like them, and here she was—just like them.

"I'm gonna gets me some sleep." Nadine took a last toke of her cigarette before putting it out. She walked backed into the house, heading for her bedroom upstairs. Celia and Russell occupied her grandmother's old room down stairs. She was glad. She wanted to be as far away from Celia as possible.

Celia followed close behind Nadine.

"You know, if you really want to find your son you need to speak with your father," she called up after Nadine.

"He's not my father," Nadine quipped over her shoulder.

"You know what I mean," Celia said. "Talk to Theo. He can help you if you let him."

"I don't have anything to say to that man," said Nadine, stomping the rest of way upstairs. "As far as I am concerned, he is dead to me."

Celia shook her head. "You ought not to say things like that, Nadine. We all have our demons. You of all people should know that. But my brother loves you...you hear me?" Celia stated.

Nadine stopped for a moment and turned around.

"He does, you know?"

"He sure had a funny way of showing it."

"Listen; we all are sorry for the past, Nadine. No one more than Theo. He's a changed man."

"Yeah, prison will do that for you!"

"Whatever, Nadine. But if you stopped being so mean, and high and mighty, you'd realize that Theo, of all people, could probably best tells you where to look for your son."

Nadine didn't respond. She looked at Celia, and then continued to her room.

Celia shook her head. "Suits yourself. Don't say I never tried to help you!" Celia walked towards the kitchen. "Damn girl! I needs me a drink. Comin' in to my house...that's right—*my house!*—and acting like she the Queen of Sheba...somebody need to knocks that chip off her shoulder!" Celia poured herself a glass of whiskey. "Mm...just what the doctor ordered." She closed her eyes, taking in the intoxicating aroma. She walked towards the living room, stopping in front of a mirror. "You looks good Celia Jackson! Yes you do," she said, touching her short Afro. "I got's to take me a trip soon," she smiled to herself. "I think it's about time to pay an old friend a visit. Damn Russell is boring me to death! Money can't fix *everything!*" She smiled wickedly to herself, as she finished her drink and sashayed into the living room, plopping down on the sofa, and turning on the television.

Nadine lay across her bed. Her head pounding, she ached for a glass of Jack Daniels. But she knew she couldn't. That would just lead her down a darker path—a path she no longer wanted to visit. Celia was right: she needed to see Theo. He was the best person to talk to. She wondered how she would feel seeing him after all these years.

J7R

Nadine rolled onto her side, glancing at the photos that adorned the wall. Yes—she would go and see Theo. She had to start somewhere...

CHAPTER 35

May, 1975

ALBERT WATCHED JAMES AND JOE. He laughed to himself, remembering when he was their age. No twelve year old boy wanted to be spending their summer working. He knew the two would rather be fishing, or getting into some kind of mischief at Miller's Field.

"Hey, you boys c'mon over here, and gets some of this sweet tea."

Both boys dropped the hoes, and ran towards the gazebo.

"Thank you, Mr. Albert," James and Joe said in unison.

"You boys 'bout finish?" he asked, handing each boy a tall glass of tea.

Both boys nodded, as they gulped down the cool tea.

"Slow down, slow down," Albert laughed.

"Yes, Sir," said James, trying to catch his breath.

"Now, I bet's the two of you won't go tramplin' throughs my yard no times soon, huh?"

"No, Sir," Joe answered.

"No, Sir, Mr. Albert," James agreed.

"The next times you two want to take a short

cut, don't use Mama's garden as your paths," Albert laughed. "You two lucky it's me out here, and not her."

Both boys nodded. They knew that Emma would skin them alive if they'd tried that again.

"Lucky for you, James Perry, she's your god-mama. And lucky for you, she likes you," Albert said, raising an eyebrow at Joe.

James and Joe bowed their heads.

Albert loved messing with them. They were fine boys, though. No more trouble than half the boys in town. At least they were respectful, and had good mama's looking after them, and a father in the home. Although, Emma would disagrees with him concerning Reverend Washington and Joe's father, Mr. Knight. Emma didn't have such kind words for neither of them.

"So, let's see..." Albert looked at his watch. "It is now, ten o'clock. How about we go do some crabbin', and sees if there any fish left?"

James and Joe looked at one another excited. They loved going on Albert's boat. "Yes...yes, sir!" They chimed.

"Alright. Go on, and put them tools back in the shed. James Perry?"

James turned around. "Yes, Mr. Albert?"

"You go inside and gets that basket from Mama. Tell her we ready to go now."

"Yes, sir!" James answered happily, as he bounded down the garden path to the back of the house.

"...I don't know. I guess maybe—"

"—Mr. Albert—" James came barreling through the back door.

"James, now I know you got better sense than that! You don't come charging through no one's door like that!" Lynorra scolded him.

"Sorry, mama...sorry, Ms. Emma." James apologized.

Emma laughed. Albert must have told the boys he was taking them out on the boat. "It's alright, Lynorra," Emma said. "You all ready to go, James Perry?" Emma always called James by his first and middle names. To her, he didn't just look like a James; but a James Perry.

"Yes ma'am," James nodded eagerly.

"Now you know, Emma Jean, you are just, too, soft on that boy," said Lynorra.

"Oh hush! That's my baby, and he's just excited. You leaves him alone." Emma smiled at James. "C'mon on over here, and gets this basket, baby," Emma pointed to the basket on the counter behind her. "You tell Albert I said only *two* cupcakes for him. And I'll know if he had more than that," she said, raising her eyebrows.

James laughed. Ms. Emma and Mr. Albert were funny.

"Did you do a good job in Mama's garden?" Lynorra asked her son.

"Yes ma'am," James answered, picking up the

"Okay."

James started to walk out the door when Lynorra stopped him.

"I knows you ain't fixing to walks out that door without giving me a kiss good bye, do you?" Lynorra asked him.

James smiled. He put the basket on the table and gave his mother a hug and a kiss on the cheek.

"That's what I'm talking about," Lynorra smiled. "Now, go on over there and gives Mama a hug, too."

James went and gave Emma a hug, and a kiss, as well.

"Go 'head, baby. Albert probably wonderin' what's takin' you so long," she smiled at him.

"Alright," said James, picking up the basket. "See you later," he said rushing out the door before his mother stopped him again.

Emma laughed. "He couldn't get through that door fasts enough!"

"Who you telling? That boy would do anything to go on Albert's boat, and goes fishing..." Lynorra said, shaking her head, "...thanks for talking with Albert."

"Oh honey, please. Albert loves takin' them boys out on that boat, as much as they like goin'. Also, he gets to get away from all the women folk for a while. He ain't foolin' no one!" Emma chuckled.

Lynorra laughed. "Yeah, you right!"

Emma walked over to the stove, and put the

Southern~421~Comfort

coffee pot on. "Hell, Albert's been lookin' forward to this the whole week."

Lynorra stared out the window. "I'm glad. James has wanted to go fishing for some time now... Lord knows, Artie ain't gonna takes him," she said, with disgust.

Emma looked at her friend with concern.

"So," Emma began, sitting across from Lynorra, "you decided when you goin'?"

Lynorra nodded. "Um-hmm...next week. I'd figured we go before Memorial Day weekend." Lynorra picked at the muffin on her plate.

Emma sat quietly, discerning her friend's changing mood. She wished she could do more for Lynorra.

"Sorry we gonna miss the barbeque," Lynorra said, softly, half lost in a thought.

"Oh Chile, please. Same ol' greedy Negroes. You won't be missin' nothin. Now, you jes makes sure you back here before the fourth of July...now *that's* the party you don't wants to miss!" Emma chided, trying to lighten her friend's mood.

Lynorra managed a small grin. "No, never that..."

"You think a month is long enough? I mean, I'm gonna miss you as it is," Emma confided.

Lynorra looked at her friend and smiled. Taking her hand she said, "I'm gonna miss you, too, Emma." She held onto Emma's hand a bit longer before letting go.

Lynorra stood, and walked towards the back door, looking out at the garden. "A month is all I need. I'm only staying that long for James. He really misses Matt and Lynnie-Mae. I want him to enjoy at least *part* of his summer. Artie's been making it real miserable for him." Lynorra sighed heavily. She walked back to the table and sat down. "I'm telling you, Emma—something just ain't right...I can feel it in my bones."

Emma went and got the coffee pot, pouring both her and Lynorra another cup. She sat down across from her friend. "Has that grimy heifer been back?" Emma asked.

"Not as I know of," Lynorra shrugged.

"What did she say her new name was?"

"Woodrow. Celia Woodrow."

"Hmm...well, if she so happily married, what in the hell is she doin' comin' 'round here? I mean, she caused enough hell as it was the first time 'round!" Emma was disgusted. She had nothing but contempt for the likes of Celia Jackson—or Woodrow!—whatever the hell she was calling herself these days!

"Your guess is as good as mine," said Lynorra, equally disgusted. "It just boggles my mind; the audacity she had sashaying herself to the church in the middle of the day, where anyone could have seen her? You know, people around here don't forget nothing! And they *still* talks about her to this day." Lynorra was incensed just thinking about Celia, and the trouble she caused when she was last in, Busby. Although she knew it was a sin, and that the good

Lord frowned upon it, Lynorra hated Celia. She hated Celia with every fiber of her being. Lynorra never forgot how she almost killed Celia and Artie when she found them together all those years ago... in her bed!

Lynorra had been visiting one of her sisters, Mel, in Mississippi. Her sister convinced her to leave Matt and Lynnie-Mae with her, and go back home so she and Artie could have some time alone. Things had been a little hectic with the building of the new church and the forming of a civil rights team. She and Artie hadn't had the chance to spend quality time alone. Money was a little tight, but she scraped up a few dollars and stopped at the butchers and got a nice steak. She had enough left over to get a new nightgown from the five and dime. She would make a nice lemon cake, with some berries. It wasn't much; but she wanted to surprise Artie. He'd been working so hard, and getting involved with the civil-rights cause. She wanted to show him how much she loved him, and appreciated all he was doing for their family.

Lynorra was under the belief that Artie was still in Memphis at a district meeting, and wouldn't be back until the next evening. That would give her ample time to surprise him. However, it was she who was surprised.

When Lynorra walked into the house that morning, she thought it strange that the back door was opened. She didn't see Artie's car. He must have been in a rush, and didn't check to see if it was closed all the way. When she came in the kitchen, there were a couple of dirty glasses, and dishes in the sink. Again, she figured Artie had some company before he'd left.

"He could have at least cleaned up." She placed her packages down, and started to clean up when she got this strange feeling in her gut. Lynorra felt compelled to go to her bedroom. Not thinking too much about it, Lynorra picked up her overnight bag, and headed towards her room. When she opened the door, she froze in her steps. Her mouth opened, but no sound came out. She blinked hard a couple of times, as if to blink away what she was seeing. Lynorra began to shake all over. She couldn't even recall walking, or making a move at all. But before she knew it, she was next to her bed beating the hell out of Artie, and this dark skinned hussy, lying in her bed.

Artie and Celia were wrapped up in each other's arms, like it was the most natural place to be. Lynorra saw red. She hadn't cussed so much in her life, as she did that day, or screamed. Her screams were so loud, and her anger so fierce, that Celia ran out the house naked. Although she was twice as small as Artie, Lynorra whipped on him like she was a man.

"Has James Perry seen her since that day?"

Lynorra was lost in her thoughts. She hadn't even heard Emma speaking to her.

"Huh? What?" Lynorra shook her head, trying to shake her thoughts. "I'm sorry, what did you just say?"

"It's alright, suga. I understand. I jes asked,

has James Perry seen her since?"

"No. I don't want to asks him out-right; but, he'd tell me if he'd seen her again. Especially since he didn't get a good feeling about her first time around. She disturbed him. I dare not tell him anything."

"Oh, no. You can't do that."

"I just hate the fact that she has the nerve to show up; and be anywhere nears a child of mine! I'm telling you, Emma; that's who been calling and hangin' up!"

Emma didn't say anything. Her eyes growing wide over her coffee cup, as she took a sip.

Lynorra looked seriously at Emma for a moment. "Has...has Macon heard any more from Nadine? I mean, I know you said she was staying in, Beaufort with Celia."

Emma slowly shook her head. "Not since the beginning of this month. You know—when I received those trust papers from Nathan."

"That's right," Lynorra remembered.

"She'd written Macon about two letters since March. However, this last letter was from an address in, Georgia."

"Georgia?"

"Um-hmm. She told Macon that she needed to take care of some things that she left undone when she left."

"Really? What do you think she meant by that?"

"I think she's going to look for that Chile they took from her," Emma said.

"You think so?"

"I do. I know she wrote tellin' Macon that she's been clean and sober now for nine months. She said that she was finally getting her life together, and becoming someone she could be proud of. She said she could only do that in Georgia, though."

"Do you believe her?"

"I wants to...for Macon's sake, *and* Nadine's, too. I told you she wrote me, tellin' me that she didn't want the trusts fund that Nathan left her? She wanted it to go to her grand baby."

"Yeah, I remember you telling me that. Do you think she meant it?"

Emma pursed her lips, and held up her hand flexing it. "Hmm, I believe so. Only because I know she's in Georgia. In order for her to go back there; that means that she was ready to face her past. Time will tell. I jes pray she don't get disappointed and turns back, you know?"

"How?"

"I jes prays that who she lookin' for, wants to be found," Emma said.

Lynorra nodded. "I see."

"Yeah."

Lynorra stared into her coffee cup, watching the whirlwind affect her stirring was causing.

"What is it, Sistah?" asked Emma, reaching for her dear friend's hand.

"I'm just tired, you know?" Lynorra sighed

deeply, "...tired of pretending that everything is alright; tired of lies; tired of Artie's treatment of James; tired of damn church folk!; tired of the gossip; tired of the wondering." Lynorra shook her head, a tear escaping her eye, running down her cheek.

Emma's heart ached for her best friend. "I know you are. I know. But you ain't alone...never alone," she reassured Lynorra.

Lynorra smiled, and looked at her dearest and oldest friend; sadness filling her eyes. "I know. And I couldn't have asked for a better friend than you. You're more my family than my own blood. You know more about what's going on than they do. And I thank you for being here for me. I don't know what I would have done without you all these years." Lynorra broke down crying.

Emma handed Lynorra a handkerchief. "Don't worry; it's clean!" She joked.

Lynorra managed a laugh, as she wiped her eyes. "Oh, Emma! You are a mess! Leave it to you to make me laughs, in the midst of all this," she continued laughing.

"That's what sisters do," Emma smiled. "We have to make one another laughs in the midst of all this crazy stuff—husbands acting a fool, kids goin' and losin' they damn minds, and church folk actin' like they servin' the devil himself! You know you means more to me than jes a friend, Lynorra. You are my family. And I loves you as the day is long," Emma said, standing. "Now gives me a hug before you starts me cryin' 'round here!" she laughed.

"Alright, sistah," said Lynorra, standing, giving Emma a tight hug. "Mmm...I don't want to sees you crying no more! You have done cried enough for both of us!" Lynorra chided.

"Girl, who you tellin'? I swear, even my bags had bags," Emma laughed.

Lynorra shook her head. Leave it to Emma to make her laugh when all she really wanted to do was cry.

"Listen," Lynorra said, "...enough about me. What's happening with that stubborn son of yours? Is he coming for the holiday?"

"No. He's more stubborn than a mule!"

"He can't still be upsets with you?"

"A little bit. But I think it's more his pride that's gettin' to him."

"He needs to cut it out! Have you at least spoken to him?"

"Mm-hm," Emma nodded. "Last week, matter of fact. He was gettin' ready to pass the phone to Anna-Leigh, and I tolds him, his Mama was back, and I ain't gonna keep havin' him not talk to me."

"What'd he say?"

"He didn't say much; jes *yes ma'am*. I told him I loves him, and he don't has to come this time; but he'd better has his black behind here, come the fourth of July!" Emma said, rolling her eyes.

Lynorra chuckled. "I know that's right!"

"Calvin will be okay. He jes one that holds onto stuff for a while. That boy can hold a grudge! But I know one thing..."

"What's that?"

"He better not keep my grand baby from me! I miss that little girl."

"How is, Ella?"

"Oh, jes as precious as she wanna be! Lookin' jes like her Grandma!"

"Oh shoot, Emma! Everybody look like you!" Lynorra laughed.

"I can't help that!" Emma laughed. "Anna-Leigh sent me some photos last week with Shelby. I'll go get them!" Emma said, going to the den.

"How are Shelby and Richard doing?" Lynorra yelled.

"They doin jes fine!" Emma yelled from the back. "Girl, wait to you see these," said Emma, walking in. She handed an envelope to Lynorra. "Yeah. Richard and Shelby are doin really well. They loves it out there. And Lord knows, Anna-Leigh enjoys the company. So does Calvin. He jes won't admit it."

Lynorra took the photos of Ella out. She covered her mouth in awe. "Lord, Emma you were telling the truth this time: this baby look just *like you!*"

"I told you," Emma beamed.

"God help them!" Lynorra laughed loudly.

"You got some nerves!" Emma said, unable to contain her own laughter.

CHAPTER 36

June, 1975

NADINE FELT LIKE A FISH OUT OF WATER. She couldn't remember the last time she went to church, and it had nothing to do with a funeral. She fidgeted with her clothing one last time before walking into, Mt. Carmel First AME Zion church. Her stomach was doing back flips. She started to turn and leave when one of the mothers from the church approached her.

"You okay, sweetheart?" The woman had to be in her seventies. She wore a hat large enough to fit two heads.

"Oh...yes. Thank you...I'm fine," Nadine stammered.

"This must be your first time," she smiled. "It's okay. We get plenty of visitors. Although, I must say you sure do looks familiar to me?" she said, studying Nadine's face.

Nadine became increasingly uncomfortable. "I guess I just have one of those faces," she laughed nervously.

The old woman smiled. "Yes, that's probably it. Well, don't feels bad..."

"Excuse me?"

"We ain't but a few minutes late. I had to waits for my grandson to picks me up," she said, pointing to a gentleman walking up the steps. "The only way I can gets him to church. I has him pick me up," she chuckled.

Nadine smiled.

"Sorry, Ma'dear. I had to find a parking space." The young man stood next to his grandmother. His smile broadened when he noticed Nadine. "How'd you do?" he asked, extending a hand.

Nadine shook his hand. "I'm fine...thank you," she said, barely audible. This was definitely not why she came to church. There was only one reason for her being here today; because she found out her baby boy was a member of this congregation. The people that adopted him were the Pastor and first lady. She didn't want to seem rude, but she preferred to cut the niceties short.

"I guess I'd better be getting inside," Nadine said, walking towards the door.

"Oh, yes," the young man said, opening the door for his grandmother and Nadine.

"Thank you," Nadine said, walking in.

The old woman grabbed Nadine by the arm. "Wait a minute young lady."

Nadine looked at the woman puzzled.

"You're sitting with me today."

Nadine tried to protest. She didn't want to sit by any one; especially if she wanted to make a fast exit. "That's—that's all right..."

"No. The good Lord wants you sitting next to me! And whatever the Lord wants, the Lord gets! Now c'mon here...by the way, I'm mother Buckner," she said, taking Nadine by the hand.

"I—I'm Nadine."

"Nice to meets you," Mother Buckner smiled, pulling Nadine along.
"That's Darius, my grandson." Darius had a smirk on his face, trying not to laugh.

Nadine tried to protest; but the Lord must have given that old woman the strength of ten horses!

Oh no! What in the—sorry Lord! No she ain't going to the front of the church! Nadine turned to the grandson, for help.

Darius smiled at Nadine, shrugging his shoulders. "Sorry," he mouthed, before taking his seat in the back of the church.

I can't believe this! I just had to be late. Oh God, not the front. Nadine felt as though every person in the church was looking at her...and they were. Nadine kept her head down, and focused on the back of Mother Buckner's huge hat.

"C'mon, baby. You sits right here next to me," she smiled up at Nadine.

The usher waited for both Nadine and Mother Buckner to sit. She handed them a program, and two envelopes.

"Thank you, Lorlean," Mother Buckner said.

"Is this a guest of yours?" asked Lorlean, smiling at Nadine.

"Yes she is," Mother Buckner smiled wide.

"Well," she said to Nadine, "can I have your name please?" giving her a piece of paper and a pen.

"We like to acknowledge all of our guests," she smiled, looking Nadine from top to bottom.

Oh hell! Sorry Lord! I don't want no one knowing my name!

"It's Nadine," Mother Buckner stated, smiling at Nadine. "What's your last name, baby?"

"Cooper," Nadine said, softly.

"Come again?"

"It's Cooper, Nadine Cooper." Nadine wrote her name on the paper and handed it to the usher. *So much for asking for Your help, huh? I guess I ain't got any business asking after all the sinning I have done.*

Nadine sat back, and lowered her head. All she wanted to do was see her baby boy. To see what he looked like. She wondered if he favored her. She was too nervous to look around the church. She wondered if one of those young people in the choir stand was him. She searched the faces to see if she could pick him out. She couldn't. She wondered if he was even here.

This was a mistake. I shouldn't be here. I must be crazy. Nadine started shaking her head, and her eyes began to fill with tears. The adult choir was singing, but all Nadine could hear was her own thoughts, and the beating of her heart.

"You all right, baby?" Mother Buckner whispered.

"Huh? Oh, yes. I'm fine."

"It's all right; God got everything in His hands.

It wasn't a mistake in coming. You'll see. He'll work it out for you, if you let Him," she said, smiling. She grabbed Nadine's hand and squeezed it. "Trust me; God ain't finish with you yet!"

Nadine looked at Mother Buckner in amazement. *How does this old woman know anything? She doesn't know me, and all the things I've done. I'm surprised lightning didn't strike the moment I touched the church steps.*

Nadine shook her head, a tear escaping her eye.

"Here you go baby," Mother Buckner handed her a handkerchief. "You know, God loves us no matter what we do? Yes he does," she said, assuredly. "Sometimes we go through so much hell on earth, and thinks God don't love us. But I tells you the truth, God loves you more than you know. You wait and see; He got something real special for you today." Mother Buckner smiled, then turned around and started clapping her hands, and singing along with the choir.

"I'm gonna lay down my burden...down by the riverside, down by the riverside, down by the riverside. I'm gonna lay down my burden, down by the riverside..."

Nadine was speechless, and a bit freaked out. She wondered how this old woman could say such things so confidently. *Was she right? Did God still love her? Did He have something special for her today? Was it her baby boy?* Nadine shook her head. She'd given up on miracles a long time ago. She just wanted to see her son, and know that he was okay.

She had stopped hoping long ago to be a part of his life. She was too ashamed of her life, and she didn't want to ruin another one of her child's life.

Nadine had fantasized and dreamed of becoming one great family; her, her son, Macon and her grand baby. However, she knew that was *only* a dream. She had screwed up; too, many times to have that happen.

It took a lot for Nadine to go and visit with her Uncle Theo. She had not seen him since the day of her grandmother's funeral, fourteen years ago. She never attended Claire's funeral, or his trial. She discarded every letter he ever wrote her. After a while, he stopped writing altogether. Nadine harbored ill will towards Theo; for the abuse he caused in her life; for his hypocritical attitude; for the lies he told, and for taking away her son without her consent. She couldn't even say she hated him; because that would suggest she had some kind of feelings towards him.

Celia was right about one thing: Theo had the answers that she was looking for. Nadine had finally mustered up enough courage to go and see him in April. The last place she wanted to be was another prison. But she had to know if Theo had the answers she'd been searching for.

SHE waited for him to be brought out. When she saw him, her stomach dropped. He was nothing like she remembered. Prison had aged him fifty years. But when he spoke, there was something different in his voice.

"Hello, Nadine. It's so good to see you after all these years."

Nadine nodded, not sure what to say.

"I'm sorry to hear about Nathan. He was a very good man."

"Yes...yes he was," she managed to say.

"It's been quite a long time. I can't say I blame you for not wanting to keep in touch..." he put his head down for a moment. A long, awkward silence hung in the air before he continued. "...I want you to know how very sorry I am for all the heartache and...and pain that I have caused you..." Theo's voice began to crack.

Nadine couldn't look at him. She concentrated on the phone cord, as she ran her fingers up and down its length.

"You know, I don't have nothing but time in here, and I've done a lot of searching. And you know what? I'm a better Pastor now than I was on the outside," he laughed. "It's something how God works, isn't it? I know you are still hurting and suffering from the things that Claire and I put you through. I know I don't has a right to ask; but I ask that you would forgive me...forgive us for the hell we put you through? Life really is short, Nadine. And un-forgiveness just leads to resentment; resentment leads to anger; and anger leads to death—physically and spiritually. I don't want that for you, Nadine. I'm living proof of what can happen. Even as a preacher, I still harbored hatred and bitterness in my heart for things done to me. And all I did was pass it along.

I'm sorry, Nadine. God knows, I am so sorry. You deserved better. Much better than I, or Claire gave you." Theo looked at Nadine, hoping he was reaching her just a little.

Nadine looked up, and into Theo's eyes. She could see the remorse; but her bitterness towards him remained, and the coldness remained in her eyes, and in the tone of her voice.

"Listen," she began, "I just want to know where my son is. Who did you and Claire give him to?" she asked, coldly.

Theo nodded. He understood. He could only hope that one day Nadine's heart would be free from all the damage that he and Claire caused.

He took a deep breath. "He's right here in, Georgia. In fact, he's in, Macon."

Nadine's eyes widen. To think that all that time, her baby boy was in the same city. She should have known that Claire had lied when she said they'd given him to an out of state family. All these years—seventeen years to be exact—and her son had been in Macon, Georgia all this time. Nadine felt her heart beat quickly. Her eyes burned with tears. She looked at Theo and asked, "Who's he with? What family?"

"He was given to a Pastor and his wife who couldn't have children."

Oh God, not a Pastor. What if they were like Theo and Claire? Nadine's heart sank.

"Don't worry," Theo said, as if reading her mind. "Pastor Samuels and his wife are good people.

They were far from who I, or Claire was. They were an older couple; very much respected in their community."

"What's the name of their church?"

"Mount Carmel First AME Zion Church."

Nadine's heart raced. She hoped that Theo was telling her the truth.

The guard came just then, and informed them that their visit was up.

"I love you, Nadine. I pray that everything goes well for you," said Theo, before hanging up the phone.

Nadine just nodded her head. She really didn't have much else to say.

Theo watched as Nadine walked away, and he was being taken back to his cell. He prayed that everything worked out for Nadine. He didn't tell Nadine that he received a letter from the Samuels a few days ago. Nadine's son had expressed an interest in finally finding his birth mother. He'd write to the Samuels and explain everything. He thought it would be better this way. Nadine deserved a few good surprises in her life. Perhaps this was one of them. It was the least he could do for all the hell and heartache he'd caused in her life.

NADINE jumped when Mother Buckner nudged her.

"Stand up, dear," she said.

"Huh?" Nadine was confused.

"Stand up. They're announcing the visitor's

names."

Nadine forgot all about that part. The last thing she wanted to do was stand up, in the front row, nonetheless. However, she complied. There were at least ten other visitors. She was glad she wasn't alone.

"On behalf of our Bishop Samuels, First lady Samuels, and the rest of the Mt. Carmel family, we extend our greetings to our visitors, and hope that you enjoy the services, and are glad that you chose to fellowship with us today. Please feel free to come again," the church announcer said, looking at each visitor.

A few Amen's, and Praise the Lords, were echoed throughout the congregation.

Nadine sat quickly. She felt like she was on display. Nadine looked over at the pulpit. She gathered that the gentleman in the robe was Bishop Samuels. And from the size of the hat, the peach colored suit, and pearls, the woman sitting to his right was the first lady. How befitting: a Georgia peach, Nadine laughed to herself. They were a fine looking couple, Nadine thought. They were older; old enough to be her parents. She wondered where her son was. She still couldn't pick him out.

Most of the service, before the sermon, were a blur to Nadine. Her mind was in so many different places. When it was time for the sermon, Bishop Samuels came to the pulpit. He was a rather large man. No doubt, first lady Samuels was an excellent cook. He was very distinguished looking. His Afro,

JC

shaped neatly, a salt and pepper gray. A trimmed goatee, all gray. His voice was deep and booming; much like many Southern preachers. His eyes sparkled when he smiled, and he looked you in the eye when he spoke. A few times, Nadine found herself bowing her head. She felt as though he was speaking right to her.

"*We thank God today for His blessings! For God has been very good to us! Hasn't He church?*"

The congregation answered with, "*Amen. Yes Lord!*"

"*We know that if it had not been for the Lord, who was on our side, we would be lost today!*"

"*Praise the Lord! Hallelujah!*" someone hollered.

"*Mt. Carmel, visitors, I want you to know, that God hasn't forgotten you today! No, no, no! In fact, God has prepared a feast just for you!*"

"*Amen, Bishop!*"

"*God knows where you've been! He knows what you've been through! He knows what you've done! And He still loves you! He wants you to come on home! He wants you to stop feeling bad about yourself!*"

"*Glory!*"

"*Yes, church! There is forgiveness for you today! There is redemption for you today! There is reconciliation for you today!*"

"*Amen! Hallelujah! Praise God!*"

"*Oh, c'mon now! I ain't even get to my texts yet...*"

"*That's all right, Bishop! Let God use you!*" one of the church mothers yelled.

"*It's just that, there's a message in my soul today. God is telling me that somebody here needs to know, that God still loves them! That God hasn't forsaken them! That God forgives them! Ooh, Jesus!*"

"*Praise the Lord!*"

"*I don't know who you are; but you know who you are! This is your day! This is your day for a miracle from God...*"

Nadine sat still. She had never been so affected by preaching, as she was that day. It was her the Bishop was talking about. She felt a stirring in her heart that she had never felt before. She could feel the tears burning the back of her eyes. She could feel the lump growing in her throat.

Mother Buckner reached over and took Nadine's hand in hers. She patted it softly. "It's all right, baby. God got you. I told you...God has something special for you today," she said softly, her eyes still fixed on the Bishop. "Hallelujah!" she shouted, waving her hand in the air. "Yes Lord! Do it! Do it!"

Nadine felt a burning in her chest. She wanted to believe every word Mother Buckner said. She wanted to believe with all her soul that the Bishop was talking to her.

"*If you will, please turn in your Bibles to Luke, the fifteenth chapter, beginning at the eleventh verse. Oh thank you Jesus! Somebody's about to be free today!*"

"Hallelujah! Thank You Jesus!" someone from the back hollered.

"We gonna talk about the Prodigal son. But please know this also refers to prodigal daughters as well..."

"Amen!"

"Now, verse eleven reads as follows: 'And he said, a certain man had two sons: And the younger of them said to his father...'"

Nadine felt a warm sensation come over her body. She felt it from the top of her Afro, down to the tips of her stocking feet. She couldn't explain it right then; but it was as if she had just taken a hit a heroin. She'd never experienced anything like it outside of drugs. She sat there listening intently, as the tears streamed down her face. She held onto to Mother Buckner's hand.

Mother Buckner smiled. "It's okay, baby. God done worked it all out..."

Nadine's heart was filled with joy for the first time in years.

"Before we end this service; I want to know if anyone wants to know Jesus today? Do you want a personal relationship with God? I ask that you would think about it for a moment. I want to give you some time to think. So, I'm gonna have my son, David, come forth and render us a selection. David?"

Nadine sat up straight, she followed Bishop Samuels' gaze to a young, lanky, boy walking from the other side of the church, near the organ. Nadine held her hands to her mouth, trying to stifle her tears. There was her son; her baby boy, all grown up. "He's so beautiful," Nadine whispered to herself.

"Church, remember we're going to be praying for David as he goes off to college this summer. The first lady and I are very happy and sad at the same time. It won't be the same around the house, or in the youth group. But we know that God has special plans for his life; and we're just happy to have had these seventeen years." Bishop Samuels' voice started to choke. "C'mon on David, sing for us."

David smiled at his father. "Praise the Lord, everyone!"

"Praise the Lord!"

"God has been very good, and I just want to thank Him."

"Go 'head and sing, baby," one of the ushers shouted!

David smiled, looking to the organist, he nodded his head.

"*Oh happy day! Oh happy day! When Jesus' washed...oh, when Jesus washed...He washed my sins away...*"

The youth choir stood and joined David signing.

Nadine was frozen in time. She watched her son singing. Her heart felt like it stopped for a moment. He was so handsome. And when he smiled, Macon looked just like him. He had Nadine's almond shaped eyes, and hazel eye color. He had her complexion, and her dimple on one side. His voice was like an angel. He reminded her so much of Macon. All she could see was David. Everyone else disappeared. It was just her, and her son.

Nadine couldn't recall much of what happened after David finished singing. It was as though she had left her body, and someone else had taken over. She remembered going forth when Bishop Samuels called for the altar call. She didn't even know how her body moved; because she couldn't feel a thing. She recalled repeating the sinner's prayer, then being taken to the back with Mother Buckner for counseling. It was at that time that Nadine broke down. She couldn't hold it in any longer. A few other church mothers came in, and began to pray for her. They covered her with a sheet as she fell to the floor.

Nadine didn't know how long she was out; but she knew that she was different once she got up. The first face she saw was that of Mother Buckner's. An usher helped her up.

"Hello, baby," she smiled. "I knew there was a reason that the good, Lord had you sit with me."

Nadine sat down in a chair next to her. The other mothers had gone. The usher left her, and Mother Buckner alone.

"How you feel?"

Nadine couldn't say.

"It's okay. God got a plan for you, Nadine. Now I know where I seen you before."

"Huh?" Nadine was confused. She didn't recall ever meeting Mother Buckner.

"Your face...it's just like my grandson's."

Nadine was confused. Darius and she didn't

look anything alike.

"No, not Darius," she stated, as if reading Nadine's thoughts, "David. He has your eyes, and your smile," she said, beaming.

Nadine was overwhelmed and confused at the same time. "I...I don't understand?" she stammered.

"I knew God sent you here for a reason. I told my grandson that God was gonna answer his prayers."

Answer his prayers?

"Do you know how long my daughter and son-in-law have been looking for you? And here you are! The Lord sends you right into the church! I tell you, God is good!"

"Your daughter?"

"Yes. First lady Samuels is my daughter. This makes David my grandson!"

"They...they've been looking for me?" Nadine was surprised, to say the least.

"Oh, honey, yes! You can't deny that David comes from you," she said, reaching out and touching Nadine's cheek. "You are beautiful!" Mother Buckner smiled.

Just then, Bishop and first lady Samuels walked in. David walked in behind them.

It was all that Nadine could do to keep from exploding into a crying fit. She stood slowly. She could feel herself shaking. *He'd been looking for her. He wanted to meet her. He didn't hate her.*

"Well, isn't this a day of blessings and miracles?" Bishop Samuels said.

First lady Samuels walked towards Nadine, holding out her arms. "We have been praying for this moment! God is so good!" She wrapped her arms around Nadine.

Nadine melted into the woman's arms, and began crying again.

"Well mother, looks like you were right again: God brought the mountain to us!" Bishop Samuels bellowed.

"God don't lie!" Mother Buckner said.

First lady Samuels stood back, taking Nadine's hands in hers. "God has definitely answered some prayers today, hasn't he?" She reached up, and wiped a few tears away from Nadine's face. She looked at David, then back at Nadine. "We see now, where he gets his beautiful eyes from." She smiled.

"I...I don't understand. How did you know? I mean..." Nadine was at a loss for words.

"Pastor Jackson wrote us," Bishop Samuels said. "We had written him a few months ago, inquiring about David's birth mother..."

Nadine looked to David. He was lovely.

David smiled at Nadine.

Nadine's heart melted.

"...he told us that you had visited with him, inquiring yourself. We prayed on it, and felt in our hearts that is was best to wait on you. When you were ready, we were sure that you would seek us out. Theo did tell us your name." Bishop Samuels smiled.

David walked towards Nadine.

First lady Samuels released Nadine's hands, and walked towards her mother. She gave her mother a kiss, and held her hand.

Mother Buckner kissed her daughter's hand. "It's all right, baby. This is what he wants. You will always be his mama. He has more than enough room for both of you," she whispered to her daughter.

"Thanks Ma, you always know what to say."

Nadine could feel her body shaking. Nadine wasn't sure what to do, or what to say.

David smiled, and stood in front of Nadine. He was about a foot taller than she. He looked her in the eyes and said, "Now my family is complete." With that, he wrapped his arms around his mother, and hugged her tightly.

At first, Nadine was too scared to move. Slowly, she raised her arms and touched her son. *Was this really happening? Was he real? Was she actually holding her baby boy that was taken away from her so long ago?* Nadine felt herself wrap her arms around her son. When she did, she cried out.

"Oh God! Oh God!" She had waited for this moment for seventeen years. "I love you! I love you so much," she cried.

"I love you, too," he said in her ear.

Bishop and first lady Samuels, and Mother

JR

Buckner quietly left the room, giving reunited mother and son some privacy.

Nadine held onto David with all her might; too afraid to let go for fear that this was some kind of dream, and she didn't want to wake up if it was.

David pulled back for a moment. He looked Nadine in the eyes. It was like looking in a mirror. The tears streamed down his face, as he smiled.

Nadine took his face in her hands, wiping the tears away. "I have prayed for this day so many times," she whispered.

"So have I."

Nadine pulled David into her arms again. It was real. It was real. God gave her a miracle. "Thank you God! Oh thank You!"

CHAPTER 37

July 4th, 1975

EMMA WAS EXCITED. More excited than she had been in a while. All her family was coming, and other guests, as well. She wanted everything to go perfect. It was ten o'clock; she'd been up since three o'clock that morning, cooking, cleaning, and preparing the house. Albert had gone fishing at four o'clock. Junior, James Perry, and Calvin had gone with him. She was so happy that she and Calvin were speaking regularly again. He was still a little distant; but nothing like he was months ago.

"Woo! I am blessed! You hear me Gertie?" Emma said, to her hanging philodendron. "Gertie, we gonna has ourselves a party! You hear me?" She watered the plant.

Emma's spirits were soaring high. She walked around the kitchen humming and singing. One of her favorite songs came on. She turned the radio up. "Sing it, Al Green! You better sing that song!" Emma started singing along with the radio. *"Love and happiness...something that can make you do wrong, make you do right...Love...Love and happiness..."*

Emma danced around the kitchen. She hadn't noticed that she had an audience. Macon and Deeney, holding Nathaniel and Ella, watched as Emma danced and sang around the kitchen; both trying to stifle their laughs. It was just good to see Mama happy again. They went unnoticed until Nathaniel and Ella started singing along.

Emma turned around. "How long you been standing there?"

"Long enough to sees you get your grooves on!" Deeney laughed. Ella squirmed in her arms.

"Look at that," Emma said, as she walked towards Ella and Nathaniel. "My babies know good music, too! Give 'em here," Emma held out her arms.

"Nathaniel's kind of heavy, Mama. You sure you want to hold this butterball at the same time?" Macon asked.

"Yeah, Ella ain't light herself!" Deeney laughed.

"You stop talkin' 'bout my babies like that," said Emma, in a baby voice. "Give 'em here. They wants to dance with Nana. Don't you babies?" She took them in her arms.

Both Nathaniel and Ella squealed with delight.

Emma danced around the kitchen with them in her arms, singing. "*Love and Happiness...*"

Macon and Deeney laughed.

"Did you see that?" Macon laughed. "They're singing with her!"

"I know! I have to get the camera for this!" Deeney ran to the family room.

Emma continued to dance around the kitchen with her grand babies in her arms. Nathaniel and Ella were laughing and singing, trying to mimic

Emma.

Deeney ran back in with the camera going. "Smile for the camera!"

Macon laughed, and jumped in the shot, dancing around. "Smile for the camera, Nathaniel. Smile, Ella."

Emma turned the babies around to face the camera. "Go head, Nana's babies. Sing...sing," she laughed. "I told you; nothin' like Al Green to make you feel good!"

"What's that about Al Green?" Albert said coming through the back door. "I thought I was the only Al that made you feel good!"

"Oh God," Junior said. "Not in front of the children!"

Emma laughed. "Hey, you know you number one, baby!" She danced over to Albert and kissed him.

"That's what I'm talkin' 'bout! What you all know 'bout that there?" He hit Emma on the backside.

"Pops! Stop trying to corrupt my daughter and nephew!" Calvin laughed.

"Oh please," Albert said. "Ain't nothin' corrupt about this here! Jes pure love, son. Pure-d love!"

Emma continued to laugh and dance with her grand babies, as they continued to sing with her, laughing.

"Whew! You ain't lyin'...these babies ain't light!" Emma handed Nathaniel to Macon, and Ella back to Deeney.

Deeney put the camera on the table. "Uh-oh! I think somebody still wants to dance." She danced around with Ella in her arms.

"No, she jes sees her daddy, that's all," said Emma.

"Daddy will get you in a minute, Ella. Let me get cleaned up before your mother says something!"

Albert laughed. "I remember those days. Don't worry son, it gets better after the first one!"

"First one?" Calvin said. "Slow down Pops! Give us at least another year!"

"I don't know...Anna-Leigh lookin' mighty fine. Got her little shape back and everything!" Emma raised an eyebrow at Calvin.

"Mama, don't you start!"

"I don't know...I had me a dream about some fish last week?"

Everyone in the kitchen looked at one another.

"Well, it ain't us," Calvin said. "You better look at Junior!"

"Oh no, brother! Not this way!" Junior raised his hands.

"Well, I don't know who it is; but somebody got some feet in the oven!" Emma sashayed over to the stove.

Deeney and Macon both declared at the same time, "It ain't me!"

"C'mon, Ella. Let's get out of here," Deeney said laughing.

"I'm rights behind you!" Macon said, following Deeney out.

"You sure knows how to clears a room, woman!" Albert laughed.

Calvin and Junior went to clean up.

Emma laughed, turning around. "Well, how else was I gonna gets you alone? Lord knows we got a house full," she said, looking at Albert coyly.

"Now, don't you starts your mess, Emma Jean!" Albert laughed. "I'm smellin' like fish and all, and we got all these folks up in here."

Emma stood in front of Albert. "Well, tell you what…you makes sure you cleans up real good, and meet me tonight at our spot." She nodded her head towards the gazebo.

"Oh yeah?"

"Yeah. As soon as everyone goes home, and everyone is settles in here; me and you gonna have our own fireworks display!" Emma leaned forward and kissed Albert passionately.

"Woo-Hoo, Mama! Now you talkin' my kinds of talk!"

"You better believe we won't be doin' no talkin' tonight either!"

"Have mercy!"

"I got a little, somethin'-somethin', waiting for us, too."

"Is that right?"

Emma nodded her head, smiling like a Cheshire cat.

"Woo, woman! You sure know how to get me started! Let me gets out this kitchen before I does somethin' nasty to you!"

"Ooh!" Emma hit Albert on the backside.

"Alright now, woman!" Albert laughed leaving the kitchen.

Emma laughed to herself, shaking her head. She felt so good. This was going to be a wonderful fourth. She could feel it in her bones. There wasn't a cloud in the sky. The sun was shining bright. Her family was with her. Shelby and Richard were on their way. And even a miracle had happened. Nadine was coming...with her son, Macon's brother. God, she felt good! "Thank you, Jesus!"

"Well praise the, Lord!" Lynorra said walking in the back door, holding two large trays.

"Hey Sistah!" Emma helped Lynorra with the trays. "Now you know you didn't have to brings nothin'!"

"I know; that's why I didn't tell you!"

"What you got in here anyway?" Emma peeked under the foil. "Ooh, Chile. Tell me this isn't your banana puddin'?"

"Yes it is!" Lynorra laughed. She knew that it was Emma's favorite.

"Girl, hush your mouth! Now you know I ain't puttin' both these here out!"

"Emma, you are a mess!"

"Don't I know it?" Emma laughed. "How's you doin'?"

"Girl, I'm fine! By the way, I'm gonna get that

Albert. James came running into the house, all excited, carrying all that fish and crabs! Talking about he's going to clean and gut them himself. *Mr. Albert showed him how!"* Lynorra shook her head laughing.

"Oh no! I can see your kitchen now!"

"Who you telling? I told that boy don't he touch that fish. Leave it in the refrigerator in the garage until tomorrow." Lynorra rolled her eyes. "So," she said placing the trays in the refrigerator, "I see you in mighty fine spirits!"

"Yes I am, Sistah. Yes I am." Emma grabbed the coffee pot, and two cups.

Lynorra took the cake dish from the counter, and grabbed two plates and the cake knife. She smiled lifting the cake dish. "Can't have coffee without your seven-up cake!"

Emma laughed. "Go on and cuts me a slice. I've been so busy this here mornin', that I ain't has time to eat nothin. Jes been tastin' this, and tastin' that!" Emma poured two cups of coffee, giving one to Lynorra.

"Thanks," Lynorra said taking a sip. Lynorra lifted her brow, and looked at Emma over her cup.

Emma sat down across from her. Feigning ignorance. She asked, "What? Somethin' wrong with my coffee?" Emma smiled sheepishly, taking a sip.

"Well, no—if you likes a little mulberry in the morning! Emma you a mess! No wonder you dancing and singing around here all happy!"

"Chile, how else you think I been able to stay

up all this time? Shoot! I needed me somethin' a little stronger than coffee!"

"I know that's right!" Lynorra ate a piece of the cake. "Mm," she said closing her eyes. "Emma, this is so good and moist! You the only one I know who can makes this cake better than I do!" Lynorra shook her body like she had a shiver.

Emma laughed. "Thank you! But, I still ain't got nothin' on your banana puddin'." Emma placed a forkful of cake in her mouth.

"Yeah, well, this mulberry wine really makes it taste even better!" Lynorra took another sip. "Mm. So, is Nadine still coming?"

Emma nodded her head. "Uh-huh."

"I still can't believe it. Who'd of thought six months ago, you'd be happy to have her in your house?"

"Talks about it!" Emma shook her head. "I still has to pinch myself."

"Is it for real?"

"Shelby and Camille believe so."

"How's Macon?"

"She's good with it. Camille went to see Nadine two weeks ago. She said Nadine really seems to have turned the corner. It's like; her finding her son was a great turning point. Girl, she even found Jesus!"

"You told me! Wow!"

"Camille took Macon to meet her last week. They met at her church."

"Really? How'd that go?"

"It went pretty well. I mean, Macon was fine with it. She didn't take Nathaniel, though. She met her brother...David."

"Wow!"

"I'm tellin' you; it's a miracle! Talk about shocked? I damn near fell off my stool when her Pastor called me. I was like, *who? What? How? Come again!*"

Lynorra laughed. "What was his name again?"

"Bishop Christopher Samuels."

"*Thee* Bishop Samuels, from Mount Carmel First AME Zion church?" Lynorra put down her cup.

"Yup!"

"Wow! He is a strong preacher. He don't mess around. He tells it like it is! That's why Artie don't like him...he has called him out more than a few times."

"Oh, *that's him?*"

Lynorra nodded her head.

"Girl, then I know Nadine gonna be all right!"

"Oh yes. This is a miracle!"

"Thank you, Jesus!" Emma lifted her hands, and laughed.

Lynorra laughed at her friend.

"He was the one that adopted her son."

"Really? Look at God. He couldn't have been in better hands."

"I know. When he called here on behalf of

Nadine; I ain't gonna lie, I was a bit skeptical and all. All things considering, you know?"

"Who can blame you? This is Nadine we talking about."

"But, when he started sharing with me about the change in Nadine, and what he and his wife have witnessed...I don't know, somethin' in my spirit jes clicked. Like, I needed to believe him."

Lynorra shook her head. "Mm, God certainly do work in mysterious ways, don't He?"

"Yes He does. I spoke with him for a good while. And do you know, Nadine told him everything?"

"Get out of here!" Lynorra hit her hand on the table.

"Mm-hm. I knew then, that somethin' really was different. So I gave him Camille's number. Shelby and Richard went to church with them when she took Macon down there. Shelby said I wouldn't believe the change. I'd have to see it with my own eyes to really believe it."

"That's amazing. For Shelby to say that? Hm."

"I know. You know Shelby was ready to kill Nadine. But she swears Nadine ain't the same person. Macon said the same thing. In fact, it was her idea to invite Nadine and David today, so they could meets Nathaniel. They're coming in with Shelby and Richard. They should be here by one."

"Emma, I am happy for you; especially Macon. That child has been through so much, to be so young."

"Yes she has."

"But I'm so happy she has you in her life. God only knows what might have been..."

Emma was quiet for a moment. She knew better than anyone, how blessed she truly was. "Well, enough about me. How you doin'? I missed you somethin' terrible this past month. Lord, Albert had to drags me out to church! Although, I did manage to get one Sunday! Jes wasn't the same wit out you." Emma smiled.

"I'm doing much better. So is James. He had a ball in, New York. He really hated to leave..."

Emma studied her friend. "Looks as though someone else hated to leave?" She smiled knowingly at Lynorra.

"Yeah, I guess so. It was good to get away for a while; but running away don't solves nothing. But, I'm okay. I know God is working it all out. I'll tell you all about it later." Lynorra waved her hand, not wanting to dampen Emma's high spirits.

"You sure? I always has time for you, Sistah."

Lynorra smiled. "I know you do, and I couldn't love you more. But really, I'm fine. Nothing that can't wait. We got plenty of time. We can go shopping this week."

"Alright. I like the sounds of that. I got a little stash I been itchin' to spend!"

"I know you do!" Lynorra shook her head. "Emma, you are too much!"

THE BARBEQUE WAS IN FULL SWING. Emma watched from the back porch. Her heart felt good. Everyone was eating and drinking, and playing cards. The children were running around, playing hard and laughing, having water-balloon fights. Albert was just about finish frying the last of the fish he and the boys caught that morning. Emma watched as each person laughed, and filled their bellies.

What warmed Emma's heart the most, however, was seeing how happy Macon was. Lord, she never thought she'd see the day—she prayed for it!—but she'd never actually thought she'd see the day when Nadine was so happy and acting like she had some sense. Lord, what a sight! Emma watched as Nadine *oohed* and *ahhed* all over Nathaniel. Nathaniel took right to her. Nadine cried and cried. It warmed Emma's heart. And to see Macon sitting and talking with her mother; it was what Emma had hoped for. She knew that Nathan would be happy. She could feel him smiling down on them.

And David! He was a handsome young man. (She could tell Deeney had a crush on him!) He looked just like Nadine. When he and Macon smiled, they looked like twins. He would be turning eighteen in another week. He asked if Macon and Nathaniel could come to Georgia. His parents were giving him a birthday-slash-going away party, and he would love for his folks to meet them. Emma said yes, as long as Macon wanted to. He even asked if Deeney could come! Lord, the boy was smitten with her, too! Emma knew that not, too much, longer Macon would be leaving. She was okay with it, knowing that Nadine was doing so well. She would miss her and Nathaniel terribly; but she would never deprive Nadine from being the kind of mother she always dreamed of being, and grandmother to Nathaniel.

"Hey Miss Emma!" one of her neighbors yelled out.

"Hey, baby! You enjoyin' yourself?" Emma smiled waving.

"I sure am! When you gonna come and play a hand with us?"

"What? So you Negroes can whine 'bout me takin' all your money?" Emma laughed.

The neighbor laughed, waving their hand at Emma.

Emma shook her head. Black folk! *"Lord, give 'em a good party with some good food...and somethin' to drink, and they loves you for life!"*

"Hey Mama, what you doing?"

Emma turned to see Shelby. Lord, her baby was lookin' jes as pretty as she wanted to be. She knew Shelby was the fish in her dreams. But Emma was content on waiting. She'd act like she didn't notice that the child's breast were getting big!

"Hey baby!" She leaned in and gave Shelby a kiss. "I'm jes watching these crazy Negroes out here!" She laughed.

"Yeah, you're right about that: they some crazy fools out here!"

"Yeah, but they havin' themselves a good time; and that's what I like to see."

Shelby wrapped her arms around her mother's shoulders.

"You and Pop always did have the best barbeques. When you two gonna stop working and moves to, Georgia? You know, Deeney be grown soon enough, and leaving for school. And we know Macon won't be here forever."

Emma nodded her head. "I know, I know. But this is my home, Shelby. This is where your daddy and I raise you chilren, and planted roots. Roots are important, you know? Me and your daddy worked hard for what we got." Emma turned sideways, looking at Shelby. "And, what makes you think that me and your daddy gonna be so lonely?"

"I—I was just *suggesting...*" Shelby shrugged her shoulders.

Emma patted Shelby on the arm. "I know baby. But me and your daddy are far from being put out to pasture. We's got a whole lot more life in us yet. Hell! I'm only fifty-three!"

"Soon to be fifty-four next month," Shelby said, stroking her mother's hair.

"I know. And I still looks good!"

"You sure do, Mama. You sure do."

"You know," Emma looked around her backyard, "there's a whole lot of history in this place; history that I wants to share with all my grand's and great grand's. Your daddy and I has built us a legacy. We didn't has that from our folks. You know 'bout my family. And your daddy was raised by his Aunt Lorelei. When we got married—it was us. He didn't have to come to, Busby, you know? Uh-uh. He came here for me. He knew I didn't know no other place. And New York was jes, too, fast a place for me." Emma laughed to herself. "Besides; I don't think your daddy wanted me to be lefts 'round all those fast talkers whilst he was in the service. Yeah...your daddy said that down south was where we belonged. It didn't hurt either that his Uncle, Lorelei's father, left him the store, and Lorelei gave him this land. A hundred acres between this land here, and the lumber mill, and furniture store. Yes, we was bless to holds onto it. Many tried to pry it from our hands...but *your daddy*? He wasn't gonna let none of that happens. No sir. We paid our taxes. Even when all we had to eats is what we grown in the garden. We rented about twenty acres out to some good people. God has really blessed us. Busby may not be as fast or happening as Atlanta, New York or even Charlotte; but it sure is home. Nah, I could never leave this place."

Emma looked around at her family and friends. This was what life was about; Family and friends, coming together in the good times and the bad. Sticking up for each other; looking out for each other's children. Emma was content with her little town of Busby. It was all home to her.

Shelby listened to her mother speak. And for the first time she really understood what her mother was saying. She had not realized that she had begun to cry.

Emma turned around, and placed her arm around Shelby's waist. "You alright, Baby?" She took a handkerchief out of her pocket, and wiped her daughter's face.

"Oh yeah, I'm good, Mama. Just happy, is all. I'm glad you and pop have this place. I'm glad you have one another. I'm glad we have this home to come back to. We may not be the Waltons; but they ain't us either!"

Emma squeezed Shelby tight to her. "I hear you, baby. I hear you!"

"Hey Mama, when you and Pop get a chance, Richard and I want to talk to you. We got in a little later than we expected today, and didn't have the chance."

"Okay baby. Your daddy should be finishing up with that fish. As soon as he is, I'll finds you."

"Uh? I think Pop is finished!" Shelby burst out laughing.

Emma turned around, and saw what Shelby was laughing at.

"Lord have mercy!"

Albert was in the middle of the yard dancing with Lynorra.

"Oh Lord, Pop went and started a Soul Train line! I have to get the camera for this one!" Shelby ran into the house.

Emma nearly bust a gut. Now Albert knew he had no business trying to dance to no fast song! He knew the rule: slow songs only! Emma laughed until her sides hurt. Lynorra was doing her thing; but Albert? Good Lord!

"I got it!" Shelby came out with the camera. Richard and Junior right behind her.

"Oh, look at Albert!" Richard laughed.

"Go Pop! Go Pop!" Junior shouted.

"Please, don't egg that ol' man on!" Emma laughed.

Albert turned around, and started waving his hands in the air.

"C'mon, Mama! Get on over here and show these young-ens how it's done!"

Emma waved her hands. "You crazy, ol' man!"

"Only 'bout you!" Albert said, continuing to flail around like a fish out of water.

Emma shook her head.

"Go ahead, Mama!" Richard said.

"C'mon, Mama! C'mon so I can get you and daddy on film!" Shelby said.

"C'mon Emma!" Lynorra yelled. "I ain't gonna dance all night by myself!"

"Hey, what am I?" Albert asked.

Lynorra stopped and put her hands on her hips. "...Like I was saying—I ain't gonna dance all by myself, Emma!"

The crowd broke out in OH's!

Emma laughed, as Junior pulled her by the hand.

"Go Mama! Go Mama! Go Mama!" Everyone cheered!

Emma let loose! She started dancing and shimmying, and shaking her backside. She laughed until her sides hurt. And danced until her hips hurt!

"Go 'head baby! Shake a tale feather!" Albert hollered. "That's my baby!"

Everyone was clapping and jumping, singing and dancing. Emma didn't know when she had more of a fine time. They partied all night; all the way into the wee hours of the morning.

ALBERT WATCHED EMMA SLEEP. She looked so peaceful and happy. He'd been lying there, watching her breath in and out. He guessed it was about seven in the morning or so. The sun was hot already. He didn't want to disturb her rest. When he looked again, he thought he saw a smile.

"Emma, you awake?"

Emma started laughing. She couldn't feign sleep any longer. She'd been awake for a while now; but she knew one of Albert's favorite things was watching her sleep. He would joke with her and say it was the only time her mouth wasn't movin'!

"How long you been awake, woman?"

Emma opened her eyes. "Long enough, man!" Emma propped herself up on her elbows, making sure the sheet covered her breasts.

"Why you gonna cover them now?" Albert laughed. "I kind of enjoyed the view from here," he said smiling.

"You so nasty!"

"Yeah, but you likes it!" Albert laughed.

"Yeah, you right about that! But, it ain't darks no more, and the sun is up. I don't want none of them kids wanderin' out here, and catchin' us in all our glory!"

"Too bad! Ain't nobody tells them to come to this gazebo! They knows!"

"Yeah, but we has guests."

"And? The kids will let 'em know. Besides, all them Negroes still sleepin'."

"Yeah, you probably right. What time did we finally comes out here?"

"I think it was two or three?" Albert surmised.

"Yeah, they were still talkin' in the living room when we lefts them." Emma lay back, turning to her side. She took Albert's hand and kissed it. "So, *grandpa*, we gonna has another grand baby, huh?"

Albert lay back, resting his hand behind his head. He lifted his other arm, as Emma laid her head on his bare chest. "Yes, *grandma!* Our baby is havin' a baby!"

"I'm so excited for them! Shelby's so happy! Did you see Richard fallin' all over himself?"

"Yeah. Good thing he a doctor!" Albert laughed.

Emma rubbed her hand over Albert's chest.

Albert took her hand, and kissed it. "We done

really good, Mama. The good, Lord has really blessed us."

"Yes He has. If you would have told me a year ago, six months ago, that I was gonna be this happy, I wouldn't has believed you."

"Me neither. I *hoped*, but I had my doubts. But look at God. He's always on time!"

"Yes He is!" Emma smiled.

Albert looked down at Emma. "What would I do with outs you, woman?"

"You never has to know, baby. You never has to know."

"Is that a promise?"

"I promise."

Albert leaned over and kissed Emma. "You thinks we have times?" He raised his eyebrows, smiling.

"*You such a dirty...ol'...man!*" Emma giggled.

"Yeah, but I'm *your* dirty ol' man!" Albert laughed, and wrapped his arms around Emma, pulling her close to him.

"I love you, Al-B," Emma whispered, barely getting the words out.

"Woman, you don't has a choice!"

"Mm. I like it when you take charge, daddy!"

CHAPTER 39

August 3rd, 1975

EMMA LOOKED OUT HER KITCHEN WINDOW. "I don't know Gertie? I don't like those clouds one bit! Those are trouble clouds! Nothin' but troubles, and a whole lot of it!" Emma picked up her plant and opened the back door. "Here you go girl. Get you some of this natural water...least you won't get into no trouble."

Emma sat her plant down on the porch step. Just as she was standing, a lightning bolt lit the sky, with loud thunder following soon after. She stood up, and looked to the sky. Emma's hair started rising.

"Oh Lord, who's goin' home now?"

Emma's children always teased her about her superstitions and old folklore. But Emma took it seriously. She knew for certain, her hair rising like that meant death was soon to come. A chill rose up Emma's back, causing her to shiver.

"Woo, Lord! Keep my family safe," she said rubbing her arms. Although it was still hot and humid out, Emma suddenly felt chilled to the bone. She looked towards the sky again before going inside. It had gotten even darker in the past few moments that she had been on the porch.

Emma had already turned all the lights out,

and unplugged the radios and television sets. She wasn't taking any chances. She sat down at the table, and poured herself a glass of sweet tea. The house was so quiet. Albert forgot something at the job. (Probably was her birthday present!) Deeney, Macon and the baby were still in Georgia. They'd be back tomorrow for her birthday. Emma was alone. She couldn't say she much liked it. It was a little, *too, quiet!* But she shouldn't complain. It gave her sometime to think.

One person who weighed heavily on Emma's mind was Lynorra. She was very concerned about her best friend. Lynorra had shared with her about her troubles with Artie, and his continued poor treatment of James Perry. She didn't know how much more Lynorra could take. Emma also didn't trust Artie. If he felt in any way that Lynorra was leaving, she was afraid of what he might do.

Emma never cared for Artie. He reminded her of a slippery snake. But she loved Lynorra and those kids. And as long as Lynorra wanted to stay, she would support her. However, she would be damned if she stood by whilst he put his hands on her. Emma didn't go for that; nor did Albert. It incensed Albert to no end to hear, or see a man put a harmful hand on a woman. "I swears, Emma. I don't care who the man is! Pastor, policeman, doctor, factory worker! Don't let him put his hands on no woman in my presence! Especially no son of mine! And ain't no man better not attempts to touch one of my girls! I'll kick their ass from here to kingdom come!" It took a whole lot to make Albert cuss. *And, a man putting his hand on a woman?* That was at the top of the list!

A loud, crashing, thunder shook the sky. Emma jumped. Heavy rain started to rain down.

"Woo-wee! You means business, huh, Lord?" Emma looked out the back door. It was a heavy down pour. *Good,* she thought. Her garden could use the rain. They had a dry spell the past couple of weeks.

It rained for quite a while; letting up for moments at a time, then down pouring again. Emma sat at the table reading a book. Looking up at the rain, she wondered if Albert was going to be able to take her to the movies tonight. They were supposed to go see that flick, *Let's Do It Again,* starring, Sidney Poitier and Bill Cosby. It finally made its way to, Busby. She hardly saw movies when they first came out. She doubted if they were going anywhere, though, if it kept raining like it was. That's okay, she resigned. There was always next year. Emma continued reading her book, when she heard a knock at the door. She forgot that she'd put the latch on, to keep the wind from blowing it open.

"Emma?"

"Lynorra, what's going on?" Emma unlatched the door.

Lynorra walked in, soaking wet, and crying.

"Lynorra, what's the matter? What happened?"

Lynorra looked into her friends face, and shook her head, overwhelmed by emotions. She fell into Emma's arms and sobbed.

"C'mon, sits down. Let me makes you some tea."

Lynorra sat down. "No, no. I—I can't stay. I have...I have to gets back home before James..." Lynorra shoulders shook from her heavy sobs.

"Okay. But you sure?"

Lynorra nodded. "Yes. Yes," she said trying to compose herself. "I'm sorry."

"For what? You know you can always come here!"

"I Know." Lynorra shook her head. "He did it again," she said, in such a whisper that Emma barely heard her.

"Come again?"

"He...Artie...he...did...it...again! He cheated... with Celia!"

Emma's mouth flew open. She swore she heard her jaw hit the floor.

"Are you sure?"

Lynorra laid a manila envelope on the table, and pushed it towards Emma.

"It's all in there!"

Emma opened the envelope. Inside were photos of Artie and Celia; at the church; at a restaurant; a motel; and at Lynorra's home. Emma covered her mouth. She was sick to her stomach. She reached out her hand to her dearest friend.

"Where'd you get these?"

"Celia's husband. Apparently, he's been having her followed. She sure picked a good one this time! He has money, and he knows how to use it!"

Lynorra shook her head, and cried some more. "In my home, Emma! In my home, where our kids live; where we live; where *I* sleep! Nasty! Just goddamn nasty! All that time I was in New York, he was bringing that heifer into my home and playing house!" Lynorra screamed. "Damn him, Emma! Damn him! And damn me for being so stupid!" She pounded the table with her fists.

"Now wait a minute! You did the best you could! I'm not gonna let you blames yourself for that slick mu—" Emma stopped herself. "Lord! Forgives me! Sistah, you ain't gots no reason to beat up on yourself! You hear me? God gonna take care of him! You watch and see."

"I can't stay there, Emma. I can't. I'm just afraid of what I might do!" Lynorra was shaking all over.

"Don't. You go ahead and gets some of your things. You and James Perry can stay here until you decides what you gonna do."

"I can't do that! You don't needs my mess on your doorstep."

"Uh-uh!" Emma shook her adamantly. "You are my family, Lynorra. My home is your home. And I won't takes no for an answer. And this way, if Artie has a problem, he can takes it up with Albert!"

Lynorra wiped her face, trying to compose herself. "Alright," she finally said.

"Let me comes with you," Emma said. "I don't want you to be there alone." Emma walked towards the mud-room to get her raincoat.

"No, no," Lynorra said standing. "That's alright."

Emma turned around. "It's okay, I don't minds. You don't needs to be alone. I'll help you get your things," Emma persisted.

But Lynorra wouldn't hear of it. "No. That's alright. I don't want to alarms James, none. He should be walking in the house any minute. I'll be finish getting a few things together before Artie gets home, anyway. We just need an overnight bag until I decide what to do next."

Emma didn't like that idea; but she didn't want to push Lynorra. "Alright, I'll jes put on some food for you, and gets the room ready. I'll see if Albert will take James Perry to the movies tonight."

"Oh no, Emma. This is you and Albert's night. You see, I'm already disturbing you?"

"Hush now! I don't want to hear that foolish talk. You know right well, that me *and* Albert would do anythings for you. Besides, it will give us a chance to be alone and talks. You know James Perry; if he even senses you upset, he'll be upsets."

Lynorra nodded. Emma was right about James. He was very sensitive to her.

"Okay," Lynorra resigned. "Give me half an hour. I want to make sure I have everything." Lynorra zipped up her rain coat, and picked up the envelope with the pictures off the table. She wasn't exactly sure what she was going to do with them, or with *Artie*, for that matter. She needed some time to think. Emma was right; she couldn't stay in that house—not tonight. She and James would stay with

Emma and Albert...at the most a couple of days; then she would know what to do by then. But right now, she needed to get back to the house before James did, and get a few things.

"You know if you ain't back here in exactly twenty minutes; I'm comin' over there to gets you?" Emma said.

Lynorra managed a laugh. "I know you will," she said. "Don't worry, I'll be back in no more than twenty...I promise. Just make sure you have some of that mulberry wine waiting for me."

"You got it," Emma smiled.

Lynorra sighed deeply. "Thank you, Emma. I don't know what I would do without you. Did I ever tell you how much I love you?" Lynorra said, as a tear escaped her eye.

Emma embraced her sister. "All the time. All the time." Emma rubbed her back. "I loves you, too. You and those kids are my family. You all mean as much to me as my own...so don't you ever forgets that. I'll give my life for you," Emma whispered in Lynorra's ear.

"I know you would. That's just who you are... good people." Lynorra pulled back, and stared at her friend for a moment. "You are the best, Emma Jean Watson."

"So are you, Lynorra Louise Washington."

Lynorra cringed. "Did you have to say *Louise*?" She laughed. "God, what a name!"

Emma laughed. "Okay, *Lynorra Washington!*"

JR

Lynorra smiled, and walked to the back door. "I'll see you soon."

"Okay. I'll be waiting."

With that, Lynorra walked out the door.

Emma shook her head. She didn't have a good feeling about none of this. She picked up the phone to call Albert.

"C'mon baby, pick up. Pick—Albert? Hey baby, you got to come home now...I has a bad feeling...its Lynorra. I'll explain it when you gets here...please Albert, come now...Okay. I love you, too. Hurry." Emma hung up the phone. She didn't want to disregard Lynorra's wishes; but if she and James Perry didn't walk through her door in the next eighteen minutes...she was going over there! She had a feeling that Artie was going to start some mess. He'd probably be knocking on her door, demanding Lynorra to come home. She was glad Albert was coming home soon; then he could deal with him. She wasn't averse to using her pistol, either! She'd do what she had to do to protect her family. And that's what Lynorra and her children were; family.

Emma looked at the clock. Only ten minutes had passed. Yet it felt like an eternity. Emma waited anxiously. "What is takin' that man so long to get home? I tolds him to hurry?" Emma started to call Albert again; but then hung up the phone. She'd just called him five minutes ago, and there was no answer. "Lord, this is worse than waitin' for a Chile to be born." Emma paced her kitchen floor. She went out to the porch a couple of times. She thought

Southern~477~Comfort

she heard Lynorra coming. But when she looked, it was just the wind blowing the gate.

"Lord, Emma Jean, get a holds of yourself." Emma went to her pantry and took out her stash of mulberry wine. She poured some in her coffee pot and warmed it.

Sitting down at the table, Emma's legs were shaking nervously. Uneasiness was growing quickly in her body with each moment the clock ticked. She took a sip of the warm wine, glancing over at the clock. *Five more minutes,* she whispered to herself. Just then, a loud crash of thunder shook the house. Emma jumped; her heart nearly in her throat.

"Oh for heaven's sake, woman; get it together!" she scolded herself.

"Mama! Mama!" James came barreling through the back door, stumbling. "Mama! Mama!"

Emma dropped her cup of wine, jolted by James Perry. Emma jumped up. "Lynorra!"

"Mama, come quick! He's gonna kill my mother!" James was crying hard, barely audible.

"Calm down, Baby! Calm down!"

James shook his head furiously. Grabbing Emma's hand, he pulled at her towards the door. "Please, Mama! Please," he cried. "You gotta come now! He got a gun!" James let go of Emma's hand and ran out the back door.

"Oh sweet, Jesus!" Emma ran to the phone. She dialed 911 as fast as she could. "Hello! Hello! Yes, this Emma Jean Watson. I need the police at 546 Winterbourne Street! Yes! Someone has a gun, and he's threatening to use it! Oh hell, woman! I don't know! Jes sends the damn police!" Emma hung up the phone and ran out the house. "Oh Jesus! Oh Jesus! Please!" Emma ran as fast as she could. "Oh God, Albert, where are you?"

The rain had started pouring again. Emma could barely see in front of her. She didn't even see Albert's car pulling up as she was turning the corner. Emma was running as fast as her legs would go. She ran so fast, she ran out of her shoes.

Albert jumped out his car when he saw Emma.

"Emma! Emma!" he hollered. "What in the hell?" Albert took off running after her. He knew there was only one place she could be running that fast to—Lynorra's.

Emma was within five feet of Lynorra's back porch when she heard Lynorra scream.

"Nooooo! Jaaaaames, mooooove!"

"Oh Jesus!" Emma rushed up the back steps; a loud pop stopping her in her tracks. She knew what it was. It was a gunshot.

Emma heard James Perry scream.

She rushed into the house; into the kitchen. "Oh my Jesus," she cried covering her mouth.

Artie and Lynorra lay on the floor. Artie was on top of Lynorra. Lynorra looked up into Artie's face.

He looked at his wife.

"No," he whispered.

A tear rolled down Lynorra's cheek.

Artie rolled off top of his wife. There was blood all over his hands. It was Lynorra's.

James ran to his mother. "Mama! Mama! No!"

"It's all right, Baby." Lynorra's voice was weak. "I'll be okay. Mama loves you."

That was the last time James ever heard his mother's voice.

Artie sat with his back against the kitchen sink, crying; mumbling incoherently.

Emma rushed to Lynorra's side. She grabbed a couple of dish towels.

"It's okay, Sistah. It's okay," she said through blinding tears. "Emma's here. Emma's here now." Emma tried to apply pressure to the wound. But she couldn't even tell where the wound was, due to all the blood. "Hold on, baby. Hold...on..." Emma almost broke down crying; but she couldn't. Lynorra needed her.

"Emma!" Albert came rushing through the back door. He froze when he saw the scene. "Oh God," he whispered. He rushed over to Emma. "Mama...let me, baby." He tried to take the towels from Emma.

"No! No! She needs me! She needs me!" Emma kept her eyes on Lynorra, while trying to stop the bleeding.

Sirens could be heard getting closer.

Lynorra opened her eyes briefly. She looked Emma in the eyes. She moved one of her hands, and tried to speak.

"Shush...shush," Emma said softly. "Saves your strength...the ambulance will be here soon." Emma tried to smile through her tears. "You gonna be alright, Sistah. You'll see." Emma grabbed Lynorra's hand and squeezed it. She brushed her other hand over Lynorra's forehead, stroking her hair. "Okay, Sistah? You holds on..." The tears were stinging Emma's eyes.

Albert went out to meet the police and the ambulance.

James stood by, crying, scared and confused, in shock.

Lynorra looked at her best friend, tears running down the sides of her face. She tried to speak, but no words came out.

"Shush...don't...don't speak, Lynorra." Emma continued to apply pressure to Lynorra's stomach area, but the blood kept coming, flowing heavier and heavier. "Oh God..." Emma cried, as she looked at the blood. She looked back to Lynorra. "I'm sorry, baby. Jes hold on. Please hold on," she begged her dearest friend.

Lynorra shut her eyes for a moment, and then opened them again. She looked at Emma. She struggled to move her lips. *My babies,* she finally mouthed.

Emma nodded her head, understandingly. "Don't you fret 'bout them. I'm gonna...I'm gonna... takes...good...care...of them...'til you...gets better," she said between sobs.

Lynorra smiled one last time at her friend, and then closed her eyes. Her head gently lay to the side, and her hand went limp in Emma's hand.

"Lynorra! Lynorra!" Emma screamed.

Albert came rushing back in with the ambulance and police.

Albert had to pry Emma away, so that the EMT's could attend to Lynorra.

Emma went in the ambulance with Lynorra. Albert took James with him. They followed them to the hospital. The police stayed behind to question Reverend Arthur Washington.

Emma knew that her best friend was gone the moment she closed her eyes. She felt the exact moment her spirit left. Emma knew in her heart that Lynorra wasn't going to make it; especially when she saw all that blood. She knew what most others didn't: Lynorra was a hemophiliac.

♔

CHAPTER 40

November, 1975

EMMA LAY IN HER BED, WRAPPED UP IN HER BLANKET. The television was on, but she barely watched. The Macy's Thanksgiving Day parade was on. She could hear the family in the rest of the house. The children were fussing. The girls were arguing about watching the March of the Wooden Soldiers, as Junior and Calvin wanted to watch a football game. Emma couldn't bring herself to come out her room. This was the first Thanksgiving in years that she hadn't cooked. She didn't feel like cooking. She didn't feel like doing much of anything. Everyone tried to get her out her room; but she refused. She just didn't have it in her. Her heart was still, too, heavy from missing Lynorra. No matter how many times Albert tried to convince her, she still felt responsible for her best friend's death.

"Now Emma Jean, that's a bunch a foolish talk! Me and you both knows who's responsible for this here tragedy—and it ain't none of you!"

"I don't care what's you say, Albert. My best friend is gone, 'cause of me! Don't you see," Emma cried looking into Albert's face, "I never should have let her go back home by herself. I knew it in my gut that somethin' wasn't right." Emma shook her head. "I felt it, Albert. My hair was rising, and I knew death was comin'."

Albert rubbed his hands over his face,

breathing out deeply. "Look here woman, there is no way on God's green earth, that you gonna convince me, or anyone else for that matter, that you are responsible! You ain't God, Emma!" he raised his voice.

"Hell, I know that!" Emma yelled. "If I was, my friend would be alive! And that waste of flesh, by the name of Arthur Washington would be burnin' in hell right...right...now." Emma began crying again.

Albert sat down on the bed next to his wife. He wrapped his arms around her, trying to comfort her. But nothing seemed to work. Not him, the children, the grandchildren. He didn't know what else to do for her. He did all he knew to do. He even asked Camille.

"She's has to go through certain stages first. It sometimes takes some people longer than others. Emma's been through an awful lot in the past year. She was just *beginning* to really deal with the whole ordeal with Macon. And the fact of the matter is; she never really gave herself a chance to grieve for Nathan. So what you see now is kind of like a crash. Everything has finally come to a head. Lynorra's death just pushed her over the edge...emotionally speaking."

Camille was right. Albert knew that Emma really didn't handle Nathan's death as well as she said. The whole fight with Calvin, and Shelby moving away: it really had been much on her emotionally. He worried about her. And no one seemed to be able to get her out of this depressed mood. Lynorra was always the one who did that.

JR

Emma turned off the television. She lay down and pulled the covers over her head, trying to drown out the sounds coming from outside her door. Her heart ached more than she could stand. She was feeling a bit better a few weeks ago; but then the holidays started coming, and Lynorra's birthday would be soon. She just didn't understand why all the good people had to die so young; her father, her sister Clarisse, Albert's Aunt Lorelei, Nathan, and Lynorra. All of them taken in such harsh ways. It was just too much.

Emma threw the covers back and ran to the bathroom. She locked the door behind her. Sliding to the cool tiled floor, she wept. She brought her knees to her chest and wrapped her arms around them. She rocked back and forth. Emma cried out from her soul.

"Lord, Emma Jean here again. Father, I jes don't understands it. I jes don't understands how you can allow such things to keep happenin' to the folks I love? I know we ain't supposed to questions you; but I jes has to know, Lord. Why? Why my son? Why my best friend? They were good people, with good hearts. They loved You and always did they best." Emma shook her head, beating her fists on her legs. "God…I'm so angry! I don't understands how Lynorra is gone, and that monster…that monster is left here. And Father, he calls his self a Chile of yours? He calls his self a man of the cloth—a man of God?

"Lord forgives me. You tells us not to be judgin' no one; but this jes ain't right. He more a man of Satan than anything! God forgive me for

Southern~485~Comfort

what I'm 'bout to say; but You already's know my heart. You know what I be thinking...I know he over there in that house sick. He's over there, wastin' away. Everybody at that church thinking he grievin' over losing Lynorra; but You and me know that ain't the truth. I swear; if it wasn't for Lynorra's babies, I'd let the lot of them Negroes know what really happened! But I won't do that to Matthew and Lynnie-Mae. And James Perry's too fragile as it is. But we know the truth, and so does he. That's why he wastin' away over there! It's all that evil he done did. It's 'cause he killed one of your precious daughters! You says we ain't supposed to hates no one; that we supposed to love our enemies. I can't do that, Lord. I jes can't. I hate that man right now. Forgives me; but I do. I can't lies to You. You knows the truth already. I can't hides nothin from You."

Emma ran her hands through her hair. She rocked her head back and forth against the bathroom wall. She looked towards the window, where a few rays of sunlight had managed to shine through.

"Lord, You got to help me. I'm barely holding on. I don't know how much more I can take before I finally loses my mind, and am no goods to anyone. Father, what do I do 'bout this pain? Please help me, Father. Please."

Emma leaned, resting her head against the wall. She stretched her legs out in front of her. She closed her eyes, praying that God would talk to her; let her know that everything was going to be alright. At that moment, Emma felt a gentle breeze blow across her face. She opened her eyes and looked towards the window.

Emma sat still for a moment. She closed her eyes again. This time, the breeze was a little stronger. Emma opened her eyes again. This time, goose bumps rose on her arms and legs. She stood, and went to the window. The window was closed. The curtains were still. Emma looked puzzled. "What in the..." Emma looked around the bathroom. The door was still shut and locked. She sat down on the edge of the tub. She felt a breeze again; much like the first one, however...gentle. She felt it across her face, chest and arms. Emma's heart began to pound. Then all of a sudden, the scent of Mulberry wine filled the bathroom. Emma stood up. Tears began falling from her already swollen eyes.

"*Lynorra?*" she whispered. Emma looked around the bathroom. She knew for certain she didn't have any Mulberry wine in there, or anywhere in her bedroom. In fact, she hadn't had any Mulberry wine since the night Lynorra passed.

"Oh, Sistah, is that you?" Emma began wringing her hands. She wasn't sure what this meant. Suddenly, she felt Lynorra so strong, as if she were right there in the bathroom with her. Emma unlocked the door and opened it quickly. She stepped into her bedroom. There was no one there. Her bedroom door was still shut. An overwhelming urge came over her just then. "*The Gazebo,*" she said softly. She had to go to the gazebo. Emma hadn't been to the gazebo either, since Lynorra passed. She just couldn't bring herself to do so.

Emma slipped on her flats. She opened her

bedroom door quietly. She didn't want anyone to see her. Most everyone was in the den, or in the kitchen. She would slip out the front door and goes around the side of the house. Emma could hear everyone chatting about. She was able to make it out the front door quietly without anyone seeing.

A few feet from the gazebo, Emma's legs grew heavy. It was much harder than she anticipated it would be. She willed herself the rest of the way. Emma took each step up the gazebo slowly. She looked around. Nothing had been touch. She looked to the left, on one of the seats. There was Lynorra's quilt. Emma picked it up. She draped it around her shoulders, and breathed in its scent. It smelled just like Lynorra: *Honeysuckle.* Emma shook her head. Sitting down, she exhaled deeply.

"Oh Lynorra, I misses you somethin' terrible," said Emma closing her eyes, rocking. "There never was a sweeter soul than yours. And you always knew how to makes me laugh. Yes you did." Emma opened her eyes and looked around. "I'm so sorry, Sistah. I wish I could go back and...but we both knows that wishing never made a damn thing so," she smiled sadly. "What am I gonna do with outs my best friend. You helped to keep me sane...you know, he don't say it much; but then again, I guess I hasn't given him much of chance to grieves himself; but Albert really misses you, too. Yes he does. It hurt him real bad..." Emma sat quietly, running her fingers over the patches of the quilt. "Girl, what am I gonna do?"

A gentle breeze blew through the trees.

Emma watched as the tress bent towards the wind. Then she heard something. She didn't know if it was the wind, or a memory in her ears. *My babies,* she thought she heard twice. Then Emma remembered Lynorra's last request: her babies. She wanted Emma to take care of her children.

Emma bowed her head and cried. Here she was, so caught up in her own grief, that she had neglected Matthew, Lynnie-Mae, and James Perry. A pain shot through her heart. "I'm so sorry, Lynorra. I've let you down, again." Emma had not spent much time with the children. Not because they didn't want to; but because she couldn't handle it at the time. They looked so much like their mama. But how could she be so selfish? Matt and Lynnie-Mae were at home; she often heard when they came over. Sometimes she would hear Lynnie-Mae crying. Yet, she couldn't bring herself to comfort her; because she felt so guilty. James Perry was in Mississippi with his, Aunt Mel. He refused to go back in that house. Emma couldn't very well blame him.

"I'm gonna fix this, Lynorra. I promise," said Emma lifting her head.

At that moment, Emma thought she heard someone coming. When she looked, she couldn't believe who was standing before her: James Perry!

James stood at the opening of the gazebo, just looking at her.

"James Perry," said Emma softly. Emma could see his eyes glistening with tears. Emma stood, and opened her arms wide. "James Perry," she repeated.

James ran into Emma's open arms. He

wrapped his arms around her waist, and buried his face in her chest. He cried, and he cried.

"Oh, James Perry, it's gonna be alright. Mama's here," cried Emma.

Emma continued to hug, and rock James, for as long as he needed her to. Finally, she walked him over to the bench.

James pulled back, and wiped his face. He looked up at Emma.

"I missed you," he said quietly.

"I missed you, too. Do you like staying with your Aunt Mel?"

He shrugged. "I guess so."

Emma reached over, and placed her arms around his shoulders. "Did you come to see Matt and Lynnie for Thanksgiving?"

"No," answered James shaking his head. "I came to see you."

"Me?" Emma was surprised. "Why?"

"Mama told me to come. She said I needed you, and you needed me," he said, with his head lowered.

Emma understood. James Perry was a very special boy. It was one of the reasons his father mistreated him. He didn't understand James Perry, or the gift he had. James Perry had the gift of seeing. And it scared his father to no end.

"Well, when did she tell you this?"

James looked up, into Emma's eyes. *"Then you believe me?"* he asked surprised.

"Of course I do, James Perry. If you say your Mama told you that; then that's what she told you. And I believe you; because it's true." Emma smiled.

"My Aunt didn't believe me. She said that I was just having a dream. But I know the truth…and I knew you would, too." James managed a small smile.

"So, what's we gonna do 'bout this?" Emma asked.

"Can I live with you, and Mr. Albert?"

"I thinks we can arrange that. After all, we are your god-parents."

James smiled wide. His face lit up, as though the weight of the world was just lifted off his shoulders.

When Emma saw his smile, she felt the exact same way.

"Mama?"

"Yes, James Perry?"

"I think Matt and Lynnie wants to live with you, too."

"You think so?"

James nodded. "I heard them talking about it with Aunt Mel."

"We'll see what we can do 'bouts that, too."

James smiled, and then got serious.

"What is it, baby?"

"I didn't tell Matt or Lynnie the truths about what really happened. I didn't even tell Aunt Mel. I didn't want them to hurt any more than they already do."

Emma nodded understandingly. "Okay," she said softly. "We'll jes keeps that between us, then, okay?" Emma pulled James closer to her.

"Okay," James whispered, leaning his head onto Emma's chest.

"Well, do my eyes deceive me?"

Emma and James looked up. Albert was standing there, smiling.

"I should have known he'd be the one to finds you. Mama, you had everyone worried. We didn't know where you slipped off to. We didn't even sees you leave," Albert said concerned.

"I'm sorry, baby. But I jes had to be by myself, you know? And then my buddy here founds me," Emma smiled at James, squeezing his shoulder.

Albert nodded, and then his face got serious.

"Did James Perry tells you?" He looked at James.

"Tells me what?" Emma looked from Albert to James.

James bowed his head. "No, I didn't."

Emma looked at Albert. "What is it?"

Albert sighed, "Artie passed an hour ago..."

JR

EPILOGUE

August 4th, 1976

THE WEATHER WAS BEAUTIFUL. It was a perfect day for a wedding. Emma squeezed Albert's hand. Albert reached into his pocket, and handed Emma his handkerchief.

"Thank you, baby," whispered Emma, taking the handkerchief. Emma blotted her eyes. Her heart was overwhelmed. She couldn't believe her baby boy was getting married. "Isn't Junior handsome?" she said, leaning into Albert.

"Jes like his pops!" Albert smiled.

"Lord, you is a mess," Emma chuckled.

"Look at 'em, Mama. Did you ever think we'd live to see this day?"

Emma smiled. "It was roughs there for a minute. But as soon as I met Camille, I knew she was the one for him..."

"You sure did. You didn't wastes no time in makin' sure they got together," Albert laughed.

"That's a mama's job," said Emma, matter-of-factly. "Besides, you saw those girls that were after him? Uh-huh," Emma shook her head. "I had to makes sure my baby got the best. And Camille is the best. She smart, pretty, and most of all, she loves our baby for real."

"I know that's right."

Emma looped her arm through Albert's.

Albert patted his wife's hand. He was so proud of Junior and Camille. It was such a beautiful thing to get married on Emma's birthday. And to think; It was Junior's idea. He wanted to do something special for his mother, and gives her a good memory. Yes, Junior turned out to be a fine man. Just like his father.

Emma couldn't have asked for a better birthday. This was definitely a day that she would never forget. Although, her heart still ached. It didn't ache as much. She was surrounded by so much love, and so much family; it made her heart soar. However, she could never forget what happened the year before. She chose; however, to no longer dwell on it as much. She was going to dwell on life, love, and her family. And the three beautiful children that Lynorra left in her care.

So much had happened in the past year. And for once, it wasn't all bad.

Emma stood in the gazebo, overlooking the reception. She looked at the faces of her family and friends: old and new. It warmed her heart to see the smiles, and hear the laughter. Junior and Camille were married, and they decided to stay in, Busby. Hallelujah! Junior was going to open a law office in town.

Shelby and Richard are doing well. Shelby gave birth to twins on Valentine's Day. Richard

Alexander the II, and Clarisse Rose. They are beautiful. Then again, Emma felt all her grand babies were beautiful, and she dared anyone to say otherwise!

Calvin and Anna-Leigh are expecting their second child.

Calvin has really changed the most over the past year. He's much more relaxed, not so serious. Emma gets a kick out the fact that he calls her every day just to tell her he loves her.

That Ella is something else, too! She's running around getting into everything! And she loves to eat! Good Lord!

Deeney will be leaving for school next week. She got a full scholarship to Howard University. Emma wasn't surprised. Deeney's a smart girl. But Emma ain't anybody's fool either! She knows that Nadine's son, David, goes there as well. They've been seeing one another for the past nine months. He's a good kid. Emma likes him a lot. So does Albert. Good thing for Deeney!

Macon and Nathaniel are doing so well. It was hard for her at first; but Emma knew it was time for Macon to be with her mother. Nadine really is doing well. It's amazing what *really* having Jesus in your life will do. She's even got herself a new man, honey! Darius Buckner, Bishop Samuels' nephew. Lord, he's so crazy about Nadine; he gets to church early now!

Macon and Nathaniel still come every other month. Emma especially missed that little boy, with his handsome self! He has the cutest smile, and the deepest dimples! Right now his favorite word is, no. Lord, if he ain't like his grandfather!

Emma's house is full—somewhat. In a couple of weeks, however, it will just be her, Albert, and James Perry. Lynorra's children moved in with her after Artie passed. It was where they wanted to be. Matt waited a year before going away to school. He'll be going to a University in North Carolina. Lynnie-Mae is going to New York. She has a need to spread her wings, and connect with who her mama was. Emma understands that. She gave her, her blessings.

James Perry is one special child. Emma couldn't love him no more than if she gave birth to him. He definitely has Lynorra's spirit. He loves himself some Albert! Those two must go fishing every weekend! It's good to see him and Albert get along so well. He needed a loving father-figure in his life.

Emma laughed, watching all the children running and playing; all the family getting together; Junior and his in-laws. Emma was going to have to loosen them up a bit! *Northerners!*— she laughed.

Emma could actually say she was happy. There was nothing more precious than the comfort of one's family. To know, that no matter how low you get, there is somebody there to pick you up, and loves on you. Yes indeed, Emma felt truly blessed.

"Hey, Mama. You hiding back here drinkin' that Mulberry wine?" Albert wrapped his arms around Emma's waist from behind.

"No. I'm saving that for later," she smiled at

him sideways.

"Umm, talk that talk, Mama!" Albert placed a small kiss on her neck.

Emma laughed, closing her eyes, leaning back into Albert's embrace.

"So, what you doin' here by yourself?"

"Oh, I wasn't alone. I was jes thanking God for His many blessings, and for the love and comfort of a family."

"Amen. We've certainly been blessed in that area."

"Yes we have. And you know what?" Emma turned to face Albert.

"What?"

"I couldn't have made it without you," she smiled.

"I couldn't have made it without you, either," he said, kissing Emma gently on the lips. "You were this city boy's, Southern comfort."

Emma smiled. "You really know how to butter a sistah up," she laughed.

"I'm serious. My Uncle told me before he passed: *'Albert, don't mess with none of these fast city girls...you get you a girl from downs South. They knows how to treat a man. They got that good comfort that men like us long for'*."

"You ain't ever told me that before."

"I can't be tellin' you *all* the men's secrets, now!" Albert laughed.

Emma raised her eyebrows at him. "So, is this what you told our sons?"

Southern~497~Comfort

"I sure did. And I'll tell it to James Perry, too!"

"Man, you too much!"

"Yeah, but you love it!"

"I sure do man. I sure do!" Emma wrapped her arms around Albert's neck and pulled him into a long, passionate, kiss.

"Ugh! Get a room!"

Albert and Emma turned around to see Junior and Camille snickering.

"Yeah?" Albert said. "You can't wait for me to say that to you!"

"Camille, you'll see...the apple don't fall too far from the tree!" Emma laughed.

"I'm sure it doesn't," said Camille giggling.

"Okay, Mama...no corrupting my wife!" Junior laughed. "Hey, we're ready to take some more pictures of the parents. We need you and pop."

"Okay. We'll be right there."

Emma watched as Camille placed her hand in Junior's, and kissed it. Junior kissed hers back.

"They are beautiful," sighed Emma.

"Jes like us. C'mon Mama, we got some pictures to be in."

Emma stopped and touched her hair. "Wait, how do I look?"

Albert smiled. "As beautiful as the day I married you," he said, placing a kiss on her cheek.

Emma eyes filled with tears "C'mon man, you know you gettin' some tonight," she laughed.

JR

"Have mercy!" said Albert, taking his wife's hand in his.

Emma lifted his hand and kissed it.

Albert did the same.

"What would I do without you?"

"You never has to know."

"Promise?"

"Promise," Emma smiled.

Ruthe McDonald

Southern~500~Comfort

JR

Southern~501~Comfort

Ruthe McDonald

Southern~502~Comfort

About The Author

Ruthe McDonald is the author of **This Christmas: A Short Story Collection, The Devil's After Me (Released in Spring 2012),** *Non-Fiction Inspirational books:* **Reflections: Encouragement in the Face of Adversity Volume I and Reflections: God's Grace is Sufficient Volume II.** *Her work has also appeared in Mused Literary Magazine.*
Ruthe is a freelance writer and editor. She continues to be involved in her community through Ministry, motivational speaking, counseling and promoting activities that help to aid those that are in need. She is a Board Member for a Non-Profit (UNCDC) that builds and rehabs affordable housing for low income and moderate income families. Ms. McDonald is the current editor at BellaOnline.com for it's African American Culture site. Read her Reflections Blog at: reflections4life.gather.com or visit her website: www.ruthemcdonald.com

www.ingramcontent.com/pod-product-compliance
Lightning Source LLC
Chambersburg PA
CBHW030924020726
47498CB00001B/96